1

Ralph Trout
is the author of four fictional novels,
one non-fiction, and one reference book.

The Wreck

Soucouyant – The Caribbean Vampire

Something Fishy

Soon Come

Non-Fiction
Road Trip Huautla: The Mushroom Cult

Reference
The Caribbean Home Garden Guide

All titles are available at
Amazon.com and Barnes and Noble.

SOMETHING FISHY

By

Ralph Trout

There are only a few sports a man gets better at as they age, playing pool and fishing are two. I'm fortunate to be hooked on both.   **Ralph Trout**

Dedicated to my fishing buddies

Raised in Japan Petey, Smiling Frenchie Mike, Connecticut Chris, Hungry Harry, Rocky Mountain Earl, Al Petrosky, Orlando Brook, Russel the Muscle, Spike, Florida Nick, Oregon Mike, Diverman Hankster, Teacher John, Coki Pete, Suki, Trinidad Andy, Barnacle Bill, Tortola Johnny, Big Mike, Texas Chris, Lovely Maureen, Christoff, Herbert, Jimmy Straka, Westline Jon, Dick Hoyt, Roz, Texas Mary, the Gings, the Hudaks, the Weslies, Joe Burke, Compound 28, Rum Ed, For Now Mark, John and Michael Lanser, Fiddling Dick, Carriacou Hope, Max, Alex, and Bayaleau Dave

and to my father who initially addicted me to fishing.
I raise my rod and reel in a happy salute.

Thanks, gratitude, and affection to Dr, Claire Hu for her patience while helping a dummy with Photoshop.

INTRODUCTION

What is sportfishing? Dictionaries define it as: fishing done for sport and recreation that often includes tournaments. Big-game, blue water fishing is done from classy boats, usually far offshore in warm, saltwater areas. Sportfishermen seek big fish that do not easily come to the boat including dorado, tuna, and billfish, especially marlin.

Commercial fishing catches the most and feeds the world. Every country with a shoreline has a fishing fleet and entire villages catch fish to survive. They are not fishing for sport. Fish are measured by weight and are only a commodity to be eaten and sold.

Fishing for sport easily becomes an affection, and addiction, often to the extent of an affliction. Competitive fishing is about prizes and bragging rights. The techniques involved to catch an enormous fish begin with high-priced boats armed with expensive rods and reels, large attractive live baits, and fancy lures. Sportfishing with heavy-duty saltwater gear doesn't come cheap. The unique sound of the screaming reel as a large game fish takes line is the best alarm clock that immediately stirs ardent fishermen's central nervous systems.

Trolling baits across the salty depths was new to me, a Pennsylvania farm boy accustomed to fishing for trout with light gear. Muskellunge or muskies were the biggest fish in local waters. After spring trout season, my father's summer and autumn interest was casting, throwing a lure, for hours hoping to hook the largest member of the pike family. The world record musky was caught in 1949 and was five feet long and weighed sixty-seven pounds. My father's biggest trophy musky measured fifty-two inches and weighed 34 pounds. In my early years, a musky had to be at least thirty inches long to be legal. My biggest was thirty-four inches, but as the fish swirled, hitting the lure hard, it also hooked me to seek bigger fish.

My first sportfishing outing was to the North Drop in the US Virgin Islands. One of the many Caribbean meccas for chasing bill fish, the Virgin Islands' North Drop is twenty miles north of St. Thomas. It runs ten miles east to west along the Puerto Rico Trench before it takes a dogleg turn to the north. It is this area, known as the Saddle, which attracts fishermen from all over the world. It is reputed that marlin choose the August full moon to spawn there. Needing extra energy for marine copulation, these billfish feed heavily during the day. The combination of tidal currents and temperature convection; deep, cool water rising to the surface, heated by the summer sun, produces schools of baitfish.

In the early eighties, the fishing hadn't yet been severely impacted. Back then, I had no idea Zane Grey, the author of so many westerns, had spent his riches scouring the world for better fishing grounds and bigger fish. I'd read The Old Man and the Sea, by Hemingway, but I never comprehended the size of that fish or the fortitude of Santiago.

That first day, prime-time August, I first realized there were two distinct types of fisher-people, salts and pukers. Salts smile and are late to advise possible pukers. Once the gagging begins, the salts recommend ginger, Dramamine, and behind the ear Scopolamine patches. All are used to prevent nausea and vomiting caused by motion sickness. Nothing drives newbies away from blue water fishing action faster than a severe case of the upchucks, hours away from blessed, non-rolling land. Off balance due to wave motion, the smell of bait often combined with a heavy scent of diesel, after late night libations can bring intense stomach problems.

Usually, blue water or open sea fishing is far offshore and out of sight of land. Few great fishing areas are within an hour of the nearest port. For example, the USVI's North Drop fishing area takes a regular boat about four hours to traverse the twenty miles of sea. Weather and sea conditions always can change with the wind. Often, within an hour, a brilliant light blue sky can switch to dark purple cracking with lightning. Flat seas can first gain choppy white caps and then uncomfortable rollers.

We pooled our money and chartered the least expensive boat in St. Thomas' Red Hook charter fishing fleet. We left late, at eight, on a Sunday morning. The old wood-hulled boat stank of mildew and stale fish. Soon we had to return to the St. John dock and drop off two pukers who couldn't handle the conditions. By ten we were heading north… again.

The mate rigged baits alien to anything I'd ever seen. They used ten-inch, thin, silver fish called ballyhoo, skewered on a five-foot-long wire leader. A frilly, fringed plastic 'skirt' slipped down the leader and shrouded the silver bait. These ran on the surface as the boat lumbered barely five miles an hour over good seas.

The boat dragged four baits on stiff rods equipped with huge Penn Senator reels loaded with eighty-pound test line. First, we caught a few small kingfish, which seemed large for us landlubbers. We heartily congratulated each other on fish that barely weighed twenty pounds. We finally reached the North Drop at one in the afternoon. That gave us only one hour to troll the edge of the celebrated drop off before we had to return to reach the dock while there was daylight.

In those days, I didn't know about prime conditions, locations, seasons for marlin, or any fish migrations. I'd never heard of the best moon phases for fishing. In rapid succession, we hooked and lost two billfish and landed what we thought was a huge yellow fin tuna, thirty-five pounds. We were so tight in those days; we didn't tip the crew. But I'd be back. The line peeling off the reel, making that high-pitched whirring sound, the sight of a fin, then a bill slashing through the water took a grip and forever held my attention. Fishing, and living on islands where I could fish, became my life.

My father visited months after my initial outing, and by then I had friends with nice boats. We took him out on a thirty-six-foot Topaz. His first outing to the North Drop, he lost one marlin and on the next hit landed a nice blue. On his second trip, a few days later, he lost the battle with a bigger blue and landed a nice sixty-pound wahoo. He couldn't see any reason for all the hoopla over marlin fishing. He went out twice, hooked three and landed one. That was a considerably better average than with his freshwater musky expeditions.

A friend and fishing mentor, Al, had his own small, four-slip marina in the lagoon on St. Thomas' south side. His boat was beamy (wide) and slow, but had four fighting chairs to relax and sunbathe. When we'd leave the dock, he'd always ask, "Do you want to catch fish, or go after marlin?" As soon as there was a hookup, he'd yell, "Are you a farmer or a fisherman? Reel, reel, this is what you came for!"

A great friend, Connecticut Chris, wrote for Power & Motoryacht Magazine and in 1993 he arrived to report the USVI Boy Scout Tournament. He traveled out to the drop for the first two days and the fishermen he accompanied had hooked nothing. I suggested he join on a friend's boat. Russ is an incredible fisherman, sort of the Clark Kent of sportfishing. His calm demeanor changes to superman when he boards a boat. Fishing is serious business. It was Sunday, the last day of the tournament. I expected to meet them for drinks and dinner at the awards ceremony.

Five o'clock was the time set for all boats were to be back at the dock. Five, six, and seven passed without my friends' return. Russ had hooked a monster marlin slightly past noon. It leaped only once and everyone, including the International Game Fishing Association (IGFA) judge agreed the fish was a thousand pounds or more. One photo exists.

If he landed a fish over a thousand pounds, he wouldn't only win the tournament, but also win a new Mercedes Benz.

The marlin fight of all time continued with Russ reeling in a foot and the blue monster jerking back six inches. It lasted over eleven grueling hours! In the dark of night, Russell finally brought the monster fish to the surface almost close enough to tag and release. A large, rogue wave hit the boat and snapped line. Connecticut Chris' magazine article told the story and Russ earned the moniker, Russell the Muscle.

In 1994, I decided to live my dream and fish the Caribbean. I had a funky trawler that was fuel-efficient. The small Perkins Diesel traveled four miles to the gallon. The meager thirty-four-foot live-aboard offered everything necessary. I was almost thirty-eight and it was time to live the Jimmy Buffett lyrics, 'But I've got to stop wishin, got to go fishin,' from, A Pirate Looks at Forty.

Ignoring the hurricane season in favor of the best fishing, my eight-month sabbatical included hop-on, hop-off visitors, 'just a few friends.' I left the Virgins in August and only encountered tropical storm Debbie. From Virgin Gorda we caught large rainbow runners, amberjacks, and lost a billfish in the corncob-rough Anegada Passage. Anguilla brought wahoo, a big marlin off Antigua, and big bull dolphins on the Saba Bank. Leaving Nevis passing Boobie Rocks, I hooked my biggest marlin, estimated by the length at five hundred plus. We caught, ate, and sold fish. Tuna, yellowfin, blackfin, and albacore, plus sailfish and sharks were daily exercise in the Southern Grenadines.

I found many spectacular fishing spots while dragging baits. One unique location was Chatham Bay on the leeward (west) side of Union Island. Then it was the last undeveloped bay with zero electric lights on land in the Caribbean. It has a great sandy bottom anchorage. There wasn't even a lean-to beach bar among the palms. Primo blue water fishing, three hundred meters deep, was only thirty minutes away after hauling anchor. Sunset Bay is based on that location for this fishing yarn.

Something Fishy is about the misfortunes of a sportfishing family in the Caribbean. Labeled 'sportfishing,' it's a business that can burn people out and disrupt families. Also, it's a fantasy lifestyle for many passionate fishermen until Mother Nature and human greed intervene. But that's life, and a bad day fishing is better than an exceptional day at work, unless your work is sportfishing.

"Many of the most highly publicized events of my presidency are not nearly as memorable or significant in my life as fishing with my daddy," Jimmy Carter.

Many fish bites if you got good bait,
here's a little tip that I would like to relate,
With my pole and my line, I'm a goin' fishin',
yes, I'm goin' fishin,'And momma's goin' fishin' too.
1911 by Chris Smith

My father and his first blue marlin

IN THE BEGINNING

The sky and sea melded into a continuous calm blue. A pink sun slowly materialized and created a median. The ocean had barely a wrinkle. They'd come to fish. Through the tranquil night, the fishing boat drifted without incident. It was June, four days after the full moon. Early, just after six. The morning was chilly, heavy with a salty dew. Far away from man's shore-side influences and pollutants, the breeze was slight and the air smelled only of a clean ocean.

The older man had spent part of the previous evening educating the boy on the stars. Every cluster had a fable and every story added to the fisherman's lore. It was good to know how to follow the constellations home. The boy was eager to learn until he was too sleepy to listen. After midnight the youth curled under a canvas tarp and slept soundly, the boat slightly rocking.

The man intently watched the sea's surface and shook the boy awake. As the youth rubbed his eyes, he followed the pointing arm. The iridescent fin of a billfish disturbed the glassy sea ten meters off the port side. The boy stood rigid, mesmerized by the rainbows of the new sun spiraling off the tall, translucent fin. His father's finger went to his lips and they silently watched as the huge fish methodically swiped its long bill back and forth, slashing the myriad of silver fry that leaped out of the water like a reverse rain to avoid being sucked into the big fish's gaping mouth.

The marlins' dawn feeding spectacle always entranced the father, who wanted to create a taste for natural beauty in his son. The older man had enjoyed the spectacle countless times. Last night had been chilly, yet the boy never complained. He loved the ocean and even though he was young, he was a passionate fisherman.

It was in his DNA, only from his father's genetics. His mother hated boats: the expense, the smell, and mostly the never-ending motion that made her so sick. The sun, the water, the fishing, all the smells were uncomforting to her. Hers was an uncompromising position, but it was his father's love and livelihood.

Neither father nor son moved until the billfish swam off in pursuit of more breakfast.

"You see that, son? Yes, sir, that's a big one. Shh, be as quiet as possible. You know, those big fish can feel slight vibrations. One calm day, rare on the Gulf Stream, I took a few friends out to drift fish and found a big swordfish sleeping, just lying there on the surface. We watched it for a long while until one guy bounced against the gaff and it hit the deck. That gigantic sword rolled over and immediately disappeared."

"This one, the fin, the dorsal, the one sticking out of the water; that belongs to a great-grand-daddy sailfish marlin. Uh-huh, son, that's a breeder. He'll make many baby marlins. So, while it might be great excitement to hook one; you always want to release them. Them guys we know back at the marina, they're killing them for nothing, nothing but pictures. They don't even want to taste them. Grind that beauty into cat food is what they do. No respect for nature at all. That's not how we think, is it, Harry?"

"No, dad, we always want to fish another day. Catch and release. So, like you say, the next generation will have the sea's beauty to appreciate."

"Right son, the sea's one of God's genuine miracles. Scientists say we walked out of the sea. So, we'll always have some saltwater in our hearts as long as our brains are in the right place and we don't think only about our pockets. Recite it with me now, Harry."

They said it together, smiling, "God called the dry land earth, and the gathering of the waters He called seas; and God saw that it was good."

"Harry, the sea is our life, our occupation, how we pay the bills. Now, where are we?"

"On our boat, *Passion*, dad," Harry replied.

"No, Harry, exactly where is *Passion*?"

"Oh, you mean in the Gulf Stream between Fort Lauderdale and Bimini."

"Yes son, this is some of the best fishing in the world. But the knuckleheads are killing every fish they can. Son, you and me, have to be conservationists. Save the fish, play only catch and release. Time might come when we there's no more fish to watch like the one out there this morning. That would be a shame, wouldn't it?"

"Yes sir, it would." Harry politely replied. He always was polite, no reason not to be. His dad had instilled in him to love all, hate none. He had to be strong enough to stand alone; think for himself, and never let a group persuaded him. His father was known as Charlie the Redman or Fish Hawk. His father always looked as if he was sunburned with a red face, redder neck and arms. These were the days before sunscreen became a necessity. Every day he donned the same work outfit, khaki long-sleeved shirt with long pants. As a younger boy, Harry had been confused with his father's name because every piece of clothing was embroidered with 'Dickie.'

Harry believed many of the other captains around the dock hailed his father by Fishhawk, because of his father's great eyes and ability to locate birds and schools of fish. When they visited granddad's grave in a small town southeast of Tampa, he learned that his father's hometown was Fish Hawk, Florida.

The boy always remembered that morning, or rather couldn't forget it. Passion was tied to the dock by nine and they were home by ten. His mother was gone, not to the supermarket or beauty parlor, but gone. Harry didn't realize it was for good. She'd left a note only saying not to look for her. She didn't even write an extra line to Harry. In a few words, she explained how her life was horrible, always waiting for the boat, and hating when it finally arrived. Harry never saw the note that had been wedged in the front door until years later. He watched his father snatch it before it fell to the porch.

Charlie, his dad, read it, sucked in his breath, and bit his upper lip shaking his head. Like a blind man, he stumbled and plopped onto the rusted metal glider. The scarred, always red, permanently sunburned hands pulled Harry to sit next to him.

There were no words for several minutes. Harry felt it was best to sit quietly and listen to his father's heavy breathing. He'd figured out something bad had happened, but didn't know what. Without moving, sitting rigid, staring ahead as the glider moved back and forth, his peripheral vision watched Charlie read the note again, calmly fold it, and place it into the right chest pocket of his khaki work shirt. Every millisecond of that moment was indelibly etched in his memory. So was the soundtrack that followed.

"Son, you're eleven, and we are the family," his father coughed back what was perhaps a sob, paused, and took a few deep breaths. "Harry, we'll be bachelors for a while." Charlie rubbed his eyes. "Your mother has taken a vacation. I can't say how long that vacation will be. But you and I are men," his father gave a slight laugh and rubbed Harry's crew cut. With a sad smile while looking blankly into the distance, he said, "You might be a little young to stand for yourself." He sighed deeply again, "I'll get us some help when we need it. Bacon and eggs, sloppy joes, fruit, and cereal, we'll get by. Always we'll have plenty of fresh fish on the barbecue. You can handle that, can't you?"

Harry didn't have an answer; he had no idea what to expect. Intuitively, he knew some things would fall into place and some wouldn't. Trust was the essence, and he trusted his dad. Had to, the older man had taught him everything, except beginning algebra.

Charlie hugged his son as never before and held him tight as the glider moved under them. "Everything just changed, son." He wiped an eye. "They say death and taxes are the only things guaranteed in life. They should add change to that list. Harry, everything changes. Some you can expect, like the weather. You know, some changes, like seasons, are predictable." The older man pursed his lips, "Some ain't; changes catch you when you least expect." He turned Harry to face him. Charlie's head was cocked slightly, chin pointed up, with a genuine grin.

"Son, you're going to mature sooner now, grow up. There'll still be baseball, girls, and, of course, fishing, but there's also going to be laundry, dishwashing, cooking, and house cleaning. This house," he stopped, "this home is going to be the same as before, clean, really clean… and respectable. Me and you are going to be clean."

The boy closed his eyes and merely accepted what was to come. Another long hug. They sat back and listened to the glider squeak.

"That was a huge fish this morning, wasn't it, dad?" Harry finally broke the silence.

"Yes, it was son, a really big one."

His mother never returned. Within months, rumors told Harry she'd run off with the blond, wavy-haired, life insurance salesman. To his recollection, he or his father never mentioned again her name. She was never forgotten, as she had forgotten them; she became a ghost. As his life progressed, Harry smiled when he thought of her and how she'd freed him to enjoy a unique life.

The family of two were fishing folks. Dedicated, almost compulsive, and always competitive, especially among themselves. Harry worked toward being as good as his father. Life was simple, opening cans of soup, Minute Rice, and bartering fish for chicken, pork, and beef, but they ate a lot of fish, a hell of a lot.

Possessions onshore rusted and living became condensed. In problem times, weaker men turned to the bottle, and others found strength while singing hymns. Charlie, that's the name his son used, and Harry turned to fishing, an art form that swallowed them. He filled junior college with diesel maintenance, logarithmic tables for celestial navigation, meteorology, and marine biology. At nineteen and two months, Harry had his captain's license.

But his father taught the best lessons. Charlie preached everything was in a state of constant motion and you can only trust the sun to be there tomorrow when it goes away at night.

CHAPTER ONE

The wide, sandy-dirt track dropped into one of the few low spots where none of the water surrounding the island was visible. No sea views. During the seasonal drought, this stretch of the path was almost a desert. Wilting, thorny scrub bush lined both sides of the narrow track. It wasn't wide enough for a conventional vehicle, just bicycles or motorcycles that could maneuver through the ruts. It was always hot. This morning had enough of a breeze to create small, spiraling dust devils along the pathway.

It had been four years and as many months since he'd been home. Sadly, he considered what he was returning to. It wasn't a funeral, not yet, and no one was ill; anyway, or not any more ill than usual. There was always confusion; the family seemed to enjoy and even thrive on disorder. Maybe every family was similar. He couldn't say; this was the only family he knew.

Growing up on the island had been good. He sighed; concerned for everyone who was no longer 'here,' but instead, 'somewhere.' He'd never thought he'd ever live anywhere else. His family owned the grand expanse of Sunset Bay. One time, living on the secluded west side of Union Island had been as good a life as he could ever imagine. It still was, but damn chaotic.

As he hiked up the next slight rise in the sandy trail, he heard a familiar sound and turned to see an inter-island turboprop bringing in another dozen tourists to the asphalt strip just east of the never-bustling town of Clifton. Those small planes had fed their sportfishing resort with an almost continuous supply of anglers. He wondered what had happened.

At the dock, east of town, next to the petrol storage tanks, he could see the small fuel tanker that brought in petrol supplies from Venezuela and had been his transport home. He arrived and cleared immigration following the morning's brilliant sunrise.

The familiar spidery pathway had many entrances around the village, but only one destination, his family's homestead, isolated Sunset Bay. Clifton, the island's only town, which faced the sunrise, was slightly less isolated. From this viewpoint, he could see daybreak kite surfers shredding the shallow turquoise waters. Boats were anchored where the sea's blues became darker, probably taking snorkelers or grabbing lobsters. Of Clifton itself, he could only make out rooftops and a few trucks. Not much had changed, except what was changing, and that's why he was back. There'd be plenty of time to walk the few streets and renew the friendships.

Another deep breath and this one brought a grin. Dag started homeward again, with a little more swagger in his step. Why not grin, life had been good. It could always be better, but damn well it could have been worse, much worse. All of his possessions were stuffed in his blue canvas duffle. At twenty-eight, slim, standing six feet with sun-bleached hair, shrouding a deep tan, he was proud to be an island boy.

Dag had wanted nothing else except to be a fisherman. He looked the part. He lived wearing khaki shorts and a shirt with many-pockets. His black web belt carried his Leatherman and phone pouch. Maui Jim sunglasses dangled from a neck lanyard. The unkempt blond curls were tucked under his faded blue cap, which bore the name Penn Fishing Reels. His well-worn deck shoes were dedicated to wide feet that were meant to be bare.

The 8 AM church bells clanged in town. Twenty more minutes, one more rise, and he could see the glint of the steel roofs on their bay. A few mango trees, heavy with fruit, and greener bushes told that more fresh water was on this side of the island. Another sigh brought a wider grin remembering the idle days of scrambling up the branches to grab a sack full of sweet, juicy, grafted Julie mangoes.

Walking farther, a few yellow-brown mangoes littered the roadside. Dag stooped to grab one, peeled it with his teeth bending forward so the dripping juice didn't spoil his already rumpled clothes. Two bites in as many steps and he stopped; the sight ahead was sweeter than the fruit. It was home, the end of this path, Sunset Bay.

A few more meters and the vista widened. It was like one of those paintings; what was that guy's name, ah, Norman Rockwell, but this setting was pure Caribbean. The big, two-story frame house had once been bright blue, a shade resembling the noon sky. That's when the fishing business and the family were both going great. Dag remembered helping paint it; all the kids had stroked a brush. On the left bottom corner of the front porch, they'd signed it. It was their painting, 'a house on the bay.' His sister had practiced it on canvas over and over, selling all sizes and variations to visitors who only came to fish. Anywhere the sun and rain had hit their home had faded to gray. The windows and their shutters still held a semblance of dull white.

The corrugated roof had some rust that blended with what had once been painted rust-repellant, zinc red. The repellant part must have expired. Rust never paused next to the sea. The house had three gables, a hot attic bedroom for each child. Another grin, remembering they were usually up and out before sunrise and seldom upstairs again till well after dark. When they'd exhausted their youthful energies, mom would tune the single side-band radio to the world news or to a cricket or football match. Every Sunday evening, they had to sit while she tuned in their weekly dose of Jesus from the St. Vincent evangelist.

The porch where they'd often sat hearing mostly static from far-off places had been edged with his mother's ceramic pots filled with bright flowers. Along the top edge of the wood pillared porch, he could still see their crude attempt at gingerbread trim from when he and his younger brother had tried to spruce things up. They'd traded a couple of lobsters for a used hand jigsaw from a yachtie anchored in the bay. They'd begged the pieces of wood and white paint from their uncle and surprised mother with a rough design nailed above one section of the porch. She always wanted nice things, but there were too many demands for her time and the family's funds. That gingerbread had faded.

Their yellow Lab, Duke, a silent partner in many escapades, had passed long ago. "I wonder if Redbeard, our macaw is still alive. Haven't thought of that mean bird for a while." Dag muttered and looked at the scarred tip of his ring finger. "That red bastard taught me a lesson, not to poke him when he was eating a mango. Damn, that bird liked mangos as much as I did. Shouldn't have teased him. God, that hurt, and I got spanked, not the damn bird," he chuckled.

"Couldn't have had a better youth," somehow slipped out.

He'd been Huck Finn, his brother Tom Sawyer, and his sister became the tag-along Becky from the Mark Twain books mom had read to them. School was always an afterthought; thought about after everything else the tropical days held.

School in Clifton was basic, basic torture. They had to wear shoes. Their family was a third of Union Island's whites, old-time, island white. His mom was a born local; his dad arrived later. That always created some friction with the 'barne heres.'

Enough of those back-in-time thoughts; Dag was certain there would soon be plenty of reminiscing. Chores, maintenance, and a general cleanup were first on his agenda. He felt his pocket full of folded help. It all needed paint; he did a visual survey. Everything needed the rust and the gloom removed. Couldn't see anybody. Dad was probably working on the boat, or just on the boat. In her last email, his mom had said the restaurant was doing good business, occupying all her time. She and dad hadn't been pulling together for a while, a long while. They'd had big problems for almost a year.

His nodded as memories flooded in from every part of the property. Mother's shady-side-of-the-house flower garden had a few blooms still battling with weeds and taller grass. Didn't look like there'd been much recent maintenance. Off to the left was the tall, spreading silk cotton tree with roots that ran like snakes. His sister had always begged her brothers to push her on the single rope swing. They'd tried to frighten her with stories of the jumbies, ghosts, who lived up in the branches, but his sister never had any fear. All three siblings were brave and immortal.

This sigh was the deepest as his eyes trailed along the wooden dock. Dag shrugged and grinned, again thinking of all the times they'd jumped into the cool bay with a running start to see who could dive the farthest. His quick sprint and lanky body always won.

There she was, anchored ten meters off the dock, their sportfishing boat. The grimy hull looked like it was also low on the maintenance list. He loved that boat almost as much as he loved his family. It was their center and that may have caused the problems. Other families revolve around the father or mother; theirs revolved around the fishing boat because it was their sole provider.

He dropped the duffle, sat on it, and meditated the scene. How could everything so positive become so negative? "Changes," he muttered, "everything always changes. I've been seeing it for a few years, cycles. Like dad always said about the seasons. Then, I could see the difference between the rain and the heat, but now it's the subtler things, the currents, wind blowing out of a different direction, the Sargasso weed. Families, people, shit, we're all having seasons. This is just one of them cycles."

Bob Marley came to mind and Dag started singing, 'Everything's Gonna Be Alright.' He chuckled, "Could be I'm finally wising up. That's what Cheesy used to say, 'Wise up kid, would ya just wise up, instead of being a wise guy'." Cheesy, the thought of their wonderful friend and fishing mate brought a bigger smile.

Dag closed his eyes, breathed deeply, and enjoyed a flashback. His mother was repotting plants in the flower boxes that lined the wooden porch. Redbeard, the scarlet macaw, squawked an alarm from his hanging roost as the Lab puppy, Duke, dug out freshly planted marigolds. Dag was sitting on the dock fishing between his brother and sister, bragging about that morning's boat trip. It was always such a big thrill if the paying customers didn't mind if he came along. He tugged his spool of hand line and jerked a wiggling, spotted moray eel onto the wooden dock. His four-year-old sister and six-year-old brother screamed. Never any fear, Dag safely snatched the black eel behind its head and slowly chased them. They ran up the path, to their home, and, as usual, they cowered behind mama while he howled with laughter.

He remembered how pretty his mother was and wondered how the four years apart had treated her. Then he was nine, so mama must have been thirty. That day she was wearing a T-shirt advertising FineBraid fishing line and jean cut-offs. Her long, naturally curly, dark brown hair was sun-bleached to a rusty blond and contained by the customary white-triangle cloth. Slim and six-foot, his mother was beautiful. Dag measured all women against her.

Cassandra, mama's Christian name, was the eldest daughter of a prominent local family, the Scarbeaux. Their skin was shades lighter than the descendants of the Africans, but their lineage was a complicated blend. It had taken two centuries to combine the genetics of the British, French, African, Portuguese, and Spanish. The family was known to everyone because her father, Grandpa Curly, owned the hardware store and Grandma Gretchen operated the first bakery, which had evolved into the first restaurant.

Each child had grabbed one of their mother's legs for a shield. His brother and sister squealed in fear while Dag taunted them with the squirming eel. He remembered that day because between his left thumb and index finger, the scar where the eel had latched on and locked its jaws still showed. Then it had been his turn to shriek in pain and plead with mama for help.

Mother Cassy thought quickly and sliced off the body with her garden shears. Then she carefully pried the eel's small jaws apart. If Dag had pulled on the eel's body, the razor-sharp teeth would have severed the flesh and muscles. The semicircle scar taught a valuable lesson, always beware of sharp teeth no matter how small the eel or fish was. Dad had taught him to be wary of the sharp bills on marlins. He didn't need a scar to believe in the damage they could do.

Opening his eyes, Dag pulled his cap's brim down to fight the glare as he assessed the present scene. The breeze had died and he was sweating. Sunset Bay was glassy flat. No waves washed against the shore. Another sigh, quiet was nice, but out of place in their bay, which usually echoed with voices, music, and motors. To the left, west, beyond their house and directly ahead on the far side of the bay, were lofty brown cliffs that provided protection from heavy weather. Past the cliffs, Sunset Bay opened to the blue Caribbean and probably the best, yet still unknown, billfish area.

Grandpa Curly had made Sunset Bay his daughter's dowry. It wasn't publicized or she would have had even more suitors than her beauty attracted. Gramps must have really liked Dad and known he would take excellent care of his only daughter and the pristine bay. Dag didn't remember but had listened to the stories of how his father had built their dock working from a small raft made of oil drums lashed together. His father-in-law supplied the greenheart lumber from Guyana. Now the dock was badly in need of repairs. Nails had rusted to just a stain, boards were visibly rotten, and some were missing. Beneath the slats, he could see gray mullet swimming above the white sand.

A hard swallow followed a long groan. Dag removed his cap and ran his fingers through his hair. There floated the family's pride and joy; its identity. The family's boat, a tuna-towered sportfisherman, lay slack on her mooring twenty meters off in bluer water. It was his father's only inheritance and may have been the correct bait to buddy up to his future island relatives.

The story was, Grandfather Charlie St. Claire had fished with the rich and famous in Lauderdale and West Palm Beach, Florida. Then the boat was named *Passion*. She was an elegant 36-foot Rybovich, built-in 1975 of Honduran mahogany coated with West System epoxy. Dag had only seen photos of his dad's father, but genetics had given them the same piercing blue eyes, designed to see fish. The family's fishing ancestry had great-great uncles who'd fished with the greats and traveled the globe as sportfishing charter captains searching for the next world-record fish.

Around the same time as his father's arrival in the Southern Caribbean, he renamed the sweet boat *Sassy Cassy* after mom. Dad knew on which side his bread was buttered and exactly who buttered it. In 1983, his father had sought fishing opportunities outside the USA and slowly dragged baits south and east through the chain. Sidestepping Cuba, the trail began on the north coast of the Dominican Republic off Samana, then Puerto Rico, staying too long in the Virgins along the North Drop, across the Anegada passage to Anguilla. He'd found Antigua and the French islands already had developed charter businesses. The Grenadines were pristine and emerging as a tourist attraction. Sparkling clear water with abundant fish caught his eye, only slightly before the willowy, bushy-haired woman.

Dag knew the story word-for-word; he'd heard it so many times. Dad tied to the fuel dock outside Grandpa's hardware store and mom came to the pumps. Did mama fall in love with the boat as Grandpa Curly liked to say, "Every islander loves to fish and loves fish to eat. Your mama," Curly would pause and snicker, "and your dad each saw free rides. Your mama filled the sportfisher's tanks and hooked two that day. Your pa took her fishing to the west drop, and she caught two bigguns on the same run, one 60 lb. wahoo and the other a 160 lb. American skipper!"

^^^^^^^^^^

Sassy Cassy was now a sorry sight; she'd seen better days... but Dag knew it would sparkle and shine again. Thick, dark brown algae covered the mooring lines and the boat's bottom. It looked like the cabin-cruiser hadn't moved in a while. No one had scraped the bottom in at least a year and it needed anti-fouling paint. The sweeping hull needed repeated polishing with rubbing compound, followed by several applications of wax. No scrapes, or worse, were apparent. From the stern cleat a small, badly painted, square-ended blue dinghy rode slack on its line. Only one homemade oar, a flat board nailed to bamboo, was visible propped over its stern.

Dag blew his nose and rubbed his closed eyes as he remembered 'that' day. Some memories never fade, but only get better, enriched by adding the imagined 'what should have happened.'

First, he recalled that the sun's glare had been brutal in July of '99.' It was a scorcher and mama had lathered the three children and herself with sunscreen and made them all wear long sleeved shirts. His eyes had watered from the sweat mixed with lotion. Dag pulled hard on the brim of his ball cap to keep focused on the baits dragging three waves behind the stern as she trolled far west of Canouan Island. He'd been out on day trips with his dad as soon as mama permitted it after his sixth birthday. Now, he had to compete with Tim who had just received the same B-day present.

Four deep-sea rods were securely lodged in their holders. Three had black Penn 8-0 reels rigged with skirted ballyhoo, but one was his father's prized gold Penn International. It was baited with a small bonito tuna. His father had taught him to snap the larger bait's backbone and thread it with a longer needle than was used string the sleek, silver ballyhoo. This was their 'secret' trick to get the bonito to correctly trail without flopping through the wave troughs. The three-pound, small variety tuna was a teaser and lurched through the water another wave distant from the other baits.

That day the entire family was aboard, sitting on the lower deck bench seats that bordered the door to the interior V berth. Mother and daughter were on the port side bench while the two boys sat rigidly silent on the starboard. They'd been taught to be polite, only speak when asked a question. It was torture, watching, and not being able to participate. But even that was better than staying at home.

Every time Dag started to rise, his mother would point at him to sit and keep quiet. This was a charter, a moneymaker. Never distract, dismay, or interfere with the angler who was paying for the trip. July meant raising many fish every day. This week only one man, a foreigner with a weird accent, was staying at their fish camp. The previous day they'd had seven hookups, and twice as many fish had been seen.

The stiff, Scottish angler had lost all but one. He'd caught a 70-pound yellowfin tuna, and they had grilled it for dinner. As they all did, he had come for billfish. The marlins and sailfish were there in numbers during the late summer months. Dad said it was their season. Spring was for the mighty, leaping golden dorados. Then May brought the deep-running schools of wahoos. Heavy tunas and bigger sharks were always lurking along the western drop off.

Cheesy had been the first mate almost since the beginning of Sunset Bay and that was before Dag's time. Eric Chessman was a large, hulking, red-faced, never-tanned man from London. He always wore the official khaki working man's outfit. The shirt sleeves were neatly rolled up and the outfit was topped with a blue Penn cap. This week he was coddling Mr. Mac Dougal, a middle-aged, now sunburned tourist from the continually mentioned 'much more temperate bogs.' The Scot's nose and ears smeared with bright white zinc oxide were a stark contrast to his deeply sun-reddened cheeks and neck. Cheesy had provided a wide-brimmed, sombrero style straw hat creating a humorous caricature swaying in the centered fighting chair.

Father, Captain Harry, was attired identically to Cheesy, but wearing a white captain's hat that had seen better days. They were a team and dressed the part of expert, well-worn fishermen. Cheesy provided the small talk and an infrequent cold drink, if the paying angler had adequate sea legs and wasn't blue in the gills. Harry stayed quiet, aloof, and aloft in the upper steering station. Both, constantly wary, watching for birds. Birds followed small fish; big fish followed smaller fish. This was the essence of the Caribbean Sea's food chain.

Harry waved his cap and Cheesy approached the seated angler with the gold reeled rod and placed it into the chair's gimbaled holder.

"Better get ready, sir, Harry sees a billfish working close to the bait," Cheesy quietly said. Never taking his eyes off the stern wake, he reached and flicked the drag a few seconds so the reel free spooled about ten meters farther back. Harry slowed the engines so the bait would sink.

"Really?" The Scot-infused accent asked, "Really, he can see one coming?" At that precise moment, the rod bent and the reel screamed as the angler was jerked forward to the task.

All eyes widened as a huge blue marlin rocketed out of the water thirty meters behind the boat and tail walked, splashing fine rainbows, another twenty meters across the stern wake before diving into the cobalt depths.

"He's sounding, going deep; hold on. Loosen the drag, Cheese!" Harry shouted from the tower as he throttled back. The engines were quiet, only the reel squealed as more monofilament line peeled out.

"No, don't crank the reel, just hold on," Cheesy said, busy cranking in the other reels to prevent a tangle. Then Cheesy tried to clip the straps from the chair's harness to the reel, so it couldn't go overboard if the angler lost his grip, which they often did. The intent angler pumped the arched rod and told him to hold off and back away.

With each pump back and forth, the Scotsman grimaced; his butt sliding in the varnished oak fighting chair. Again, the spectacular fish shot up out of the sea and plowed through the waves. Marlin were probably the strongest of all the game fish, continually rolling and lashing their bills as a bull would thrust its horns when it entered the ring facing the matador. The angler was tied to the monster fish by a thin, almost invisible line. This was a war of muscle.

The Scotsman lurched, twisted out of the fighting chair. Cheesy flung his arms around his shoulders and pulled him back into the seat.

Mama Cassy, sister Mia, and brother Tim all stood silent at the spectacle, mouths agape. In the action, the tourist's straw hat went with the breeze. Then he lost his grip on the rod and reel, later blaming sweaty hands. Luckily, the line snagged in the transom gate and rod tip eye wedged on the deck with the reel still screaming, stripping the line. Cheesy helped the flushed angler.

Dag scooted across the stern, grabbed the rod, and cinched it tightly with a line from a fender float. The nine-year-old knew enough that if the expensive equipment went overboard, Pop would be pissed. The boy smiled as he looked for confirmation from a scowling Harry who was climbing down the ladder.

"Someone damn well better grab that rod!" Harry proclaimed loudly as he snatched it himself. "Cheesy, tend to the customer's bruises. Dag, get in the chair. Let's see what you can do!" Harry untied the rod and loosened the drag lever. With the line free spooling, there was no pull from the marlin. He could lock the rod butt to the chair.

Dag remembered and reveled at his first slight taste of early maturity as his small left hand grabbed the stock of the rod above the reel before Harry switched the drag lever back on. Dag's right hand made a few easy cranks rolling in the slack line before he felt the weight of the fish. It wasn't his first big fish, but it was his first huge fish. His toothy grin quickly changed to wide-eyed gasps. Harry slipped into reverse and adeptly backed down, chasing the marlin in reverse so Dag could rapidly reel in line.

A full smile returned as he remembered his mother's arms surrounding his small body, trying to lock him to the seat as a human safety harness. Cheesy found a few seconds to snap the safety clips on the reel before returning to their anguished guest.

Everyone watched Dag on center stage fighting his first big blue. His small arm muscles strained as sweat soaked his shirt. The Scot had enough composure to rummage in his shoulder bag to find his movie camera. He began filming while still being braced by Cheesy.

Dag's small hands quickly cranked the reel as the reversing boat cut the distance to the billfish, but his arms were aching. Waves hit the transom and made a continuous prism.

"Harry! Harry! Don't!" he remembered his mother shouting, but he didn't know why. Even then Dag knew the worst that could happen was he'd lose the fish. And what were they going to do anyway except release it? He concentrated on cranking in the line.

"He's old enough. Let him try," he heard his father's reply and it elated him. Harry's words provided more energy to pump the rod and crank the reel. Tim and Mia each sat low, between the chair and the transom. They helped push the rod up so Dag could wind in a few more meters of line. All knew their family was about fishing and fishing was the family.

Harry upped the throttles in reverse. The fish's dorsal sliced through the wake, twenty meters off the stern.

"Pull boy, pull. Mother, get the camera. This is one of those Kodak moments if there ever was one," Harry proclaimed.

Cheesy snatched the leader's swivel, meaning this was an official catch. Harry came down and grabbed the rod, "Son, step on the dive platform and get your picture taken. Be careful, don't slip off. Sharks undoubtedly lurking."

"Harry!" Mother yelled.

"It'll be okay. This blue played himself out. We gotta get the boy some pictures."

Cheesy had a good grip on the leader as Dag carefully walked through the stern gate and onto the dive platform. The Scotsman's Honeywell-Pentax 8mm camera had captured the struggle on celluloid.

The family's Instamatic clicked as the fish thrashed. Dag jumped, stumbled, caught his balance, and then dove over the transom to the safe deck space. Cassy wrapped him again in her warm arms and the two, mother and son, rocked back and forth. The boy felt young and protected, yet also mature and immortal.

Dag remembered beaming more at this catch with the family than when he officially experienced sex for the first time. Next, his father's arm was wrapped around him and carried Dag again to the fish still resting on the diving platform. Brother Tim took another two photos, looking down from the tuna tower. Spectacle finished; they pushed the fish back into the sea.

They all saluted as it swam away into the deep.

After the release, "Son, you did good, really good. Mother, don't coddle the boy. Let him be, he did great. That's your first blue. Probably goes 300 plus, but, you know, we had to release it." Harry glanced, smiling at the Scotsman, "If you were a paying customer, we'd might have killed it, and given it to Otto, the taxidermist. Then, you could have a dust-collecting trophy to brag about. But, as it is, you'll have the photos to show your kids one day, like you've seen mine with my dad. Maybe this man will be so gracious, and he'll send you a copy of the movie."

The Scot winked with a nod and a thumb up. Years of watching that film wore it out until they had to splice the pieces together with clear cellophane tape.

Harry tussled Dag's shaggy hair. "Hey, Mr. Mac Dougal, you don't want to call it a day, do you? Cheesy, get set up. Check all the baits and get the lines back out. Set up the International with another bonito. What do you say?" he shouted, "Let's go fishing. I can smell another big blue out there 'specially for you. Let's go raise another big one. Hell," he glanced at his watch, "it's only one, we got time to raise another half dozen!"

Harry grabbed a Budweiser long-neck from the ice chest and toasted, "This one's for you." Dag knew they said it to him. Mr. Mac Dougal believed it was meant for him, but Harry had raised the brown bottle to Neptune and Poseidon, the fishing gods and ushered his usual fish prayer, "Jesus, Jehovah, Neptune, Poseidon, Allah, Mohammed, Buddha, Confucius, please give us a fish. I think I covered them all. Oh yeah, please give us a big billfish."

Cheesy readied every rod again. The Scotsman was back in the chair and Dag was enjoying hugs from tiny sister Mia. Tim slapped him on his back. "Knew you could do it, bro; never doubted you for a minute." They all laughed and then sat back and quietly watched the remainder of that afternoon's late show.

That had been an exceptional day. Things were different now as Dag surveyed the bay. "It will be the same again," he muttered as he stood up. "Hello! Hello! Anybody?"

Harry appeared on the boat wearing a ragged, stained tank top and the usual faded blue Penn Reel cap. While still tall, the lanky part had slipped into a round belly. The new, scruffy beard added to the long hair that draped around the balding spot Dag knew was hidden by the hat.

"Who's making all the noise, disturbing the fine quiet of nature?" He shielded his eyes from the bright sun and saw only a silhouette on the dock. Harry looked at his watch. "What do ya want? It ain't even 9 AM yet."

"Hello, it's me, your son."

"Think I'm that bad off? I can see who you are. Early to collect your share of the inheritance, aren't you? What ya want?"

"Will you row in or do I have to swim out to talk?"

"I'd row in, but I think I lost a paddle somewhere. Don't think I'm up to swimming this early. So, if you want up close and personal, you'd better be the one getting wet."

Undressed to his jockies, Dag swam and pulled himself onto the dive platform. Harry had opened the transom gate as a slight welcome.

"Wow!" Dag whispered, catching sight of the mess.

"Wow... wow what?" Harry said regally from the fighting chair.

"Wow, dad," he moved to hug his father who shot up an arm to foil the embrace. "What have you been up to? Been a while, huh?"

"Well, son, look around. Nothing good's been happening."

Empty beer and rum bottles littered the deck space. Electrical wires were visible, pulled out of their chase from under the deck rail. The starboard engine cover was propped open. He peered below into a greasy, sloshing bilge below the huge Caterpillar diesel.

"So?" Harry snorted.

"It's good to see you again... Dad." Dag gave Harry a good scan. His father's eyes were still beaming bright blue, but surrounded by deeper and grayer sockets. His father's hair had thinned and grayed, but the older man managed to beam a true, welcome-home smile.

"Save it, boy. You didn't come just to say hello. These days everybody wants something. What do you want? Where you dragging baits now? You're still fishing, aren't you?"

"Dad, I really don't want or need anything. I'm fishing, running a boat out of Puerta Caldera, Costa Rica. Life isn't too bad."

"What type of fishing you doing?"

"What I know, what you taught me." Dag smiled and patted his father on the shoulders. "Same as this. Catch a lot of marlin, tuna, wahoo, and dolphin when they're running. The businessmen from San Jose all want a trophy."

"Killing what you catch?"

"Depends,' Dag paused, "mostly yes. But it doesn't make much difference, because all the long-line trawlers are hauling them in. At least, my crew releases some."

Harry slammed his fists on the arms of the fighting chair. "Damn fools. Big old billfish are too tough to eat and the small ones ain't bred yet. Those imbeciles probably selling the next generation's best fighting sport fish for cat food. Tried to tell them, all of them, only so many ocean gar out there. Look at what they've done to the swordfish. All that's left of them is babies. Now they're killing all the sharks for fin soup. Hell!"

"Yeah, Dad, I know, but after that record fourteen-hundred-pound blue the guy caught off Brazil, all the rich boys want to get their names in the book." Dag started filling a five-gallon bucket with trash. "What have you been catching lately?"

"Look around, boy," Harry picked up an empty rum bottle. "All I been catching is bad luck and trying to chase it with a good buzz. Been a shit storm up here lately." His tone lost the harshness. "So, why are you here?"

"Cheesy emailed me about the situation."

"Damn meddling Limey!"

"Cheesy's a friend, our best friend. He mentioned problems and that you could use a hand with the boat."

Harry puffed up his chest. "Me, needing your help? Boy, I don't know?" he slumped against the back of the chair holding his head in his hands, shaking back and forth. "Cheesy's right about the problems, but it was wrong to call you. You left the family," Harry mumbled.

"You chased me away."

"Broke my rules, boy. Got to abide by the rules or the entire family could suffer."

"That was a long time ago. I've forgotten about it and hoped you would have. You're my father and I'm here to help my family, no more, no less."

"No more or less, huh? Did Cheesy tell you what's going on around here? Your family, hmm, part of our family is the problem. Your Uncle Sammy is a leech, trying to suck the blood out of this bay since your Granddaddy Curly died. You didn't even come to pay your respects!"

"No one told me until I got a letter from Mom. By then, Granpop was already buried. Dad, let it go. Please, life's short. I miss you and Mom. Let me help. What do you need?"

Harry laughed, "What don't I need! A winning lottery ticket would help." He looked at Dag with sad eyes. "They got us in a bad way. Somebody monkeyed up *Sassy*'s engines. I think they spoiled the fuel."

Harry stood and slowly climbed to the controls at the upper steering station. "Look at this mess. They pulled the wires out of all the gauges. "Had her tied to the dock and somebody did me dirty! That's why I moved her off to the mooring. Made it this far before the engines conked. Checked the filters and they got some sludge. Ain't made a cent in months! Still getting messages, emails, and letters from people who want reservations, but can't accommodate until I get both *Sassys* fixed. This one, and your mom."

It wasn't hard to see the complete body shiver that overtook his father. It was either alcohol withdrawal, lack of sleep, or sadness. Dag assumed it was a total combination. "What do you think it will take to get her back in shape?" he asked.

"Money. Time and money. Maybe some magic," his father returned. "That's for the boat; who knows about mother?"

"Let me help. Come on, it's no biggie. We can tear the diesels down, flush out the tanks. We both know these Cat engines like the backs of our hands. I'll intervene and bring peace between you and mom."

"Good luck with all that! You probably got better things to do. Starting to sound confusing already." Harry paused and rubbed his beard. "But okay. I'll admit, I need help. Your mother will be glad to see you."

"One thing, Dad, cut back on the boozing. I can't take it, and won't take it. We get to it and stay at it until we get everything straightened out."

"Already giving orders! You are your mother's son. R-I-T-A!" Harry grabbed another rum bottle off the deck and slowly said, "Boy, this has been my only friend lately. Rita, R-I-T-A, rum – is – the - answer. Can't say I'll succeed, but I'll try to dry out. I'm ready to try a lot of things." He shook out the few remaining drops from the bottle over the side.

"Rita has chased away a lot of people," Dag added.

Harry gave another body shudder and grabbed Dag in a hug around his broad shoulders. "It's great to see you again… son." They broke apart, each looking different directions while wiping their eyes.

"Let's go get some food, get cleaned up, and make a plan. I'm hungry. Been traveling since yesterday. You know it isn't easy to get here. Where's Mom? I hallooed, but got no answer."

"That's another problem. Your mother, well Cassy and me aren't getting along. Nah, it wasn't the rum, well maybe, sort of. Hell, I don't know. I'm stubborn, she's stubborn, and we ain't talking. I got some canned beans here. Will that do?"

"Let's go ashore and figure out a plan while we eat something."

"Have to cook it yourself. Your mother's back working at the restaurant."

"Everything starts here, huh, isn't that what you used to say? Everything starts with the *Sassy Cassy*. Well, this is the start!" Dag playfully shoved Harry over the side with a big splash. "You said you only had one paddle for the dinghy. Got to swim for it, Dad."

"Damn kids, should have had a vasectomy!" He rubbed his face in the saltwater. "Okay, okay, I'm swimming. Son, I'll try, but trying might not fix all that's broke. Ya know what I mean?"

Dag made a shallow dive and popped up close to Harry. "Depends on what all's broke. You and I can do this. *Sassy*'s one of the family. She just needs a transfusion." He pointed back at the fishing boat. "We'll put some money in there. With fresh fuel, we'll get her purring again."

"And we'll have to sleep on her, to keep the bastards away," Harry concurred. "Someone's up to mischief and I'm pretty sure it's your uncle Sammy.

They were both treading water. Dag asked, "Pretty sure, but not certain?"

"Unless I catch him red-handed pissing in the tanks, he'll always be your mother's half-brother. But things have changed on Union Island. You'll see. Hey, I'm swimming in. You can do whatever, but I'm swimming in. You're right, a good meal after this sea bath and we'll make some plans."

Harry stroked ashore while Dag swam farther out to see the cliffs and the bay's mouth out to the Caribbean Sea. Everything beyond their homestead had stayed the same, natural and pristine. He could see the pebble beach where they'd snorkeled as kids. Rapid Point trailed into the blue sky as the north border of their bay. Dag smiled, "Aren't many people who can say they owned a bay. Looks like we've got to hold on to this one."

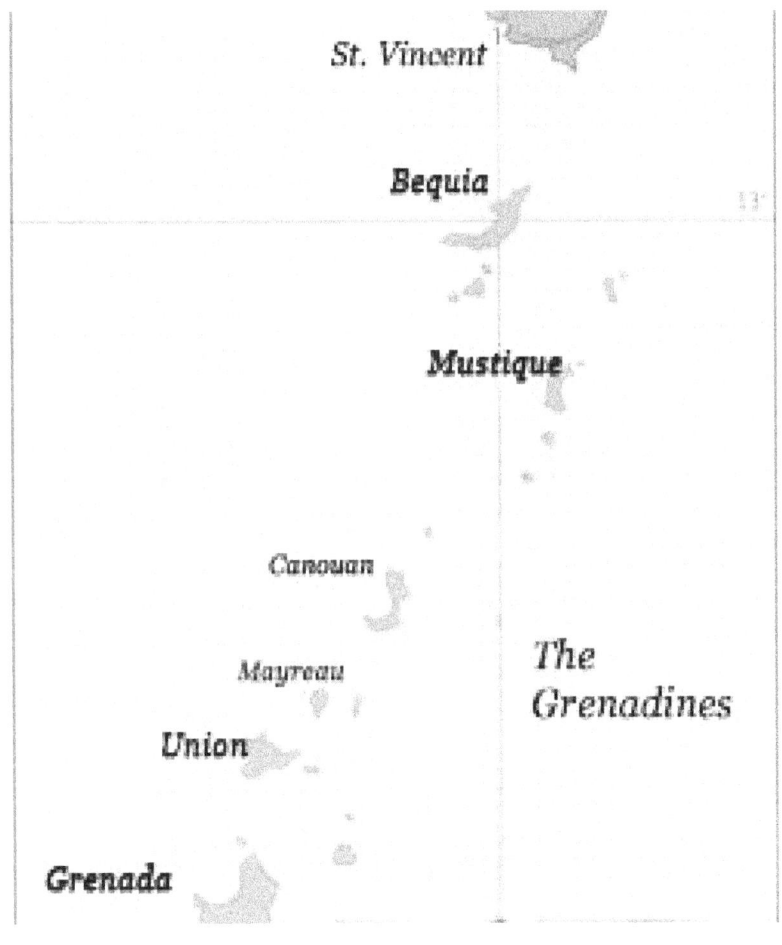

CHAPTER TWO

Harry was singing a Jimmy Buffett tune as he used the garden hose for a freshwater rinse. "… she was looking for a man of strong bond, any direction he sailed would be fine… that's about all I remember of that tune." Harry turned to Dag, "You get married? Knock up any senoritas? So much for the small talk." He shook himself to dry in the afternoon sun.

"No, dad, been playing it pretty slow, mostly fishing. Got ladies I date. Nothing serious. Fishing is serious. Living on the boat, saving money. Get paid in pesos, but usually tipped in dollars. No overhead. Been able to sock a good bit away. Figure it will come in handy now."

A squawk interrupted the conversation.

"Can't be! No way, Redbeard's still around?"

"Yes sir, that bird's too mean to croak. He'll probably squawk at both our funerals. Guess he heard your voice. Them birds are too smart," Harry wiped his face. "Just like your mom, never forgets a thing. I'll see if I can roust up some clean towels."

Dag grabbed his bag from the dock and stood for a moment to let it all sink in. Watching the porch, Harry'd left the front door ajar and he could see that little of the interior décor he remembered had changed.

He walked into the entry alcove and found it still plastered with framed family photos from babies to graduations. His sister Mia was the only one who'd married, but there weren't any shots of her and the lucky gent. He turned into the kitchen.

Redbeard squawked again and fluttered his red wings when he saw Dag. "The Hell you say! Argh! Fish on! Cheesy get that rod!" The bird mimicked.

Dag carefully approached the big, sergeant macaw who appeared to be dancing on his post, raising one leg at a time. "You miss me, you mean bastard?"

The bird rolled his head and warbled, "Hello! Hello! Redbeard wants a cracker."

"Give you a cracker, my ass. I know you just want a chance to get at my flesh again." Dag shook his scarred ring finger while he looked for a suitable treat. "Here's a peanut, bird."

The macaw grabbed the peanut with his left claw and said, "'Thank you, too." Before he peeled the shell.

The old-fashioned kitchen still had the gray wainscoting, but the flat white walls had been turned a slight shade of orangish-tan from the sun coming through the now curtainless windows. This room was another mess, with dishes piled in the porcelain sink with more where they'd been used at the table. Pots and frying pans crusted with curdled grease sat on the splattered gas range. Dag removed everything from the sink and began by scrubbing the basin clean. The solar hot water still worked and one pot at a time was scoured and hung at its place on the wooden rack above the stove. Then the stove and table were cleaned and Dag was mopping the white tile floor when Harry reappeared, clean-shaven with an almost fresh towel on his arm.

"I still got good timing, huh? Always wait 'til most of the hard work is finished." He traded the towel for the mop. "Best you use the garden hose outside. Otherwise, we'll never get anything in our bellies 'cause you'll want to do the happy housemaid routine in the bathrooms."

"That bad?" Dag asked and headed to the garden without waiting for an answer. He headed to the garden.

While he was gone, the mop swirled and scrubbed a few stains, then rinsed and scrubbed again.

"Now that don't look too bad, does it, son? Guess things got a little ahead of me."

"Just a little," Dag shrugged, toweling his hair. "No biggie, but let's get the house spruced up to smooth things with mom."

"Son, things are a bumpy road between me and your mom. Might need a D-7 bulldozer to smooth it down. I agree, but my eyes ain't as good as they used to be." Harry squinted, "As you can tell, I can't see much of a mess anymore." He laughed.

"I remember; you had two disabilities," Dag replied. "Couldn't see and either didn't hear or didn't listen."

"Well, you kids were the troops sent in when the action was tough." Harry wore a broad grin. "Looks like the same now. Not to worry, I'll help. Kitchen looks okay, but your mom will always find fault. I got to agree with your program. It ain't made noon yet. I'll take the upstairs bathroom; you take the downstairs. Pile up all the dirty laundry and I'll call Verena, Cheesy's wife. She'll come and take it in their skiff. Better to pay her and get it done without involving dear mother." Harry playfully punched Dag on the shoulder. "Yes sir, you are a sight for my sore eyes. We'll get our boat back in shape and you know damn well that red-faced English bloke is gonna be in the engine pits with us twisting spanners."

Just then Redbeard squawked, "Cheesy, where the Hell are you?"

"Damn bird, never forgets what he hears."

"Far as food, didn't see much in the fridge or in the pantry," Dag commented.

Harry pursed his lips. "Told you, I had a can of beans on the boat. Without it running, I haven't been out and about too much. Common sense said I should stick close to home. Going into town would only mean arguments. Either be disagreeing with mother or her damn brother. Cheesy brought me rum, mind you only for medicinal purposes, and Verena kept me in eats."

"Yeah, I can see," Dag spread his arms wide, "you didn't cook much."

"Well, she helped when the freezer was empty." They both laughed and headed to tidy the bathrooms.

An hour and two large piles of dirty laundry later, Dag said, "I'm starving; still a growing boy. What say we trot to town and see what mom's cooking? I'll surprise her and we can have a good lunch and chat. Come on, Dad?"

"I think I can tell you how that's gonna go, but like I said I'm ready to make some changes, necessary changes. I'll bet that lunch won't be relaxing. Better I stay here and chow on beans." Harry grabbed Dag in a tight embrace. "Sorry about the words earlier. Hell, I'm so happy to see you. First bright spot in months. Wish it was better days."

They looked at the road back to town. Dag put his arm around his father's shoulder and in a Bob Marley voice said, "Don't worry 'bout a ting, now, everyting, gonna be all right." He pulled Harry close and their blue eyes met. "Better days are just around the bend. Come on, come with me to see mom. She won't be out of sorts seeing me. You get a free pass."

"Son, you haven't figured it out? Harry never gets a free anything. Okay, okay, like I said, I'm willing to try a lot of things."

^^^^^^^^^

The long walk to town became their primary planning session. First, they'd need Cheesy. He was almost family, a talented mechanic, and knew the *Sassy* as well as they did. He also had a good skiff and that would be needed to dispose of the old diesel once they drained it as the initial stage of the recovery process. If they were lucky, and Harry pessimistically predicted they wouldn't be, the diesels would run smoothly again after all the filters were changed and the fuel lines flushed.

"Nice to be optimistic, son, but pretty clear the injectors and pump are fouled."

"Might be, but we got to start somewhere. Come on, dad, think positive."

"I agree. I'll change the oil, everything, so it's all up to par when we crank her over. Have to burn the old fuel on the pebble beach. Gonna have to cut inspection ports on top of the fuel tanks to swab them out. Damn, sorry I didn't catch the bastards."

"Sure, Pops, we've been living here for thirty years. Bet they'd still throw your old white ass in jail for even punching a 'barne here' vandal."

"Yep, ain't it great doing business in the Caribbean!"

^^^^^^^^^

Clifton in the afternoon was heated and dry. Both Dag and Harry were sweating heavily after the half-hour walk to reach the family's restaurant on the quiet Main Street.

"Not much traffic today. Guess nobody knows Dag St. Claire is back in town." Harry laughed. "Think the girlies would be washing out their best panties. What happened to that girlie-friend you had here? What was her name?"

Dag swallowed hard, knowing dating a local woman of color had always been a sore spot with his father. "Rosa. You know it well and probably know better than me what she's up to these days. I heard she married last year."

Harry feigned a frown, "Must have gotten tired of waitin' for you."

"Probably. We kept in touch, but I bounced around fishing from Grenada to Venezuela before all that political shit hit the fan. Calling from Costa Rica isn't easy."

"Don't we know; your mama's been worrying between your every-other-month phone calls. That was when we was still talking…"

"Shh," Dag put his finger to his lips. "We're here. I want to try to surprise mom"

"Try to not surprise her too much. Cassy ain't as young as she used to be," Harry grinned.

The St. Claire family's restaurant was open to the street, one building upwind from the ferry dock. A block away on the waterside of

Main Street was Curly Scarbeaux' Grocery and Hardware. Both sides of the street were lined with many small stalls displaying t-shirts, conch shells, jagged shark jaws, and wooden model sailboats. Both businesses were monuments to the Scarbeaux family.

The restaurant, Granma's, was the pride of Curly's second wife, Gretchen. A wide awning of thatched palm fronds supported by thick, rough wooden columns shaded its front. All the windows had shutters that were hinged at the top and doubled as nighttime security. The tables and benches were of the same rough hardwoods. Importing lumber from South America had been the family patriarch's main moneymaker. Decades ago, local boat building had been a big industry. It was necessary for fishing.

The hardware store had grown with the fishing industry and had the only marine fuel pumps on the island. Presently, Scarbeaux Hardware sold outboard and inboard motors and every necessary marine after-market part, besides cement, nails, and finished lumber.

Aromas from the big, stone barbecue grill that sat at the street's edge were the key attraction after reasonably priced, cold beer. The grill man, big, dark, West Indian Honoré, moved to embrace the young man, but Dag waved him off. He peeked around the corner and didn't see his mother. There were two tourist couples and a few locals at separate tables enjoying beers and sandwiches. He chose a seat with his back to the kitchen.

"Hey, can I get some service? Anybody working today?" Dag shouted as the other customers cringed.

"Well, if you're in a hurry, you're on the wrong island," came a familiar return shout from behind the bar. "Be with you in a minute."

"Come on, will ya? Always the slow island service…"

"Hey, you can always take your business elsewhere." The voice laughed, "If you can find 'elsewhere' in Clifton." Cassandra St. Claire swayed through the kitchen door draped with a curtain behind the small bar. She looked at least a decade younger than her forty-six years. Genetics provided a permanent tan highlighted by the long, sun-streaked hair pulled into a ponytail. Her light green eyes gave a searching look. "Who's complaining about my service?"

Dag stood and turned.

"Oh, my God! Dag, Dag, is it really you? It is so good to see you, son." Her six-foot slender frame leaped upon her son, crying, amid hugs and kisses. The outburst startled the tourists, but the locals stood and approached, politely waiting for Cassy to disengage once her motherliness ran out.

"What are you doing here?" She said, as she let go of her son to wipe her eyes. "I'm so glad to see you. I've missed you so much." Cassy sank into a chair, patting the table for her son to sit.

Squeezing her hand, Dag smiled through his explanation. "Home to help. Heard this might be a time to lend a needed hand."

"Oh, dear Lord, we've got..." Harry turned the corner into the bar, waving a hand back and forth like a railroad signalman.

"What are you doing here?" Cassy uttered in a completely different, much colder tone.

The older man shrugged and pushed his hands deep into his pockets. "Ah, I don't know. I really don't know." Harry's tone took on a bit of a growl until he read a pleading look from his son. "Oh, with the boy here, appearing like a good surprise, I thought..."

"You thought what?" Cassy snapped, "Exactly what conclusion did that rum-soaked brain of yours formulate?"

His lips grew a long frown. "Well, I thought..."

Dag cut Harry off before inciting an argument. "Mom, I talked dad into coming to get lunch and thought we could have a reunion."

"Okay," Cassy shot a produced smile at her husband, then stood, moved behind Dag so he separated them with a 'no-fight' zone. She hugged her son, pulled off his cap and ruffled his long hair. "Okay, honey, it is so good to see you."

Pointing to a larger table and the local fishermen watching, "Take that one and you guys, you know my... hmmm... our son. Come on, happy hour started early this afternoon. Honoré, help me out with the bar and come sit with us."

Skeptically looking at Harry, "What can I bring you to drink?"

Harry beamed his version of the produced smile, "Bring us all club soda. I feel like a club soda." He beamed to his wife and accented soda, "You know how I like my club soda, on ice with a piece of lime."

"Oh yes, Harry's special soda, coming right up." Cassy twirled the cloth she used to wipe tables. "Beer okay for the rest of you?" was met with affirmative nods.

Sonny, a very large–bellied dark local, asked as he extended his hand, "Been awhile Dag. Good to see you. How you been keeping?"

"Things are good, for now. Working hard; fishing. How about you and the boys? Things good, I hope?" Dag rose and shook every man's hand.

"Things slow, partner, but I guess Harry here told you that. Season wasn't much." The other two men quietly nodded. "We sellin' our fish up in Canouan, to the big resorts, but they ain't paying shit. They know we desperate. Damn, we hurtin' for water here, and dey got enough to keep a golf course green."

"Yeah, be good if we got something like that here. Some development, you know. Bring in a de-sal plant. You must be dealing with hotels in other places, ain't you?" Sambal, the Trini Indian asked. "I come up here 'cause crime so bad down my way. Dangerous place now."

"That's what development brings." Harry started, "Things good, then things terrible."

"But you…" Sonny began.

"Hey guys," Cassy appeared with beers, "Would you mind letting us have some family time? We haven't seen our son in a while." She handed the beers. "These are on the house."

The three men shuffled away again after shaking Dag's hand, ignoring Harry.

"Harry, don't stir the coals. You know what that will start," Cassy insisted.

"Ah, you're right. Today, I'll keep my trap shut. Son, we're both," Harry nodded to Cassy, "so happy to see you. Might mean a new day has dawned for the St. Claires and Sunset Bay. Here's a toast to better days." They touched their clear sodas. Harry took a gulp and his wince was noticeable. He smiled at Cassy, "See, Mother, a new day has dawned. I'm trying all kinds of new things."

"Bullshit, we'll see how long this one lasts. Got some nice yellowtail snapper fried in my red Creole sauce with green banana and yellow rice." She looked only at Dag, "Hungry?"

"Absolutely, mom."

"Me, too, mom," Harry stammered.

An hour later their table was cluttered with empty plates, most piled with fish bones. Harry pushed back his chair and rubbed his belly as Cassy talked about the other children.

"They're all about as communicative as you."

"Tim is in England, some sort of accountant or something in a big bank. I guess he's doing well. You know how smart he is with numbers."

"And everything else he tried," Dag added.

"And Mia's in," Cassy sighed, "or rather, on a charter yacht somewhere in the Caribbean. We saw her when they anchored off last summer. They came south in the hurricane season. You heard what happened to Kurt, her husband? We met him once; shot himself, despondent, or something."

"Yeah, I heard all that. We try to stay in erratic touch via email."

"Despondent," Harry laughed. "Despondent my ass. Making a living off a yacht in the Caribbean with our sweet Mia as crew." His face grew serious, "I guess that could make you despond. Huh? That guy was never right. She met him when he was an Elvis impersonator on a cruise ship. Despondent my ass!"

"Shh!" Cassy looked away, shook her head to clear the moment of sadness, and suddenly reached for both Harry's and Dag's hands. "We're a family and always will be. When one hurts, we all feel it. Tim's like us, tough, can stand alone against anything. Mia… well, Mia isn't that tough. She never liked…" Cassy cleared her throat, "She wanted more than fishing and living on a small island."

"Tim, too," Harry said solemnly, "But at least he didn't marry up with a nutball."

"Shh, Harry. Timmy got scholarships, free getaway tickets."

"Mom, dad," Dag said, "it is what it is and only what we make it. No more, no less. All of us know how lucky we were to live together on Sunset and have you for parents. This is paradise."

Cassy smiled, "Thank you, Dag. The way all of you disappeared, well, we have to think you didn't want to be here anymore."

"No mom, I made a little mess and needed to get away for a bit, you know, gain some perspective." He slapped his father's hand. "Right dad, you said I needed a different perspective?"

With his lower lip pushed out, Harry tilted his head and sang a couple of lyrics, "You don't know what you got 'til it's gone."

"Surprised you can remember any words," Cassy said. "I'll clean up while you two chat. Honoré, give me a hand. Good thing business has been extra slow."

"Yeah, only today," Harry smirked.

"You heard Sonny; it's been a bad season."

"Season ain't got shit to do with it. People ain't coming to Curly's like they used to 'cause we don't want… nah, because we're fighting development."

"Hush, someone will hear. This isn't the time or the place," Cassy argued. "Everyone wants a change. That's what we're just talking about, you and Tim and Mia just wanted to get a change. Look around different places."

"Yes, mother," Harry spoke condescendingly, "But they traveled off-island for a change. These morons want to change our home and it won't be for the better."

Cassy clattered some plates into a plastic tub. "Don't call our friends and neighbors morons!" She traipsed the load to the kitchen.

"Okay, dummies," Harry gulped the club soda and gagged. "Gonna be hard, son, gonna be hard."

"Let's change the subject," Dag offered, "Costa Rica has lots of big boats. For a country so poor, they sure have a lot of wealthy fishermen."

"So, what do you figure the biggest blue you caught so far?"

"Big, but not that big. We caught one eight-fifty. Seen a lot of fifteen-foot, thousand-plus pounders in the freezers of the longline boats. You know, I still think the one we hooked off of Diamond Rock is the biggest fish I've ever seen."

Harry rattled the ice in his glass, "You remember that?" Harry chuckled, "Junish, remember that fish? Had to go twenty or more fat feet. He bent our outrigger at twenty-five feet with his bill, and his tail wasn't far from the water."

"Not far at all. Junish dwarfs any fish I ever even heard of. Dad, I don't tell people about that fish."

"Good. Don't want them to come trying for it," Harry said.

"If we can't catch him, nobody... But it would be embarrassing; nobody would believe its size."

Cassy brought another tray of club sodas and watched Harry wince. "Junish, did I hear Junish? That day almost chased me off the water for good." She draped her slender arms over Dag's shoulders. "It is so good to see you. I guess the first thing your father told you was about Sammy trying to get our bay. You can see, I'm back to working here trying to reduce expenses."

"Uh-huh," Harry commented, "Uh-huh, you're really reducing expenses."

"So, exactly what did your sorry ass decide to do, stay drunk and sleep it off through the eviction? We were lucky to get a lenient six months to pay the fines. Then they become overdue and the government will repossess. And there's the past five years of license fees staring at us in the face. At least, they didn't order an immediate shutdown."

"Dag, I dug a deep hole and they're filling it back up, burying us."

"Judge Abraham gave us a break," Cassy added.

"Some break," Harry spurted.

"He said that our title was solid but..."

"But your uncle, your mother's half-brother, got them to find us in violation of a license."

"Never knew anyone needed a fishing license here."

"No, for a guest house," Cassy explained.

"Well, Abe's been out fishing on *Sassy* several times and knew we had fishermen stay overnight. The damn airport here; no one can get in and out when they want."

"They fined you? What's the big number?" Dag asked.

Harry made a long whistle, "Let's see, even though we been operating here twenty-plus years, Abe fined us for only the last five years, one hundred grand a year. The license is another one hundred grand. That comes to six hundred with three more zeros. And, we're required to pay next year's license before the end of this year. Another one hundred and that doesn't include fixing the boat or any of the necessities to live."

"US or EC?" Dag inquired.

"East Caribbean money," Harry answered.

"That's not half so bad." Dag grabbed his mom's pen and waitress pad and did some math, "Two point six seven to one US. Holy shit, we owe the St. Vincent government over two hundred and sixty thousand US!" How soon is it due?"

"I've been paying what I make, a sort of good faith, here but they're calling it due December thirty-first. The year ends and so do we, if…"

Harry interrupted his wife. "They sabotaged our operation, five months with a boat that don't run."

"We can sell some stock," Dag offered.

"I thought about stock, memberships, partners, but that takes more organization than I've got these days. And it means being owing to strangers. Never know when one of them is going to decide to sell you out," Harry sadly lamented.

"No, I mean me, Tim, and Mia will become your silent partners. We don't have enough, but we can stall the machine. Have you tried talking to the Prime Minister?"

"Oh yeah, yes, I talked to Simon, Simon the politician. Hmmm. I thought Simon was a friend. He'd been fishing with us more often than I can count. He…"

"He is why we got the rest of the year to pay the arrears." Cassy cut Harry off. "They could have thrown us out as undesirables or unmentionables."

"Un-hoteliers. They want to buy the bay for five hundred grand. I… we paid two hundred thousand, twenty more years ago without the house and dock." Harry threw back the club soda like it was alcohol.

"We wouldn't sell, anyway. Where would we go? This place, our bay, is everything to us, all we have. They'd mash it up!" Cassy gasped.

"Development," Harry coughed. "Progress."

"I'm sure you've considered it," Dag said.

"See, son, we've already been considered out. But not counted out. Not yet, anyway. Everyone wants that hotel built. Good for business. Business! Look at this place, T-shirt City. Nothing makes this place different from any other saltwater rock. Nothing except the fishing." Harry grabbed and gulped Dag's soda.

"Everything will be okay. You're here." She reached across the table and clasped Dag's hands. "We'll work at it. Maybe now your father will be able to see beyond the bottom of a rum bottle. I hope you can show me how to do email. Cheesy's wife, Verena, has a computer. I'd like to be closer to Tim and Mia."

"No problem, Mom. But I think they'll be much closer very soon. I let them know that I was coming."

"Holy Jesus! My other two are coming back. What about Mia's Kurt? We can't be taking time to nurse someone. We got plenty of our own grief to deal with," Cassy said.

"Kurt passed over," Dag explained.

"You mean Elvis' left the building, the boat, or whatever?" Harry smirked. "Never liked that guy."

"I never met him," Dag replied. "Whatever."

"Too much soda, gotta bleed some out." Harry found the bathroom.

"Tim and Mia are returning? I can't believe it, my little girl… You know the only reason your father wants to keep the bay is so he doesn't have to start over and actually has to go to work again. I want it for you three and your families. The Scarbeauxs, my family, have been here since the first settlers came south from Martinique in 1780. We've always been fishing folk. Guess that's why I was so attracted to your father. I think my brother, Sam, started with good intentions." Cassy paused, "No, I can't say that. Sam smells money and we're in his way."

"I can't believe that he'd do this. I know you and Dad were paying on it."

"Big money back then, five hundred a month, two-day charters. More money than anyone else here saw. I guess that's why they're so spiteful."

"Things are slow on Union Island. Maybe a hotel would liven things up."

"Your father's seldom right, progress is okay, but the business, the hotel and tourist type, is not good. Look at what it has done to every other island. Drove them into debt, crime, and drugs. More people coming does not mean progress. Conserving the Caribbean would be progress."

"We're better off than most other families," Dag replied.

"Better off? We don't pollute with a car," Harry preached as he walked from the bathroom. "Your mother, all of us, ride bicycles, always did. We recycled before it was recycling. Hell, I stack up the bottles to make walls. I think we are the only bay anywhere in the Caribbean without some hotel polluting the water."

"Pretty hard to hold back progress. See it everywhere. Even the far-out sand spits have rooms to rent," Dag said, "Desalination plants are all over. Freshwater is progress. Once they got that, high-rise concrete seems to follow."

"Hopefully not here," Cassy said as she rose from the table. "I'm so glad you came back. I'll get some conch for dinner. I know that's your favorite."

"Let's go back to the boat and start making a list," Harry moved towards the street. "Hmm, that club soda ain't so bad. I've still got motivation."

"See, dad, you can adapt."

"Yes sir, when duty calls your old man, Harry, is up and at them. By the way, how much can you lend us?"

The two men made a direct return, constantly planning the resurrection of Sunset Bay Fish Camp. Having his eldest back on the island had rejuvenated Harry.

"You know, son, everything just kept mounting until it seemed like too much for me to handle. I was just spinning in my tracks; couldn't get started."

"Dad, you should have called us."

"Well, you know me, I couldn't do that. I'm the father. Like my father, I'm supposed to handle the problems and protect the family." He slung his arm over Dag's shoulder. "I'm glad you came back. Cuts the workload in half. You think Tim's gonna show?"

"Definitely. But why didn't you start with Cheesy?"

"It's what we told you, charters been slow, and more than friction with your mother. The government says we are running an illegal hotel and hits us with a big fine, then the other Cassy has problems. No other way to say it; I got weak and succumbed to demon rum. Chessman started preaching one day when I was hungover, and that was enough to tip the scales. We ain't talked much since."

"You're on the outs with Cheesy, too?"

"Not the outs son, more like a lover's quarrel. You know how me and him are; we're friends even when we ain't talking."

"Dad, that's number two on our list; tonight, we patch that up. First, we hit the boat hard with what's left of today. I'll start scraping her bottom. Can you scrape and polish the props?"

Hours later, as darkness spread over the eastern lowlands, the father and son team, wearing only bathing trunks, were slowly tugging the sportfisher to the dock. They wrapped the long anchor rope around a dock post and gained a few feet with every huff and puff.

"Heave and pull; heave and pull," Dag sang like a seasoned sailor on one of the old three-masted sailing ships. "Come on, another half-hour we'll have her to the dock."

"Whoa, boy, I need a break. Hitch her off for a few minutes. You're forgetting the age difference. Your old man hasn't had much exercise lately."

"You got the props shining again. I got about half the bottom scraped. When we get her running good, we'll take her down to Grenada, get her hauled, and paint the bottom."

Harry scratched at his chest hair. "Yeah, and got them damn tiny shrimp crawling all over me like lice. Probably got some other icky-shit inside my ears. Might have been better to wait until we had the full bottom scraped; it wouldn't be so hard to pull."

"Not to worry, we'll get her in. Me too, I got the creepy-crawlers, but, hey, we made some progress. We'll scrub down and find some peroxide to clean out the orifices. You just tail the line, dad, and I'll walk and pull, I want to keep the momentum going."

"Okay, okay, but I'm supposed to be the slave driver, not you," Harry chimed. "Yes, it feels damn good to be getting back on track."

In another twenty minutes, darkness had descended as they cleated the *Sassy Cassy* to the dock. Both men sat with legs dangling over the water, admiring the elegant hull. Darkness descended, marked by the planet Venus.

"You know, she wasn't the only thing I got from my father. He bequeathed knowledge of fishing, the weather, and celestial navigation. Not to mention good will. When my pop passed," Harry looked up into the starry night, "he was one of those very few who no one could say a bad word about." He shrugged and sort of deflated, "Not like me, huh? Well, some of these rich dot-fucking-com idiots think they can buy a boat and gear, and bang, they're in the sportfishing business." Harry paused, "Sure, some are lucky and get by for a few years. Look at how long we've been here, 29 years. Making ends meet since day one."

"Having Curly for a father-in-law didn't hurt."

"Don't even go there, son. It was more your mother than her father. Cassy drew a lot of business. While I was building this dock we're sitting on, she was still pumping fuel and working in the hardware. Mom steered lots of paying tourists to fishing charters." Harry scratched his head, "Damn shrimp. No disrespect to Curly, he sold us this bay, but it was mom who kept our business going. You know that all the while, 'til we built this house, me and her shared the V-berth. Yeah, she'd line up the customers and I'd motor around and pick them up. Without her, I'd never have hustled up as many clients. Once we had the house up with rooms and her cooking, they kept coming back."

"I remember that Elks Club group, the four fat guys from Tennessee that came every April. They brought their own bourbon, got shit-faced drunk, and beet-red sunburned every time."

"But I got them to hook fish, your mom kept their big bellies full, and they tipped extremely well. Them and gangs of Detroit auto workers and all wanted the yearly bragging rights for the biggest billfish. Think we can get them back? I think I got their address and maybe phone numbers somewhere."

"That would be great if you could sort that out tomorrow morning. You're moving back into your house and I'll be the watchman," Dag wrinkled his nose and grinned, grabbing his father's hand, "You keep smoothing that rough road between you and mom."

Harry returned the grin, "Running them boats, got ya used to giving orders, huh? I'll see what I can do. Think your mom knows where the client lists are."

"Dad, can you imagine if the Internet would have been around back then. You'd be famous, might have your own TV show."

"Don't understand much of that Net shit," Harry laughed, "I'm better with a gaff." The older man giggled, "Fish we catch are too big for a net."

"You think mom's coming home tonight?"

"Dag, you're the only reason she'll make a show. I think she's been sleeping on a small cot in the restaurant's office. She's gonna bring us a sweet dinner, you can bet on that. Mama's gonna take excellent care of her firstborn. I heard her say conch."

"So, what's happened between you and mom?"

"Not now. Save that for another day. Looks like with you, Tim, and Mia making a homecoming, she just might let 'ol Harry outta the doghouse."

"What's on the agenda for tomorrow?" Dag asked.

"We can get fresh diesel and try her engines. I'll get Cheesy to bring around two drums and some spare filters. Better him to deal with your uncle."

"We'll need empty drums so we can pump them full of the shitty fuel. Then Cheese and me will horse them ashore. Tomorrow night we'll have a bonfire. How full are the tanks?"

"I had them filled to the brim. I finished a charter and took the clients around to the ferry dock and topped off the tanks. Bought a bottle to celebrate. We caught seven wahoos, nice ones, that day. A few locals were scoping me out. Didn't think much about it. Got up a little late and had her idling at the dock while I cleaned her up. Ran her for a half-hour and then she started to sputter." Harry winced, "Your mom's right; if I hadn't been boozed up, I might have heard them pricks."

"Maybe we should get another dog, a yapper? Early warning."

His father sighed deeply, "Lots of things I let go slack. Be nice to have a good hound around again. Looked at the filters and saw, well you saw the white sludge. That's something more than just water. Not condensation either. I use that fuel additive with every fill-up. To answer your question, 200 gallons of spoiled fucking diesel worth $1600, I ain't got. Damn, my luck."

"It's all small things, dad."

"A mountain of small things." Harry reminded, "Got to be careful not to get a slick on the water. Next thing, the environmental department will be on our asses with another fine. I got some of that good dishwashing liquid that'll hide it."

"You really think so? Think we're being watched?

"Hell yes, your Uncle Sammy wants our bay by hook or by crook. Personally, I don't believe he'll stop at anything."

"Why?" Dag asked.

"Sam's never been happy that your mom and me got this place. Sure, he smiles and did the family thing while Curly was breathing. It has a lot to do with having different mothers. Luella, Sam's mother, did something. I never heard what; it was a big secret, but she was out. He kept Sam because he wanted a son and then married Cassy's mom, Gretchen. Gretchen treated Sam good, and as you know, she was white, a Brit. Gave 'em both a dose of European culture."

"Oh, heard nothing about that. Wow!"

"Wasn't common talk. In those days, most had outside women, but the rule was no diseases and no unwanted babies. Oh, Curly took care of them all. God knows he was making a ton of money. Sam was the son, but he did right by Cass. Gave her this bay as a wedding gift. I had to buy it, 'cause that's how Curly was; nothing for free. Now, with Sammy, he's always had a grudge against me. Ain't been invited to anything he's had going on for a few years. He's joined the never-enough-to-be-satisfied-club. He's making good money at the hardware. Got no overhead, could run for governor. But he wants more and more and more…" Harry paced and looked around at the bay. "We got to watch they don't try it again."

"I'll stay out here. You try to patch things up with Mom."

"Be easier fixing this boat. Be careful where you go. Sam's got almost everyone on the island against us."

The men began scrubbing the grease and grime with dishwashing soap. Dag handed the bottle to his father. "I'll be careful, you be sweet."

"Hello, hello, you still working? My, my, Dag, how did you build a fire under your father?" Cassy rode up to the dock on her bicycle. The front basket was loaded with sealed plastic containers of food. The enticing aroma got the men up from the dock. "Get bathed. I'll have dinner on the table in about twenty minutes."

"Wait 'til she sees the kitchen is cleaned," Harry slapped Dag on the back. "We'll get it done, son."

The front screen door slammed and about a minute later, "Oh, my god!"

"Yep, mom's happy."

"Yeah, she can see the floor again." They both laughed.

The screen door slammed again. Cassy was dragging a long extension cord. "I knew you'd need this to charge the batteries. Come on boys, dinner's ready."

Harry took the cord and plugged in the battery charger. With a smile, nodding his soapy head, "Woman always did know just what to do."

The night grayed into dawn. The smell of coffee was the best alarm clock. "Well boys, I figured you'd want an early start. Scrambled eggs and toast on the table," Cassy shouted from the doorway.

Dag wandered in from the dock and Harry appeared, hair uncombed, from the bathroom. He gave his wife a playful squeeze that was met with a stern look.

"You're still sleeping on the couch. You can clean the house, fix the boat, and do a million other things," She gave him a good-humored shove, "but you're still gonna be sleeping on the couch."

"Ah, give a guy a chance, will ya?"

"Had your chances," but she cracked a bit of a smile as she swatted at his jockey shorts. "Gotta get going and clean up the restaurant. After you left had a lot of customers, mostly women," she smiled, "think they heard Dag is back. What do you say, son, maybe we schedule an appearance of Union Island's most eligible bachelor? I could make a poster?"

Dag pushed out his lips and cocked his head. "Island women or island girls? Be a while until I don't smell like rotten boat-bottom algae or diesel." He laughed, "Maybe just collect their phone numbers."

Cassy light-heartedly slapped his long hair, "It was the women's chapter of the Lions Club. Yes, we have advanced to not only have that club, but a Rotary, and a Chamber of Commerce."

"Uh-huh, yawn, what have they accomplished lately besides having a sit-down dinner at your restaurant?" Harry muttered.

"Couch agreeing with you, Captain Harry?" Cassy joked. "It's a start. Hopefully, they can agree to have a definite area for the souvenir stalls, set up taxi stands, and train people to be professionally hospitable."

"That'll be the day taxi drivers on this rock are hospitable to tourists. They're all rude bandits, gouging, and getting as much as they can get."

"Well, duh, Captain Couch, isn't that what I just said. I listened to the Rotary speaker who came in from Kingston. They're going to rate and inspect their vehicles. If they work the airstrip, they must have good air conditioning and no more charging for extra pieces of luggage."

"Sounds reasonable," Dag interjected. "Is Guido still working or has he retired? He was pretty fair carrying our fishermen."

"He was at the meeting. Guido asked when we were getting busy again. So, Captain Couch, when are we getting busy again?"

"Hmm, where's the sugar?" Harry asked. "

With a pointed finger, Cassy smiled and said, "Haven't you figured it out yet, no sugar for Harry. Here," she handed him a plastic bowl, "same place it always is, in the fridge to keep the ants out."

"Cold, seems, all the sweetness on this rock is giving me the cold shoulder these days."

"Soon we'll have *Sassy* warmed up and running smooth again." Dag said as he gulped breakfast. "You talk with Chessman yet?"

Harry licked coffee from his lips, "He contacted you, right? So why don't you call and chat him up." He wrinkled his nose, "Another unfortunate bad rub in my social abilities."

Do not tell fish stories where the people know you. Particularly, don't tell them where they know the fish," Mark Twain.

CHAPTER THREE

Erik and Verena Chessman sailed into Union Island shortly after Harry had begun the fishing charter business. In the early days, Harry did everything, bait, scout, and captain, steering the boat while scanning the seas to locate fins or birds. The locals proved to be 'irregulars' as he called them. Their appearances for work were totally irregular. The men he hired all liked the sportfishing work, knew the routines, and loved the fresh fish they brought home, but they weren't dependable.

The Chessmans had left a thriving boat building business along the Thames in London seeking better weather. Erik and Verena were a team. They'd met when he studied as a shipwright in Denmark and she learned clothing design. Verena became his logistics and sales manager, locating the materials and the buyers. After twenty successful years, Chessman's hand-laid fiberglass yachts were recognized as strong, dependable, world cruisers easily capable of a safe circumnavigation.

Finishing their twentieth year, it had been their intention to sail their custom 44-foot sloop to greener and warmer pastures, but they were met with a series of international problems. In Algeria, the customs authorities argued over a rifle and a handgun they had declared. But Erik wanted to keep them on board for protection. The weapons were confiscated and Erik jailed until their cash kitty had been drained of 20,000 £.

With the Mediterranean and Africa soured, the couple sailed across the Atlantic hoping to purchase a marina on Grenada, one of the Commonwealth islands. The legalities of the purchase and transfer of ownership to non-residents depleted even more of their finances, again with no success.

By chance, they sailed north and met Cassy St. Claire pumping diesel at Curly's. The two women started chatting, comparing stories and boats. Forty gallons of diesel and two beers later, they became friends. The Chessmans gratefully took the offer and grabbed the extra mooring at Sunset Bay. Over dinner, two nights later, Harry hired Eric as mate and maintenance. That same night, three-year-old Dag tried to pronounce Chess, and it came out cheese. He decided Eric was Cheesy, and it stuck.

Together, Harry and Eric kept detailed written logs, correlated the dates, the moon, weather, sea conditions, with the type and quantity of their catch. Seldom did they return empty. After several years, The Sunset Bay Fish Camp could predict when the fishing would be best for various species. Both families ate fish, fish, and more fish. They socialized, partied, and celebrated until the bad luck tide turned against the St. Claires almost five years ago.

The fraternity of the families seemed to dissolve as the St. Claire children came of age. Each sibling wanted something more. Dag didn't want to push Cheesy out as mate. He wanted his own boat, but knew there probably wouldn't be enough business. Tim knew he was brilliant and desired a position making serious money; that wasn't available on Union Island. Mia craved the bright lights of bigger cities, any cities. Her gaze led elsewhere; she stowed away on a visiting cruise ship.

The morning sun was almost overhead when the father and son mechanics heard an outboard enter the bay. Harry bent lower in the smelly engine room and coughed, "Guess that's Cheesy. You talk, my throat is feeling kind of hoarse."

A small wake rocked *Sassy*. Dag crawled up, on to the deck, wiping his hands with a rag. He waved. Cheesy cleated his skiff, jumped aboard, and hugged the younger man.

Breaking the embrace, Dag managed, "Good to see you Cheesy. You're lookin' good. Verena must have put you on a diet."

The red-faced man pushed out his gut proudly. "Plenty of time later to tell you some of my misadventures." Dag's back was to the engine compartment; he mouthed Harry was below. "Are you available; we could use some help?"

"Let me see," Cheesy quipped counting the fingers on one hand, "Yes, son, nothing scheduled for the next... say, few weeks. Where do you need my assistance? By the way, where's that cantankerous father of yours? Probably still sleeping it off after draining another rum bottle, I presume. Left you here to do the literal dirty work."

Dag was signaling with his finger across his throat to quiet him, but Cheesy continued, "Yes, son," he draped his arm over Dag's shoulder, "your father told me, in no uncertain terms, my services were no longer required in Sunset Bay."

"He did, did he? No way, you're like brothers," Dag moved to stand over the opening above the starboard engine, looking down at Harry's wild-eyed grin from the bilge, "What pissed him off so bad? You two are a tight fishing machine."

"Wrong day," Cheesy recalled. "It was the wrong day. I tried to provide some sound advice, and it was rudely rebuked. I offered to take your father sailing, blue water, out of the sight of land for a week to ten days so he could dry out. He'd been hitting the rum hard and… well, wasn't making decisions. Everything was just sitting there, not a thing getting fixed. Ol' Harry didn't want to hear one more word. So, he's got you working alone?"

"No, not alone."

"Look at you. Back, what, one day, and up to your ears in motor oil!" Cheesy shouted.

Harry barked angrily as he made himself visible in the engine compartment. "Hey, you coaxed him here. He's not working alone, you, you English crumpet. You should have told him what to expect."

"Dad, I didn't have to be coaxed. You're lucky Cheesy respects you enough to want to help."

"No, he's not!" Harry stuck his grimy head above the deck. "We're working together and Mr. Chessman, we would appreciate your help. You'll be compensated."

"Surely, you know I am here to lend a hand and my skiff. What are we doing?"

"You brought two 55-gallon drums, didn't you?"

"Yes."

"Then you know damn well we're draining the spoiled fuel. Hey, Cheesy, I know I'm an asshole when I'm binge drinking." Harry raised his voice, "And you used to put up with me… and my rum tantrums."

"Yes, yes, Captain Harry, I'm accustomed to your temperament. And yes, I brought the drums and a pump."

"Well guys, times wasting," Dag interrupted, "my skin doesn't like diesel and the hot sun. Give me the pump and I'll connect it to the batteries. Dad, you wedge the hose in the port tank and Cheesy, you keep the output hose in the plastic drum."

"Fellows, I think we should only partially fill the drum and make more runs ashore to dump, they'll be lighter to move, and the fiberglass on my skiff won't get badly dinged," said Cheesy.

Dag agreed as Harry returned to cleaning the bilge. It took eight trips to dump all the rotten fuel. Using a broomstick and several rags, they swabbed the interior of the tanks through the inspection plate. Harry remained silent and scrubbed the engine rooms and bilge until they were spotless and he was filthy. Then the captain grabbed a scrub brush, the dishwashing soap, shed his shorts, and dove into the bay.

As he scrubbed, "Cheesy, get us a drum full of sweet fuel at Sammy's. If it was glass calm, I'd say buzz over to Petite Martinique and get it. That way we'd keep some privacy."

"If they're really watching, someone would probably see the skiff with a barrel, anyway," Dag replied.

"Oh, they're watching. You can bet your ass they're watching. I know both of you probably think the rum's made me paranoid, but be realistic, here we are fixing our fishing boat after serious mischief. Nothing was wrong with the fuel. This boat is our cash cow and all the other legal shit that's started. If they think they can buy an entire beautiful bay in the beautiful Southern Caribbean for only half a mill, then there's a lot of money to be made. That means greed with a capital 'G.' Dag, think it over, might be wiser to stay and scrape the bottom. Let Cheesy get the fuel alone," Harry reasoned,

"Everyone knows Cheesy and his boat with a 55-gallon drum of diesel heading back to Sunset; nah, no one will figure it out."

"Just be careful, that's all I'm saying," Harry preached. "Things are different around here now, son. Just be careful."

"You're right, dad. Do you think you're okay to get it yourself, Cheese? I think it's best if I stay close to home and work cleaning the bottom. If we're lucky, after the fuel change, *Sassy* will purr to life again."

The skiff with the prominent blue barrel slowly motored out of the bay. Harry sank dejectedly in the fighting chair and stared after his friend. "My mouth always seems to work backward, instead of bringing people home, my mouth drives them away."

"I'm back," Dag answered.

"Yeah, but Cheese called you back. I didn't have the nerve."

Dag walked up behind his father and put his hands on the older man's shoulders. "Look, I understand you have a hard time asking for help. Me too, mom probably does. It's from living on Sunset and being almost self-sufficient. Hell, dad, we didn't need anyone," he laughed and gave a slight tug on Harry's hair pulled into a ponytail. "Except now we need a bank where we can stash all the money we're gonna make."

They both laughed. Dag grabbed his mask and snorkel and splashed in to continue scraping *Sassy*. Harry sat looking into the blue distance, "Yep, we'll make some money, damn well have to."

^^^^^^^^^^

A sleek, shiny white Hatteras sportfisher named *Temptress* rumbled up to the fuel docks in Clifton. A tall, lean West Indian with short, fashionable dreadlocks waited and grabbed the dock lines, cleated the bow, and stopped the boat's forward momentum as the skipper throttled up in reverse for a few seconds.

The motor yacht nestled snugly against the dock. The big inflatable fenders gave a few squeaks as the craft aligned with the pilings.

The attendant assisted three passengers. They made it obvious they were moneyed people and used to a good life with constant personal attention. The men, all in their forties, were dressed alike in loose white cotton pants, open white shirts displaying thick, gaudy gold necklaces with flashy watches and sunglasses. Each wore a red ball cap displaying a big gold crown, Crown Hotels.

"Where's Sam?" the shortest man with the thickest mustache asked.

The West Indian stood rigid, as if at attention, and answered, "Inside."

"Let's go, boys," he smiled, nodded, and slid open the glass doors to the hardware and marine store.

Sam, a stocky man with a lifetime tan, sprung out from his office chair. "Mr. Van Gell," Sam tried to hug the man, but was rebuked with one raised arm. "Yeah, ah, we were, I was expecting you. What do you need, fuel?"

"Sam, good to see you," the men ritually extended hands to shake. "Sam," Van Gell tilted his head to different angles as if to gain a fresh perspective of the scene. "Sam, haven't heard much from you lately. That worries me. Yes, we need fuel for the boat and for our pockets, money, moolah, dinero. What's happening with our project at Sunset Bay? I hope you have good news."

The three men in white stood with clasped hands in an 'at ease' stance and nodded in unison, almost choreographed.

Wetting his lips with his wandering tongue, Sam reacted as if shocked, "Mr. Van Gell, same as when we last talked, nothing changed. They have a while until they're evicted, but it will be legal, every bit of it. The government will be seen as the bad guy. We must let, ah, due course, yeah, everything in due course. I, ah, or we, have an inside track to purchase the tract from the government at the exact price due on the levied fines. After all, as the older brother, I will get it."

Van Gell tapped the tanned man's shoulder, "As the eldest, it should have been yours, bequeathed to you." They stared at Sam.

"Yes," Sam quietly answered, "But it's coming to me now and then to you. They can't get that kind of money in time to stop the proceedings. The sportfisher where they made their money, past tense, is broken... I believe beyond repair. They had a minor accident with the fuel I supplied them. They got a free special additive that should have ruined the engines enough to need a complete rebuild."

"So, they're not fishing? You've been checking?"

"Of course, I'm the only fuel. You know, marine supply on the dock and autos on the street side. If someone came in a boat or a van wanting twenty gerry jugs filled, my men are on the alert to notify me. Then, we would proceed with the next stage. I'm ready, but like I was saying, they don't have adequate funds to pay the fines or repair the fishing boat. They need that boat for paying charters." Sam shook his head, "Hasn't been a new fisherman at the airport in over four months." He sniffed and moved his head to look each man in their eyes, "I gave them a one-two punch. It was a knockout." Sam pulled his mouth into a smug grin.

"We just hope there won't be any surprises. Right boys," to a double nod, "You'll make money on all ends. We need you, Sam, as much as you need us. You'll make a nice profit transferring the title to Crown Hotels, middle a good bit of the building materials, and," Van Gell smiled, "You'll have first dibs on as many concessions as you want, bars, restaurants, diving, fishing. You'll do well. The island will do well. They might even elect you boss, ah, mayor, or governor or whoever runs this island." He patted Sam on the back while reaching to pump his hand, "This is gonna be a very, very good thing. Lots of jobs, while we are building and even more when the hotel is operational."

"I know, and I appreciate your trust in me. I will make this happen." Sam swallowed hard and cleared his throat. "It's something my father would have wanted. Ensure the Scarbeaux family dynasty continues."

"How many children do you have, Sammy," Van Gell inquired.

"Ah, none, I'm a bachelor," Sam shyly answered. "I like to play the field."

Van Gell gave him a wide-eyed look with a grin, "You've hit fifty? Bet that field keeps you busy. You might start late, but you can make up for lost time, huh, bang, bang, bang. A son is a wonderful thing. Well, as long as the hotel is on Sunset Bay you can fill many prominent positions. I promise that."

"I know, I know, Mr. Van Gell, I'm working at this project every minute. I have eyes watching, ears listening. My sister's restaurant is barely afloat. Not many residents will buy dinner from someone who's impeding progress."

"Sure, sure, Sam, sure. We know. We're staying up on Canouan, at Trump's Pink Sand Beach. Sam, it's over $1,500 USD a frigging night. Buddy, we'll build it better here. The money is there from all the ritzy schmucks with rich bitches who want the next elite, exclusively private, no paparazzi, location."

Sam coughed loudly, "Wow! That much a night? At a hundred rooms, Jesus, that's $150 large a night!"

"We'll start with fifty excellent rooms," Van Gell wrinkled his nose, "a hundred won't ensure the privacy our clientele craves. Our aim is to sell units that will become another of their many homes away from homes. In that sheltered bay, you'll be in charge of a first-class mega-yacht marina. It's all planned and on the drawing board. Just waiting for you to give us the thumbs up-go ahead."

Again, Sam unsuccessfully reached for Van Gell's hand to shake. "I'm on top of it, sir. When I know, you'll know."

Van Gell cut Sam short, "I know, but we feel we must remind you time is of the essence. If you perceive some way you can expedite this, move it along faster, that would be fantastic. There are many bays all over the world that are competing for Crown Hotels." He nodded, turned, and rapped on the glass door. The West Indian dock man had a questioning look until Van Gell pointed to the door handle.

With a broad smile towards Sam, the three left without another word, got aboard the running Hatteras. The dock man almost curtsied as he released the lines on signal and the boat rumbled gracefully from the dock.

Everyone on the yacht presented the courteous and necessary goodbye wave that curled into a salute.

"What the fuck is with them guys?" The dock man complained. "White-assed-fucker points at the sliding door handle like he doesn't have a fucking clue how to slide a glass door open."

"Kalaloo, that guy, Mr. Van Gell, probably hasn't had to open a door for himself in a long, long while, if ever. Those guys are cared for, watched over, coddled like babies. They live that way because they're rolling in money. Looks like we might get some of that down here."

A skiff with an upright, blue fifty-five-gallon barrel wedged where a seat should have been, slid up to the dock. "Please fill it up with your best diesel, Kalaloo." Cheesy smiled vacantly as the sun was to the Kalaloo's back. "Some kind of special boat just fueled, huh? Saw that sportfisher heading out. They catch anything?"

"What's up, Mr. Chessman?" Kalaloo asked as he inserted the nozzle into the barrel. "Who, them guys? Probably wouldn't fish 'cause that would get the deck bloody. They just cruising the islands."

"Must be nice… or rather it was nice, quite pleasant actually, when you have money." Cheesy drifted, "Careful don't run it hard so the fuel suds up. Then I got to wait for the foam to settle or take the time to clean the smelly diesel off my skiff."

"Sure thing, no problem," and he aimed the nozzle at the tank's sides. "So, you been catching fish? Ain't seen the *Sassy* around for months."

"Nah, Harry got called to the States on an emergency. I'm running the boat, keeping her tidy until Harry returns. No business when the skipper's not home. This is for a sailboat that floundered in the Bay. Out of fuel and out of talent."

Kalaloo topped the barrel off and screwed on the cap. "So, it's for a sailboat?"

"Lots of the Clorox bottle boats only motor sail. Like I said, lack of talent." Cheesy gave a wide, toothy grin, "Picking up some spare change, helping a bloke. All right, Kal, here's two Bens that ought to cover it. The remainder is yours."

"Thanks," the attendant said as the skiff slowly motored away.

Sam walked out on the dock watching the small boat disappear. "Working on fixing Harry's boat?" He asked.

"Probably, 'cause he give me some bullshit about helping a sailboat."

"Later, just before the sun sets, take your boat around, get a peek. Put some rods in the holders so it looks like you're trolling. Take my good binoculars."

The water around the dock was teaming with small, bright reef fish feeding on the algae Dag had scraped off *Sassy's* bottom. It had grown four inches thick along the transom. It still needed a final cleaning with a green scotch pad. He knew there would be time for finishing touches later, after she was running again. He enjoyed the shade of the cabin while chasing the wires that had been ripped from the dashboard gauges.

Harry was sitting in the fighting chair fondling a cup of coffee. "In two days, we did a hell of a lot of work. Still plenty to do. Fingers crossed, she'll run okay. Good idea you had using the compressor to blow out the fuel lines. Changed all the filters. Don't want to be a pessimist, but all that shit-sludge in the lines is in the injectors and pump." He raised his head, "Then again, we might get lucky. I'm feeling lucky these days. Your mother left a pot of coffee and sandwiches. Yeah, I'm feeling lucky."

"Here comes the big test," Dag said, watching Cheesy's skiff nose around the south point of the bay.

They quickly transferred the fresh fuel without talk until Cheesy had the siphon hose set and the fuel was flowing.

"Nice sound, fuel going in the tanks." Harry stepped into the engine room and loosened every injector. "Got to bleed her good."

The evening stars were sparkling in the red dusk when each man crossed his fingers as Harry turned the key to try the starboard engine. Dag opened and drained the injector pump and every injector.

Finally, after long minutes of cranking, the engine sputtered and caught. But, no matter what adjustments Dag and Cheesy tried, nothing could level out the big six-cylinder diesel. Harry pushed up the throttles and the engine sputtered and spread a cloud of thick black smoke.

They shut it down. Sad eyes avoided other sad eyes.

"No sense in even playing with the port side. Take both sets of injectors and the pumps and get them calibrated. Fly 'em to Trinidad. They got a lot of injection specialists there, reasonable, too. Let's see, been about, ten years since we did that. You remember Cheese?"

"I remember everything. You finally relaxed and shut down in February 2009. We knew it was always a lousy month. Yes, Harry, we took off a month, but we were back dragging baits for puking anglers two weeks later. Your father complained the entire time that he had to pay me to help even though we weren't making any money."

"Probably my own drunken, depressed old ass's fault. If I would have drained and flushed the system sooner."

"I agree," Cheesy concurred.

"About the system needing drained?"

"No, about it's your own pickled fault. At least you take the responsibility; that's a step in the right direction."

"Ah, come on, Cassy was giving me problems and all the heavy-duty legal stuff," dejected, Harry slouched in the chair, pulling his knees up with his arms into the fetal position.

"Look, we expected this. After a fuel system rebuild, these engines will purr again. I'll fly everything to Trinidad tomorrow and then we'll know everything is right."

"Dag, you just came. Do you have to leave again so soon?" It was his mother, Cassy, who they hadn't seen arrive during the engine trials.

"He's only going for a few days, right?" Harry said. "You know we could ship 'em down on the plane and they'll have somebody pick them up.

"I'll carry them and stand there until they're finished. Wouldn't want these to get lost."

"If you desire to continue the family reunion, I could go," Cheesy said.

"Cheesy, you've done plenty already," Harry answered.

"Think it might take you a day to clean up enough so that the other passengers on the flight won't think the fumes off you will explode." Cassy pointed out, "You need about four good scrubbings."

^^^^^^^^^^

"What's happening? You see what they're are up to?"

"Boss," Kalaloo's gold incisors flashed, "Dem ain't going nowhere. We chanced it right an' got there to see," he laughed loudly. "The cloud of smoke coming out of their boat was like a volcano shooting off. Relax, that boat needs new engines."

The author with 21 kg bull dolphin.

CHAPTER FOUR

Torrential rain rushed the passengers into the terminal at Piarco, Trinidad. Dag half jogged, swinging the rucksack with the injectors and pumps. Once inside the terminal, he stopped to adjust the shoulder straps when a man intentionally bumped into him.

"Hey! Excuse me. Hey!" The other man squeezed him in a powerful hug. "Tim! What are you doing here in Triniland?"

He let go and shoved his older brother. Both laughed as Tim said, "There's no excuse for you! Ah, a safe bet would be the same reason you're here, family." His main family resemblance was his piercing blue eyes, but he had the reddish-blond hair puffing around a pale, baby-face, which he tried to hide under a scruffy beard.

"Look at you, bro, the Euro-businessman."

Tim wore a tailored gray pinstriped suit and carried his jacket on top of his oxblood leather suitcase. His white polo shirt was stretched with new muscles.

Dag grabbed Tim by both arms and looked him over. "Holy Jesus, are you trying to become a replacement for the Hulk? Wow, Tim, are you the muscle-man-banker or what? Gray pinstripe! Leather bag! Muscles bulging!"

"Not so loud," Tim asked as he flexed his well-defined arm holding the luggage, "Got tired of being referred to as Tiny Timmy. Yeah, Dagger, this is coincidence-city. I flew in from Heathrow on the red-eye. It was the only way not to waste a day with connections. Sounds good. My plane to Union is supposed to leave in an hour, if it isn't canceled. You know these puddle-jumpers better than me. What brings you to this garden spot of the Caribbean?"

"I'll tell you over a beer... after we catch a taxi and drop-off all the injection equipment. Cancel your flight. Hang here with me for a couple of days. It will be safer for us to return together."

"Safer? Oh?" Tim deflated. "I get you. Mom and dad, huh?"

"Yes, oh, not so long of a story, but better told with hops suds. Not much to do back there until we get these pumps rebuilt. Then... then there will be plenty to do. I'll tell you all about it."

Tim wrapped his free arm around his brother, "I have a feeling this is a story that's going to require several beers. Everyone all right at home or do I need Scotch whiskey sedation?"

"More or less, usual chaos, wait for beers." They laughed.

Tim waved his credit card, "I'll rent us a car," and proudly said, "and I have a driver's license."

At a roadside bar, after finding a good injection service lab in San Fernando, they relaxed. "Boy, oh boy, Trini traffic is tough, like a road race," Tim said as they tapped bottles.

"Man, you look a shade lighter than white bread, boy," Dag harassed.

"No beach in London," Tim dropped into a British accent. "Bloody awful swimming in the Thames and all that muck." (He laughed and started using the accent of the islands. "Really good to see you. Thought the next time we'd meet would be a funeral. Glad I was wrong."

"I don't know, the wake might have already started. Things are bad with the 'rents.' You'll see. So, talk to me. Tell me what you're into now. Last I heard, you were some sort of investment broker. Not too communicative with those not too frequent and always intentionally vague emails."

"My good man, at twenty-three, I am the youngest department head at Shearsome Bank. I manage the Communications Division." Tim clowned again with the Brit inflection and dropped it. "Got a real break getting a scholarship with Granpop pulling the strings. Computers, Bro." He flexed his arms above his head. "Got that down. Man, the things I can do; it still amazes me. So, what about you?"

"SOS, same old shit, different boats," Dag regaled his brother with Spanish. "Muchos botes de pesca, grandes, mi hermano. Abundantes peces grandes en Costa Rica. Hermosas mujeres y cerveza fría.¿Qué más puedes pedir? {*Lots of big fishing boats, my brother. Lots of fish in Costa Rica. Beautiful women and cold beer. What more could you ask for?}*" He paused for a gulp of beer. "I'm not doing anything that amounts to a hill of beans. Working someone else's boat. Same as always."

"Same here. Making serious cash for some other guy I never see," Tim lamented. "It's a drag. Never feeling the warm sun is a bigger drag. I know I'm young, but I've already learned that paying dues is tough."

"Mom and Dad are still paying. Seems the entire island has them backed against the wall wanting to build a hotel on our bay."

"Maybe that's where we got it wrong, might not be 'our' bay, Bro. Got to see the big picture," Tim argued.

"Whoa, that's been in our family forever."

"Yeah, since Jurassic Park! Maybe that's what the family has become, dinosaurs." Raising his glass, he spoke like Churchill, "Can't hold back progress and all that rot, governor. Dag, I've planned out a rescue. Numbers are our strength. I can demonstrate it to everybody."

"If they'll listen."

"Get Mama or Dad on the soapbox and the whole island will listen," Tim reasoned.

"I've only been back a few days, but believe me, the cold shoulder is like an iceberg that's drifted in," Dag said as he waved to the waitress for more beers.

^^^^^^^^^

The weather was nearly perfect in Clifton, Union Island. Sam sat in his old oak swivel office chair with his bare feet propped on his ancient roll-top desk. His new stock girl's smile was a combination of gracious and seductive, as she adjusted the floor fan so her boss could enjoy the air.

Today was Annie's second day working at the hardware end of Sam's business. On her first day, Sam had made it clear that he was a 'touchy-feely' boss. Swats on her tight denim stretched posterior amid continuous complements, she'd smiled and returned the obvious flirts. Sam wasn't nearly as bad as her previous fat boss at the airport who'd been grabbing at her since day one. She'd been lucky to sidestep his rude advances for a few months and finally find another job.

Annie handed the pricing sticker gun to Sam, who demonstrated how to make changes. "See, darling, turn this and insert the red tape here and it comes out there... with the correct price."

"Oh," She raised the plastic gun, "I see, you hold it just so." She played with the knobs, "turn gently so you get what you want." She gave a flirtatious smile, "Don't want it going off too quick..."

Sam grabbed her wrist and pulled her towards the desk when Kalaloo bounced through the door. Annie pulled her hand away and moved out the door, flashing Kalaloo the same smile she'd used on her new boss.

"Don't you ever think I might be busy, but you just barge in. What's up?" Sam asked.

"Sorry, sorry, boss, didn't think you was getting busy with that sweet young thing yourself. Just wondering if you heard any more from the big guys?"

"Not for you to worry about." Sam rubbed his hands together, "Everything be sweet and smooth just like I'll bet Annie's backside is. Soon as we claim the bay, life will be much sweeter. I, we, got all the concessions plus the... never mind, your only concern is that everything's going to be good after this. Really good. Harry refused their offer in writing and that played right into our plan."

"How's that?" Kalaloo sat on an upended Guinness beer crate.

"Well, my young protege, Grenada, with their greedy government, reneged on the big guys' plans to build a hotel on the south side. Those white dudes are seriously pissed. They'd spent real dough optioning the land, did all the necessary surveys. Soil tests. Paid the bribes and then got fucked when the government canceled the contract. Said the proposal had a negative environmental impact. Them white guys aren't spending a dime until they, we, own Sunset Bay. I might also add that since all the shit came down on Harry for having an unlicensed guest house, Sunset is now zoned for a hotel. No other changes are necessary. Our friends are excited. The deal is as good as gold."

Sam reached into the air as if to grab the prize when Annie returned with a questioning look and handed him the pricing gun. He grinned at her, "I'll give you more instruction on this later. Now shoo, we in a business meeting. Shut the door please." He turned to Kalaloo and said, "You remember what we're talking about here is secret. You pick the right time to chat and when we do, you close the fucking door! Got me?"

"Yes, I'll knock, and you be sure you don't knock up that sweet thing with the big butt. By the way, Dog-boy is back."

Sam returned his bare feet to the desk, "I suppose we'll see all of them between now and the New Year. They've got some time to try to raise money to pay the fines and buy their new license to operate." He winked at Kalaloo, "Lots of jumbie problems gonna plague Sunset Bay between now and then."

"You can always count on me for help," the younger man assured, "if I can count on you."

"Sure thing, Kal," Sam winked. "You're done, over the hump, made your breaks. Our connection is good and always will be. Just help and you win; win big."

"Sure Sam, sure, but I ain't no kid. I'd better be seeing some money. I ain't talking 'bout small money, either."

"Kal, Kal, you're like a son to me," Sam sat straight in the chair and swiveled towards him, "You get the water sports deal, concession, whatever, you got it. You're the man who rents all the sailboats and diving stuff. And jet skis, don't forget about them. You'll be right there on Sunset Beach with all those babes."

"Like I said, I ain't no kid. So, don't think you gonna play me. If I'm getting those, what you call concessions, let's get us a paper signed." Kalaloo grabbed and shook the hand Sam extended.

"Yes sir, business is business. I'll get a contract drawn as soon as I talk to my attorneys in Kingston. Be next week. Yeah, next week."

^^^^^^^^^

After two solid days of waxing and polishing his beloved fishing boat, the view of the bright sun reflecting off the tranquil bay had helped Harry doze off in the usually uncomfortable fighting chair. His faith was being slowly restored as he brought the sportfisher back to life.

Even Cassy noticed that her errant husband was attempting to change. Their fishing boat was nearly pristine again. Every day since Dag had left for Trinidad, Harry had worked from before sunrise to after sunset, cleaning, wiping, and waxing. The topsides and hull had to be done before and after the heat of the day.

First, his duty was to scrub the fiberglass with a brush and Ajax powder to remove the dirt and grime. Then, he used rubbing compound to remove any stains, and finally applied Simonize paste wax, and polished with the big buffer. His arms and back ached, but the payoff was *Sassy Cassy* was shining. The topsides had been easier than the hull. In the past, he'd run down to Grenada and have the boat hauled out, and have the bottom painted at the same they waxed the hull. Working off a rolling scaffold was quicker than out of his wobbly dinghy. But the boat wasn't moving yet, and even if it had, he couldn't spare the cash for a haul out. When they'd been flush with cash, he'd gladly pay a local to do it while supervising, sipping cold Heinekens. Now they had to make do on a tight budget until they got some charters. Dag needed to return pronto with the cleaned injectors to keep the rejuvenation rolling along.

Every morning Cheesy appeared with his stainless thermos of coffee and busied himself cleaning the below decks in the forward cabins. Months lacking proper attention had spawned a serious case of mildew. The Brit scrubbed and wiped with straight chlorine bleach. It was nasty work, but with all the hatches open and the white cushions out on the rear deck drying in the sun, the boat was almost spiffy again. Cassy had contributed some scented herbal sachet packets to combat chemical odors until the boat could run with the forward hatches open to better ventilate and chase the odors.

Harry's head hung tilted over the back of the fighting chair; his mouth open, snoring. Cheesy was sprawled in the shaded part of the decks on the V-berth cushions, sleeping peacefully.

"Hey, is this what I'm paying you blokes for?"

Both older men jumped, startled by an English-accented voice, and twisted to find its origin. Tim came into sight, walking down the dock, past the side of the cabin. His bag slung over a shoulder, he approached, arms wide open. Wearing a white shirt and khaki shorts with hard shoes, his skin was almost the shade of his wide-brimmed Panama hat. Tim was pale and with so much sunscreen slathered on make him appear even paler, like a ghost. He jumped on to the boat and hugged his father, amid salutations combined with humorous curses.

"Finally getting some needed rest and you wake me up? Come here, Tim," Harry said, "Give me another hug. When did you get in? Why didn't you tell us you were arriving; we'd have met you at the airport? Hey, get those hard-soled shoes off; I just scrubbed the deck."

"Just came on the spur of the moment and, by coincidence, ran into this guy when I was about to make connections in Trinidad a few days ago."

Dag followed down the dock carrying the box of injectors. "Yep, there he was, Tim, the businessman. What a sight, so white he almost blinded me." They laughed. "Got him some Trini sun. Now he's at least red, ah, maybe pinkish."

"Don't matter if you got polka-dots, let me shake your hand, Tim," Cheesy extended his hand and hurried to pull the younger man into a hug. "Good to see you, good to see you." He broke the embrace and stood back, "You are more limey white, but where did all those muscles come from?"

"I was about to ask that," Harry chimed

"Not much to do in the dreary land of fish and chips except work out at the gym. A company benefit, so I take advantage."

"No one's going to recognize you on Union," Dag said. "Even when you get some color, people will be shocked at how the boy has grown. I didn't even know my own brother, bumping into him at Piarco Airport." Dag poked at Tim, "Should have seen him all prettied up in a three-piece suit."

"Wait, you wearing suits in these tropics, son?" Harry asked. "That shitty foggy weather make you go daffy?"

Tim feigned a few jabs around the group. "All part of the businessman act, a uniform, no more, no less." Now in shorts, he pushed out a pale leg and in his British accent, "My good men, when in Rome…"

They all laughed.

"So, what's on the agenda?" Tim asked.

"How'd it go with the injectors?" Harry quizzed Dag.

"They had to soak them overnight. That's what took the extra day. The technician said it looked like someone has tried to run the engine on paint, thick paint. He cleaned them with ultrasound and then recalibrated the pumps. I'll get busy installing them. Should have our boat running today, if luck is with us."

Harry clapped his hands. "I don't ever count on any luck, except bad luck. But that sounds good. Think I'll figure a way to lock the fuel caps to stave off those buggers." He rubbed his jaw. "They'll be back. You can bet on that." He pulled his two boys into a bear hug and dragged in a sheepish looking Cheesy. They huddled for a few seconds and separated, all somewhat embarrassed by their visible emotions at the reunion.

Sniffling and wiping his eyes, Harry gave directions. "Dag, you get the injectors bolted up. Tim, how about testing the gauges and ignition wiring? You feel up to that? Cheese, get these cushions back onto the bunks. I think this sweetheart will be purring in a few hours and we'll want to try her out. And me, I'll help whoever needs it."

"I'll need a second set of hands as I check the wiring harnesses," Tim reported. "We'll check each gauge from the sender against the mechanical units."

Cheesy offered, "Dag, throwing these cushions back will only take a minute. I can do one engine while you do the other, or we can work together?"

"Yeah, rather work together, like the old days."

"Hell, you ain't old enough to even say 'them old days'!" Harry piped. "You two are still pups, me and the Chessman; we're the old dogs in this kennel."

The gauge panel was finished, screwed back in place, then Harry and Tim checked all the running lights.

"Looks like everything is a go, Dad. What's next?"

Soaked with sweat, yet beaming a smile, Dag crawled out of the engine compartment. He and Tim extended hands to assist Cheesy who once on deck burst into the old Jack Horntip song, "Roll me over in the clover, roll me over, lay me down and do it again."

"What? The heat and exertion finally get to you, or what, Chessman?" Harry called.

The red-faced man said, waving his hands as if conducting an orchestra. "Time to roll *Sassy* over. We done our best. We're in the clover."

"You hiding a bottle down there or something? Cheese, you're too happy."

"No sir, just seeing these two youths back is revitalizing me. Been a while, a long while since this bay's heard genuine laughter."

"Oh-oh, I'd better warn Verena," Harry chuckled, "Sounds like she's in for a good one tonight, talking about roll me over."

Dag nodded his head, "Well, gang, are we ready?" Pointing to the ignition, "Dad, you deserve the honors."

"Don't know about honors; with my luck, I'll fuck something up. Okay, okay," Harry slid behind the controls. He turned and waved both hands with fingers crossed in the air. He solemnly put them together and mouthed a silent prayer, crossed himself, and twisted the key for the starboard engine.

Everyone waited silent and rigid as the engine cranked for about half a minute, coughed, caught, sputtered, and then caught again, the RPMs revved and then leveled out. Harry's eyes stayed closed, listening. Then he broke into a wide grin, turned to his jubilant crew, his right arm shot up clutching a handful of satisfaction.

"Okay, we're halfway back to Eden. One more to go," Harry twisted the port side key. As if rehearsed, the big Caterpillar coughed, sputtered, caught, coughed again, and finally roared to life.

Tim grabbed Cheesy and arm in arm they broke into a rough semblance of a jig. Dag hugged Harry, who again was wiping away an errant tear. He slowly pushed the throttles forward. Gray smoke funneled out of the exhaust. As the engines growled the smoke vanished. Harry reduced the rpm, and they all heard the engines idle evenly.

"Sounding damn sweet, if I do say so," Cheesy assessed. "Damn sweet."

"Also, a damn good effort, I might add, even if I came in late in the game. We're back. Can't stop team Sunset Bay," Tim was jubilant.

"Get the fishing gear in order, some oil, and check the line on the reels."

Tim made a sour face." Let's wait until we have some hookups. If they break the line, then we know we need to replace it. We should be conscientious on expenditures."

"Sunset Bay's new accountant," Harry's arms stretched to straddle his sons' shoulders, "What say, shall we take *Sassy* for a spin?"

"Sure," Dag agreed, "Let's blow her out."

Tim opted out, "Sorry to be a party pooper, but dragging baits tomorrow morning is soon enough for me. Think I'll hike to the village and see if any of my old school mates are still hanging around. You know, I'd like to walk Mom home; been a while, give her a little surprise."

"Gotcha, son, be careful with surprising Cassy. She's had a good week seeing Dag again, and," Harry touted and nodded, "and me, I'm on the wagon."

"Again," Cheesy and Dag combined with a laugh.

"Yeah, again, but I think this time I'll stay with it. Seen the errors of my old ways and all that. Son, you go along to town, but hey, the family ain't held in good stead anymore. Bit of friction, Dag probably filled you in."

Cheesy offered, "I could head that way in my skiff, if that would help you out?"

"What? Not going for the trial run with us?" Harry asked.

"Think I'll wait till tomorrow, the wife's got something planned for this evening. But I'll be here, break of dawn and plan on eating fish tomorrow."

Tim ducked below and reappeared wearing a white polo shirt, carrying his briefcase.

"Ain't we spiffy?" Harry commented, "You always was the smart dresser, now the consummate businessman. I got an idea about the business you're up to; what was her name? Roslind? Or was that your girlie friend, Dag? Looking up old school chums, huh? I'll bet. Well, go ahead; mom finishes 'bout six or so, depending on if there are beer drinkers hanging around. You got a couple of hours." He hugged Tim again, "Be careful, okay? Times have changed. That's all I got to say. People ain't happy with us for refusing that hotel's offer."

"Ah, that's kind of what I want to get a feel for," Tim replied. "If we want to beat them at their own game, we've got to get an idea of what they are up to."

"No good, that's what they're up to, no good," Harry answered. "Fire her up again, Dag, let's go blow off the stink. Let these two deal with Clifton."

"Need anything, Harry?" Cheesy asked.

"Always the same, buy us a winning lottery ticket, Cheesy."

Cheesy fueled his dinghy and parted company. "Mind what your father said, people have been, let's say, to be nice, a bit stand-offish of late. Watch your back, son."

Flexing a bicep, "Not to worry, Chessman, not to worry." He turned and looked down an unusually vacant Main Street. At the dock were some fishermen he vaguely recognized, unloading their pirogue. After wiping his face with his handkerchief, he turned and walked up the steps to Scarbeaux Hardware. His Uncle Sam had been watching from the door.

"Timmy," Sam shook his hand, "it has been a long time. What? Six years?

"Almost eight, four in school, and stayed to work in London, but that's not news. You're looking good, Uncle. The store looks good, you're making Granpop proud." The younger man beamed a broad smile. To him, the store was as comfortable as a worn sofa. As a child, it had been one of his playpens, because his mother carried everyone to work with her. Granpop Curly occupied them with board games like Monopoly. Tim gained his love of business from his grandfather, combining learning to count while helping with the monthly inventories.

There were changes, but the worn wood floor still had its oil sheen. They had changed the shelving that held everything most island families needed. It had been plywood, renovated to metal sprayed a more sanitary appearing bright white enamel. The music no longer was Granpop's beloved country and western or rhythm and blues, but bass pounding Caribbean soca.

"Thank you, I appreciate the compliment," Sam turned and led Tim into his private office. A blast of almost frigid A/C hit as they entered.

"Wow, you could freeze meat in here. Like the way you opened the office with all the windows." Tim patted the roll top desk. "If this could talk, huh, Unc. I can see Granpop wearing a stained tank top, chewing on a stogie. Don't think I ever saw him in this store without chewing on a stubby cigar."

"Yeah, but he was never permitted to have one around the house," Sam grinned, "Glad you like the changes, the boss got to have some luxury. I spend too much time here. Have a seat. Relax. Must be sweating up a storm, coming all the way from England."

Tim accepted an offered cigar.

"Monti Cristi Number Three," Sam snipped his and handed the cutter to his nephew. After a deep pull, "Figured all you would return to help Harry." Sam shook his head disapprovingly, "Your dad's made a mess out there on Sunset."

"Well, what's going on?" Tim inhaled and almost blew a full ring of smoke. "Thought I should speak with you first. Guess you're now the patriarch of the family's holdings."

"That's very kind of you to say that," Sam smiled. "Seems Cass and Harry forgot they were operating a guest house. Even St. Vincent has rules and needs money. There are taxes and licenses that needed to be paid." He took another long pull on the cigar as he relaxed into his padded leather chair. "These days everything's got to be inspected."

Tim smiled, "Understood. There's a rumor a big hotel chain wants to buy our bay."

"The Caribbean is booming. Union Island is missing it, stagnant. Tourism is the only hope we have for improvements. A hotel would mean a higher standard of living."

"A new school with more subjects taught, a hospital, a library?" Tim asked.

"Probably, at least improvements to our funky little clinic."

Standing, Tim pretended to swing a golf club, "And a golf course or the hotel like they got two islands up in Canouan?"

"Maybe. You play? Yep, most new hotels have golf."

"Unc, where could you squeeze a course on Union?"

Sam fidgeted, "I don't know, never really thought about it. Harry's right, though. Guys have been scouting all the islands for sites. Seems a big deal fell through in Grenada. Sunset Bay's prime. They mentioned half a million."

"Oh, you're negotiating for our bay?"

"Tim, it was always 'Scarbeaux' Bay." Sam rolled out authoritatively from behind the desk and stood sucking on the cigar. "I'm the eldest Scarbeaux, like you said, the patriarch."

"Where'd that come from?" Tim politely asked smiling, "Mom and dad bought it from Granpop."

Sam had turned his back and stared out the glass doors. He gave a nervous laugh, "Tim, we got to see the big picture. It's not your bay or our bay. We got to consider the island."

"Yeah, sure," Tim answered by pulling a manila envelope from his shoulder bag. "Unc, my business is business." He fanned papers onto the desk. "We compiled this report in 2015 as back up for financing of a group of resorts." He lifted the top sheet, "Potential income per capita of residents, negligible. The overall standard of living increase is negligible until nine years pass, then a twelve percent increase, which is negated by a twenty percent overall increase in the cost of living." He pointed to other papers, "Education…negligible. Crime, an increase of eight percent starting with initial construction, increasing to plus thirty-three in just four years. Medical… better services on the island, yet in most cases not available to all island residents, only employees. Employment has an incredible burst at construction with untrained lift and carry jobs, but drops to only an eleven percent increase within three years. Surface water quality sinks to unhealthy." Tim snubbed his cigar in the big ashtray. "I'd hardly call that a win-win, Unc."

"Tim, it's not me. Look around, every other island is doing it. Union deserves a chance."

"I agree," Tim replied as he sat back and relaxed. "Our island deserves better. But the impact would erase our culture, not to mention we'd lose our peace and quiet. That's what is so nice about Union. Building a resort, huh, I figure we'd be better getting hit by a tidal wave. Then we could rebuild. With a hotel, you can't unbuild."

"Boy, what are you talking about?" Sam almost barked, "You know Harry will pull it out. No worries, we're all behind him, ready to help." He nodded to Tim, "You bringing in investors?"

"Wow, it's a strange thing, Unc, you're talking like it's okay for you to get investors for big hotels, but not for small operations like ours. That report," Tim pointed to the papers, "sounds bad, but the hotel is presently being built on St. Lucia."

Sam nervously scratched his neck. "Uh-huh, that's business, and I got to get back to mine." He extended his hand. "I got to get back to this store's business. You can count on me, Tim. Come back anytime. I'll look forward to more corporate board room discussions. Yes, I will."

As Tim opened the office door to leave, Kalaloo bounded in, startling everyone.

"Kid Kalaloo, long time." Tim put out his hand to shake, but the West Indian passed on it and stood squarely blocking the doorway.

"Well, well, if it ain't Tiny Tim."

Laughing while flexing his arms, "Yes, Tim, but not so tiny anymore."

"And I ain't no kid," and pushed his way past Tim into the office.

Tim shrugged and left. Somehow, he hadn't noticed the sun had slipped below the horizon while chatting in the store. His mom's restaurant was shuttered. He walked home.

^^^^^^^^^^

"Thought you said Verena had something special planned for tonight, Cheese?" The two couples were sitting on Harry's front porch. Dag was off to one side, the only chair with a view of the bay. Redbeard, the macaw, sat on his shoulder preening through his long hair.

Cheesy rolled his head. "You're my boss part of the day when the missus, Verena, lets me out. She said she had plans and didn't mention what or where. I just follow orders. When she's finished sewing, we hop in the dinghy and she points, I navigate. "

"Harry, this is a special evening," Verena spoke softly, "You have the boys home. It's nice to have you back, Dag. Where's Tim?"

"Good question, he said he wanted to walk Cassy home. Must have snagged his line on something," Harry said as he raised the glass of tea Cassy had just poured. "Look, here he comes now."

Tim broke into a trot at the gate and swept a crying Cassy off her feet. "Mom, what are you crying about? I'm so sorry I missed you at the restaurant."

"Happy tears, Tim, happy tears." Cassy shot a glance at Harry, "Don't get many of those around here for a while." She hugged him tightly, "Wow, look at these muscles! You aren't on those steroids pills, are you?" She stepped back and inspected her son, "My goodness, you look like that Terminator actor."

"No, just regular daily workouts. Not much to do in that horrible climate. Either the gym or the pub; I chose to get fit over getting fat." He moved on to the porch and hugged Verena, "Pretty as ever, Cheesy's always been a lucky man."

The slight, blond woman stood and politely kissed Tim on both of his cheeks. "So, Timothy, you haven't found a proper young English lady for a wife? How are you acclimating to British life?"

He cleared his throat and slightly blushed, "Everyone wants to marry me off. No, no plans as of yet. I keep busy with work; lots to learn. With the financial markets, everything is always fluid and changing."

"Yes, I can understand and agree," Harry said, "fluid and changing. It's sundown and my fluid has changed from rum to iced tea." It brought a chuckle.

"Ah, as I remember the clammy fog, all the better reason to find a suitable lassie," Cheese added.

"There's plenty of time to get snagged on a reef," Harry mumbled.

"Oh, so you got snagged on a reef?" Cassy snapped.

"No, no, you caught me fair and square. Damn good bait," Harry smirked.

Cassy elbowed him in the ribs, "You better say that."

"I keep telling myself that," Tim answered. "Oh, there are a few good lookers who frequent the gym, but there're lots of other fellows standing in line."

"Well, the Missus and I got at it right away, at sixteen," Cheesy grinned, holding Verena's hand, "and been at it ever since. You'll know the right one when you meet her."

"I'm just happy you and Dag got to spread your wings before one of these local girls trapped you by spreading their legs."

"Harry, how can you be so rude?! That's probably what you say about me," Cassy exclaimed.

"No, ah, come on, let's not. You know you played hard to get." He rattled the ice in his glass, muttered, and smiled, "Played me like a big fish on a light tackle, you did."

"What was that? Talk up unless you're making rude comments."

"Oh, now, after almost thirty years of glorious marriage, nothing but good, no, great times with a great family to show for it all," Verena sermonized, "Thank God for all his good grace."

"Yes, Timothy and Dag, hey you're being quiet over there, behind every successful man is a…" Cheesy was interrupted.

"Pile of debts," Harry interrupted.

"Oh, you, you," Cassy sucked her teeth loudly, "Does anyone want more tea? I'll get it?" Verena rose to help her.

"Dad, you certainly have a way with women and words," Tim said.

"Your mother doesn't recognize a compliment when she hears one. Always got her ears cocked the other way."

"Sir, really, that was quite the compliment. Pray, what do you tell her on Valentine's Day?" Cheesy joked.

"You all know our story. I met Cass when she was pumping diesel on Curly's dock. When there was no boats, she was helping her mother, Gretchen, God rest her soul, cook at the family restaurant. That was a blessing 'cause the woman I love is both beautiful and a fantastic cook," Harry smiled. "Hey, you in there, are you listening to these real compliments? I'm sober as a church mouse, swear."

He rattled on, "From the moment I saw her... and when she saw me, we both knew this was the big one. I couldn't let her break the line, escape, so to speak. Without her and me, well, working together, hand in hand, like ring and finger, none of this," Harry rose and spread his arms, "none of these glorious things would have happened, none of you children or this wonderful place we are lucky enough to call home."

"Here, here," Dag tinged his tea glass with a spoon. "I never thought I'd hear that come out of my old man. Wow! There's still sides of you we haven't seen."

"You're right there, kiddo. My water runs deep. Right now, I got to let some of this water out." Harry retreated to the side of the house.

"And you'd have been a rummy," Cassy called after him as she came out from the kitchen. "My man has his sweet moments, but damn, too many sour ones."

Verena hugged her, "The sour only makes the sweet sweeter, and sometimes, the really sour can make even usual average compliments seem endearing, darling."

"You two amaze me," Tim muttered.

"Yep, this is another of those Caribbean Norman Rockwell moments," Dag added. "Next thing, we'll all be on the cover of a magazine."

"Yeah, Mad Magazine," Harry quipped returning from his relief station.

"Harry, you have a certain way of interpreting things unique only to you," Cheesy laughed.

"The St. Claire family is even too weird for Alfred E. Neuman," Tim said, and he stuffed his hands in his pockets and walked off towards the boat. "I'm hitting the sack. I'll rack out in the V-berth."

"What's wrong, did I say something wrong?" Harry asked and looked around.

"My dear husband, if your lips are moving you are usually offending someone."

"But Timmy? Who knows me better than my family? Hell, yes, I have a wry sense of humor."

"Tim isn't Timmy anymore," Dag replied. "I'm hitting it also. Fishing at daybreak, huh?"

"Righto, champ." Harry gave Dag a hug. "Great to have you two back. Could never have done this without you. You guys know that, right?"

"Yeah, dad, we know it. Goodnight. See you in the AM." Dag said as he disappeared into the house.

"Did I say something," Harry asked again. "What got into them? Thin-skinned, I guess."

Cheesy and Verena rose to leave. The Brit lightly tapped his knuckles on Harry's forehead, "Hard-headed."

"Boy, did you ever hit that nail on the head, Cheese," Cassy remarked. "Thanks for coming. We're all family."

"Yes dear," Verena agreed, holding her flashlight walking towards the dock.

"Be careful, no moon tonight," Harry said.

"Hadn't noticed, Cappy."

"If I fished only to capture fish, my fishing trips would have ended long ago," Zane Grey.

CHAPTER FIVE

Quiet. An hour and a half before dawn, Sunset Bay enjoyed pure quiet. It was the quiet almost everyone had lost or forgotten. Few in the modern world had ever even experienced it, even for a sparse moment. Most places have constant background noise, usually from transport. But not Sunset, no noise; it was naturally quiet. Sunset enjoyed it only during the early morning intermission before the airplanes and water taxis started moving. The gulls were still perched, the sea was almost perfectly calm, and the shore was stock-still.

The ageless darkness matched the natural quiet. They always reminded visitors that the bay was the last in the Caribbean that could be completely dark at night, with no streetlights, and no cars. Natural darkness shrouded everywhere and everything when they turned off the one pole lamp on the dock. It gave stargazers rapture. Getting accustomed to the wasted, extra lights was difficult, similar to sleeping next to a boom box.

Like everywhere, humans generated the main noise, if not the only noise. Dag rolled out of bed, hit the bathroom for a minute, and brushed his teeth on the way to the dock. He absolutely loved to fish and hadn't been getting enough the last few weeks. Today was the first of many payoffs for his greasy work. As much as he loved fishing, he hated the necessary maintenance, especially on a dirty boat as *Sassy* had been. But the engine room, in fact, the entire 36 feet was about as spotless as it could be. When a boat is working, out on hire for many days fishing, you're exhausted on the return. No one refuses a charter to stay tied to the dock and scrub.

There wasn't much better fishing anywhere, what they called 'deep-sea.' Dag had dragged baits nearly everywhere in the Caribbean. Some drop-offs on the east side of the Saba Bank, far from St. Eustatius, were usually smoking with game fish because they were so isolated. But places like that also held lots of negatives, the possibility of foul weather, pirates, and, or the Dutch Navy.

The shelf went deep off the west side of Union, very close, only two kilometers from Sunset, a relatively short distance in sportfishing. Dag understood fishing as well as anyone; achieving the art of having fun, while making a good living, and doing it as a business. There were so many aspects of why the fishing was so great close to his home.

It was his home; he always had bragging rights. He was a natural, had fish sense; that's what Harry called it. Family owned the fuel docks and the parts supply. That is if the family still pulled together. With Sam's connections, they could get any part in a few days, little downtime. In Costa Rica, he was at the mercy of the marina manager's mood, and most often it required a bribe.

This is all he wanted, to get paid for doing what he loved and was so good at. What else could you ask for? Maybe a nice house, nice woman, nice dog. Remembering his youth, and sure kids, two boys. And he needed his own boat. That was the first requisite. Money, it always came down to money. Working for somebody else, living close, saving every dime... centavo.

"Hey, hey," he knocked on the hull. "Get your lily-white, Liverpool-living ass up. We got fish to catch. Hey bro!"

"I'm awake, I'm awake!" Tim shouted from below. "Did you ever consider my body is still living in bloody England, five hours difference? I've only been back for three days. Five in the morning here; my brain is sipping a pint at 10 in the evening." Tim coughed, "Haven't had a good night's sleep. But I'm ready to fish."

He came up with four rods that Dag grabbed. Then Tim carried up a plastic toolbox. Opened it and surveyed the contents. "Hasn't only been Dad that gotten rusty. Look at this stuff."

"Yeah, there's got to be a file or a wet stone in there somewhere. Sharpen up four long shank hooks."

"Aye, aye, skip. I'll make a half dozen rigs. Hey, where are we getting bait?"

"Brought some bread. Turn on the spotlight and I'll bring up some ballyhoo. I saw a throw net stored under the bench seat." He opened and grabbed it. "This is basically how I have to do it in Papagayo Bay. Not enough boats to get the locals interested in supplying bait."

Tim adjusted the drag on each reel as he put the rods in their holders. "I thought there were a lot of boats working around the area you're in now?"

"No, not that many. Most of the serious fishing is by foreigners who bring their own boats with captains. They come and go, passing through, like here. My bay, maybe ten, twelve other boats. It depends on what fish is running." Dag threw some breadcrumbs into the spotlight's circle and waited a few minutes. Then he expertly twirled the throw net off the port side. The yellow mesh fanned out into a perfect circle. The drawcord was nearly perfect in the center.

He let the net sink, always counted to fifteen, as Harry had taught him. Then, hand over hand, he pulled it up, "Look at that, got some fat nice ones, bro, going to be a good day. I can tell. Hardly even a breeze. Once Cheesy shows up, we hit it. Dad will be here by then."

"You sure about that? I guess, yeah, he's sober. He'll be here. What's that cliché? A bad day fishing is always better than a good day at work." Tim was busy with pliers making wire leaders, "You still make them 6 feet long?"

"That would be good. Keep the loops slim."

"I envy you. Truthfully, I hate what I do, rather be fishing, but there's already one too many fishermen in this family."

After two more successful tosses, Dag had twenty long needle nose baits. Ballyhoo was considered 'the bait' for big game fish. Bigger, but still slim, natural fish baits, other than mullets or bonito, were very rare. Because this bait was so long and thin, marlins would slash through the school, chop a lot apart, and return for the self-serve ballyhoo buffet. game

It was probably the same with squid. Those schools were thick. The slashing beak would make chopped calamari salad. Dag had seen schools of squid off Venezuela that had been acres in size. They were easy to see at night because they gave off a phosphorescence. Most fishermen slipped a plastic skirt over the nose of the ballyhoo that looked like a squid, but few ever went out and used real squid for bait. The big, slower variety was called cuttlefish. He'd used a big four-pounder on a downrigger off Panama and brought up an appropriately named five-hundred-pound Goliath grouper.

"Yep, three's a crowd and Cheesy is a great mate. He loves the work. Who wrote, you can never go home again?" Dag said starting the engines. "Dad'll be here in a minute. You know he'll be at the helm."

Tim chuckled, "You get your chance to show your new lessons. Don't worry. Can never go home again, that's Thomas Wolfe. Make your mistakes, take your chances. That's exactly what we are doing. I know I can't come back. I've changed too much and Union, by the grace of God, has changed little. Hey, listen, there's Cheesy. Everyone's chomping at the bit to drag baits. I know I am. This has everything to make it a classic day, like a time machine."

"Except we're short mischievous Mia," Dag mentioned while stringing the wire leader through the bail.

"She's coming, but don't say anything. Might spoil the moment."

"What? Really, Mia's coming back? Holy shit! Ruin what moment?"

"Both now, when Mom and Dad get morbid about all her blah, blah, blah. You know, they talk the same morbid, flew the roost, shit about me and you. And then it will be anticlimactic when she arrives. We'll be listening to reruns."

"Nothing is anticlimactic with sister Mia," Dag grinned. "That's great news. Mia will pump some life into this place. Hell, doesn't it feel like a funeral?"

"No, not quite, I'm seeing it as a game we can easily win and return Uncle Sam to his rightful position of island jester. You know he's such a fun guy," Tim paused, "but greedy. You should have seen him yesterday. Had his Gucci shoes resting on Granpop's roll top desk. Gucci's, I'm telling you. Got a pair myself. Damn comfortable. Wear them at the office. Unc's living large. Gucci's and saltwater." He laughed.

"I haven't heard anything or seen him yet. Wouldn't know a Gucci if it bit me on the ass."

"Also saw Kid Kalaloo last night coming into the hardware. Guess he works for Unc." Tim scoffed, "Wow, is he carrying a chip. Must be too much testosterone."

"Yeah, let's drop that subject. Why ruin a perfect morning. Oh, no, worst-case scenario, Mom's coming."

"What? That's great," Tim peeked around the cabin. "This really will be back-in-time. Our family together again."

"Save that until we return this afternoon. Then we'll know the bicker limit. I think they live off of it. Tim, you left way before me. I had to listen to them together, in stereo, and then when I worked with dad, he'd broadcast in mono. Then, most of it was about you, and never wanting to visit us, even on holiday. I don't know how Cheesy's put up with it for so long. Speak of the…"

Barefoot, Cassy bounded on deck wearing her official Sunset Bay set of a khaki shirt and shorts with the shirttails fashionably knotted. She handed a sack of sandwiches and two stainless thermoses to Tim. "Come on boys, give me a hug. This is such a pleasant morning. Remind me later to call Honoré. He can run the restaurant. Don't you think I deserve a day off with my boys?"

They obliged.

"Yeah," Harry butted in as he jumped aboard, "any day vertical is a great day. Right fellows? Been busy, huh?" Harry nodded, admiring the leader baits. "Nice work." He strung himself over both sons.

"Cheesy, you coming? Let's get this show on the road. The fish are waiting."

"Aye, aye, Cappy, ready for the dock lines?" He handed a small cooler to Tim. Cheesy adopted the perfect mate posture, hands on his hips awaiting orders. Harry slowly pushed the throttles forward evenly. The engines never coughed, just roared until he pulled them back.

"Purring like two kittens, tiger kittens." Harry slipped into the role with his practiced verses, "Everyone ready, bring everything you need, sunscreen, motion sickness pills? Life vests are in that locker." He pointed to the long bench, "we got the automatic life raft sitting up there on the bow. It inflates as soon as it hits the water. At least that's the promise, and you see the two fire extinguishers on each side."

"We'll be fishing in water a couple of thousand feet deep." He widened his eyes, "Big fish out there, really big fish. Let's go catch some!" Harry rolled his eyes, accompanied by hand gestures. "Got to practice my safety speech. Government and good common-sense dictates and all that bullshit. Let's go."

Dag gently pushed the stern away from the dock. Cheesy pushed the bow and hopped on board with an experienced leap.

Harry cupped his ear as he watched his boat move away from the dock. "Sweet, baby, you sounding sweet-sweet." Harry kissed the steering wheel, "I love you, baby. Know you missed this as much as I did."

Cassy turned, "Yes, I have. See, you can be nice when you want to, even romantic."

"Oh, oh yeah, honey, I know you was missing this type of together time."

"I really was. Remember, we'd go out when we didn't have charters and fished to sell? I missed that."

"Them days was before we spawned our crew." Harry smiled, pushed on the throttles, "We'll be dragging baits in ten minutes. Get everything ready. Since always, this has been my favorite time to fish, when the mist is still coming off the water. Could skip a coin on this glass. Look at it, wow, what a day!"

The sky brightened and by 6 AM they didn't need lights any longer. A bright coral sun inched up behind them. It would be hot in a few hours. Harry liked to fish the cool mornings. Get the anglers busy, bring in a few nice ones, if the guys weren't too lame, and then get them into a happy beer drunk. That way they went to sleep right after dinner. That was when they had paying fishermen staying at the house.

Everyone got comfortable. Harry stayed at the lower helm. Cassy was first to sit in the chair. Dag and Tim climbed up in the tuna tower. The aluminum pipe frame was equipped with an identical steering wheel with throttles and navigation systems. The tower increased long-distance visibility and helped to watch a fish once it was hooked. There's a lot of finessing a good skipper could do to help a poor, weak, paying angler. On a day like this day, from the upper steering station, twelve feet above the deck, they could see vertical visibility down at least fifty feet. Made it easy for the boat to reverse and back down, chasing a fish.

Cheesy watched the lines from his usual place at the stern while enjoying a thin cigar.

"I thought you quit, Cheese?" Cassy asked.

"Only smoke offshore, one or two at most." He used a wet finger to snuff the cigar, "Verena won't tolerate it. I know it's bad for my health, but then what isn't? Helps relieve stress."

"What stress?" she asked, "You never look tense."

"That's because I smoke one of these when we're out," he flashed a toothy grin as he poured a cup from a thermos. "Get ready. We're just going off the drop. A good place to nail a wahoo." He smiled. "Also got to practice my words."

"Birds!" Tim and Dag both bawled, "birds off the starboard bow, about a half-mile!"

"You take the control from up there, Dag," Harry yelled. "I'll help Mr. Chessman with the rods. Tim, let out the riggers."

It was a well-practiced drill, except Cheesy was accustomed to doing everything. Harry usually stayed at the helm and shot the shit with the customers. Cassy sat still while the men whirled into activity around her. The outriggers were fifteen feet long, aluminum poles supported and reinforced with thin stainless-steel cables on both sides of a boat. They usually drop from their hinged bases to be almost level with the sea. The purpose is to spread the two outside lines farther from the boat. Usually, these rods had their lines farther back and frequently got hit first. Harry took the port side and hooked a line into a special clip that popped open when it was pulled hard enough. All saltwater fish hit hard. Sometimes a dancing sailfish or marlin would smash into an outrigger.

Two pulls and the outside lines were spread. Each man watched intently and adjusted the distance. There wasn't much what could be called waves. The silver baits trailed perfectly.

"Harry, ready for these?" Cheesy asked, holding up two mirrored teasers.

"Uh-huh, put them back the usual six meters."

Modern sportfishing had evolved into whatever it took to bring fish up from the deep. Fishermen used new technology, or at least thought it was new, to attract fish. These big billfish aren't stupid, Harry thought. Once they've been hooked, they're wary, but also always hungry. A six-hundred-pound fish has to eat a lot of protein to keep its engines running.

The lures Cheesy dropped had mirrors glued on and spun on their swivels, without hooks. As they rotated, a few small pebbles inside rolled and made noise. The flashing and rattles imitated a school of sprat on the surface. The few times he'd been brave enough to snorkel through a school of fry, Harry had heard the thick schools of finger long fish rattle.

At eighty US apiece, Harry hated to lose them, but sometimes the fake baits agitated the marlin and sailfish so much that they'd whip their bill and break the heavy monofilament line that secured the teasers to the boat.

"Getting close," Dag said. "Everything ready? Wow, plenty of birds diving. Looks like yellowfin tunas cutting through the school of fry. Better strap mom in; these look good-sized."

"Aye, aye, skipper," Harry answered as he buckled a seat belt around his wife's waist, then stood ready at her right side. Cheesy was on the left. From the tower, Dag slowed and watched where the baitfish were heading. As soon as the boat came upon a school of bait out in the ocean, they pushed the fry. Everything moved constantly in the deep blue.

"Fish, fish all around the far outside lines," Tim yelled as a rod bent and its reel screamed out the alarm. "Fish on, starboard inside!" He jumped down from the tower and grabbed one of the other rods and began frantically reeling in line. A fish darting left and right could easily tangle with another line. That made it difficult to boat and could lose the other rig. Cheesy did the same as Harry, let the fish run for a half a minute, then pitted his weight and strength against it and set the hook. Watching his footing, he moved the rod across the deck and wedged the butt into the chair's rod holder. A deft, practiced move, he snapped the two straps from the harness to the metal loops built into the top of the reel. Everything was secured to the chair. It would take a monster to lose the rod overboard now.

"Cass, it's a nice one. Crank slow, if your arms start burning, I'll take it or Tim."

The woman bent about her task, dipping her back with the rod and then straightening, pumping it. Each time she cranked in a few meters of line. With a high-pitched whirring, the fish stripped more line off the reel.

"Careful now, don't hurt yourself, baby. Watch your thumb. You can lose a lot of skin very quick if you make a mistake and put it against the spinning spool to slow him when he's tugging it out. It's natural to try to…"

Cassy cut Harry short, "I know, and you know I know. Give it a break."

"Just practicing again. Must have said those words thousands of times, almost every hookup. You know, numbnuts, know-it-alls, burn off an entire thumbprint."

"I know, I know. Stand behind me and help me pump."

Harry moved behind, reached and had his hands about two feet up the rod. Cassy directed each pump and he assisted. "You know how long I've waited for you to say, 'get behind me and pump?"

"Oh, you! Be serious, I want this fish."

Cheesy grabbed the long gaff from its place clipped below the stern rail and turned to watch for the fish.

"I can see him. He's a nice yellowfin." Tim said and frantically pointed, "Oh, this is great. Mom, what can I do to help?"

"Just get the soy and wasabi ready for the freshest, raw fish snack," Cassy said between bending at her waist using her slim body against the fish. "Can you see him, Cheese?" She asked, almost out of breath.

"Oh yeah, oh yeah, it's right here. A couple more…" Cheesy said. As an expert mate, he first looked at how his feet were planted. He stretched and swung the long aluminum gaff hook. The swift movement coupled with adrenaline fueled muscles had the big tuna pitched up onto the deck in seconds. Harry bopped it a few times in the head with the small wooden baseball bat they carried for such occasions. The fish shuddered as it became part of that evening's menu.

"Yahoo! Wow! I won!" Cassy yelled at the top of her lungs as she wilted from the exertion.

Harry kissed her cheek as he bent to free her rod from the chair. "Knew you could do it, baby. Looks like we might be selling fish again. This one's at least 50 pounds."

"Come on boys, lines out. We're wasting time," Dag shouted from the upper station. "We're in a big school."

As soon as the rods were out, two were slammed by similar-sized fish. Tim pumped one rod on the starboard and competed against Harry on the port side. Cheesy cleared the way.

"Either of you want the chair?" Cassy asked as Harry staggered, tugged to the stern by his fish.

"I'm okay, I'm okay." His face was already red. The rods slammed down and more line stripped. "Yeah, yeah, maybe I could use the chair. This one feels bigger, yeah, bigger."

"Want me to help you pump," Cassy quipped.

"Always," Harry grunted.

Tim's line shrieked as the reel peeled line. The fish rocketed out of the water. "Hey, this is a sail, wow, a nice sailfish," Tim huffed. "Dad, can you get yours in while I play with this one?"

Harry pushed out his jaw, neck veins bulging, "Sure thing, kid." He pumped the rod up and down, cranking like a madman. "Cheese, snag this guy, will ya? Got a queue waiting for this chair."

"Try not to nick my line," Tim asked.

"Done this a few times before, son, only a few times," Cheese muttered, took his stance, and slung the long hook down and followed through with his weight. In an expert movement, the sharp, six-inch stainless hook caught the fish in thick flesh, just behind the gills. With both hands tightly gripping the gaff's pole, he deadlifted the unwilling fish out of its natural habitat and slammed it onto the fiberglass deck. In seconds, that fish was also on the menu.

Harry jumped out of the chair and helped Tim carefully move into the seat. Cassy grabbed Harry's rod and ducked down below the stern rail to reduce the confusion and avoid a chance of being injured.

A long sailfish spiraled up from the boat's wake and tail walked for a few seconds. It dove and then shot out again.

"Keep a taut line, Tim. You got a beauty on, probably over one-twenty," Harry knelt and whispered. Everything was quiet. Dag had cut the diesels, and the only noises other than the screeching of the feeding birds was an occasional clank from the bouncing outriggers.

Tim was in his glory, his new muscles bulging in his jersey. "Pump and reel, pump and reel," he recited again and again as he dipped the rod and steadily raised the fish.

"You know we ain't going to keep this one, right? Dag's getting some nice photos from his phone. One tuna is plenty and we got two," Harry again whispered. "Never could figure a tasty way to cook sailfish anyhow."

Harry yelled, "I can see its bill coming up the port trough. Cass, maybe you should go up top with Dag."

"Okay, good idea." She scurried to the ladder and clamored up the tower.

"Hmm," Harry whispered to Tim as he bent to snap the harness. "Maybe fishing does bring the family together?"

The sailfish rocketed again and Tim's upward thrust of the rod knocked Harry backward. He missed his footing and fell. He quickly stood and grabbed onto the back of the chair. Looked around, took a slight bow, saying, "Hey, someone's always gotta be the clown. Dag, give your phone camera, whatchamacallit, to your mom. Cass, you know how to work one, to get a video? Don't get to see tail walks much anymore."

"Yeah, dad, you need to mount a GoPro camera somewhere. We got three on my boat, starboard, port, and the one up top has the widest angle. Lots of anglers bring their own mounted on their heads or chests."

"I have zero idea what you are blabbing about, Dag. Stow it for later. Quiet while your brother lands this fish." He placed his hands on Tim's broad shoulders, "Doing it perfect boy, perfect. Keep the line tight. When he shoots towards the boat, which he will, crank your ass off."

Everything was strained, the line, the arc of the bent rod, and mostly Tim's arms. His biceps and forearm muscles burned, but he was winning the battle and that's all that was important. A foot was gained, but the fish tugged it back. Up and down, up and down, the rod tip bobbed.

"Mates, I can see its bill," Cheesy shouted.

"Me too, Cheese, I can see it," Dag agreed. "I think he's giving up. Keep cranking, bro. I'm slipping it into reverse. Think you've had enough of a workout today. Crank! Now!"

Sassy Cassy reversed slowly and Dag artfully moved to the fish. Cheesy straddled the stern; his right hand was carefully loose around the line as he waited to see the wire leader attached to the swivel rise from the water. "Okay, almost got it. Yes, touched it. Tim, you landed a biggie. Okay to cut it loose?" The Brit turned to get the okay from the angler, who nodded. Cheese's left hand thrust a pair of wire cutters and snipped the leader.

Once the fish was freed, Tim collapsed in the seat and rubbed his arms. "Can I get a water?" His father complied, and Tim took two gulps and poured the rest over his head. "Wow, that was more fun than I remembered!"

"Probably because that's the biggest fish you ever dragged in. And that's because of your extra muscles." Harry recounted, "That's the most and longest tail walks we've seen in years, huh, Cheesy?"

"Agreed, Timothy, spectacular fish. Good to have spared him to catch again. Next time he'll probably be more pissed, fight harder. When I first started out here, walks like that were common, almost every day. Then something happened, sailfish almost disappeared, and we started hooking more sharks. The tiburons probably drove them away." Cheesy patted Tim on the back, "Atta boy. Good going."

"Dag your turn. I'll take the helm," Harry said.

"Nah, I'm good. I get enough of this."

"Hey, no St. Claire ever gets enough of fishing. Get down here," Harry ordered.

"Okay, okay." Dag descended and Harry replaced him at the upper controls.

"Let's say my sail was 110, on the inside. You got to beat that," Tim boasted. "Dad and mom got theirs. Go get them slimy, scaly bastards, Dagger."

"Sure," Dag found his shoulder bag and rigged his own bait, He slipped a bright pink plastic skirt with a two-inch-thick and wide clear head adorned with big, protruding eyes down the leader, before snapping the swivel.

"Wait a minute, we all used natural baits. This is one of those fancy bubbleheads," Tim complained. "I've seen them in magazines. They use them in Hawaii."

Dag shrugged, "Yeah, they're called Hula Hookers. One of our anglers tipped me with five of them. Brought them along. I didn't hear anything in the rules…" He pushed a button on the slightly concave head. The eyes started alternately flashing.

"But…"

Tim was cut off by Harry, "Let 'em go. I heard about 'em too and like to see how they operate. Can't hurt. We wasn't betting. Already ahead, as we have fresh fish. Extra fish will always help make friends and or money. And let's face it, right now on Union Island, the St. Claire family can definitely use more of both." He sermonized with a nod to Cassy who returned beaming a smile.

They fixed two rods with Dag's skirts and each had to be adjusted a few times to have it pull correctly following the boat without twisting and rolling through the prop wake.

"Where you want to run them," Cheese asked. "How far back?"

"Well, inside lines, about halfway between the teasers and the far lines running off the riggers," Dag replied.

"Okay, you get yours set where you want it and I'll match the distance," Cheesy agreed and then said, "Maybe one in closer? You know, see where they work the best. Our water might differ from Costa Rican water." He pursed his lips, "Fish probably different, too. Went to different schools." He chuckled at his own joke. "Bet you, Pacific fish are different from the Caribbean versions."

"Who gives a shit what fish does where? We're here. Let the battle begin. It's just eleven now, and we already got three hookups, with zero losses. Somebody better be ready to tip the Skip." Harry nodded and continued, "What say we give it another hour before it gets too hot out here. Them tunas need ice. We thought of everything, but ice."

"Sure Dad, I think some long figure-eight passes, maybe ten times, and these things should bring anything up if it's there," Dag answered.

Harry looked down, nodded in agreement, and turned the wheel slightly, "Figure eight or circles?"

"Eights," Dag said over his shoulder while watching the line feed out. Tim relaxed on the long bench sipping another water, mulling, "We've got to compete against Mr. Super Lure."

"Come on, bro, if these work, more fish get caught. We get better tips. People don't mind spreading the cash around if they hookup with big, story-tale fish. You know, bar talk type fish to brag about when they're back in the Wisconsin sportsman's club. Next time we go out, I have some lead heads wrapped with really long horse tail hair, dyed black with the shit all the Spanish use on their hair. They call those lures 'bruja', witch, because they work so good, especially on wahoo. Somebody's always improving on the wheel, you know that."

"Yeah, yeah, I can appreciate that and you for sharing these advancements only when it's your turn in the chair. I brought one, but…"

"Jeeze, you can use one next time, I promise," Dag offered. "We don't even know if they work here yet. Bro, the real secret of these lures, they're named Screaming Hula Hookers. When I flicked on the eyes, there's a little chipboard in there that starts sending out two pulses, one high-treble and one low–bass frequencies. The guy who gave them to me said he was the inventor. Buddy, these raised some real serious fish. Glad I got my lures free, 'cause the new catalogs got them at $150 apiece. The kicker, another rich man's toy, they're disposable. Use them for one hookup and they're finished. Can't keep the fish from breaking them."

Harry rolled through the intersecting patterns for forty-five minutes.

"They make a nice picture," Cheesy nodded to Dag and Tim of their parents standing side by side on the tower watching for signs of fish. "Back to nautical Norman Rockwell again, boys." He nodded to them, "It was you guys coming home that did this. You get the credit."

It was a wholesome scene against the light blue sky. The sun was directly overhead, with no clouds, only solid pale blue. Cassy and Harry accidentally wore matching work uniform khaki shirts and shorts. The accident was Cassy, who favored jean cutoffs and peasant tops. Harry was into the crew routine, topped with his white captain's hat. Cassy wore a tan, straw Panama-type fedora.

Tim looked around, "Hey, I didn't notice 'til now, all of you got tan work shirts, fishing shirts, but me," He pulled on his knit shirt with an alligator on the chest pocket, "I'm Mr. Polo."

"You always were the neatest of us," Dag didn't finish as the rod beside him bent as the line sung a shrill, high-pitched alarm.

"Fish on!" All five voices shouted.

Dag flicked the lever on the right side of the big, black Penn 8-0 reel and let the fish run. "Anyone see it yet?" He asked as he settled in the fighting chair. It felt good, damn good. "Steady her, slow her down, Dad, until we see where she's going."

"Sure, son, sure, but I can damn well tell you where that fish is going, as far away from this boat as possible," Harry said. "Mom, you keep those binoculars looking around, far astern. From the way he took that bait so clean and so strong, I think this is another biggie sail. Looks like he already ran out about half the line. That's eighty-pound test, more than fifteen hundred meters on that reel. Look back about a half-mile, honey."

"Honey?" Cassy smiled with a happy laugh. "Honey, okay, honey."

Dag tenderly slid up the drag lever with his body arched in the fighting chair. He was almost doubled over. He moved his left hand to wrap the rod just below the first eye. His right hand cranked the reel. His efforts met with no cooperation from the fish.

"Better put her in reverse, Dad. This guy's speeding for China!" Dag asked.

Tim and Cheesy cleared the deck of the other rods. Harry instead steered in a wide arc to port. With his glasses, he could see the line cut through the water. Dag reeled and reeled. Couldn't let any slack in the line. A big fish could feel it and spit the hook if it hadn't been properly set.

It wasn't a fair fight. If they'd have been in a smaller boat, a fish this size would have towed them around. It was all part of the game, strategy, technique. Let the fish fight and pull until he tired himself out.

The downside of that was the fish could literally have a heart attack and die or be so tired it couldn't fight off the predator sharks. A big fish thrashing on the surface was certain to attract sharks, usually just as big.

They still hadn't seen it break water and didn't know what they had hooked. All they knew, it was big.

"Whew," Dag groaned. "No matter what I do, I can't stop it."

"Thought of all people, you'd be used to this," He teased. "I can help if you're getting winded."

"No, I can do this," Dag said as he frantically reeled. "People catch fish on the boats I run. They don't pay me to fight their fish." He kept the line tight. Harry had closed some distance and had *Sassy* in neutral.

Boom! Their questions were answered. A huge blue marlin shot straight up out of the water about a hundred yards off their stern. Everyone was mesmerized not only by its twelve-foot body, but that its broad tail cleared the water by more than the same distance. This fish was an ICBM!

"Keep 'er tight, son, keep 'er tight. Looks to be bigger than six hundred!" Harry exclaimed. "Looks like them special radio lures do work. Cheesy, Tim, pay attention mates. Mama, you got the camera?"

"Yeah mom, get good shots. We can use them in our new online brochure," Tim said.

"Hey, I got one on-the-line here. Let's only worry about that," Dag lamented. "I'm pumping, I'm pumping. He's coming. I'm gaining on him!"

"Yeah, son, he's coming straight towards us. Looks like a fucking torpedo, excuse my French," Cheesy exclaimed. "Oh, watch out, watch out, here he comes!"

First a big blue tail sliced through the water. Then the front dorsal fin was pushing six feet ahead. Ten seconds later, thirty feet directly off the stern, the huge marlin launched up, twisting, the pink lure was easy to see against the shiny dark blue head.

"There she blows, holy Hell, that thing must be fifteen feet!" Harry shouted.

The deep blue ocean opened for the darker blue monster and it plunged deep. The rod arced and the line peeled off through the roller guides. Dag pressed all his strength against it but couldn't move the rod.

"Now he's sounding, mother of God," Cheesy giggled and clapped. "Minutes ago, the bugger launched himself twenty feet in the air, arcing across the stern. This is one hell of a day. Tim, use a water bottle to soak your brother, cool him off. My money's that he'll be busy for a while. Might as well have a stallion horse on that line; it'd be about the same weight and temperament."

Dag strained, eyes bulged, his knuckles were white, and his breaths deep. He was focused. His ticket was punched. This is what he'd craved, but more than he ever expected. He was certain he could fight this marlin and win. With his feet planted flat on the chair rest, he flexed his calves and thighs and pushed up. He was lifting this fish, this giant. Nothing hurt yet. All he needed was to get his rhythm.

"Only had a few that size up out here during the last few years, lad. Mind the line, Cheesy. Whatever you do, don't let it touch the stern. Now, don't you wish we had replaced all the lines?" Harry said twisted around, watching the stern, but ready to slip into gear and chase the fish.

"Yo, Dad, this one's medium-sized compared to what we hook in Costa," Dag coughed.

"Bull shit," came the reply from the upper station. "Bullshit, bullshit, bullshit. There aren't that many of these grands left, longliners clearing them out."

"Tim, give your brother some water to drink, don't just pour it on him. Tilt the bottle," Cassy instructed.

Everyone had something to say except Tim. He watched as if it were a movie. Everyone was choreographed, knew their places, and recited their lines. He was the only outsider. Too many years away from this life, and 'this' had been the life he'd wanted so much to leave. Now it had him, hypnotized, frozen, standing behind the hunched Dag. He shook his head as if to wake from a dream. In his shorts, Tim found his phone. He stood to the left of the fighting chair. No shadows, he snapped consecutive pics of Dag struggling against the weight. Satisfied with the portraits, he retreated to the wall bench and stood on it, clinging to the tower ladder for stability, waiting to capture the fish on video.

It was quiet, like the morning again. Nothing on *Sassy* rattled. No one said a word. The well-lubricated Penn reel was silent as line was cranked in and tugged out. Dag's ragged, deep breaths could barely be heard. Tim wasn't familiar with sportfishing like the rest of his family was, but this didn't seem either normal or average. If he hadn't been so caught up in the initial hookup, he would have captured the first time this magnificent fish lunged and danced. He wiped the sweat from his jaw. "Yeah, that scene would have brought in many, many charters; I hope mom got it," he muttered under his breath.

The next half hour brought little encouragement or line back to the angler in the fighting chair. Dag arm-wrestled with the marlin and was at a standstill.

"Better hook me up in the harness. I'm here for the duration. This fish is," he was cut off.

Swift as lightning, the fish made another run to port. The chair turned to follow the direction, keeping the line pulling straight off the rod. Harry turned the same direction, trying to close the distance.

"Jesus, this fish is a locomotive, barreling on a downhill stretch," Harry bellowed. "We'll get him." And nudged the throttles.

"Watch out, dad, he might make a move and go under us. That'd be the end," Dag recommended.

Harry swallowed and grunted, "I'm paying attention, Dag. Been here, done this before. You just keep ready; this one's coming up again. Mark my words. I'm gonna get you close, but safe close. If it decides to go under the boat, I'll goose her a bit, but my business now is to keep you close."

Twenty long minutes later, the line relaxed and Dag wound in a lot, but he knew what was coming. Again, the monster was rushing up from probably thirty fathoms. Perhaps the fish just wanted to see what was taking its freedom. The marlin did its best magic trick, just powering up fantastically high, but didn't dance, just dove. The first arc was close to fifty feet. Line screamed and the crew gasped four-letter-words. Dag hung on, releasing the drag as this fish completed seven leaps clockwise around the stern. Harry kept steering counter-clockwise, trying to anticipate the fish. He never took his eyes off the spot where the line entered the water.

Mr. Sun was well heated, high in the sky by one o'clock. Tim applied more sunscreen. "Dag, you want some? You're burning, buddy."

Wrapped around the rod, buckled into the chair, he was sitting curled in a fetal position. The fish was on the umbilical. "Tim, it's only my forearms burning. Don't worry; a few beers and lots of tuna sushi will fix me up," Dag laughed.

"Yeah, well, if you don't bring that fish to the boat soon, the tuna's liable to spoil. Come on now, you're cutting into my nap time," Harry barked. "Just kidding around, son. This is one that's storytelling material."

"Hmm, like you needed facts to make a good story," Cassy laughed and nudged him. "I got some great shots. How about you, Tim?"

"Oh yeah, got that entire seven leap show. Brother, you'll be famous," Tim yelled. "Hell yeah, after today, Sunset Bay Fish Camp will be famous on YouTube. This is gonna be great for business."

"Son, we don't need charters six months from now trickling in from watching an Internet video. We needed them yesterday."

Tim was standing behind the chair, eying through his phone camera. "I know, pops, but it can't hurt. Now we got *Sassy* up and running, we can talk about marketing solutions."

"Right now, got one solution for our market. Dag, crank that bitch in. What are you, a farmer or a fisherman?" Harry joked.

That last line brought laughs. Everyone knew it came from Granpop Curly. It was his go-to line when someone had a big one hooked. It lightened the baking hot moment.

"Oh, oh, I can feel him coming up again," Dag reeled as fast as he could. His thumb kept moving back and forth, well trained to keep the line making a level wind. Otherwise, monofilament would bunch up on one side and could jam the reel. "Okay, get ready with those cameras. Make me famous."

"You're already a legend in your own mind," Tim clichéd.

To expect a fish leap was trying to prepare for a tornado. There was no way to anticipate which way it would go, except out of the water. *Sassy* wasn't moving much. Harry knew the fish was approaching again and just watched. Everyone's eyes were glued, waiting for the appearance.

Ten meters back, this monster rocketed straight out; its dark blue back and silver striped sides glistening in the sun. As it shot up, the huge dark head wagged back and forth. The long bill sprayed water, creating several small, brilliant rainbows. The fish's enormous black eyes seemed to look directly at all five on the boat. It seemed he was taking stock of his enemy.

Dag swallowed hard and kept reeling. "Cheese," His mouth was dry, he coughed out, "Cheese, can you see the leader?"

"Sure, son, it's attached to his mouth. I know what you mean, it's closer than ever before."

They could cut the line now and let the fish go, as much as saying that the fish won, over-powering the angler. Once the mate touched the wire leader, it was considered as good as bringing the fish aboard. Not that this one would fit. But the object wasn't to kill it. Tim looked at the time on his phone. The fight had moved into its fourth long, sweltering hour.

Line again stripped off the real.

"Hold 'em!" Harry shouted, "That scaly bastard is sounding straight down again, going deep. What's going on here, straight down, straight up, hopscotch across the stern; somebody inject this fish with Red Bull?"

"Can't hold him, dad," Dag gasped, "but this will probably be his last dive. He's going down, but not taking line like the other times."

"Hey, matey, that fish is a heavyweight champ of the sea. He met his match in Dag and now realizes it," Cheesy cheered. "Twenty more minutes, I'm betting I have the leader. Give it your gusto, son, finish this beast, denizen of the deep." Cheese bent at the waist into a neat bow because those were more of his rehearsed lines, to get the optimism back into the angler as the fight dragged on. Everyone always expected it to be easier. Big fish were exactly that, big. Once you hooked something your weight or bigger, they didn't come easy. That's what everybody wanted, what everyone paid for, but few of the anglers who got their wish were physically ready for the test.

Tim rubbed Dag's shoulders in silent reassurance. As the fish started to slowly rise with every pump, he moved to the stern, and kept his camera ready. Cheese would cut the leader. This fish had given a noble fight, a classic Triple-A, Five-Star, Ali - Frazier struggle. Dag wound line slowly. He was smiling. He started to laugh, first nervously, then snorting a howl as he could feel the enormous fish had given up. It was coming to the boat.

Ten meters behind the stern all eyes were on where the monofilament line met the water. The tip of the blunt, grayish-blue bill rose from the water. It was done thrashing until it got closer. Then the fish would give all that it had to escape the ultimate penalty. Every wild creature and even the not so wild humans knew to give it their all, fight to survive, when it got close to lights out.

He knew he was being cheered, but Dag couldn't hear the exact words. It was all jumbled around him. The fish had drained him. If the positions had been reversed, if the fish had made one more run, he would have had to pass the rod to Tim.

This fish was being gracious, giving up, coming in just when Dag's leg muscles were cramping.

"I can see it, ten, fifteen more feet, drag it in, boy, drag it in!" Cheese yelled. Tim was hanging over the stern. He knew it was dangerous, but the contagious adrenalin was overwhelming. Marlin were known to have killed fishing crew by stabbing with a solid thrust of their bill. Hell, that's why they were called swordfish. But he got the shots and videos of Cheesy touching the leader, recorded the rousing cheers, and captured the confused, forlorn look in the marlin's eyes.

"Done, and done," Cheese said as he snapped the side cutter pliers and watched as *Sassy* drifted away from the fish. "I think it's all right."

Everyone watched intently. The fish flexed its long body, snapped, and disappeared.

"You did it!" Tim was slapping high fives with Dag, who couldn't believe he could raise his arms.

"You did good, Dag," Harry piped, "Let's go home, unless you want a chance for a biggie, Cheese?"

The Brit was already organizing the rods, unsnapping the leaders. "I'm good, boss. Dag breaking that beast, yes sir, that was good enough for me. I'm ready for a cold one. Anyone else? Brought a quarter crate, or, to you, a six-pack."

Cassy looked at her husband, who waved it off. "No, I'm on the wagon. Be awhile, if ever. Got a Pepsi in there?"

"Yes, I do." And a perfect pitch satisfied the captain and his wife. They shared the soda and the warm satisfaction that their family was back together.

"Nothing's easy, Cass," Harry said low enough that those below wouldn't pick it up over the diesels. "Nothing is easy, but I'm trying." Harry caught her arm and turned her to him and looked Cassy directly in her eyes. He slowly said, "I know I made some mistakes. I am so sorry."

She hugged his arm, "I know, I know." She turned to watch her sons regale with laughter at that day's fish stories while sipping their beers. Things were changing and for once for the better.

"Mom, Dad," Dag, Tim, and a sheepish Cheesy, raised their beers to salute. "Yahoo! Team St. Claire is back."

Harry grinned and flashed his Pepsi in reply.

"If all politicians fished, instead of spoke publicly, we would be at peace with the world," Will Rogers.

CHAPTER SIX

During the hour-long run back home, Dag and Cheesy reorganized the fishing boat and washed the decks with buckets of sea water. Tim inspected all the rods, lubricated the reels, and kept busy making a few more rigs. This was the standard routine.

The day had been gorgeous, even better than the usual spectacular Caribbean days, cloudless, constant bright blue sky, but with a broiling sun. The heat finally dropped off about five with a breeze from out of the west. Once at the dock, Harry shut her down and finally relaxed. He would never have admitted that he'd been nervous, wondering if the engines were dependable. Currently unpopular, it might have been hard to find a tow if one or both of the diesels had problems. Once all the action ceased and the boat was empty, he opened the engine hatches and did an inspection.

It felt good; he was into the skippering routine again and would do this before and after every charter. Better for Harry to catch a problem early than it caught him and bit his ass through his wallet. No oil was leaking, belt tensions good, and no water in the fuel filter separators. The dipsticks showed a perfect oil level. *Sassy* really was back.

Harry relaxed in the fighting chair, sober, soaking in the evening. It felt good, wholesome for once, listening to his family and good friend, Cheesy, echo across the bay, their bay. Harry could see all the way out, beyond the brown cliffs; not another boat in sight. His leathery face formed a self-righteous grin.

The boys cleaned and chopped the tunas into reasonably sized chunks. More beer accompanied the freshest sashimi. A few burps punctuated the evening from the over-spicy wasabi paste. Cassy was in her glory, sitting between her sons. Cheesy returned with Verena and a barbecue ensued. They pried tales of Costa Rica from Dag and of Fleet Street from Tim.

It was happening again; things had almost returned to the way it was meant to be before he'd screwed it up. *Sassy* had become the time machine that righted Harry's many wrongs. Hell, he'd had to study and take a coast guard test to skipper a boat, but nothing to be a father. Ah, he shook his head; the timing had been all wrong. Things happened too fast or he'd been too slow; too much fishing. The kids cost money while building the dock and then the house. That took charters, and that included drinking with the customers. Fuck it. He'd been weak, but he'd caught fish and made St. Claire's Sunset Bay famous. Well, sort of famous, and look where it had gotten them.

Cheesy had seen the reckoning near at hand and had the guts to call for reinforcements. They were giving him a chance to bounce back and dry out from his rum-soaked days, maybe the last chance. Listening to the easy laughter at the house, Harry tenderly patted the fiberglass hull as he stepped off the sportfisher on to the dock.

"You worked wonders, girl. Now, I have to." He took a deep breath, straightened his shirt, and issued a long, contented sigh before heading to the house party with a rare bit of bounce in his steps.

^^^^^^^^^

"Just like old times, huh?" Tim remarked.

"Yeah, kinda, sorta," Dag agreed. "Today was fairly remarkable. The bicker quotient was negligible. Mom never bitched once. And Dad refused a beer on a smoking scorching day after catching fish."

"And would rather have a fucking Pepsi!" Tim howled.

They both laughed. Tim had convinced Dag to make a trip into town. Said it would be good for both their sore muscles. Dag had found his rusty old Raleigh bicycle, hosed it off, and pumped up the tires. Tim borrowed Cassy's bike.

"Not so bad, worse case, the tires go flat and I got to push it home, no biggie," Dag said.

As usual Clifton in the evening was dead except for the few beer joints. They pedaled along the small waterfront park and found Clarence's Shaved Ice cart. Clarence was an institution and his beat-up, stainless pushcart, with the Campari umbrella, was a landmark. The old island man was stocky; probably his girth equaled his short stature. He enjoyed his own product. The story was he'd learned to make custard when he was in the Merchant Marine working with an Italian crew. First, he called it gelato, but no one knew what that meant and shied away. It became Clarence's Coconut Custard.

The West Indian elder greeted the brothers as if they'd visited every evening. The sense of yesterday disappeared.

Grabbing their tall cones, Tim pointed farther up the waterfront, to a bench near the gate to the airport. As they got busy with their dripping custards, a twin-engine prop screeched onto the landing field.

Slowly licking the cone, Tim managed, "Takes you back, right back to where we're 7 and 8, sneaking down here every time we got some spare change from one of the charter fishermen. Nothing like good homemade custard. This was our secret bench. I know you brought your girlfriends here to neck."

"Had to hide, kissing with a local girl must be a well-kept secret. Her parents wanted an island beau, and ours wanted an off-island white or tan. Anyway, that's what I thought back then. Everything was a secret. I kept breaking this streetlight for more privacy," Dag confessed.

Tim stretched out his legs and changed the subject. "Remember when Granma would get that hand-crank freezer machine out. So infrequently that we always had to scrub the dust of it."

"Not so infrequent, for each of our birthdays, don't you remember?" Dag asked. "Granma just liked everything spotless. She always had a thing about germs. Probably because she was a Brit in the islands. Everything was d-i-r-t-y. What a great old lady she was. She had Dinah, her housemaid, polishing, scrubbing. The kitchen in the restaurant shined, even in those times."

"Yeah, I think mom's mom lived on chlorine bleach. And Granpop Curly, what a guy; he never cleaned the store. You could always tell what didn't sell by the thick layer of dust."

"We were blessed to grow up here. Might not have felt like that when we were finishing school. Bored and cramped. Too much of 'everyone knew everybody and knew everything.'" Dag licked at his cone, "Now who cares?"

"But they might know something that we don't, bro. Lots of things we must find out, investigate this hotel group."

"Tim, you investigate, I say fuck it. Fishing will get us through this. After today, you post those videos on YouTube and we'll have charters out the ass. I brought some pesos and can help."

"I got some other ideas, better. But we need to change the opinion against our family. I brought money, but, bro, unless we change the attitude this is never going away. It'll fester and eventually nasty shit'll happen," Tim warned.

"Yeah, I know, but I don't know, and don't know if I want to know. I know fishing. I'm still a kid, haven't grown up, and don't plan on doing that mature thing for a while. You got that three-piece suit thing locked and loaded?"

"Got to do what you got to do. You're a fishing whore and I'm a banking whore."

A voice erupted from the darkness at the airport gate. "You'd think they could spend a few fucking dollars on lights. You're talking about me, poor little Mia, doing the nasty-nasty? Isn't that what people call me, a gold-digging whore?" She laughed, dropped her bags, and ran to them.

"Great!" Tim bounded off the bench and hugged his sister.

"Mia!" Dag shouted as he surrounded all in the embrace.

"Hey, don't wrinkle the merchandise. It is me or do you guys smell like fish?"

"It's you," Dag laughed, "No, it's us; we caught some fish today, nice fish." He sniffed the air, "And you got a scent, what is that?"

"Sunflower perfume, asshole, not fish guts. Let me look at you two. Holy shit, Timmy, what the fuck happened? You must have been eating your spinach." She felt his biceps and then ran a fingernail around his pecs. "Nice, nice. My goodness, you, you... holy shit, you got big! I would rough you up for calling me a fish whore, but..."

"Little sis, you're looking good." Tim returned. "Not too shabby."

Mia posed, feigning surprise, one hand on her hip and the other in the air. She looked spectacular wearing tight black short shorts and a white halter top.

"Nah, come on, we were talking about how 'we' had sold out, whores to banking and fish."

"Look at you, Dag, you're even more handsome. Wow, tanned and with that long blonde hair, wow. You're both like movie stars. And look at drab, little old me." She opened her arms and fluffed her short hair. "Like the haircut, easy to take care of. Like me, a little pixie, huh?"

"Oh, you're a sweet little pixie, a regular Tinkerbelle," Dag replied.

"Yeah, I just flew in from Puerto Rico. Thanks for coming for me. I hope to make my grand entrance and surprise everyone at breakfast."

"We didn't..." Dag looked confused.

"I didn't know for certain, so I planned to be here every night. The only time the commuter comes in," Tim winked at Dag. "We heard and are so sorry about your husband."

They strapped Mia's bags on Tim's bike. Cassy's bike's side-baskets, designed to carry produce from the market, fit the job. Mia wiggled her little butt and got reasonably comfortable riding on Dag's handlebars.

"Oh, I've had a horrible year. A fucking weird year, but then again, I'm a magnet for weird. What did anyone expect marrying an Elvis impersonator? With mom and dad, they raised me to appreciate weird and feel comfortable."

"Hey, what's weird about growing up on Sunset Bay?" Dag asked.

"Don't get me started. Please, it was okay for you two, Huck Finn, who never came off the water, and Einstein, who never put down a book. I was supposed to be choir girl, gardener, chief cook, and dishwasher."

"You make it sound... Nah, maybe it was confined..."

Mia cut Tim short, "Confined? Mom had all my clothes made by Jessie, the seamstress. You know how much I hated checkered blouses and knee-length skirts?"

"So, you broke away. We all broke away. Now, we're back together as a family."

"Whoa there, Timmy, I'm back. I'll get some balance and then I'll be looking for newer faces and places. My life's gotten weirder and weirder in the last six months."

The boys stopped peddling when they could see the tall lamp at their dock. Mia got off and continued her story.

"First, beloved Kurt's depressed, then he tore two groups of charter guests new assholes because they requested he does a few songs dressed like 'The King.' Duh, hey, that's how we got the money to buy the yacht. Photos of him in costume everywhere. Don't think it would have been worse if he'd have been a drag queen. So, we had to make refunds. Then, 'blewwie!' I'm a widow and had to hire someone to redo the cabin. Think the son of a bitch could have shot himself on deck."

Her laugh was contagious.

"Hardly a rich widow, but a very in-debt widow who probably must sell her boat." She paused, "How you like my mourning clothes?"

"Anyway, we're all sorry. No one should have to go through all of that," Dag hugged his sister.

"Being raised here, I don't think I'll have much of a problem with it." She unzipped her waist bag and pulled out a cigarette.

"Got that habit? Better be discrete."

Mia inhaled deeply, looking at the building's silhouette. "But I'm back to finish my Devil's Island sentence and pay off my debt to Harry and Cassandra."

"Things have changed. Dad's on the wagon," Tim answered.

"Again?" was her reply.

"Hey! He's trying. Tim and I just got the boat straightened out. Cheesy and Verena are helping to get things back on track." Dag announced, "And you better get with the program. The island's got our balls in a vice and cranking it tight."

Her smile could be seen in the cigarette's glow, "Then, I'm lucky I was born without testicles."

"Caught a nice sail and two big tunas today," Dag said.

"Yeah, and your brother forgot that he boated a six-hundred plus blue." Tim bragged. "You should have been there. We were the team again. Mom and Dad never argued once. Can you believe alone for nine hours on the boat and they were nice to each other?"

"Which one, or are both taking tranks?" Mia giggled. "I promise I'll be the perfect daughter, Rebecca of Sunnybrook. I won't let them catch me smoking and try not to embarrass anyone in town. I promise."

Dag cocked his head, "Mom will probably want you to help at the restaurant. Some quality mother-daughter time. No excuses. We're doing the same with Harry."

"And we got him in excellent spirits. He's cleaned up his act. We owe this all to Cheesy." Tim added.

Mia flicked her cigarette away. "Wish you would have waited for me. I miss fishing so much. Can't really fish properly from a sailboat, even a catamaran. And when you're chartering, you always have to consider the mess. Lots of people don't like to see fish die. I guess they never figured out where a McFish sandwich comes from, huh?" she laughed.

"Oh, we'll be back out there again, catching more," Tim said. "The way I've got it figured; we have to catch a lot of fish quick."

"We're going to sell fish? How are we going to that if the villagers hate us?"

"Oh, don't sound melodramatic. No one hates the St. Claires. No, no, I'll explain it all. It'll take some time. More like selling mucho charters and then selling the fish we catch that the anglers can't take home. Best, optimum profit is if mom sells our fish cooked at the restaurant. Lots of details to work out."

"You always were the brains. I want to hear all about London and the shopping! Let's get going. Remember, I've got to be smiling, well-rested Rebecca in the morning when I make mom and dad choke on their coffee," Mia smiled. "Who am I bunking with?"

"Me," Tim quickly answered. "On the boat. Tonight only, if you don't mind. I'm sure you'll get your own room back."

She made a face, "Maybe we could share the boat. That old room was so damn hot! I still sleep in the buff 'cause of that oven. That won't bother you, Timmy, will it?"

"Same with me. But I pull a sheet up. *Sassy* gets a breeze through the forward hatch and it's cold. We can share, but I know you'll want a better bathroom. I just wiz over the side."

"Like I can't squat and aim?" Mia posed. "You must have forgotten your sister's abilities."

Dag slapped her protruding butt. "Come on, enough talk, you're both tongue-waggers. Save it for tomorrow."

^^^^^^^^^

The morning sky was beginning to brighten. Everything was standstill quiet. Light, wheezing snores came up through the front hatch. Brother and sister were content in their separate dreams.

"Cluck, cluck. Cluck, cockle-doodle-doo!"

Mia suddenly sat upright and screamed as she wrapped her head with two small pillows. "When did we get fucking roosters?" She fumbled around and found her belly bag and retrieved her phone. "Holy shit, it's not even six yet. That fucking bird is gonna be soup."

"Shh, not so loud. There's no noise out here. You know everything echoes," Tim reminded. "Chicken must have walked the distance from town especially for you. Never heard him before."

A knock on the boat startled them. Tim put his finger to his lips and, wrapped in the sheet, peeked out the hatch to see a smiling Dag. The older brother crowed again.

"Pretty good, huh? Figure you'd want to greet it early. I got a pot of coffee on. Getting ready to scramble some eggs. Thought we needed some strategy on how to sneak in little sister."

"Could have waited another hour," Mia said from below. "Rather have the heat wake me."

"Yeah, but you're forgetting we're a fishing family, up before the sun. I'm sure Harry followed me downstairs. Here's an idea; while we're eating, slip around to the back of the house. Wait until we finish breakfast and Tim and me will get them out onto the porch. I'll give you a shout; how about another rooster crow? Then you stroll through and come out the front door like you were there all the while. How's that?"

"Not bad, but probably well-practiced from the guy who was banging all the local girls and sneaking home at daybreak." Mia laughed, "Think they didn't tell me, bragging about that white boy…"

"Okay, okay," Dag stuttered. "Enough of that crusty talk. Come on Tim, we're the diversion. Pull on some drawers. You toast the bread."

"Save some breakfast for me," Mia said as she lit a cigarette. "I'm a growing girl."

"Don't worry, they'll be enough. I'll cover your plate with a towel. No one will notice," Dag assured. "Do you have to? Dad can probably smell it. Try to keep it all on an even keel. Okay, for a few days anyway? Please?"

"I'll do my best," Mia promised as she wet a finger and snuffed the cigarette.

An hour later, the family was on the porch and Cheesy had joined them for coffee. Dag topped off everyone's cup and sat with Tim on the first step. "Made you all guess this morning, right? The rooster? Come on, you had to hear me, spot on," Dag crowed again.

Cassy scratched her head, "That was you? Some of us like to sleep to a reasonable hour."

Tim caught Dag's eye with a wink and both grinned.

"Yeah, got to hand it to you, this is a wonderful idea, boys," Harry proclaimed. "We don't enjoy this porch in the morning. Fact is, unless we're grilling, we don't eat outside that much. We should appreciate the cool early morning weather. Right, mom? We talked about how nice it would be to have a porch that wrapped around the whole house."

Cassy coughed and chuckled panning for the group, "Yes, father, I agree. More enjoying the outside, chewing flies and mosquitoes."

No one turned as the screen door opened. Mia stuck out an empty cup, "Can a girl get a refill?"

"What? Where?" It seemed to be the universal response by the three unknowing on the porch, but all five pivoted towards the voice. And, as if on cue, they all shouted, "Mia!"

Wearing a set of bulky white cotton shorts and a matching tank top over her halter, Mia posed with a shy, meek look, but ready to accept the accolades she knew were coming.

Cassy bolted up and grabbed her daughter with a combination of sobs and laughs. Harry and Cheesy stood waiting for a chance to embrace Mia.

"Oh mom, come on, you're crying. Aren't you happy? I'm home again."

Cassy buried her face in her daughter's shoulder. Her back rippled, convulsing with sobs. "Oh dear, oh, Mia, you'll never know how I've missed you." She wouldn't break the embrace, so Harry hugged them both.

"We all missed you, Mia," Harry got out, trying not to show the true depth of his emotion.

"Flew in last night and by coincidence met these two. Slept on *Sassy*. Thought I'd surprise you. Did it work?"

"Oh, my dear Mia, it worked. Thought I'd have a coronary when you talked," Cheesy contributed. "You look good, no, you look absolutely marvelous."

"What's the news, guys?" Mia directed at Harry and his first mate.

Harry cleared his throat and turned away, flicking something from his eyes, "Damn bugs, always flying in your eyes. Not much new, you know, the usual. Except for this unscheduled family reunion. Same old, same old. Right Cheese?"

Cassy hadn't broken the embrace. Mia was stretching her neck as if she needed air, but wore a big smile.

Redbeard, the red macaw, squawked from his perch as if he was the wrestling referee telling Cassy to break her hold.

"Hello to you too, Redbeard," Mia said.

"You have been losing weight?" Cassy asked as she pushed away from her daughter. "I'll make sure you're eating better now, plenty of fish, I must get some pasta for you. Girl, you're hardly filling out those shorts."

"They're Timmy's, mom," Mia smirked and pulled the drawstring tighter. "I'm traveling light. Got some shorts and tops, but this combo is Sunset Bay comfortable."

Harry hugged them both again and solemnly said, "My deepest sympathies and all, ah, for your loss."

Mia sighed deeply, "You always said I could drive someone crazy."

"Well, I didn't mean…" Harry stammered.

"Anyway, I think it was the anti-depressants Kurt was taking. Next topic?"

Dag brought Mia her breakfast from the kitchen and passed around another pot of coffee. Cheesy relinquished his seat to the new reigning princess.

Mia sat back and forked her scrambled eggs. "I heard yesterday was great fishing. When are we going again?"

"You name it. Tomorrow, if you can fit it into your schedule?" Harry replied. "Now that the entire crew has returned, I think we can make anything happen."

"Well, daughter, it is so great to find you in good spirits," Cassy was wiping her face wet from tears. "Sorry, you're all visiting because we're in this mess, especially after your tragedy. Looks like we have to meet a deadline with a sizeable check."

"Are we going to lose this bay to a hotel?" Mia blurted. "That's what you wrote, Timmy."

"Oh, it's bad, but not that bad. We can still save it," Harry huffed. He hated talking about the situation. It was as if he didn't mention it, it would just go away.

"Now's as good as any to hear your plans, Tim," Dag said.

"Okay, okay," Tim began with his British accent. "I've been working in the most advanced section of Shearsome Bank. My department is staying constant with the wave of technology. Internet banking is a new thing. People can move money easily. With their money is advertising. Banks hate to spend a dime, so they offset all their expenses, staying current with the tech by selling space to every type of merchandise."

His family watched as Tim stood with a coffee cup in hand. He spoke with confidence as though he was instructing a board of corporate directors. "I know computers. Here, in the bay, with my laptop, and a good Net connection, I believe I can work a link with every compatible site: vacations, cruises, fishing tackle, movies, you name it. When someone is interested in a parallel subject, I can make Sunset Bay also appear on their screen." He stretched and yawned, "Without a good Net connection, I can use the satellite phone Shearsome," Tim grinned, "and connect anywhere on the planet."

Harry scratched his head, "Son, I can't lie. I'm totally out of touch and want to stay that way. Kind of lost me at Net connection. Satellite phone, huh? Parallel, compatible, you got to break it down some more, so we can digest it easier. I finished high school in '89. There wasn't a computer yet.

Tim took a deep breath. He'd known this wouldn't be easy, but he was also prepared to be a one-man show. He'd reasoned that's the only way it would work. They knew how to hook game fish. He knew how to hook the anglers for the charters.

"Okay, I'll start at the beginning." He spread his arms wide, "In the beginning, God made the sea... now God has made the worldwide web, a network that goes everywhere. Never mind how it gets to every nook and cranny of mankind, just believe me; it does. It's here, even in the boondocks of Clifton, Union Island. See that big dish antenna on top of the telecom building, that's bringing the Internet here."

"I checked before I boarded the plane; we can get Wi-Fi, even out here. But it will be a much better connection if I can work out of your restaurant, mom. Just need enough space for my briefcase..." Tim hesitated and then laughed, "And a fan. I remember how small Granma's office was, and that was when I was much smaller."

"Sure, sure," Cassy affirmed. "Whatever you need. We're all in this together. I'm busy cooking. I only stack the receipts in the old file cabinet. Feel free to make yourself comfy." She reached and grabbed Mia by the ankle, "Hoping you could take some time and hang out with me. Got some new recipes. What do you think?"

Mia wrinkled her face. "Dumb question, mom, I'm here to spend time with you, but I want to go fishing. I know some of this Internet shit; I can lend a hand with Tim. The important thing is we save our bay."

"Here, here, that's all the right answers," Harry chimed, raising his empty mug.

"Okay, back to my plan," Tim continued, now dropping into his island twang. "Like I was saying, we connect to everything, every site. We put adverts everywhere. The adverts are the videos of catching fish, like yesterday. Now we can show exactly what are the accommodations, *Sassy*, and our incredibly experienced crew."

"Wait a minute; that might not be such a brilliant idea. We got no A/C. The place is a bit frumpy," Cassy interjected.

"Don't worry, mom, I made our sailboat attractive, and that took magic. Here we got a lot more to work with," Mia was invested. "If Jesse's still sewing, she can stitch some new curtains." She wrinkled her nose in a semblance of agreement and grabbed her mother's arm. "We'll work together. Clean the rooms real nice, spruce it all up and air them out. It'll be fun."

Cassy almost swooned from the unanticipated offer of help. "Yes, we'll make it fun. And if it's not, let me know. Promise?"

"Back to his program," Tim explained, "I'll spend the first days connecting with every tour operator on the mainland and throughout the islands and offer a big twenty-five percent commission."

"Whoa, that's a chunk of change to give away." Dag countered. "Fifteen's what we pay. On a good charter, twenty-five can translate to losing a grand."

"That all takes time, it's a damn good effort, but we need cash now," Harry reminded.

"I've already started and got some bookings." He walked over and roughed Dag's hair. "I knew Dag and you would get our boat fixed quick. So, we got two, five-thousand-dollar-weekends starting next Friday. I got credit card deposits. No commissions."

"You got five grand for two-day trips?" Harry was flabbergasted.

"Three days, I offered them what I felt we could afford."

"And I'm gonna kick in some cash, Dad," Dag offered. "This is our lifestyle, our heritage that we're looking to save."

"Gracious, your education wasn't wasted," Cassy put her arms over her Tim's big shoulders. "Lots of hugs going around this morning," she looked at Mia. "We'll have to get the rooms ready, pronto."

"That's just the first part," Tim continued. "Mom, you and Dad have to speak to local groups, like churches and schools and anywhere else you can think of. Turn their thinking so they'll work with us. I've got numbers that should convince everyone that the hotel is an awful idea."

"Not to be a party-pooper, but your Uncle Sam's got them all believing that this hotel will be a godsend. It'll make everybody rich," Harry said. "Money for all is damn convincing."

"That's why we go to the churches first and explain all the downside, crime, drugs, gambling, prostitution," Tim replied. "Then we talk to the educators, about dropout rates."

"I'm willing to try, but churches? How about the fisherman's association?" Harry was serious.

"That too, talk with everybody, you, mom, and me, but we have to change opinions. I have all the facts and figures that a hotel will be bad for our island. I'm certain we can save Sunset from development. But when we do that, unless we change the thinking, the average Union Islander will hate us."

"Tiny Tim, I think you're on drugs. Can you see Harry in the pulpit?" Mia rocked with laughter.

"Your sister's right; that could be dangerous. Sam's got these island pick-a-ninnies believing a hotel would be a blessing."

"Shush," Cassy shouted with a stare. "That's the kind of talk, using words like that got us in this predicament."

"Wait a minute," Harry barked back, "It wasn't 'my' talk, or 'the' talk, or the words. It was your greedy-assed brother. We're crackers, rednecks, whitey-cheese. Everyone knows all that's in fun. They're nappy, spear-chuckers," he forced a laugh.

"Shut up, just be quiet," Cassy growled. "We take those comments, but I didn't like it then, never have. Because someone else might have those feelings, we don't have to play tit-for-tat. Remember, I barne here, raised here, lived here all my life, 'cept for a few brief vacations. My family worked with everyone. You know Curly fed and clothed people who didn't have a cent. Why? Because we all live on one small island. Goodwill goes a long, long way. Get with the program, Harry. Tim's right, we must change their opinion."

Cheesy had sat quietly until then. "Well, we have to teach them, persuade them. Must be level-headed. Can't talk any trash." He stared directly at Harry, "Everyone deserves respect. Me and the missus are white bread limeys. Might be said with a smile, but we know it really means we will never exactly fit in. We always will be outsiders."

"Might be easier with a lead pipe," Harry muttered.

Cassy stood and poked him in the ribs as she gathered the coffee mugs. "Lose that attitude. We all have to work together."

"Okay, Mother. Like I was saying, I'm willing to try anything. But trying to talk sense over greed, well... I'll give it a try."

Their offspring were nodding to each other, calculating the current bicker quotient.

"Dad, I agree, we need to put on our nice-nice face. Don't give anyone a reason to feel we are better than anyone else." Dag contributed.

"Look son, and son, and daughter, Cheese, and Cassy," Harry stood and knocked his hand against the house. "I agree, but it's like an election and someone already bought their votes. I, we, worked hard to build this house, this business. People are naturally unhappy when they got less. Now, look at this rationally, they had the same opportunities as we did and came up with less."

Cassy was shaking her head. "You really don't see it, Harry, do you? Your daddy gave you our boat. My daddy gave us this bay. How can other locals compete with that?"

"Okay, I stand corrected," Harry seemed genuinely apologetic. "Whatever it takes has always been my motto. Go out and drag baits when the weather's been grim and the sea's rough as a corncob." He had a broad smile, "Well, I'm in this to win friends and influence people. Whatever it takes to save our bay."

"That's the main no-no." Tim instructed, "Whatever you do, never call it 'our bay', say Sunset."

"Right-o, champ. I read you loud and clear," Harry clapped his hands. "Chop-chop, we got a lot to get organized if we got clients coming on Friday?"

"Yes, sir, I received their confirmation and payment in full before I left Heathrow. These are younger guys, our age, coming on a charter flight Friday early. Don't know the precise time. They'll

WhatsApp me in the next few days. I agree; everything needs to be ready. Stock up with food. Liquor and beer; they pay for every drink."

"I'll bartend," Mia offered and laughed. "And you're already eighty-sixed, Dad."

"Okay, I'll do the menus. They ask for anything special?" Cassy asked.

Tim shrugged his shoulders, "Fresh fish."

"I'll make up a bunch of rigs," Dag said. "Cheese, you going to help?"

"Sure; thought I might shuttle over a couple more drums of diesel. Wouldn't hurt to keep it on hand. And the dock needs repaired. I'll get a few lengths of lumber when I get the fuel."

"Ask them to bring the wood to your boat. Never take your eyes off the fuel, Okay?" Harry recommended. "Remember, this will always be spy versus spy. Fuel has proven to be our weak spot. Good thinking, Cheese, bring the fuel to us, so fewer know our exact business."

"Angling is extremely time consuming. That's sort of the whole point,"
Thomas McGuane.

CHAPTER SEVEN

Stuck on the refrigerator, in broad print, Cassy listed and categorized the house chores. Her second day back home was busier than ever anticipated by Mia, who became the basic one-woman house cleaner. The common feeling was it was too early to bring in outside help. The family needed all the money and there was the constant espionage syndrome. But she got into the mood, drank a pot of coffee herself, and tore the rooms apart. Mia had a lot to work out of herself. The exertion and attention to detail was therapy. It was common knowledge that when mom was happy, everyone was happy.

There was one restriction, only four anglers per charter. Harry had what was called a six-pack license: six passengers in total. It didn't matter, *Sassy* could only handle four comfortably, and any over four fishing was usually utter confusion. Ideally, one hardcore, deep-pocketed fisherman was the perfect charter. It all depended on what species were running. Saltwater fly fishermen loved to fight the high jumping dorado, mahi-mahi, in May. During February and March, Sunset Bay Fish Camp could almost guarantee anglers to tie into a grand fight with big wahoos. Some wanted only sailfish and others would rather troll for a massive blue. The latter two were only catch and release. Anglers got first floor rooms with twin beds and all meals. Seldom did a 'romantic' couple charter, and if they did, the beds were pushed together.

There was an age requirement, six years to eighty. The youngest Harry's ever carried was nine, a respectful kid, big for his age. Cranked in a nice sailfish. The kid would talk about that fish forever. The eldest, well, he broke his own written rules and took out a return client's father at 93. Harry admired the man who refused to go sit in the rocker. With all the new technological whistles and bells, hell, every angler instantly produced his own movie. They had all sorts of phone and camera mounts that they either wore or clamped around the boat. Harry had never considered buying one, but when he saw what his own family had filmed, he started thinking. During the following evenings, Tim edited all the grand action scenes of the perfect Caribbean fishing day, tunas, a sailfish, and a blue marlin.

Back in the early 90s, Sunset Bay depended on a solid telephone connection, and faxes. Ten years later it was all Internet. The kids learned how and taught the parents. Cassy kept at it regularly; the restaurant had a reliable connection, close to the telecommunication office. Even Harry could send and receive emails. Two years ago, the house got a Wi-Fi router. Now Tim tried to explain how he was building a website, but his father decided it would be easier just to watch the end product. Dag also worked on it. It seemed everyone traveled with their laptops. He'd noticed it with affluent clients, but his own kids?

People didn't come to Sunset Bay to indulge in luxury; they came to fish. The flight arrangements were usually daunting. The major hub was Antigua. If lucky, they might connect in a few hours to a flight to Union. One flight could easily include a grand tour of the Grenadines, St. Vincent, Bequia, Canouan, and maybe even a stop at hotsy-totsy Mustique. Many chartered a direct plane, no wasted time from serious fishing.

Cassy was busy readying Granma's for the inflow of guests. Harry would bring *Sassy* around and drop them off for dinner. While there, he'd fuel, arrange for bait, and unload that day's catch to butcher and sell. The routine was the anglers could choose to enjoy their catch for dinner. It was easier to feed them dinner in that professional client atmosphere and charge for the drinks. Her help got good tips. Meals were included in the grand fishing tour. Cassy did breakfast by request, pancakes, eggs, and omelets. They packed the lunch the night before at the restaurant. It was all combined with thermoses of coffee for the way out and chilled beers for the return.

Granma's Restaurant was also receiving a much-needed facelift. Honoré assisted in the scrub and polish process. His wife, Mammie, touched up with some bright paint. The big islander was all smiles watching Cassy, his boss, return to contentment. When the boss is happy, everyone's happy.

After she'd stripped all the rooms of bedding and drapes, Mia washed the salt-streaked windows, polished the dusty furniture, even oiled squeaky hinges, and then swept and mopped while the linens were drying on the line. Twice a day at lunch and before dinner, Mia would slip away to the bayside and inhale some delicious nicotine.

The men put together another list. Tim and Cheesy worked refurbishing the dock, which became a much bigger project than expected. Once the top decking boards were removed, both sides, the long lengths of the main framing, were replaced. Luckily, Curly's Hardware had suitable lengths, but this meant drilling and bolting to the pilings. It also meant people would know the St. Claires were rebuilding. Tim pushed, and it was getting done. Everything was on a time limit to finish in four days. Nothing in the Caribbean moves fast. The fishing boat had to be kept off the dock while repairs were being made. Dag dove and decided the dock pilings would be okay, and then replaced the chain and shackles on both of their moorings.

With the boat in top running condition and men working on the dock, Harry had become the 'lend a hand' guy and the gardener. Cutting grass and weeding the flower beds wasn't something he was fond of, but it needed to be done. Every aspect of Sunset Bay was being rejuvenated. Using an annoyingly loud weed whacker, Harry widened the track to the house and leveled out some ruts so a taxi would have a decent ride with as few bumps and holes as possible.

Harry was in the running for 'good man' of the month. He knew how to self-promote; every evening weeding the flower beds that lined the porch scored him a lot of points with his wife. He raked Sunset's small beach and shored up their picnic table. Everything looked and was good. He couldn't see any single point of failure among the boat, the house, and the restaurant. The fish would cooperate. Almost everything at the bay was repaired to 'as good as new', well, maybe, 'as good as it can get.'

It was time to confront public opinion. Wednesday evening was choir practice. None of the St. Claires had been singers. Church was required for the big holidays, Easter, Christmas, New Year, births, baptisms, deaths, and marriages. On Union Island, everyone knew everyone, Minister Harris was a friend. Harry and Cassy worked and contributed to his projects to help the youth.

The island didn't have a great disparity of incomes. Everyone was only three or four notches above poverty. A combined population of three thousand didn't make for many opportunities outside of either fishing or working for the government. Neither paid well, and the former depended on the latter to buy fish. Trickle-down economics really dribbled on this island. But they accepted their lots, and there had been universal contentment. People were happy until the Internet. The Worldwide Net connected everyone and inflated dormant jealousy and envy. Relatives living in the US or UK had only told stories of their lifestyles and flashed a few Kodachromes. Now, everything appeared on Facebook and then Union Islanders felt they were missing something.

Suddenly, people desired more money. A few resorted to the black market. Smuggling among the islands was a way of life, mostly cigarettes, and alcohol. Drugs had become the most valuable commodity. There was no way to hide a ganja garden on Union. It came in by boat and everyone knew who was doing it and few cared. Everyone took a toke now and then, you know, for relaxation. Coke appeared with guns and bad manners. Minister Harris was the island's primary defense. The police were better paid regularly to look the other way rather than to make one arrest.

Harris' sermons foretold of the imminent apocalypse if drug use continued. It was a virus and incredibly contagious. He was a one-stop man of the cloth; he performed ceremonies from day one at birth to the end of days, dust to dust, and everything in between. Every summer, the church ran a camp where they taught valuable skills. It helped monitor the children and their biggest influences. Swimming was one he personally taught. Few islanders felt comfortable in the water. Harris got them paddling around before the children hit their teens. He probably saved more lives with the Australian crawl than counseling drug addiction.

Union Island's Calvin Church was one of the few architectural landmarks. The sparkling white, two-story clapboard was attached to a slightly slanting stone bell tower. Rain, accompanying a hurricane in the '30s, soaked the island so bad that the east side of the chimney sank four inches. It pulled away and pointed to the sunrise. More than twenty rough storms had hit the island since then, and the church held tight.

Deep breaths followed by long sighs, Harry was pouting because he had to become political to enjoy his home and business. It was mandatory that he be the speaker on the family's behalf. He was the father, the owner, and the boss. Tim put the words in his mouth and accompanied them. Dag and Mia stayed at home. Each had their own island baggage they'd rather stay forgotten. Harry was the man for this job, standing at attention with one of the island's favorite daughters, Cassandra.

Looking the part of the village pastor, Theo Harris was a thin, almost gaunt, six feet. He was dark-skinned with kind, reassuring brown eyes. His broad forehead led all the way up and over, almost receding to his neck. A two-inch band of white, cottony hair wore like an angel's halo. Matching, long, fuzzy, mutton chop sideburns framed a thick, white, Fu Manchu mustache. His weekday wardrobe was always the same, white, short sleeve shirt, denim slacks, and shiny cordovan penny-loafers.

That's how he was dressed as he met the St. Claires at the side door and led them to his office. "The last time I... we were back here, Theo," Harry smiled, "remember Cass and I were asking if you'd marry us. Now, look, we made the long run. We want to chat about gaining your help to change the opinion about the hotel planned for our, ah, Sunset Bay."

"Harry, Cassy, and Timothy, I'd be happy to have you address our congregation, but I'll be honest; I'm for the hotel. I'm so sorry, but your bay is the only place it can fit on Union. Think of the jobs, the benefits."

"Well," Harry cleared his throat, "You really think our little island would benefit from a large hotel? They're talking sixty or more rooms to make it profitable. This isn't planned to be a small, tasteful boutique, ten-roomer. We've researched, well; Tim researched and found there is definitely a downside that outweighs the cash. Come on, Theo, that's the only thing it's about, money. People think money is the answer to their problems. Our numbers show it is only the beginning."

"You're saying we should fear development and the better services it will bring with more opportunities?" Theo Harris asked as he took a seat and offered water. He clasped his hands together, raised off his desk, as if always in constant prayer. "Everything has a downside. People even say life is a terminal illness. But it is what we do, what we create, what we make that matters. And I think we, combined, could make something very good on Union with a new injection of jobs and money."

"Hmm," Harry murmured. "After this, the island will need an injection of antibiotics for STDs!" That was followed by, "Ouch!", after he received a backward heel kick from his wife. "Wait a minute, everyone wants what 'they' want; what about us? Where do you plan for us to relocate? That's our home, everyone else is so free for us to give away."

The minister wrinkled his face in a sneer, "Come on Harry, Cass, you've done well, better than almost everyone else. You'll be more than adequately compensated."

"Compensated by who? And where would we get another place that we can work out of for sportfishing?" Harry was getting riled. "Everyone wants better, but it means we get the royal shaft. How's that fit into Jesus' plan?"

"I don't know, probably under sacrifice for the greater good," Harris was quick to reply.

"That's exactly what we came to speak about," Tim began. "There are no greater good, only negative changes."

"Yeah, negative changes, changes not for the better," Harry ran on. "You, like my brother-in-law, Sam, see only the ear of corn on the stick, but can't see it jammed up your island ass." That was followed by another, "Ouch! Damn it, quit kicking me."

"Then stop the profanity," Cassy roared. "This is a house of worship. This was my Sunday School, and I made my first communion here. He married us outside on the steps; Minister Harris baptized each child at the beach. So, cool it, Harry." Her husband sank into the chair. "Okay, Tim, it's up to you. Tell them what happened on other islands."

"Oh, I'm aware that development, such as a hotel, will bring certain demons, but all islands are benefiting from the resorts," Harris reasoned. "But being stagnant, as Union seems to be, is definitely not good. We need to grow, catch up with the other Caribbean."

Tim stood up, "No, we don't! If we change, we lose our uniqueness, our quaint, small island mystique. There's an entirely alternative approach being taken by some islands who have reviewed and rejected big hotel tourism. Bed and breakfast, people renting out a bedroom, will bring in more money to the families who can do it. And with the Grenadine government willing to fund local entrepreneurship, your members can work together and better their lives directly."

The reverend sat back, "Bed and breakfast, huh? I hadn't considered that as a literal cottage industry. And why is that better? What do your numbers tell? Say what, wait and come back tonight. It's choir practice and almost all the prime elders of our congregation will be present. Let us practice our four hymns needed Sunday and then we will give the St. Claire family all our attention."

"Okay, Theo, that will work for us. Be back about 8?"

"Come at 7 and listen to our harmonies," the minister grinned, knowing it would be a pain in the ass for Harry.

"Sure thing, 7 with bells on," Harry forced a smile.

Cassy pulled the family together at the dining table. Verena and Cheesy joined. "This is serious business, Reverend Harris told us bluntly, he's against us. Right?" Tim and Harry nodded. "We have to show we're unified as a family. I want everyone at that choir meeting this evening. We've got an hour to get ready. Mia, Dag, you can do it. Harry, I'm warning you, put on a God damned happier face."

Harry settled with a blank stare and mumbled, "It's not fair, but let's face it, we're more white. That sums it up."

"Dad," Mia started, "I don't think white, black, tan, or any color matters except USD green. Seems like we're trying to change the ancient vice of green-eyed envy. All the while I was growing up, I felt we were special, different. Come, Dag, Tim, say you didn't feel the same? Now they want us to pay for being special. They saw us, the St. Claires, as better than 'them'. It's not our fault. Are you sure Uncle Sammy is working against us? That I find hard to believe. I mean, he's family."

Tim sucked his teeth, "Hate to say it, but yep, it's fairly obvious, Unc is leading the charge. I think he wants to live the American dream and simultaneously turn our lives, especially Harry's, into a nightmare."

"That is the new American creed," Cheesy offered with a stern look. "Not only get the money, but make certain to leave bodies behind. What did you ever do to your brother-in-law to warrant such treatment?"

Harry lifted a cocked eyebrow and tried to sound like Bogart, "Married his sister, why else? Really? I don't know. This hits me right out of the blue. I always thought we were friends, good friends. Can't remember a bad word crossed between us. Got to be he wants; what do they call it, a legacy? Craves people to consider him in the same light as his father, Curly."

"Maybe you've got something there, dad. That could be it; money isn't enough. Come on," Dag said. "Uncle Sam has always been a devoted bachelor, womanizer supremo, got beautiful women working in the store and taking care of the house. He's got all the toys, boats, jet skis, can travel anywhere. And he inherited Granpop's hillside house and business."

"Well, you could say we split the properties, but he got the higher dollar figure with the house, store, and fuel dock," Cassy said. "I got the restaurant and Sunset was our wedding present, and we paid my father for it, close to market value. Both are prime real estate."

It was Tim's turn, "Yeah, but shouldn't you at least get a share of the profits? I mean, Gram's restaurant never made big money. She did it to have something to do; no offense meant."

"None taken, dear. I know what you mean, and it's sort of that for me, too. But it is making money, as you say, a positive cash flow. We need it with the fishing charters. Having the fishermen eating breakfast at the house is a big enough pain. And we designed the kitchen for that exact purpose, but it is cramped with all of us and anglers."

"Look, all of you, I don't care if Sam needs a Brinks Armored Car to load his cash. Let him make his money. All I want, and I hope you want, is to keep our bay and our business," Dag said. "You talk about mom working to have something to do, we'll all be working there scrubbing pots if Sam has his way."

"I think Dag's correct," Cheesy offered. "Sam wants to be the power-broker on this island. He's putting everything in place, piece by piece. The hotel is not the last piece, I fear. Waterfront development, marina, condos, and then, you know what, Clifton is done; it'll be known as Sam's Town. Mark my words; I've seen it happen in other places."

All heads silently and sadly nodded as he continued, "I've only known Sam since I arrived, and it is a 'hi and buy' relationship. You've all known him your entire lives, up close and personal. He's blood. That said, Sam doesn't come across as all that smart in the big scheme of things. You know what I mean? Someone else is behind this land grab."

"Been saying it all day long, we got to research this hotel group," Harry blasted. "This has outsider written all over it. Money passes and palms get greased; that's the Caribbean way of business, but there's usually a foreigner behind it all."

"So, how do we investigate?" Mia asked. "Probably aren't too many people on this rock involved, otherwise the word would already be out. Can't keep a secret on Union, and don't I know that!"

"Darling sister, you could never keep a secret because everything you did during your teens was always in everyone's face," Dag assured. "Me and Tim pulled some pranks, but we always kept it between us. I didn't talk and if I heard about it, had to be Tim bragging."

"My stuff was girl things," Mia returned. "And that's my point, if Sam or anyone he's working with would brag to one of the island women, it would be all over the coconut telegraph."

"I think there's one island woman who should talk directly with Sam, and that's me," Cassy said. "I'm his sister and we always got along as well as brothers and sisters do."

"No, no, no!" Resounded from everyone's mouth.

Harry spoke first, "No, Cass, better to leave well enough alone. I know your temperament and," he paused "better to let one of the children do it, if anybody? Some dogs are best to leave sleeping."

"I can return and chat about business strategy. Chat him up about living in London. Sam gets off on that stuff," Tim offered. "And," he dragged the word out while making a lengthy sigh, "that's probably why he is doing this. He thinks he's proven he's a talented businessman, competing in mainstream business." Tim shrugged, "That's the way I see myself. The boy from a small island makes it good, really good. The score is measured by digits in the bank account. I'll use finesse and worm it out of him."

"Ya think?" Dag caricatured. "I'd like to tag along."

"Hey, hey, that's down the road. In an hour, we've got to deal with the Bible thumpers. Concentrate on the matters at hand," Tim took control. "Okay, we're going to learn this drill. No frowns, no mean words, no matter what. Remember the Godfather's words, "Never let them know what you're thinking. That means we only reply in certain ways, usually with another question."

"Verena and I will accompany for not only vocal support, but in a show of solidarity," Cheesy addressed. "If it wasn't you, my best friends, and it was any local, I'd also stand for that man. It's the damn principle, you can't force someone to sell their assets. The government can call the right of eminent domain, but not a bunch of businessmen. That's coercion, plain and simple."

"Plain, but not so simple, Cheese," Mia followed. "We pissed off lots of local families. The people you hired and fired over the years, your drunken rants on the waterfront. Drunk and arguing because you were too smashed to steer your way home." Her words caused snickers.

Harry inhaled and cocked his ear as if to hear better. "Yes, I have on a few occasions been well over the safe boating limit. Agreed; some of those incidents were in poor taste, but at least I had the common sense to sleep there. Damn police bothering me, not permitting me to sleep on my own boat at the waterfront." He scratched his head. "You're correct. I played the village ass."

"Not only you, dad, I broke a lot of hearts here, started fights," Mia looked up sheepishly with her green eyes wide. "Never realized what I was doing. I guess this is my apology, I made it shitty for everybody. That's why I wanted to leave so bad, and finally left this rock."

"Yeah, sister, you got me into a few scrapes," Dag admitted. "Like you said, we are the lightest skinned. You were desirable, and me and Tim had to defend your honor."

"Thank you," Mia beamed.

He wrinkled his lips, "Didn't want to, but you're our blood. That's what this all boils down to, blood. We got to stand up, circle the wagons, and keep back to back. Don't let anyone, other than family, know what we're doing."

"Wait, wait, cool it, now. We're leaving in 15 minutes. Faces washed, clean shirts. Put some deodorant on, you guys have been working hard," Cassy required. "Cheesy, go get Verena."

^^^^^^^^^^

The choir was unsuccessful in harmonizing the two hymns the St. Claire family heard. The dozen singers were trying, with good intentions, but the voices weren't there. Of the twelve members, half were baritone and half bass. The church interior was white with the usual split rows of varnished wood pews. To the right of the big brass cross, above the altar, was the choir box.

After refreshments with the usual smattering of gossip, Minister Harris asked for their attention. "Ladies and gents, we are now involved in a growing local debate, that of the proposed hotel. If one is to be built, there is a likelihood it would be built on Sunset Bay, belonging to the St. Claire family and their fishing business."

"Yes, let's talk about *your* bay, Cassandra," Myrtle Hodge jumped up. The slight lady was very dark because of daily toil in her vegetable garden. Myrtle's gardens and her hydroponic grow beds produced a large percentage of the veggies consumed on the island. "I'd like to see a hotel be built. Yes, I would. For me, I'm told, it would mean more water, and certainly a new market to sell to." Myrtle primped, "I'm a local source of vegetables, especially salad greens and tomatoes."

"Myrtle, I buy from you," Cassy replied. "Please hear us out."

"Easy for you all to sit here and chat what with you having that bay and not having to farm it or anything. You just sittin' over 'dere. The court wants you off and just so suddenly you get civically minded." Paul Liburd sneered. The willowy man was a good role model, hardworking, nothing to excess. He stuck with what he knew, goats. "My animals are thirsting to death on that little ration I get for my herd. They're tight with that tap, keep it locked off 'cept from 2 to 3. Water, we depend on rain and it comes less and less. Cassy, I know you buy from me, but really, me selling you three kilos a week for fricassee ain't buying me nuthin'. A tiny bit more feed, maybe. If they build that hotel, then I'm selling more than that every day. I can expand my herd."

"That's not fair," it piqued Cassy, "I was born on this island. You know my father helped everyone when they needed it. We used to be one big, extended family. What happened? You all want for more now at our expense."

"Your pappy, yes, but now we're starving while you getting rich," Philow Campton shouted. "I'm fishing and now you're coming back into the market. You going be taking my share, again."

"Hey, where do you see rich, huh? What part of me looks rich?" It was Harry's turn. "Myrtle, we rushed your son to the clinic in St. Vincent when he chopped himself so bad. And Philow, your granddaughter was born there because of our boat. Remember, your daughter was paining with bad complications? So, be fair and think about those kids. If you want to farm Sunset Bay, just say so and find the water."

"A minute, please, a minute, please," Cheesy spoke. "If I correctly understand this, you are saying this is about water first, money second? Well, let's petition the government to install a small, maybe 5-

10,000 gallon a day desalinization plant. I know we could swing that. Work with our bank and sell shares. Hmm?" The Englishman searched the choir's eyes. Then Cheesy grinned and said, "Truthfully, it is about the money, isn't it? Not about what you don't make; it's about what you think the St. Claire family brings in fishing."

The grumble-mumble renewed.

"That's just it," Reverend Harris pulled at his mustache. "Too many of our children are traveling to far off places find suitable employment and falling into wicked ways."

"Amen!" The choir's grumble morphed.

"Certainly, development has evils," he continued. "But our children would stay here where we could give them proper guidance. And the development would provide much more water. Water means comfort, sustainability."

"Water, my ass!" Harry spouted as Cassy gave him a seething stare. "If it wasn't our bay, ah, Sunset Bay, I'd still try to stop the progress. Have you looked at town lately? Anybody sell anything besides T-shirts?"

"I sells shirts," Monica Stout, aptly named, yelled. "What's wrong with that, Harry?"

"Curly's sells them shirts, too." Someone mentioned.

"Nothing wrong with selling souvenirs, but do you want our island to look like every other island?" Cassy lamented.

"Dearie, we don't travel to all those other places," Monica answered. "We ain't got no yacht. If those other islands are making money selling souvenir shirts to tourists, I say we get some of that money, too."

"We don't have a yacht, it's a fishing boat," Harry answered to no question.

"I got a plywood, basic canoe with a 35. Okay," Philow replied. "Harry, what you got is a floating castle."

"Everything's relative, but what happened, Philow? You always seemed content. I never touched your market, so to speak. You sell trapped reef fish, snappers, and groupers, 'cudas. I sell to…" Harry caught himself as he was about to confirm he sold to other hotels. "I sell off-island, to our neighbors. But all of you have gotten a nice chunk of fish from time to time. You giving any fish away, Philow?"

The thin man snickered, "Harry, you getting paid by the tourists to catch them and then you get to sell them. To me, Harry, you're making a hell of a profit, what 3-400%?"

Harry chewed on a fingernail and looked around the room. "Why do I have to defend my family's business to you? Union Island isn't Communist Cuba. You, every one of you, can give us competition. Except it is a business I know and am very good at, so are my sons and daughter and my wife and my friend Cheesy. We fish for a living. All of you make some money from our business," he hesitated, "and we've been friends for twenty-plus years. Now, because someone paints you a rosy tale of the profits, you want to sink us. Some bunch of Christians. I'd never pull nothing like this on you."

"You don't have to," Myrtle defended. "You have everything you want."

"But we worked for it," Dag finally spoke, rubbing his eyes. "I can't believe I'm hearing this from our friends. Myrtle, would you like it if they was going to take that prime piece of land your garden's on? See all your improvements bulldozed?"

Myrtle sort of giggled, "If they was giving me the chunk of change, like they probably offering you, I'd think I won the lotto. Boy, you broke so many hearts to be mentioning friendship. My daughter, Elizabeth was one of them."

"Who? They didn't offer us squat," Tim said. "Who are 'they'? Has there been an island meeting? Has anyone of you heard an actual name, a hotel chain mentioned?"

Cassy frowned, "This is a plot to create nasty feelings between us."

"And it's working," Philow chipped in.

"It shouldn't be. That's the first sign of the negative impact unrestrained development will have on a community, dividing us, destroying long friendships. A lot happened here when we were young, and that's what it was, being young and stupid and sometimes rude. You have a few personal, small grudges; and that should cost us our home and business?" Tim questioned. "I have a completely unique business solution. Please permit me to explain it to you."

Reverend Harris stood and raised his arms, "First, let us pray. God, our Savior," Everyone got silent and dropped their gaze. "Guide us so we may listen and learn. Present our island with options for a better future. Thank you for protecting us against the weather and the scourge of drugs. Please, Jesus, protect us from ourselves. We need healthy attitudes and perspectives. Thank you, amen."

Harris took a deep breath and looked at everyone, holding their gaze for a few seconds, breaking it with a nod. "Please give Tim St. Claire you full attention. This young St. Claire may have a good, solid business solution where we can keep control of our island. My friends, I know we need change, evolution of our businesses, growth in jobs and incomes. You are all my friends, and the other four hundred in our congregation are also our friends. The St. Claires are our friends. Everyone on Union Island knows everyone else. I'm saddened that I'm already noticing a negative attitude among you."

"Negative... attitude?" Myrtle repeated. "Reverend, we are not negative. We are positive like the top of an Eveready battery."

"Oh, Myrtle, you are positive, but if all of you are positive with a path that causes others harm, whether physical, psychological, or financial, it is a negative, or a bad attitude. Love thy neighbor, help thy neighbor. Do not push your neighbor down so you can rise up. Please listen to Tim."

"The greatest attractions to Union are its marine interests and quaintness. All the other island cities do not have the unique charisma that our island has. Ladies and gentlemen, we have not developed it to even half of its potential," Tim explained. "We have no crime, sure people smoke pot, but hey, this is the Caribbean and tourists expect a laid-back attitude. That's what they're missing in their Stateside or UK lives. If a big hotel lands here, our quaintness, our personality disappears... forever. We can never return to this peace and quiet."

Harry nodded in agreement with the others as they listened. He nudged Cassy and whispered, "Guess the money on his education wasn't wasted, huh?"

She replied with a wink.

Tim continued, "I'm talking about keeping control of our own destiny. Union Island can become a new evolution of the tourism product. We stay... like it is now, only better, and we keep control. How?"

"Yes, how do we do all that, increase our market and make more money?" Philow asked.

"Well, like everything you said before, expanding to a greater market and making more money; it takes investment."

"You mean loans,' Monica answered. "So, we go into debt. Hmm, that's some strategy."

"I can set this up for you free of charge. Union Island will have its own Bed and Breakfast website. With proper branding, we could become known as B&B Island."

"Whoa, how does B&B work?" Myrtle asked. "It means I got to have people in my house. I'll be losing my privacy."

"No, you will be making money right out of your house. You'll be charging for meals, selling beers and drinks, and arranging tours.

After I print this out," Tim waved a sheaf of papers, "everyone will understand how to keep control of our island. Keep it from changing, preserving our way of life for future generations."

"I don't see it," Philow remarked. "I'd have to build on another room and do a hell of a lot, excuse me, reverend, a lot of repairs and clean up."

"Not really, Philow, you will sell more of your fish because people will have more money. Every house will consume more fish. And buy some life jackets and take tourists on bottom fishing, trap pulling. You'd be amazed at how your usual everyday chores are interesting to outsiders," Tim said. "And, Myrtle, your gardens, those hydroponic boxes you have growing lettuce, well, I find that amazing. It wasn't long ago, the only green Union had was wild spinach."

The older lady beamed.

"Yeah, we could make it a unique island tour. That's it! That's our hook, ah, the name we want to brand, Unique Union," Tim was rising into his role. "Un-huh, T-shirts, a fresh sign at the airport. We are all unique, right? So, let's sell that, sell that we aren't like the other islands and will not commit to a hotel concern."

"I don't know, seems like a lot of debt and work, changes at this stage of my life," Billy Brandon, a new voice, echoed reciting the words twice for effect. "How you going to protect us from the banks?"

Tim puffed, "That's what I do, Bill, I'm a banker at Shearsome Bank in the UK. I run the Communications Division. I can and will help write every bank loan application. I plan on petitioning," he looked around the room, "only with your combined approval and permission, St. Vincent and the UK for financial aid to financially assist setting up our bed and breakfast cottage industry, for fishing and agricultural grants, special low-interest loans, and at least one reasonable sized desalinization plant. I'm thinking we can trap the salt outflow and with some ingenuity dry and sell it. Sea salt is a valuable commodity."

The choir's mumble became a high-toned mercenary chit chat. Momentarily, Tim sowed the seeds of optimism. He kept on, "We can do this. The internet is everything to everybody. Now, when they want something, tourists, it's all there. We, Union Island, need to be described better. The advertising execs call it branding. Believe me, with our beaches, beautiful waters, and living reefs, with plenty of excellent food, Union is highly desirable. Mainly, though, the lack of crime will be the biggest selling point. People, travelers, want to feel safe."

"Yes, by the grace of the almighty, we have policed ourselves," Reverend Harris contributed. He rubbed his mustache. "Tim, have you researched a direct comparison between the financial benefits per household of the hotel versus the home-style bed and breakfast?"

"Yes, I have, in fact, I'm glad you asked," Tim dropped into the speech he'd recited to his uncle. "Ladies and gentlemen of Union Island, I am Tim St. Claire, I barne here." He reverted to his native island accent and spoke with authority. "You know I went away to school and probably heard through the coconut telegraph; I got a job with Shearsome Bank. My business is the business of communications. Today, everything is communications. This report was done to finance a group of proposed resorts in 2010."

Every time Tim brought up a point, he waved another piece of paper from his stack. "Potential income per capita increase; negligible. Ever, that means with the hotel, Union Island residents make no more money on the average. The overall standard of living increase, negligible until nine years, then a twelve percent increase, which is negated by a twenty percent increase in the overall cost of living." He paused, "That means your standard of living will get better when your children mature, but you will pay more just to live here. Education, no negligible increase in courses or job placement. Crime, an increase of eight percent starting with construction, but increasing to plus thirty-three in just four years. Medical… better services on the island, but in most cases not available to island residents, only employees. Employment… an incredible burst at the construction stage, but drops to eleven percent in three years. There will be some jobs, but mostly for those who are willing to travel off the island to be trained by a hospitality college. There are no college courses available, even in St. Vincent. Trinidad has the closest hospitality school and we know how bad violent crime is there."

Tim surveyed the now quiet room. "The kicker is that our very limited surface water quality sinks to unhealthy. The pollution from the hotel's sewage, refined and purified with lots and lots of chlorine, will definitely kill our beautiful reefs." He paused, "I'd hardly call that a win-win."

"And you are certain concerning these figures, percentages?" The Reverend inquired. "How can we check?"

"Reverend Harris, my bank did this report for the government of St. Lucia less than a year ago. I was in charge of the research. You can check with their Ministry of Finance."

"Okay, Tim, you have given us much to think about. And you have offered to help and assist everyone. That is commendable. I truly wish you had offered under it different circumstances."

"So, do I," Tim replied. "I'm here to help. I can explain every one of those percentages I just mentioned. Once we permit outsiders to take control, a big hotel will boss everybody; we turn the page away from our unique, quaint island home; there is no saving it. What we love, truly love, we will lose forever; lost to us, our children, and our children's children."

The meeting concluded with a prayer for unity and clear minds. Reverend Harris asked his audience to consider the facts. Tim promised to have his papers copied and on the Harris' desk as soon as possible.

Harry said goodbye. "Hey, all of us still are one. We never stopped being friends. I know I played the ass for too many years with demon rum. I'm over that now. Let's work together."

"How long you been sober," Philow asked, "this time?"

Harry looked up, "three weeks, but, Phi, all of you, I'm done with it, I promise. I promised to myself, to my family." He rubbed his head and sighed, "Yeah, I'm done drinking for good, my own good."

^^^^^^^^^

The stars were growing in number as the daylight dimmed on their walk back to Sunset. Cassy and Verena chatted with Mia about her charters. Dag and Harry had their arms around Tim as they marched down the road.

"Who filled in the ruts?" Cassy asked.

"None other than your adoring and adorable husband," Harry eagerly confessed. "Everyone is busy and so am I. Thought you would have noticed it days ago. Hey, we've put enough distance between us and them thumpers; let's hear it for Tim. Son, you wowed them."

"Baffled them with bullshit is more like it," Tim declared. "All that info was real, but it applies to a much bigger area. St Lucia has about fifty times more people. Another resort won't do anything for the average man up there. Here, it might be different, but the changes, environmental disasters, those are real. Everything comes with a price tag."

"Here, here," Dag and Mia chimed.

"Brother, you can really spout the shit," Dag playfully shook him. Then seriously, "You did good, fantastic. I think you helped save our bay and our way of life. Even if, God forbid, we must relocate, the proposed hotel will mean more charters."

"See, that's where the average person goes wrong. Dag, I'm not saying you're average, but that hotel will take a hell of a commission for throwing us a charter. They'll also want freebies. Who knows, they might cut us out entirely and bring in their own fishing boat."

"Never thought of that," Harry said.

"This, ah, informing the public isn't going so good. They almost ran us out of there tonight. They already had most of the answers and weren't ready to listen, but I think you changed their mind, Tim," Cassy said. "You are fantastic at this business thing."

"It won't be easy, but you have to keep talking," Tim replied. "This is our private battle to keep our bay."

"Why didn't you two speak up?"

"Like you always said, children should be seen and not heard," Mia answered.

"They made a few stings about our boat, but that's what we'll use to win," Tim continued. "The war will be won out there on the blue Caribbean."

"I got a decent start on spring-summer-fall cleaning," Mia mentioned. "Back to being a maid again. Can't seem to get away from it."

"Mia, if it bothers you…" Cassy asked.

"No, just joking. Believe me, it's no big thing. I'm glad to be back. Really, this is something I needed."

Cassy replied with a long hug. The squeezes continued with her brothers and father.

As they turned to the house and found seats on the porch, Harry said, "About now would be beer o'clock, but I'm reformed. Time for lemonade. You guys, hey, don't reform on my part."

Dag stuck out his lower lip, "We'll respect your wishes at home. We've already decided if we want to have a few beers we'll do it in town. That way we won't be tempting you. Let's just make things work."

Tim disappeared to the boat and returned with his computer. "Okay, watch this," he said. With a special cord, he plugged a fancy phone into his laptop, punched some keys and the computer started making an almost mechanical, whirling noise.

"This is a satellite phone, special, our info is kept private. It doesn't go through the local Internet. Shearsome Bank gave this to me while I'm here. If they have questions about our systems or projects, they can contact me. But we will also use their satellites for our business. I set up Sunset Bay Fish Club as a corporate file on my bank's server."

Tim watched the somewhat startled faces surrounding his bright laptop screen.

"Look," he pointed and opened a file on the screen. "This is our confirmation. The money for our first charter is now deposited in my

London account. Friday, three men fly in from Florida and will land at seven. That gives you two days to finish all the details. What do you think, Dad, everyone?"

"I think that's damn amazing! You get all that info... from where?"

"Sort of like a phone call, but it is typed, er, a text, an electronic message." Tim struck a few more keys, "I write a letter coupled with our advert. See, this is what's called a streaming video."

In the darkness of the early evening, the computer screen radiated as a huge blue marlin seemed to leap from the screen. Harry, Cassy, and the Chessman's jerked backward as if to avoid the fish's sharp bill.

"Wow, Tim, this is the one from the other day?" Cheesy asked.

"No, this is a composite of some old photos I had, and Dag sent me a video from Costa Rica."

"Yeah, one guy on a charter let me use his camera to film them," Dag said. "This was a nice fight with the five-hundred-pound blue winning. It broke the line after a half an hour's struggle."

"You're not showing us losing game fish, are you?" Harry queried.

"No, I had to edit down and splice in some sunsets and shots of a calm sea. The entire thing takes only ninety seconds." Tim pointed to the screen, "Here's where they type in their credit card, and every charter, we get closer to being flush. I'm advertising a week for eight grand US and a weekend for five."

"Not bad. So, where's the money?" Mia inquired.

"In merry old England, at my bank. They confirm everything by electronic mail and then wire it to you wherever I want."

"What?" Harry was almost indignant. "Our money is in your account? So, son, you're running things now?"

"Kind of, sort of, Dad. I got word things were bad here and started working on a solution," Tim said. "I didn't know where you want it deposited. I thought there might be a problem with letting the local bankers know our financial status."

"Well," Harry replied in a pleasant voice. "Yes, that sounds good. No chance it is gonna get lost in them wires someplace, is there?"

"Can I try this? Are you finished with your second presentation?" Cassy asked. "Mia, you understand all of this, don't you? While the men are chatting, maybe we ladies... Verena, you get your butt over here. I'm thinking this can work for our businesses, too." They moved to the bayside corner of the porch.

The brawny young business exec continued to the men. "Not really, that's why I chose the bank I work for bank, Shearsome. I can use its influence. All you need to concentrate on is catching fish, and Cheesy, you're working for the big tip."

"Tim and I put together twenty-four thousand toward the debt after the cost of the boat's rebuild." Dag offered, "We'll roll with it, and see what happens. These charters will bring the debt to one fifty, give or take a few grand."

"And when did you become a mathematician?' Harry chuckled, grabbing both of his sons and vigorously shaking their hands. "I remember trying to get you through fractions in the fourth grade."

"There aren't any fractions in that," Dag smiled.

"We might make it," Harry beamed.

"Fingers crossed, no more misfortune," Cheesy added.

Harry took a wicker chair and pointed directions for the others to sit. Out of habit, he pulled Redbeard from his perch and started stroking his belly. "Try to keep things quiet. Tomorrow, the island will know from the choir we have an alternative plan. Our enemies will see us at the dock picking up passengers, getting fuel and supplies."

"We put together a budget for fuel, maintenance, and we'd better keep close. It's the last week of August and we have until the end of December to pay off our fines and court fees. Remember, we also must get the money for the next permit. So, we need to make about a couple hundred thousand."

"So, if we can live off half the tips…" Mia chimed in. "Just so you know we ladies of the auxiliary are listening."

"We just might make it," Dag said.

"I'm working on getting a tournament here. Spur of the moment thing, maybe in November. FineBraid Fishing Line would be the main sponsor. We'll see what happens."

"How you work something like that from here, Sunset Bay?" Harry asked. "Wow, hate to see the cost of the international phone calls."

"With that thing, I can call anywhere in the world, any time, and the message is waiting when they get to it." Tim pointed to where Mia was instructing Verena and Cassy on the laptop. "The real smarts is discovering who are the genuine power people at the companies, the top dogs, the decision makers…"

"Always liked FineBraid line." Harry puffed up his chest and tried to sound like a businessman. "Well, keep us informed of all, ah… details. Yeah, the details. Time to crash. Been a long day."

"I agree, boss. All that spouting strategy can wear a man down,"

Cheesy agreed. "Come, darling wife, your romantic starlit boat ride home awaits."

"Come on, Mom, let's hit it. I'll computerize you more tomorrow night. I'll be back to being Hazel, the maid, in the morning."

"I don't want to sit at the head table anymore. I want to go fishing,"
George Bush.

CHAPTER EIGHT

The St. Claires were once again sitting on the porch in the cool morning light sipping coffee Dag had carried from Costa Rica. "This is the best coffee in the world, if you believe the big dude plantation owner who charters our boat a lot. I like it, but a spoon of Nescafe Instant jolts me about the same." Dag said.

Mia laughed, "You still do that awful thing, take a spoon of the instant coffee straight and wash it down with water? It gags me to even think of it. I prefer Jamaican Blue Mountain."

In his British accent, Tim said, "Tea, a proper cup of tea, is what gets most of the world moving, my dear friends."

"Screw that coffee bull, coffee is coffee, hot and black," Harry added. "After yesterday afternoon you can see what we're up against. Now we all have to be really careful. These islanders smell money. They might be our friends, but the promise of money will make some of them do crazy things. We got to be constantly aware."

"We're ready. One of us should to be on the boat almost every minute. That's our real weak spot." Tim addressed. "If we lose *Sassy*, even for a few weeks, we'll be down the chute. I'll keep sleeping on her, no problem."

"I'll join you there, bro," Dag agreed.

"You crowding me out? I can't even sleep on my own boat?" Harry asked.

"Probably best if you keep mending things with Mom. What happened anyway?" Tim leaned close and inquired.

"Long and the short of it, I don't know."

"You must have some idea…" Dag said.

"I don't remember. Keep your voices down. She found some photos… damn … a woman." Harry gave a shrug combined with his dumb, wide-eyed look.

"Just a woman's picture, that doesn't sound so bad," Dag said.

"Well, ah, something more than that." Harry pulled at his eyebrow, "She was naked on *Sassy*."

"Holy shit!" Tim exclaimed.

"Cheese on bread!" Dag burst. "You're lucky to be alive. Mom's been known to throw knives."

"Hey, hey, I said keep it down. Worse part, it was Beatrice

Thorpe."

"Isn't she Mom's friend from Grenada?" Tim asked. "Her husband insures us."

"What's her story?" Dag had many questions.

"She's not talking to Cass. Me, I was boozed up more often than not. Lots of things I don't remember. You'd think I'd remember getting the photo."

"All you can do is keep trying." Tim offered.

"Damn," Harry grinned. "You'd think I would remember Beatrice without her knickers…. I wish I could."

"Come on guys, Cheesy's pulling up to the dock. Let's have another cup of inspiration with him and then hit it, hit it hard a couple more days, huh, Dad," Tim said, "We only have until Friday morning. That's two days."

"Yeah, Harry nodded, "Yeah, the clock is ticking."

The Englishman walked to the coffee drinkers and handed a full cup. "Cheesy, my friend and accomplice, what's on our agenda today?"

^^^^^^^^^

The two bathrooms consumed a lot of bleach and more elbow grease. It seemed the rift between her parents had extended to housekeeping. Not one had cleaned anything in a long time, not even broom swept. Usually, she considered her mother a neat freak. It was obvious all the turmoil had caused the depression and that led to the gloomy, unkempt house Mia was now scrubbing.

She'd whittled down the pile of laundry to the last load. They'd tossed all the used bedding into a corner along with dirty clothes. Harry's old clothes, anything except his khaki fishing garb, which made up his drunk attire, were sickeningly filthy. From the number of dirty T-shirts and shorts, this feud must have been going on for months.

The only daughter understood depression. Her significant other had committed suicide with that self-diagnosis. What the fuck? How could things ever get that hopeless? Countless times, Mia had asked herself that question. She'd thought they'd been in love. Perhaps not being certain was why they weren't. Even though they'd had what they wanted, they never had what they needed, and that was good communications. She could have said more; she could have said less. Now, again and again, she relived that horrible night.

She also knew that all of this nervous cleaning activity was excellent therapy for her at this point in her life. Making her childhood home sparkle was helping to scour away her own demons. Mia chuckled, using the toilet brush to bleach the stains. She was stained and had been since she lost her virginity at fourteen. So much she wished she could erase, mostly her reputation for being wild and unruly.

There were only a few light-skinned, unmarried women on the island. The locals called them clears, red-skins, or 'they had high-color.' Girls became women early, as soon as puberty. The island rule was, you stayed a virgin if you could run faster. Most island females bred quickly and started a family to anchor a suitable man.

Commitment and marriage, well, those two words didn't apply much to down island, West Indian culture. Men were always on the prowl to feed their egos by lying to sweet, naive girls. They promised a house, car, and definitely to divorce the current mate. And women were not much better, always looking for some action, sneaking around, but everyone knew who did who.

She smiled and hummed the Trini song, 'Shame and Scandal in the Family'. She sang, "His papa said son, I have to say no, this girl is your sister, but your mama don't know." Grinning, she removed the rubber gloves that had protected her from the household chemicals and rinsed her hands and face.

Mia stared into the medicine cabinet mirror. "No age marks, yet," she whispered. "Mirror, mirror on the wall, who is the fairest of them all?" Her grin stretched. She'd always asked this to the same mirror growing up. While she'd never been exactly Snow White, from her childhood, she was even lighter-skinned than her mother. Harry's genetics had given her the edge. Dad's family lineage had also provided a fine nose, but mommy's side contributed lush hair, skin that tanned rather than burned, and gorgeous full lips. She kissed the mirror, leaving the lip print.

Her brother, Dag, had been lucky to inherit the best of both parents. Mia thought he was a lady killer; she was the *Temptress*. Dag had grown over six feet tall, lean, but muscular. He'd never done an abdominal exercise in his life and was born with a perfect six-pack.

Tim had sprouted slowly, only to her height of 5'9". He got the fairest complexion that sizzled in the heat with his dirty blond hair. The tropical sun was his enemy, so he stuck to the shade and consumed books. Dag was the outdoors, all-rounder who read nothing except instruction manuals, unless forced.

Tim remained Timmy until he completed secondary school. By then, he was as smart, if not better self- educated, than his instructors. The youngest brother won every island brain competition from spelling to creative writing and higher math. He snagged several scholarships, and Tim was the trophy of Union Island's education system.

Harry had kept Cassy busy, pregnant and barefoot, having a child almost every year. Dag and Tim were fourteen months apart. The scuttlebutt was Cassy wouldn't quit until she had a daughter. That happened within the next two years.

Ten years later, Cassy swore that Mia was more to handle that both boys tied together. The teachers, ministers, and girl scouts agreed; Mia terrorized all.

She was last in the birth race, but got first in everything else. From a small girl, Mia had been stunning, wearing colorful frocks and buckle shoes. Blink and her feet were bare, like her brothers, and the frocks transformed to unisex cutoff shorts and T-shirts. As she grew older, the shorts and tops got skimpier. Everything about Mia seemed to flow against the island current.

Unlike Tim, she never burned, but her skin gained a light, golden glow. Her hair remained raven black, probably due to the Spanish or Portuguese genes. Mia fished, swam, snorkeled, and windsurfed with the boys. She was a ravishing tom-girl.

Both Harry and Cassy had provided 'that' talk when their children came of age. Harry also prodded the two boys to protect their sister. The astute fisherman did not require a crystal ball to foretell the future. He knew Mia would be a heartbreaker. He didn't want her raped, and that was always a possibility either by a neighbor or a stranger. His only daughter openly flaunted her beauty and charisma. To every man, Mia was a trophy to be taken... by force, if that's what it took.

Mama Cassy tried to take Mia into her confidence and prepare her for the weird rituals of island courtship. She was very familiar with being the most desired on the island. Her father, Curly, shooed local men away. It was difficult to find the perfect suitor for his only daughter; impossible on Union Island. Curly had a grand plan to add fresh blood to his family.

Curly loved both of his children with as many wives. His first wife, Laverne, Sam's mother, had been his school days' love. Laverne was as tall as six-foot Curly, slim and muscular. Then she'd been the dream girl among the island men. Curly didn't realize that she made too many other men's dreams come true.

His son Sam, the eldest, had a darker complexion with curly hair. Two years after he was born, Curly acquired a strange, burning pain in his genitals. The doctor pinpointed it as gonorrhea. Of the two, only he'd been faithful. Laverne confessed it was the product of a weekly coupling with the captain of the inter-island ferry boat. To save his own self-image and to keep the gossipers quiet, Laverne was banished from all business and family affairs. She stayed on the monthly payroll. If Sam wanted to see his mother, he had to visit her at her house in Union's 'other town', Ashton. Laverne was effectively exiled.

A successful man at 28, only a few months passed before Curly designed a new strategy to find a wife. He broadened his sights, purchased the best motorboat available, and cruised north to Kingston, the capital of St. Vincent, every weekend and holiday. He was a handsome man working well with old family money. His business connections provided invitations to society gatherings. At a garden party, he met the next Mrs. Scarbeaux. Gretchen was the niece of the previous English Governor.

The courtship was short because Phillip 'Curly' Scarbeaux made money, lots and lots of money, an excellent catch. Curly wasn't a bigot or racist; he was a local to his core, but for his second try at marital bliss, he chose a European woman with more rigid set of morals. Curly was becoming Union Island's top dog, and light skin in the Caribbean usually meant might and right. That meant European features. He wanted that for at least half of his grandchildren.

After secondary school, Cassy had no use for further education and didn't want to leave Union even though Gretchen offered a quality education on the continent. Instead, she'd work in the family's businesses, the hardware, and the restaurant. And she did well with a sweet hand like her mother for cooking and a quick mind for figures like her daddy. Out of the deep blue sea, the man of both Curly's and Cassy's dreams appeared at the fuel dock in a big sparkling sportfishing boat.

Suave Harry won everyone over with his broad, toothy smile, handing out chunks of fish to all who asked. He took his future father-in-law fishing one day and had the second facts of life explained. Curly knew fishermen. If he stayed on Union, loyal and reasonably sober to his daughter, Curly would take care of any immigration issues and give him the sweetest piece of land, for a reasonable price. The two men chatting knew exactly what the sweetest piece was.

The lanky, blond Floridian wowed and wooed Cassy. Their big common denominator was fishing. The island girl was as strong as she was beautiful. It was a splendid match. Their wedding was a memorable island event. Curly's friend, the Prime Minister, attended. For two years, husband and wife worked side by side, fishing and building their house. Following that, for the biggest part of the next four years, she had a swelled belly.

One of those few amazing women, the pregnancies didn't faze Cassy's looks or slow her down. When the children were infants, they had cribs in both the restaurant and the hardware's office. As they developed and found their voices to yell and argue, she stayed home and did the accounting for all three businesses, Mom's, Dad's, and hubby's.

In the nineties, travel agents directed the fishing charters. Over the years, Harry's father had made solid connections with agents along Florida's east coast. Expensive long-distance calls invited a group of his father's old buddies to come and fish for the big ones in the southern Windward Islands. Each travel agent returned with a good-sized game fish accompanied with a stack of the best photo brochures Union Island could produce. Word of mouth spread the info that remarkable fighting fish and a quiet island were ready for the intrepid fisherman who was willing and financially able to make the trip. In those days, the Caribbean hub was San Juan, Puerto Rico, and a trip usually required a layover, arriving and departing.

Sunset Bay was on its way to fame and almost fortune. With zero nightlife compared to Puerto Rico and the Virgins; rum swilling became hard and heavy on Sunset's porch. At first, the drinks were mild and only if the clients asked. Then Harry realized the incredible profitable mark up and accommodated matching drink for drink. At first, Cassy accepted it, even enjoyed a few Cuba Libres with the fishermen. She tried to keep it reasonable, knowing there'd be guys hanging over the side puking the following day.

Drinking is one of those vices that seldom stays reasonable. It easily becomes a habit. Cheesy tried to intervene, but that didn't work. It only created friction. The boys hated it. That was a positive point. Neither picked up the desire. Mia sipped, but inherently knew what could and probably would happen if she lost control. Mia liked to be in control. She grew into the Daisy Mae she'd found in the comics. Too young, she started searching for Lil' Abner.

^^^^^^^^^

With everything folded and a short power nap, Mia showered and put on some of her mother's clothes. She'd packed light, knowing she still had clothes she'd left at home. They were old and tighter than she imagined they would be. Mom's fit better and she donned a conservative long-sleeved white shirt over her black tank top and aptly named gray pedal pushers. With her hair tucked under another Penn ball cap and wrap around shades, she was ready.

From her bedroom window, she watched the four men putting

the finishing touches to the dock. Without a word, she grabbed Dag's old bike and pedaled into town, hoping to continue her low profile. Maybe she could help Mom close and get some leftovers. Four consecutive days of cleaning had wiped her out, and she was hungry.

Honoré was mopping up, and she snuck up and gave his big butt a pinch.

"Oh my God, it's Miss Mia, how are you. I was wondering when you'd come by. No customers after six this evening, so Cass decided to shut her down," Honoré spoke rapidly and then wrapped her in a bear hug. "Darling Mia, how you been?"

"I missed you, big man. And I miss your good cooking. Anything left? The family's back together and I've been the housekeeper, too tired to cook and so is everybody else."

"Well, dearie, I can find you something, but Cass had the same idea and cooked up a batch of fish and rice and carried it home." He opened the big fridge and scrapped a few pots together and set the microwave to heat. "You would like some of my cornmeal coucou? I got some fish and green bananas."

She stretched up to the tall West Indian and kissed his cheek. "That sounds delicious. So, how you getting along?"

"Me, I'm okay, the family's okay, everything pretty much cool for the time being, anyway. How's things with you?" He asked. "Heard you had some turmoil. Sorry to learn about your fellow."

"Hey, you know me, no stranger to, ah, turmoil. Like they say, everything passes. Yeah, it feels almost like home again."

"Gonna be here a while? You need anything?"

"Not really, just hungry," Mia grabbed his arm, "Company. I wanted to see some more of the island. Been busy… catching up… at home. Been with the family."

The tall man scratched his neck, "Lots I hear about Sunset Bay and the St. Claires. Everybody talking about the changes coming. Hell, what's wrong with the way things is now?"

"Nothing, nothing that I can see. I didn't realize how much I missed this place."

"You know what they say, Miss Mia, absence makes the heart grow fonder."

Suddenly, arms encircled Mia's waist and lifted her off her feet. Kid Kalaloo kissed her neck as she squirmed.

"Always fighting the best thing you ever had! You talking 'bout me, absence and fonder?" he joked.

"Whoa, hold it, put me down," Mia requested. "Nice to see you, too, Kid. But I'm about to have some dinner," she caught herself, "alone with Honoré."

"Come on, girl, what's it been? Lots of years, come on for old times' sake, I'll share a beer with you."

"Sorry Kid, the bar's closed," Honoré spoke. "Boss closed up and locked up."

"You mean you can't even grab one beer?"

"Nope, no sir, every cooler got a padlock. Someone was coming in, drinking it up for free. That was a while back; so we've been locking."

"An' you ain't got no key?" Kalaloo sighed, "Okay, I get your meaning. Anyway, sweet ting, at least come look at my new boat."

"Kal, I hoped I'd see you." She pushed his arms away and then gave him a hug, "How you been?"

The West Indian had matured since she'd left the island. His shoulders and chest had filled out. His dreadlocks reached his hips. He even braided his beard. Mia circled clockwise, and he followed. Kal pushed his lips out and tilted his head as he examined her. With a swift move, he stooped and scooped her into his arms and continued spinning her around. Honoré watched them as the microwave sounded.

"Better now! Real better now!" Kal shouted as he carried Mia across the street to the waterfront. "That's my boat."

Tied to the pilings was a long, thirty-foot go-fast painted in the Rasta colors. The sleek boat's foredeck was a brilliant red, even in the dusky light. The hull's sides were bright yellow, blending to green just above the waterline.

"Sweet, huh, like you," Kal smiled. "Let's go for a ride."

"Can't, not now anyway," Mia quickly answered. "Wow, where are you working to afford that?"

"Nah, not for… with… that's a tool." He turned and saw the big Honoré watching, arms folded, from the restaurant porch.

"Miss Mia, your dinner is ready."

"So, what do you do, speedboat tours?" Mia inquired. "Anyway, whatever, good to see you."

Kid Kalaloo gracefully hopped onto his boat, loosened the dock lines and fired up the three big outboards. "Take you on a tour. Anytime you like."

"Sure, well, maybe. I'm kind of busy at the parents."

"Heard all of you came home," Kal said. "Don't know if it'll help. Big tings going on here, these days."

"You got an interest?" Mia asked.

"It's a small island; you got to back the long shot."

"So, who's the long shot, us or the hotel?" Mia again. "Oh, are you saying I must back my family and they're the long shot?"

"You figger it. See you soon." Kal flicked a switch that bathed the boat in white light. The sleek craft chugged away into the night. She followed its lights and then Kalaloo must have punched the throttles for effect, doused the lights and disappeared.

Mia sank onto a bench next to the cook. "Honoré, what's that all about? How'd he ever get enough money to have a ride like that?"

"Loans, dearie, loans," he said. "These days, it's best to keep quiet and watch. Me, I'm a spectator, not an accomplice, or an accessory after the fact." He nudged her with a broad smile. "Know what I mean?"

She shoveled down the cornmeal and boiled fish. "I guess I know what you're saying. Best to not know, huh?"

"That's right, dearie," he answered. "Best to wait until you hear it on the evening news."

The moon was two days after full, but crested bright and high over Sunset Bay as Mia hit the last bump on the way home. Tranquil was the best description, but as the islanders always added, 'for now.' The conversation with Kid Kalaloo had shaken her. Was her family considered the long shot?

What was that saying, possession is nine-tenths of the law? She looked at the unspoiled setting. It was all natural. There was a time when she hated this seclusion. Now, just the opposite. The style of their house was old-style Caribbean, not ostentatious like many other homes on private bays. And this bay wasn't private. They'd chased no one away, never had to as far as she knew. Everyone was polite. Islanders of the same mind came and appreciated it, quietly; no music except nature and maybe a boat coming and going. Laughter usually made the best echoes.

And they came when the family would have a lights-off festival night. Tim started it when he was 'small Timmy.' Harry taught them about the constellations. Tim was always inquisitive and researched at the school library. Things had changed little with the constellations over a few millenniums. Union School had decent books on the stars. At nine years, he was giving astronomy classes for the school, Boy and Girl Scouts, and hustled yachts that anchored.

A few captains, who regularly had Sunset Bay on their weekly charter itinerary, grabbed moorings also rented by the family. Tim and Dag would come aboard at dusk, sell fish, and recite the story of all the major star clusters for the charter guests. Having a kid give a star talk gave the captain some precious self-time when he could pay to have his guests entertained. Tim, the young entrepreneur, set a fee and got tips. Dag usually got the fish money. They had few things other than basic island boy toys, like scuba gear, to spend it on.

From 12, Dag worked with a professional diving company, 'D' Diving. He started carrying tanks. That shaped his arms and shoulders better than lifting weights. The company comprised the D's, Dangerous Dave and Dennis, the DiSilva brothers. Retired from the Royal Marines, SBS (Special Boat Service), when the price was right the brothers could and would do anything underwater.

Eventually, Dag was scrubbing yachts that overnighted. Every yacht could use the algae trimmed. His 17th summer, he learned to cast big concrete moorings coupled with sand screws as the D's got the job installing moorings in Clifton Harbor. The job expanded into all the dive sites. That would at least slow the anchor damage to coral. He and Tim cast two big moorings in case of foul weather and two more to rent.

Mia felt herself grin, push back her dimples with a quick chuckle. Her hustle was painting and crafting little seashell knickknacks. She practiced painting the same scene. She sat in the same chair and painted the bay, the house, and the boat. When she got her first oil paints at six, Mia fixated on that scene and she sold every painting. She was a cute kid, rowing a cute little dinghy, peddling original down island naïve. She forged her own style in colors and shapes, but usually the same house and boat scene on Sunset. All of them had money through their own efforts. Fishing was their bread and butter, and everything else came second. That's the way it was now.

It hit her; the St. Claires had finally struck it rich, again wealthy, if only in friendship. This calamity had brought them back together. Some families aren't buddy-buddy. It had been this way when they were young. Mia and maybe her brothers had forgotten, but now it was ringing loud and clear. Each had their own issues and those could be dealt with later. The family was getting fixed while saving their fishing business. She hadn't heard an angry word. Everyone was confident, and they'd help elevate her spirits.

Harry always did his part, Mom cooked and cleaned, and they all catered to the guests. Three cute kids who respected their parents and their environment worked the anglers and warmed the scene. Mia wore was smiling as she parked the bike against the porch. Redbeard's loud squawk was the house alarm. Everyone was seated at the kitchen table listening to the BBC on the shortwave. She smiled broader. It was just like the good old days.

"What's up with you, Mia?" Cassy asked. "That's a pleasant grin; where have you been?"

"Ah, thought I would meet up with you, grab a meal and we could ride back together. How'd we miss each other on only one path?"

"I detoured to buy some goat from Paul Liburd. Thought everyone would enjoy a change from fish, fish, fish. Did you get some dinner?" Cassy smiled. "We have some leftover fish. Or, I have either cereal or eggs and toast."

"Honoré fixed me up," Mia said as she took Redbeard from his roost. The big red bird cooed and snuggled his head against hers.

"Bird always did like you the best," Harry said. "Darling, you have this place spotless. If it was white, it'd be a hospital."

"Thanks, took some work," Mia answered. "I must show you how to operate the washing machine. Bet you didn't know you had so many clothes, now that they're clean. Won't lie, kicked my ass. Had to take a nap this afternoon."

"We're done with one day to spare," Tim mentioned. "I knew we could do it now that we are all pulling in the same direction. We'll build a monument to Cheesy. That man, for his age, really busted ass. Me and him got the dock back in shape. Shouldn't have to worry about the liability of someone falling through it."

"And with Father not drinking, we don't have to worry about anyone falling off it," Cassy laughed.

"Hey, I helped. No honorable mention for me?" Dag asked. "What say we do some moonlight fishing? Anyone up for it?"

"You go," Harry replied. "Mom, you got enough gusto?"

"No, I'm drained,' Cassy answered. "You three go out and catch three big ones. Tell us about it at breakfast."

"Ya sure? Dag asked, "I brought some more lures that light up at night. Sort of cyalumes, chem-lights. Supposed to look like squids in the water."

"You use them and let me know how they work," Harry said. "In the morning. I don't need to tell you to be careful with our boat."

"Big moon tonight. Should be able to see okay. Plan to slow troll," Dag explained.

Sassy was idling just inside the drop-off. The boat was lit up by the tower lights.

"Depth's about 400 feet here," Dag read as he rigged one of the long lures. It was a cylinder with a pink plastic fringe and a double rig of hooks. He twisted the lure: something cracked and produced a dull light.

"I don't know what type of boat Kid Kalaloo has, but the only word that describes it is awesome. Big, long, stretched out, close to the water. At least thirty feet," Mia described. "Painted dread colors. Might be a Cigarette, if they still make them. Most of his boat is the stretched-out front cabin. The wheel is far back."

"Got to be the only boat like it around these islands," Dag said. "Kid must be doing something good. Gas is expensive here, like four a gallon."

"Think so? In London, it's over six dollars a gallon." Tim added. "Doesn't matter, Kid's making some big money to afford that luxury. You said he was calling it a tool? Not a taxi?"

Sitting nobly in the fighting chair, Mia sighed contently as she puffed on a cigarette. "Yeah, I promise to quit. This is cutting down," she inhaled deeply again and coughed. "And he said it in a way that was supposed to make him sound even cooler. Like he was on the inside of something and me, we, are on the outside. I'm not sure how he said it, but weirded me out. He, or I'm, backing the long shot?"

"Sounds like something he heard in a gangster movie," Tim said. "They all want to be bad asses."

"Kal was kind of goofing, laughing at me, sort of... like he knew what was going on."

"He's just like everybody else, waiting to see. Our fishing brings in some bucks that get spread around, but the hotel will make an enormous difference. If I were Mom and Dad, I'd think hard on that offer. Could be a windfall."

"Dag, I never thought I'd hear something like that from you. You were always outdoors, swimming, spearfishing... How could you think of giving...?"

"No, little sister, not giving." Dag interrupted. "Selling and moving on. Change is good; it keep life interesting. Think what our life would have been if we'd been raised somewhere.... somewhere we had more opportunities."

With a loud sigh, Dag let the line out from both reels and slid the rods into their holders.

"What?! I can't believe this!' Mia yelled. "I was the one who wanted to get out of here and you two were always either busting me or telling me how really, lucky I was."

"Dag, you really think we didn't have chances?" Tim asked. "Good chances?"

"Better than most," Dag replied. "Most of the others from our island had less, but what's that saying? I can fish, I can dive, but I can't navigate in a city. Really, I'm unprepared."

"You've got to be putting me on!" Tim said. He was at the helm, moving slow, about four knots. "Hey, I thought the only thing that you ever wanted was to sport fish?"

"Shit, that's the only thing I know. Yeah, Dad was right, I still need a calculator to add. And I can't really settle into a book if the print's small. Give her more RPMs. Keep her about 5 knots."

"Understood," Tim was curt.

"Here I am, the prodigal daughter," Mia spoke. "Hated doing slave housework and ended up doing it 24-7 on a yacht. You're always picking up, wiping, sweeping after somebody. I tried hard to get away, but this bay… this bay gets you."

"Every bay! You think you were prodigal?" Dag's tongue was wagging. "Sure! Dad exiled me to another saltwater country."

"You could have stayed," Tim replied. "All it would have taken was an apology… for poor judgment."

"Dag, you were so stubborn. But Harry was even more stubborn."

"Now, I know what I did was stupid," Dag said as he adjusted the distance the lures were trailing. "Hey, Leroy was drifting, and I was coming home from fueling. What did I know, I gave him a tow. Helped a friend, and he's got a load of ganja. Gave me a piece. Remember how outstanding that stuff was? Dad found it and hit the roof. When I explained it was only a gift for trying to do a good deed; he clobbered me."

"Dad was always good at hitting first," Tim agreed. "And then he'd ask for your side. But that was the booze. Come on, you can see Harry's trying."

"Yeah, he's trying," Dag said sullenly, "this time."

"He warmed my butt. Jeez, lots of times, but I guess I deserved it. Being a parent can't be easy," Mia laughed. "Dag, you think you're unprepared? Look at me," she flicked the spiraling butt overboard, "I'm a widow at twenty-four and in debt." She laughed hard, "Remember, Harry saw red the time I stowed away on that cruise ship."

That made Tim howl. "You pretended that you were with that German tour group on the beach, and they didn't find out until you were in Barbados. Mom had to fly out and get you."

"What were you, fifteen?" Tim inquired.

"Fourteen," Mia smiled, "a mature fourteen."

"Developed, maybe precocious, but never mature," Tim replied with a laugh. "But you almost pulled it off, escape from Union Island."

"Almost," Mia was cut off.

"Hey, hey, shine the spot," Dag pointed. "More to the right. Look, see that small wake over there; we're gonna get us a yellow fin." He pushed the reel's drag lever forward and let the line free spool out about ten meters. They all intently watched the lures.

Tim dimmed the spotlight. The big moon gave plenty of light. The props swirled up some phosphorescence. With the eerie glow of the two trailing lures, it was an unique way of fishing.

Quietly, Tim asked, "You learn this in CR? I never heard of anything like it. We used to drift with cyalumes, deep on downriggers. Remember?"

"Bro, the tech revolution is here. Fishing is evolving like everything else. Those big money fishermen guys, hell, they don't care. They drive up in a hundred grand Mercedes X and toss their gear. Don't give one shit about all the saltwater."

"Wow, I'd love to do a road trip in a Benz X jeep," Tim was just above a whisper.

"You want a road trip now? Back then I wanted to see something more than the traffic lights in Grenada." Mia replied in a low tone, "You realize that there is still no traffic light here."

"Be glad they got a stop sign at the end of Main Street," Tim laughed.

"I think that sign's what keeps so many people here," Dag said.

All three stood watching the wake. *Sassy* was moving slowly on autopilot. There was nothing in sight except the black sea reflecting the same color slightly sky illuminated by the moon and stars. Just enough breeze kept it fresh. Small fish were leaping out of the boat's wake.

The port rod suddenly bent, and the reel screamed. The quiet night was over. On reflex, Mia grabbed it, dipped the rod tip, and the pumped upward to set the hook. "Got him," was all she said and then pulled, staggering, towards the stern.

"Give him line," both Dag and Tim yelled, well-rehearsed from years of practice. "Loosen the drag. Let him run with it."

Tim moved to the wheel. Dag's arms encircled Mia's waist, and he guided her to the chair. Once the drag was off, she could move and buckle in.

"Okay, you're good. Reel that slimy bastard in," Dag coached. "You know the routine, pump and reel, pump and reel."

"Slow the fucking boat, Tim, I haven't done this in a while," Mia pleaded. "Don't need to fight *Sassy* and the fucking fish."

"My, my, aren't we excitable," Tim responded by pulling the

throttles down and put the boat in neutral.

"You could back down, bro," Mia asked.

"Come on, this is a good workout," Dag chuckled. "Fuck you. My arms are killing me from scrubbing," Mia exclaimed. She pumped and pumped the rod, gaining on the fish faster than expected. The deck lights showed her well-defined muscles flexing. "Remind me, next time to bring gloves. He's coming in, Hey, get the gaff, get the gaff."

Dag grabbed the pole gaff and Tim held the small ball bat.

"We're selling this one," Mia shouted between ragged breaths. Her slim thighs bulged as she strained her feet against the aluminum rest, jerking the rod all the while frantically cranking the reel. "Got him, got him! He's almost at the boat. Can't you see him? Gaff that mother, Dag. My arms are killing me!"

"Quit whining," Dag laughed. "I can see him, crank more."

It was as if the fish heard them, and made a surge away from the boat, stripping off more line.

"Son of a bitch!' Mia complained. "Okay, you want to fight? I'll show you." She tightened the reel's drag, and the chair creaked as the fish pulled harder on the rod.

"Watch it little sister, not too tight. Play him. Remember that tuna is fighting for his life," Dag delivered his standard fishing lines.

"I know, I know, crank slow, deliberate. Pump the fucking rod," Mia huffed and puffed.

"See, where that smoking's got you? Can't even crank in a small tuna." Tim chided standing behind her with his hands on her shoulders, lending some moral support. "And if Mom was here, you'd be choking on soap suds. Can't swear around the guests, remember."

"Well, she's not fucking here," Mia gained some line on the fish, pumping the rod up and down with serious cranks on the reel. "And you've heard worse. No anglers are saints," She got out before the fish made one more desperate attempt to pull away. Mia held firm, and that was the end of the fight. She hunched over and started quickly reeling it in.

"I can see him," Dag said, watching the stern. "Okay, a few more cranks." He adjusted his stance to get a firm footing. "Okay!" And deftly swung the long gaff hook and caught the fish perfectly just behind the tuna's gill plate. In one smooth swing, almost like a golfer, Dag snagged the fish and lifted over the transom and onto the boat's deck. In step, Tim conked the fish a few times with the bat and it stopped thrashing.

"Come on, high fives all around," Mia shouted, and she undid herself from the chair and danced around it.

"Yeah, we might be a fine trio of maladjusted, screw-ups, but damn, can we fish!" Tim howled.

"Tu-na, tu-na, tu-na!" Mia chanted in her little girl voice. "Damn straight we can fish!"

"We'd better…" Dag reminded. "A lot is riding on us dragging in a lot of biggies. Mia, this one goes a good thirty kilos." He hugged her. "You did fine. I was wondering if you had it in you since you've been living the easy life."

"Easy life?" Mia scoffed. "Hey, buddy, I carried the weight for all the years since I left. That idiot, no, I was the idiot getting hooked up with that stupid, lazy, worthless asshole. He talked me into using the money from my paintings for a down payment on the cat." She lit another cigarette and inhaled deeply. "Yeah, he worked me like a dog. I had to, floating in debt. He was the skipper, and I was the crew. Some things never change."

"Okay, we ready to head in?" Tim asked, "It's almost eleven. Be midnight when we dock and still got to clean up. You caught your fish. Feel good?"

"Sure does," Mia said between drags.

"Yeah, let's head home," Dag agreed as he secured the fish and organized the tackle.

Tim slipped the boat into gear and pushed the throttles up. "Didn't you have a thing for Kalaloo? I seem to remember…"

"You remember bull shit," Mia crabbed. "Kalaloo wanted me. They all wanted me." She presented what she thought was her best side; she bent over. "Kiss this! I admit, I still think he's handsome, but Harry would have a regular fit if he thought I ever dated a local guy."

"Yeah, Dad was always funny about that." Dag joined. "I had friends. What did he expect us to do, import them or go without?"

"Remain celibate," Tim said.

"That's wasn't of your choosing," Mia joked. "Nothing funny about it at all. Kind of sad, considering he married into an island family. You see Ursula yet?"

"Yeah, what's up with that?" Tim joined.

"Nothing's up," Dag replied. "When have we had any free time?"

"Remember when I found out that Ursa meant bear in Latin class?" Tim continued.

"Ursi's a bear all right. Been thinking about looking her up. She's probably got plenty of kids by now."

"That shouldn't slow her down any. What did you two do when

you'd sneak off?" Mia asked.

"We explored… the island. And what about you, Tim, didn't you have your heart set on…"

Tim peered into the night they were heading to. "On getting out and away from here."

The author with a 37kg sailfish and 12kg kingfish off Carriacou.

"It has always been my private conviction that any man who pits his intelligence against a fish and loses has it coming." John Steinbeck.

CHAPTER NINE

As usual, Harry changed plans at the last minute. Friday morning, he decided to run around to town and do away with the cost of a taxi. After a quick breakfast, they towed Cheesy's skiff for the shuttle run from shore. When the anglers reached Sunset, Cassy and Mai would prepare brunch and pump beers in them. Dag remained home to seine net fresh ballyhoo and mullet to add to their stock of frozen. Fresh, still swimming in the baitwell, was best.

As they pulled away from their dock, it was the beginning of another classic Caribbean day. Blue sky and billowing clouds, with a slight, fresh breeze blowing from the east, the sea was flat. The fishing boat's minimal wake gave the sailboat masts a slight teeter. Carriacou to the southeast with Palm Island and Petit Martinique to the east broke the broad, flat blue horizon.

Everyone wore their dress khakis and best ball cap. All the clothes were embroidered with SBFC, the Sunset Bay Fish Camp logo. This was a show for all to see; the St. Claires were back. Harry would not push his luck, or his try his patience, as far as tying up at his brother-in-law's dock. He knew the renewed *Sassy* would create a lot of chatter in Clifton. If Sam wasn't watching, he'd, sure enough, hear the chatter.

Plus, the walk from the airport to the beach lent more an air of adventure to the charter. Perhaps they could stay out of motor vehicles for the duration. Harry hated cars and what they'd done to the world. He'd always bring up hearing someone talk about how automobile tires were the world's biggest unsung villain. Where did the rubber go as the tires wore down? The powder flowed with the rains into rivers, lakes, and oceans.

The sea on the windward side of Union's airport was calm. No wind chop at all. Harry said Neptune and Poseidon were happy. He was radiating with new, suave confidence, ready to play his part again, the part he was born to. Shaking his head, he relished the overall improvements of the past weeks.

The crew waited aboard until the turboprop landed. Over a thermos of coffee, they started a pool on how many fish the guys would bring to the boat on this charter. Harry was high at lucky 11, Tim took 9, and the Chessman 8. Harry kept slowly circling while they headed in. Cheese stayed with the tender while efficient Tim beelined to customs and immigration.

Ten minutes later, Tim returned leading two fishermen struggling to pull their wheeled luggage on the rough surface that had once been an asphalted path. Each finally gave up and lifted their bag. The anglers were paler than expected, considering it was summer in the northern hemisphere. Typical tourists, they were in white shorts and shirts, busily wiping their damp brows with white handkerchiefs. The kicker was they had white socks, almost knee high, pulled out of white high-top canvas shoes. Tim smiled to himself. He could easily read these guys were businessmen like him. Harry would love this.

The skiff was crowded, but they made it without anything getting wet. Tim held the skiff's bow to the tuna tower while Cheesy secured the stern. Harry assisted the two anglers in getting on board. They stretched their white legs gingerly over the fishing boat's high gunwales.

"Welcome aboard *Sassy Cassy*, gentlemen, I'm Captain Harry St. Claire. This is my son, Tim, and my mate Mr. Chessman, or Cheesy. Ah, we're not that kind of mates, you know what I mean," Harry stammered, stumbling through one of his usual jokes as Tim tied off the skiff from the stern.

All hands were extended, and generous shakes went around. "You'll soon meet my real mate, our boss, the other *Sassy Cassy*, Cassandra, my lovely wife. So, where you guys from?"

One word and it was definite they were hardcore Brits. "Good to meet you. I'm Ian Mosley, and this is my brother-in-law, Carl."

"Glad to meet you. We're going on a quick run to the other side of Union Island, to our dock, and get you settled, some lunch, or breakfast, brunch, whatever, and then we'll drag some baits."

"Flight okay?" Tim asked.

"Good as one could expect. Flew up from Grenada, short forty-five-minute flight; didn't make bad time. No bumps at all in the small puddle jumper," Ian said, satisfied.

Cheesy nudged Harry, "Think they got monocles?"

"Huh," Harry was lost in nervous thoughts. This was his first charter in months. "What barnacles?"

"Gorgeous, absolutely gorgeous," Carl whispered, "Lovely place. Live here long?"

"All my life," Tim answered. "Well, not quite, I lied," Tim dropped into his British accent. "Last eight years I was in Jolly 'Ol. I work for Shearsome. Head of IT."

"Really, that's quite commendable," Carl replied. "I can see you enjoy the best of both worlds. How's the fishing been?"

Harry crowed, "Hauled in a couple of big tunas, a sail, and a big blue over six hundred all in one day during the last charter,"

"Went out last night and my sister, Mia, landed a nice albacore about seventy pounds. That'll be dinner," Tim added.

"Your sister, fishing at night?" The anglers exchanged glances. "Plenty of action, eh?"

"All you can handle, but only on the water," Cheesy returned in his best Brit style.

"Aye, another Limey?" Ian asked.

"Many years removed," Cheesy beamed as he readied the rods in their holders. "For years, the wife and I were doing a 'round the world cruise. We decided to hang on the hook here for a while. I'm originally from Brighton, you know the Pews area?"

"Why, coincidentally, yes, my wife's family is from around Brockton, not that far away," Carl replied.

The charter was off to a splendid start. Harry smiled to himself. Yep, they were back on track.

^^^^^^^^^

Sunset Bay Fish Camp poured on the charm as if this was a dress rehearsal for the real deal. The ladies had the time to make an over-the-top brunch. Healthy, whole grain pancakes and quiche Lorraine with fresh orange juice. Dag bragged they had the best Costa Rican coffee on Union Island. By the last bite, everyone was on fabulous terms.

"Now, get them out of here and fishing," Cassy whispered. "You know the routine; we clean up here and I got to get ready at the restaurant. I'm late. Hate to strap Mia with all this dinnerware."

"Do what you gotta do. Don't know if Dag's coming. Guarantee he isn't a dishwasher. Who knows? Might be a few too many captains. They're all surprising the hell out of me. Can't remember them, oh, ah, all of us getting along so good," Harry hugged her tightly. "Thanks, baby, I know I'm not easy, but I swear I'm reformed."

She gave his cheek a peck. "Get them out of here now."

Dag took the helm, following the heading to the closest point of the drop-off. Tim was in the tower on the lookout for fish. He turned in search of diving birds with small, modern binoculars. Harry and Cheesy split the numbers; Cheesy got Ian. Both fishermen were smeared with white creamy sunscreen, had long-sleeved, SPF shirts and wide-brimmed cricket hats. Each wore expensive, polarized sunglasses.

If things went as planned, they wouldn't be looking down, but at fish jumping up, out of the water.

Harry waited for his cue, and it always came; what was the biggest fish you've ever hooked and held? He skipped over the massive Junish and plowed into his repertoire of dolphins, tunas, and finally the billfish. It was early, only five minutes into it. The clients were spellbound as Harry explained the art of catching dolphin. Just as he said to keep one on the line, in the water close to the boat, brought in more; Tim shouted from above; birds were 30 degrees to port. All eyes tried to be the first to confirm. A coin flip decided Ian would be first in the chair.

"There, there, over there," Carl, the brother-in-law screamed. "Oh my god, must be hundreds of birds. What are they?"

Harry smiled because he loved to say it, "Boobies." He used his hands to pull out his shirt like breasts. "Brown boobies, we sure got a lot of them on this rock," he giggled.

Tim shouted, "I think we got tuna." And dropped into the tuna-tuna chant. "Dag a few degrees more to port."

"You picked a fine weekend, but then it's seldom we have nasty weather." Cheese offered.

"But isn't this hurricane season? We were worried, but your excellent reputation, coupled with your rates, seemed reasonable for a holiday. Left the wives in Grenada. A direct flight from Heathrow."

"Reasonable rates, huh?" Harry chirped. "How'd you hear about us?"

"Matter of fact, by surfing the Net, dreaming of a fishing vacation," Ian explained. "But then there's always the spouse to contend with. She's also a manager with a high stress level. Hit a site for FineBraid Line, don't even know how I happened upon it. Sistered with it was a group of places that offered simultaneous entertainment for the girls. Sunset offered a getaway. You know," Ian joked, "trial separation. You had exactly what we needed, we, Carl and me. The wives could sunbathe and tour Grenada or relax with cocktails, welcome to be rid of the boys for four days."

From the upper steering station, "See, I told you I could work wonders."

Harry nodded to both appreciation and in awe of the technology.

Cheesy started in, "Oh well, yes, the big storms usually head further north. Hasn't been one hit here in a dozen or so years. We get some wind, and needed rain, but do little other than clean out the dead leaves"

"I would hate to experience a horrendous tempest," Carl said.

"Bad enough viewing the devastation on the tele."

Tim whistled, "Hey, better quit the blabbing. Spot on, Dag. We're cutting the edge of the school perfectly."

Confidently, Dag said, "Just like the bigger fish swimming around the school of fry, we'll circle then cut through. I think we'll have a hit in a few minutes. Keep your eyes open, bro."

"Aye, aye," Tim paused, "look out! Fish on," he said a mini second before the rods plural, dipped. Two had line screaming off.

Harry grabbed the starboard rod and gave it a staunch set as he dropped the tip to the deck while letting loose the drag. He stopped the line, pitted his feet and did a semicircular swirl, again setting the hook in perfection. In the practiced ritual, he placed the rod into the seat's center gimbaled holder and strapped in the angler. Now he'd show his worth. Tim qualified the hookup as two nice yellowfin tunas.

Tim dropped to the fighting deck to help Carl buckle into the stand-up fighting belt. Tim's muscular arms circled the fisherman's waist as Cheesy carefully handed him the other busy rod.

"Okay, we got this," Tim assured. This was the dangerous time when a rod could get lost overboard. Tim snapped the reel to the harness, and then snapped Carl's harness to the tower. Now, nothing should get wet. Cheesy and Harry reeled in the other lines. There would be enough confusion, fighting two fish. They had to keep them separated.

Dag expertly maneuvered to help keep the fish apart and pushed in different directions.

Ian shouted, "Damn, he's big. My arms are burning. Blighters, he's taking more line. Should I tighten the drag?"

"Only if you want to lose him," Harry calmly said. "Don't think about the other fish. You listening too, Carl? Just fight yours. Like everyone says these days, focus. We'll do our best to board these. You want photos, don't you?"

Unanimously, "Yes, absolutely!" Came the cry as both fishermen dipped and pumped. Carl was staggering with the stand-up outfit. With Harry leading the cheers as Dag backed down, Tim was quick to gaff Ian's twenty-plus kilo yellowfin. They got him out of the chair and they waltzed Carl into it.

"Okay mate," Cheesy leaned to his ear and showed Carl his digital watch. "We have a rum drink bet on this; yes, we do. I'm saying it will take you fifteen or more minutes to grind this fish to the boat. Prove me wrong and I'm buying you a grog." He set his stopwatch.

Carl swallowed, "Some water. Got a squeeze bottle in my ruck." Tim attended him as he pumped and garnered distance. "Mary, Mother of God, are you certain we haven't snagged the bottom? It's not moving."

"That's called the 'tuna wall.' You still got nine minutes. We have some tasty rum. Ever sample El Dorado?" Cheesy taunted.

"Not now, not now. I think I'm permanently bent over. This fish has pulled my back," Carl bellowed.

"Maybe separated your arms from your shoulders," Cheesy gave Carl's left shoulder a squeeze. "Don't worry Timothy has all this on camera. Digital, correct?"

"Yes, forgot to mention, we have a GoPro on wide focus strapped on each of the tower struts." Tim answered, "We captured all the action."

"Blimey," Ian winced, "can you edit out the part about the ladies?"

"Don't worry, I set them with a remote," Tim flashed a small button. "Once I sighted tunas trailing the baits, I clicked them on."

Carl bent into the task, knowing there would be no chance of altering the facts. "Ugh, it's a monster, I know it." Now, hamming it up for the cameras, his upper torso bent almost double to make the longest rod pumps as possible. Ian had their camera also operating, getting close-ups.

Dag gushed and walked into the range of both cameras. "Which is my best side?"

"Not to worry, skip, these two capture the complete deck. You're in every clip," Tim assured.

"Okay, okay, are you paying attention to my fish?" Carl gasped. "I think it's close?"

Tim stood rigid watching the stern. "Don't worry, Carl. We'll keep you in the loop. You'll know he's here when you pull his nose through the top eye on the rod tip. Ease him in, easy, easy," Tim thrust the gaff and smoothly lifted the struggling fish over the transom. Harry was about to give it a good whack, but stopped to ask, "Catch or release?"

"Damn, Harry, that's the biggest fish I've ever even seen, let alone caught." Carl twisted his hand, thumbs down. "Need photos for posterity and to placate the wife for how much this expedition cost!"

"Thought you said it was reasonable?" Harry smirked.

"Reasonable is all relative. Hanker a guess on how many salon trips this equates to?"

Cheesy sidled over and pushed his watch, "Shut it off, you did it in twelve minutes. Not quite a record, but not bad." He pulled the fish up with a block and tackle scale. "Not bad. Got yourself a biggie at 41 kilos. 91 pounds.

"If you can handle it, I have soy and wasabi, freshest sashimi you'll ever taste," Tim provided, "And cold brews."

"Now you're talking!" Ian replied. "Slice off of my small one. Keep Carl's intact for photo ops."

Harry looked at Dag and exchanged broad smiles and thumbs up. Dag mouthed, "We're back." Harry nodded.

It was a fast and furious four days. Five more tunas, but Carl's first one stayed the biggest. An early getaway the third day, just after dawn, they chanced upon a school of dolphins that loved to jump. Four rods went off simultaneously. Everyone was busy, and that was the record day for catches with fourteen fish by ten o'clock and an early quit at two. The Brit anglers feigned exhaustion and sun damage.

Even the anglers didn't hit the bar too hard. Tim and Dag stayed by their word and never had a drink if Harry was around, but the third night they snuck a bottle to the dock. Mia mixed the amber juice with soda. Her brothers enjoyed their rum straight, on the rocks. All were smiling.

"Got this shit clocked, me-son. Yes sir, clocked. We can raise some fish," Dag bragged.

"I'm coming along tomorrow," Mia issued. "Wish I'd have been there today. I love catching dolphins."

"Damn, they were thick today! Massive school, a couple hundred. Biggest was twenty kilos. Never saw so many jump and dance," Dag bragged. "Hooked into school once off Puerto La Cruz in Venzie. Hauled in over fifty, but not one broke water."

"Everyone jumped today, everyone. And we got it all captured digitally," Tim reported. "Hey, you said you hated this fishing stuff." Tim's words were slurring.

"I said it was all I can do and wow, come on, wow me with a high -five, both of you. I can steer to the schools, just right to do the most angler damage," Dag continued.

"This rum's good, isn't it," Mia passed the bottle. And then sang the advert 'We deserve a break today, er, tonight. We've been really humping. Harry and Cassy nodded off early. The Brits crashed just after sunset. Maybe their snoring will die down by the time we crawl upstairs."

"We, you crawl upstairs. I'm crashing here with Timbo. Like the old days, sneak a bottle out of Dad's case and guzzle it then stick it back in the box. I'm guessing he knew how many he was going through. Didn't mind us drinking at home, alone together."

"Oh, rat's ass. I'd like to switch bunks occasionally. I like *Sassy*, too. Open-air, waking to gulls," Mia grouched.

"Bull shit, you hear them just as well from your bedroom gable."

"Well. A damn side cooler out here."

"Yes, I'll agree to that," Dag granted.

"How were your term-charters, if you don't mind talking about it now that we're a bit greased?" Tim asked.

Mia sucked in her cheeks and let out a long breath. "Who doesn't mind explaining how stupid they were? I guess I'm still involved with all that shit, so still are, am, stupid. It wasn't so bad, but to make money we were always busy. Not like you, Dag; take them fishing then have them off the boat. Your evenings were to yourself. I had them 24-7 to 14 days on charter. The only way to make money was to stay busy. We had two weeks off in seven months. I cooked, baked fresh every fucking day. And I fucking cleaned up after them, fucking constantly. Got so now, I'm a worse neat freak than mom."

They poured another round that would be the last one as Tim's drink drained the bottle. The two brothers sprawled on the benches with their glasses of rum beside them on the deck. Mia had claimed the fighting chair and swiveled directing her questions and answers to either and became the commentator.

"Saw the same string of islands in the BVI over and over. It was like being caught in the Bill Murray movie, Ground Hog Day. Remember that one?" Mia nervously laughed. "Every little rock, beach, coconut tree we stopped at, some, usually, a red-eyed Rasta type, would try to hustle something. It got monotonous quick."

"I paid the bills, dwindled down the note, and sort of lost sanity, at least lost a good bit of the other Mia. Became too responsible," she explained.

"I know what you mean, sort of," Tim said. "I've been erased. The island Tim disappeared. Feels so good to have him make a return. I pushed to be somebody else, someone bigger and better. You can imagine, everybody I work with is extremely greedy, but with the genteel touch." Tim's face grew grim, and he reached deep inside. His body gave an involuntary spasm, "Wow, rum's working. I hate it. I hate it, but it comes so naturally. I'm an over-achiever, always was. Perfect fit, but, but, but my life is drudgery. Same routine, maybe see the outdoors on Sundays, maybe," he sighed. "Seldom sunny weather."

"Wow, sounds grim," Dag commented.

"Look at me, I poured everything into the gym. The big dogs at the firm like to see self-determination. I hulked out, burnt the midnight oil, and in four years, I'm head of a department."

"If you're the head, how are you here indefinitely?" Mia asked.

"Oh, I'm working. That sat phone is my Net connection. They still get their pound of my flesh. This is a special deal I worked out with the boss, a six-month sabbatical. I didn't take any vacations in the four previous years. My boss liked the true-life sob story of a man helping his family save their livelihood. Add sportfishing in the Caribbean and they all want to rub up against me."

"I guess. Bro, you really have, what's the word?" Dag asked.

"Try sculpted," Mia said. "Yes, you have grown beyond Timmy."

"Here we are, three siblings, thrown into a Caribbean mystery," Tim said as he grabbed Mia's lighter and waved it drunkenly, "Are we the bad guys? Who are the bad guys?"

"Nah," Mia sniped. "We are not bad, we're good. And eventually, we will overcome…"

"As soon as we figure out who and what Sunset Bay Fish Camp is up against," Dag interrupted. "Maybe all this is bullshit? Harry and mom fucked up, didn't pay any license fees for years. Then Harry, the drunken Harry, pisses off everybody. The government decides we outlived our value."

"Oh, that's exactly what it is," Tim pointed out. "The government in Kingston will make more in taxes from the hotel than ever from us. The politicos are the only certain winners from this. Hey, I did a lot of research before I boarded the plane for here. Grenada just made twelve-million, and nothing happened."

"What?" Mia asked. "Who'd be that dumb?"

"Big hotel chain, Crown Vetch Enterprises, part of the Beritz syndicate. Thought they'd paid, greased enough palms, and were guaranteed a fantastic building site. The government promised to relocate people and give them a chunk of the south side. Lots of development going on there. Then one day the government decides, mind you, after 11 months, that Crown didn't turn a shovel of dirt, and cancels the deal. No arbitration possible."

"The legal scams that are out there," Dag agreed. "How come, if you know so many rich fuckers, you couldn't get us a loan?"

"Bro, you and I will loan money to mom and dad. The fuckers I know are exactly that, fuckers. They want to buy in, then we lose control. Just like my hero, Gordon Gekko-Michael Douglas in Wall Street."

"Ah, you'd never pull anything like that," Mia assured. "Tim, you have morals and scruples."

"I do, but, but, but I'm sure my department's deep into the same style. You should read the information search requests we get. They want to know down to the time a competitor was born. Every fucking detail of a man's life so they can find some leverage. That photo of the naked woman on our boat is something Shearsome would do to make a deal go through. But pops was seeing life through the bottoms of rum bottles and has memory lapses."

"This has been great. Nice talk." Mia kissed each on the forehead. "I'm hitting it. Tomorrow is these guys' last day. I give them credit; they caught a lot of fish. Didn't look that earnest at the beginning, but they stepped up."

"Still looked like white bread," Dag laughed.

"Hey, they're fishing tomorrow and flying straight back to Grenada," Tim said. "They're only taking two of the dolphin back and we're selling the rest that mom can't use. Got Dad's list of numbers for the neighboring resorts. Maybe we can make a run to either Canouan or Palm. Both resorts will snap them up. We spend the night? Huh, the three of us live it up, have a proper restaurant meal, and crash on the boat. We can work the restaurant tab in with the fish deal."

Mia jumped at it. "Brilliant idea. I'm there. That means I can wear some nicer things."

"Yeah, brilliant, Tim. Keep them coming. I'm with Mia, both on the trip and crashing." Dag headed to the bow cabin and turned, "Goodnight."

The next day Ian and Carl were dazzled with Mia's presence as a stewardess serving lunch and cocktails between hookups. She wore her khaki combination and surprised everyone by refusing an offer to reel in a fish. The Brits caught four medium, forty-pound yellowfins. By then they were old hands and cranked those babies in. It was minutes past noon, when the starboard outrigger rod went off. A nice sailfish hurtled straight up. Its tail cleared the water by at least a meter. On the second leap, the fish wrenched its body, head to tail, and spit the hook. Ian was lucky enough to catch the last jump with his camera.

The Brit puckered up and then broke into a smile. "Seeing is believing, but truthfully, I'm glad he threw it," he sighed. "It was my turn and if I fought it to the finish, I doubt I'd have enough energy remaining to give the wife what I hope she'll demand; if you catch my drift. No offense, Miss Mia."

"None taken." She wedged between the two fishermen and draped her arms over, "You must do whatever it takes to keep the wife happy." Mia lifted her hands and led the chorus that included all the crew, "If the wife's happy, the world's happy."

They laughed.

All six pairs of hands were shaken a few times around. Cheesy and Dag issued long goodbyes with babbling descriptions of one of each client's catches. The tip was huge, a grand in Euros.

Ian rationalized, "Sunset was reasonable, while not first-class luxury accommodations, it certainly felt like home." He pushed out his stomach, "And the food was sublime. We'd have paid extra and couldn't have caught more fish anywhere else."

"We'd be pleased to return and go for billfish," Carl added. "Now that we've found a way to keep our ladies smiling, everything is possible."

Harry accompanied Tim and the men to the airport dock in Cheesy's boat. The two medium-sized dorados were stretched across the bow, frozen stiff and wrapped in as much newspaper as they could gather, then taped inside trash bags. Ian and Carl were returning to their wives, bringing the evidence.

"Can't believe this excellent weather. Always another great balmy day," Carl said as the two Brits departed and headed for ticketing.

Once in the skiff, Harry beamed, "We'll get some return business from them."

"Sure, we will; I got them to write long testimonials on our social pages," Tim said.

"Social pages? Is that like," Harry hesitated, "shit, I don't know. What are social pages?"

"Don't worry about it, pop. Got it covered," Time grinned. "Facebook, Twitter, and Instagram. Our web site, Perfect Sunset Bay, connects to all three, plus a bunch of other sponsors."

"We got sponsors? This is the first I'm hearing about it. How much money we get?"

"Not our sponsors, the social page sponsors. Someone clicks on them; our site pops up. Don't worry, it's all good," Tim sighed and grinned. "It's all good, dad," he hugged his father.

Once back at the boat, "Let's fill her up at Curly's. I think we can let people see us again," Harry said.

Cheesy was quick with a return, "Seen, but you can't be heard."

"Oh, I got ya, loud and clear."

"Standing by, skip," Dag said to his father.

"Well, son, take her around, port to. That'll keep the cabin even with Sam's office and not the pumps."

"You're the captain," seemed to come instantaneously from the other three.

Dag followed orders and eased the sportfisher to the fuel dock. Harry relaxed on the bench while Cheesy and Tim placed the fenders and hopped off, each with a dock line.

Sam was sitting on the concrete steps with some local men. A bottle of rum was circulating.

Tim passed salutations with a wave and started filling his boat's starboard tank.

"Hey, you guys been out fishing?" Sam shouted. "Catching anything or just drowning baits?"

Dag hopped on the dock and embraced Sam. "Yeah, caught a few. A few always get off. You know the routine, Unc."

"Sure do, that's why I sell hardware. Tim, Dag, you boys have been away too long," Sam said as he walked and threw a switch to turn on the pumps and he smiled. "Just like a woman, you always got to turn the pump on. We could buy some fresh fish if you got it? Trade it off for fuel?"

"All, well, we release them," Dag lied. "You know how Dad is."

"Yeah. So, you busy with charters?" Sam inquired.

"Not too. Getting a few here and there. Trying."

"Mr. Chessman, how are you? You come and go so fast; we never have time to chat. I take it the wife's ok?"

"Fine and dandy, Sam." They shook hands. "We must make time to catch up."

"Getting sunburnt, Tim. Better watch out." Sam said as he turned and extended his hand to the silent Harry.

"What do you say, stranger? Harry, we see you about as much as we see your boys."

Harry didn't budge except for a barely polite wave as he said, "Give 'em the numbers for the diesel and dinghy gas. Get a case of oil."

Sam bit his lips as he walked with his nephews into the store, "Never changes, does he?"

"Dad's dad. Just that," Dag explained.

"I think he feels the island's against him. That isn't quite true. Come in some time, we'll chat over chilled greenies."

"Count on that, Unc," Dag said as he passed the case of oil to Cheesy.

"Yeah, me too," Tim smiled, "And Mia, you know she's back? But we've all been working to get the place back in shape, up and running again. *Sassy* was having problems."

"Yes, I heard both from Kalaloo, I think. About your boat and your sister."

"Hey, wait," Sam turned, "take some beers on me."

Dag opened the cooler and grabbed two Heinekens.

"Thanks."

"Take one for your father."

Tim went to the soda cooler and grabbed two club sodas.

"Oh, on the wagon again? No wonder he's grouchy. Cheesy, too?"

They did a tap toast, and they drained the bottles in one continuous gulp. Dag wiped his mouth and shrugged, "Like I said, Unc, Dad's Dad."

With practiced movements, they came off the dock with grace and style. All the crew, except Harry, who was again at the helm, stood at ease, hands laced behind their backs.

Sam let go with a loud sigh.

The author and 19 kg wahoo off St. Thomas.

CHAPTER TEN

The next six weeks had five more four-day charters. Fish were plentiful, but Harry was remembering why he drank. The steady flow of fat, usually rude, customers drained his optimism. Half the days he traded off with Dag. One remained on shore and helped Cassy with that evening's barbecue at Curly's. Each got their share of together time.

On the off days, they sold the fish and relaxed when *Sassy* didn't require maintenance, but she always needed maintenance. Cheesy would appear just after dawn and change the oil and filters. His hands were the neatest and seldom did he foul the bilge. Part of the deal, he'd stay and enjoy the offered breakfast. More than a few days, Verena accompanied.

The crew was savoring an early September morning with coffee and scones Verena had baked. The short wave held their attention with reports of another Israel-Palestine problem.

"Well, made it through another bunch of assholes, huh, Cheesy?" Harry casually remarked, blowing at his hot coffee.

"Dad, those 'assholes' are digging us out of debt," Tim reminded.

"Yes indeed. Debt that other assholes put us in! Hard work being nice and smiling all the time," Harry confided.

"For you, smiling is work," Cassy held up her hands. "I've washed enough dishes. Those last guys ate like bottomless pits."

And I've washed enough bedding," Mia interjected and then gleefully snapped her fingers. "But they tipped well."

"I'm thinking your new Sunset Bay tank top had more to do with the tip than the four blues we hooked for them."

"Whatever it takes," she smiled coyly.

"Hey, didn't I teach you better…?" Cassy prodded.

"Shh, weather's coming on," Harry shushed them. "It's that time of year again. Keep an ear tuned for our coordinates."

All remained silent. The middle of September was when the big ones came off Africa. It was time to pay attention to the storm track predictions. Each year was different, but the ocean was definitely warming. Harry and Cheesy had kept detailed logs since they started working together. Water temperatures, moon phase, wind, all were logged on each charter with species, hookups, boatings, and bait types. When they'd started keeping records, twenty-three years before, the water on the average was five degrees cooler. The warmer water confused fish migration cycles and supposedly increased storm intensity.

The last violent storms had been Ivan in '04 and Emily in '05. Both clobbered Grenada and her set of islands to the south, but spared Union. They survived both with no serious damage. There was always clean up after, but that was part of the deal, living in the Caribbean. Harry had ridden Ivan out alone, with *Sassy* on her mooring. No matter how much each begged to experience the tempest firsthand, Cassy wouldn't permit him to have the boys at sea.

She, the children, and the Chessmans made a party of it. It was common sense to leave your vessel in a blow. Cheesy had taken one of their moorings for their yacht, *Moonchild*. Harry stayed in constant radio contact.

There were always squalls and tropical depressions to contend with. Cassy hated the term tropical depression. Every island resident was tensed, depressed, out of sorts after the onset of the storm season.

They all recited it after Cassy started the rhyme, "June too soon, July standby, August must, September remember, and October all over."

With global warming, October wasn't the end anymore. They'd had ballbuster gales in late November. Even one at Christmas; it was blowing thirty-five. Gales rarely increased to the force of a hurricane, but that didn't soothe frayed nerves. Listening to weather reports three times a day, for months, kept everyone on edge.

Sunset Bay was always prepared. Harry knew the wrath of storms from growing up in Florida. It was the same with Cassy. Their house was wood, but strong, tied together with the best methods. Every window and door could be quickly shuttered. As prescribed by the old-timers, the lower bathroom, usually for the guests, was attached, but outside, protected between the house and the hillside. That bath was all concrete blocks with a slab roof. If the storm progressed from bad to worse, it was their panic room, where they would hide. In almost thirty years, they hadn't had to use it.

The BBC reported: "Tropical depression Francis might upgrade to a tropical storm by tomorrow. Present position is latitude 10.5 and longitude 55; course is north of west. Three more depressions coming off of Africa have formed; Gertrude, Horace, and Ingrid. Next broadcast at five PM GMT."

"Well, that's some relief, this one should run north of us," Harry sighed. "Sounds like this will be one of 'those' seasons where we got to worry."

"Hope so. Just about have everything finalized for an IGFA

sanctioned tournament for the third weekend of November," Tim said. "I'm calling it a Thanksgiving Tourney in Paradise."

"I thought it'd be for Halloween," Dag countered.

"Competition with St. Lucia. Besides, the moon is five days past full for ours. Should be a good time," Tim replied. "Wait a minute; I had some posters printed. They're in my bag on the boat. I'll get them."

"Go for 'em; me, I like the fishing before the moon," Dag offered.

"Before, after, don't make a damn," Harry scorned. "Tell them Cheese; everything with fishing is skill, presentation, and technique. Moon don't mean shit."

"Harry, tone it down a bit," Cassy reminded.

"Yeah, Harry, somebody ought to show you the moon," Mia said as she bent over and pointed at her butt. "Come, on mom, let's get this cleaned up. After that, we have the day off."

"Until lunch and dinner," Cassy sighed.

"More fish on the barbie," Cheesy recommended. "Me and Verena will tend it. You two, take a break."

"That girl! Between the weather and her dramatics, the government, the people hating our guts, and me not drinking," Harry whistled, "it's taking its toll."

"And you are a much better man for it," Verena chimed. "It is the hard times that define our character. More histrionic for us, mind you. Most of what we have is our sailboat. Don't want to lose that to Mama Nature."

Dag soothed her, "I checked all the moorings, as long as your cleats hold your home is safe. But we'd rather you're here with us. You know that, Verena."

"You are such a sweet man, Dag. Yes, hopefully, this season will amount to a pile of erroneous reports, like previous years," Verena replied.

Changing the subject, Tim reappeared holding one of the tournament posters. "What do you think? Nice photo of our boat with the blue jumping.

The poster circulated through the group. All agreed it was a great photo. "I think I remember that day," Harry tilted his head and pondered, "96 or maybe July 97?" He scratched his head.

"Nope, pure Photoshop," Tim explained. "These days, with a bit of computer skill, we can combine a few photos. That one is a composite of at least three different charters." Tim had a gloating smile. "This is the first of our annual Sunset Bay tournaments. Going to become a re-Union event. Get it, re-Union?"

Harry scrutinized the poster, "Yeah, yeah, the First Annual Sunset Bay Billfish Tourney, IGFA Sanctioned. And you did this photo with some new-fangled computer techniques?"

"Yes sir, technique and skill. Speaking of which, you ought to love these next guys coming in for a full week. They want to fly fish."

"Hell, been doing that for a while, Tim," Harry came back. "Fact is, we got a record dorado and a king on very light tackle"

"We know," Tim and Dag rang in unison.

"These guys are staying for a week hoping to hook into a few blues," Tim said.

"Hope they don't mind breaking some tackle," Harry calmly stated. "They'll probably hook into one, but bringing it to the boat for a leader touch is another thing."

"Our job is only getting them where they can get a hookup," Tim reminded. "We got the teasers and this is big billfish season."

"In CR, I've been backing down and tagging a few for the señores. Getting good at it."

"Well, truth be told, I like the sport of it, huh, Cheesy?" Harry confessed, "Gives the fish a chance. But they're building rods with that space-age stuff; it'll twist into a knot before its break."

"They pay more for that ultra-light tackle than good deep-sea gear. Never meant to put food on the table," Dag surmised. "But we, Sunset Fishing, are all about catch and release. Billfish anyway."

"Sportsmen, they pay for the thrill while we just change the oil," Cheesy offered. "Me and the missus are off. Thanks for a delightful morning."

"Yeah, let's get at the oil change before the sun gets too high," Dag said.

Cheesy smiled a broad, toothy grin he reserved only for the St. Claire family. "Done, done, and done. The old oil is in the buckets on the grass beside your dock. You're welcome." He tipped his hat as they headed to their skiff.

^^^^^^^^^

A storm is always brewing somewhere. Hurricanes form in the Atlantic because of unstable easterly winds coming off the Sahara Desert. Conflicting wrinkles of east-west hot, dry winds competing with north-south heavy, wet weather bands create tropical waves. Strength and duration depend on the prevailing conditions. Once the conditions become unbalanced and permit the moisture to rise, thunderstorms form. Too often in the Caribbean's late summer months, these tropical waves undulate with a circular motion causing a hurricane.

Inside Scarbeaux Hardware, Sam was conversing with the developers whom he considered his friends. Bruno Van Gell occupied his throne behind his roll-top. Sam uncomfortably stood with his arms crossed, looking out at the bay.

"Come on, Sam, don't hold back," Bruno said. "What's the status of our project? Is it a go or are we still searching for another island to construct our multimillion-dollar hotel and subsidiary businesses?" The pale, bearded man sat with a clenched jaw smirk knowing his financial syndicate was always looking into other islands.

"Everything is going okay," Sam nervously reassured.

"Good?" Van Gell scratched his head. "Do we have a deal? Let me guess; not yet, but soon. Samuel, in my reckoning, that is not good." Van Gell pointed to one of his men and was brought a bottle of water and a face towel from an insulated backpack. "Well, Sam…"

"Mr. Van Gell, can't tell you much more than everything looks positive. The government set a time limit for my sister and her family to repay all monies due by December thirty-first. They owe more than a quarter-million US."

"The clock never stops ticking." The white-shirted man took a few sips of the water, then dampened the towel and wiped his face. "I have investors dissatisfied with the outcome of our last negotiations. If I must delay construction again, and miss yet another tourist season, I'm afraid that this deal will entirely fold."

"Mr. Van Gell, you know the residents of the bay have until the end of the year," Sam reiterated. "I can't move that deadline up."

"Yes, nothing you can do with the court's decree, but I had the distinct impression you were going to, hmm, assist with their failure," he said snidely. "Sources tell me they have numerous fishing charters. In your local lingo, what's up with that, Sam?"

"Okay, they've been working, but that ain't, ah, will not get them out of debt. They need a pile of money. They're getting five thousand for a week. Subtract expenses, fuel, maintenance, wages, food; they might put three thousand towards what's due. That's nothing. They can't make the payoff."

"There's a few months left. Something can always happen. The storm season is forming," Van Gell nodded to his men. "We're taking my motor yacht, *Temptress*, to Puerto Rico."

"Hard to tell where those things will go. Might go north, straight into the Atlantic, or head to Florida. Hardly ever come through here. Better to take your motor cruiser south. Storms never go south."

"Never say never. Maybe we'll get lucky.' The man in the chair forced a smile, "Some natural redevelopment." Van Gell stood. With one gesture, all headed out the door. "I'll return when this storm season is finished," the boss said. "Sam, I'm counting on you to make this happen."

"It will, Mr. Van Gell. I'll get it done," Sam promised.

^^^^^^^^^^

The temporary respite from charters was over and the St. Claires were back to work beginning with another airport pick up. This one took extra shuttles and things went slower than usual. That frustrated Harry, who was running low on patience, especially for tourists. Three anglers arrived, each with a large suitcase, a tube for fishing rods, and a sizable tackle box between them.

This charter might be different, Harry thought; these appeared to be men who loved to fish. The three were in shape; looked like they worked out at a gym every day. All wore the same blue short-sleeved, chambray shirt with 'Team Wahoo' embroidered on the pocket. Harry did a quick assessment and realized he'd have to keep an eye on his daughter. They were handsome and looked like they had what almost every woman desired, money.

Sassy's crew exchanged knowing glances, and whispered odds on which of the trio would be the first to chum over the side. Dag took the wheel while Tim and Harry continued the pleasantries. Cheesy hung back and videoed the beginning of this charter. Three charters previous, that group had persuaded him, with a sizable, prearranged tip, to produce a rough diary of everything that happened. Cheese, the entrepreneur, with Tim's assistance had convinced each following charter that for five hundred they would have plenty of video minutes to edit into a superb journal.

Once all were aboard, introductions progressed amid a circle jerk of handshakes. Carlos was a tall, six-foot Latin with high cheekbones, raven black curly hair above dark, piercing eyes. Slightly out of place was the ebony handlebar mustache with waxed ends on a man probably under thirty years. It was obvious there would be little common about this trio. Carlos hailed from Guatemala and no stranger to blue water fishing. Guatemala was often characterized as the marlin capital of the world. But so were Costa Rica, the American Virgins, and Venezuela.

Jason, an African American, was stocky, muscled, and the youngest of their new clients. Immediately, Tim was comparing their flexed biceps in jest. Jason admitted he was not as experienced as his companions. That's why he'd signed on, to catch several big ones. This would be a test of his stamina, and he felt up to it.

The elder of the group, aged by his receding hairline, was Duncan Kelley, and he appeared to be in charge. A red-haired Irishman, with a strong Boston accent, also had a chiseled physique. The quality wrist chronometers, bracelets, and chains told Tim these guys were in the high six-figure bracket or more. Tim smiled to himself, remembering what he'd said; the scorecard in business was the bank account - always the number of digits ahead of the decimal.

Duncan had made the arrangements with Sunset to build camaraderie through a personal contest. Although a few years apart, they each had a desire for fairly safe risks and had met while taking a cost-efficiency post-grad program. All belonged to the same university fraternity, Zeta Beta Tau, at Wisconsin. They'd booked seven days and wanted to start as soon as possible.

"I thought we could forego lunch and seeing your lodgings. I'm certain everything will be more than adequate. We came to fish. Our plan is to fish hard, drink, and pass out after dinner. Can we stow our bags up forward and motor directly to the drop? Your website said it wasn't far," Duncan asked.

Carlos explained, "We've got our own private tournament planned with a sixty K purse. We each threw in thirty. Ten for the biggest fish in weight, ten for the most fish boated, and ten for biggest on the fly rod, which will hopefully be a huge, smoking blue."

"Yes, we saw your streaming videos. Wow, the blue your son pulled in was massive. You estimated at over six-hundred," Jason exchanged. "I'm the new kid, still proving myself." His demeanor was cool and calm, "Spent a good bit of money and time learning the fine art of presenting a streamer to billfish. All virtual, as you might guess."

He continued as he openly gawked at quaint Clifton's waterfront lined with coconut palms. "I've been to the Keys a few times, but found that area more barren and more hedonistic than to my liking. Had a few hookups, but this is what I've always imagined as the tropics."

"Yeah, J's not a drinker," Carlos added. "Those Key West characters can weird you out. Speaking of drinkers, Dunc and me, we could handle a beer or two."

Cheesy was quick to hand Heinekens from the cooler. The Sunset Bay crew drank water as they rounded Miss Irenes Point heading straight west into the cobalt Caribbean. The sportfisher was stocked with sizable ballyhoo and mullets. Tim and Harry fell into the usual comfortable banter while rigging the rods.

"Figured, if it's all right with you," Duncan addressed Harry, "we'd get wet, so to speak. Not waste much of today. Interested in seeing what you can bring up for us to play with."

Harry yawned, "I recommend getting some rest now, while you can. We plan to keep you busy. Lots of good-sized tuna lately, some big, thirty plus kingfish, and some big sails with a smattering of blues."

"Been hot here? I mean; you've been hooking up some blues?"

"Oh, dear me, yes. One of the best seasons ever." Cheesy extolled. "In our last three charters we've raised well over twenty and... and I must say that at least one marlin was tagged and released by each angler, plus they hooked numerous wahoo. The wahoo are running now."

"Wahoo! Wahoo!" Jason cheered. "What a name for a fish, wahoo. I love it! I thought my buds were joking when they suggested Team Wahoo."

"Wait 'til you hook into a nice one. Those blighters like to go deep and stay there," Tim fell into his UK accent.

"I really miss the salt air," Carlos mused. "I was raised in Livingston, just south of Belize, on the Bay of Honduras. Great fishing when I was growing up, but it's fallen off sharply in the last decade. We used to have ten hookups with billfish every day. I left at 18 for the university. Each summer, less and less."

Harry nodded in agreement. "Our local St. Vincent government does a decent job with the Coast Guard of patrolling and keeping out the pirate long-liners. Those guys take everything. Personally, I think they're worse than the gillnetters."

"Just as bad anyway," Duncan concurred. "We read you were catch and release. Only trophies are the photos."

"Yes, it keeps us here," Cheesy said. "Unorthodox life, and all that. If we kill all the fish, well, then we'd be like all the other boneheads. We definitely release the bills, but some yellowfin and wahoos we take home for dinner."

Dag entered, "You know, it really depends on the fish. Some fight 'til there's no life left in them. Got to respect that. No sense releasing them to be shark bait."

"A real styling existence you have here." Jason sighed, "Man, all we see is gray; skies and buildings, airports, and hotels." He rubbed his hands together. "This is gonna be great."

"What do you do that keeps you in such drab climes?" Cheesy

inquired.

"Techs. I'm an automotive designer in Detroit. Jay does security and Duncan is a quantity surveyor. We all met at the same grad school program and coincidentally were in the same frat house at different eras."

"Here's to you!" the crew toasted with their water bottles.

"Here's to fish, big fish, and bigger fun!" Duncan cheered.

"And the sea conditions?" Carlos requested.

"Lads, I think you've pulled some smooth days," Harry gave the weather report. "There are two storms moving north that have sucked the breeze from here. It should be fairly flat."

Duncan slid away from the group and joined Dag at the helm, "Hello, I take it you're one of the sons."

"Yes sir, only two of us," Dag smiled.

"Remarkable boat, Rybovich, circa mid-seventies when they first started glassing."

"Correct. 1975, my grandfather had it built and fished the Gulf Stream off the Keys. My father fished her down the chain until he stopped here. The way he tells it, the fishing was almost as good as my mother. We take good care *Sassy*." He extended his hand, "Dag."

"Duncan Kelley. You're from here?"

"When I was a kid and people asked me that, I'd say I commuted daily from NYC," Dag grinned. "Born and raised. I just got back from fishing in South and Central America, learning different techniques.

"Oh, I loved it in Venezuela before all this political strife. We bonefished at Los Roques; brought up a few blues, and a few sails just north of there."

"Yeah, well, ah, piracy has been awful down that way," Dag complained. "Real bad. About two years ago I moved up to Punta Arenas. I usually didn't have to go that far off the coast."

"I like to fish the structures, you know, seamounts and canyons. Like up in the Virgin Islands." Duncan tried to sound experienced. "But damn, it seems always rough up there."

"Can't say that I've ever been up that way. Most of my fishing has been along the north coast of South America and western Central. That's only been a few years. The rest have been right here, on this boat.

"You're the local expert?"

"No, that would be Harry, my father, and Cheesy. Isn't much they haven't seen and hooked over the years."

The wind died, and the sun was scorching. Everyone sought shade except Tim bathed in SPF 90 under a broad-brimmed hat. He rode as the lookout in the tower. Their clients switched off, climbing up for as long as they could endure the bright heat.

Each angler was asked what bait rig they preferred. All three shrugged and said to give them what worked. The tunas had hit ballyhoo strung with plastic skirts. While two anglers drained the beer supply, it became a stellar day as all three boated two nice tunas.

Cheesy rigged the biggest mullet and added ten ounces of barrel lead to keep the bait well below the surface. About four, well-baked and ready to head in, Jason got his final turn in the chair. The two anglers who drained the beer supply were busy flashing drunken grins.

Muttering a sober, "Wahoo, wahoo," Jason got his wish and hooked what felt like a submarine. The fish surfaced for half a minute flashing its side stripes and then dove.

Harry was the first to describe the catch. "Ah, Jason, I'm thinking you got lucky and hooked a big daddy wahoo. You're in for a fight. It ain't coming up easy. That's what wahoos do, they sound, go straight down." He laughed with another of his practiced lines, "I think that's where the name comes from; the first guy who landed one shouted wahoo!"

The usual repartee of pump and reel started from all the spectators. The same routine was continuing an hour later with little line gained.

"Better work on more arm curls, buddy," Carlos chided his friend. He and Duncan were slurring words and mashing their sentences together.

"Slick, come on, haul that bugger in. I thought you said you could press four hundred? Lift that fish straight up." Duncan and Carlos knelt on either side of the chair and drunkenly cheered. "Wahoo! Wahoo! Wahoo!"

"Some say it's the best-eating fish," Carlos provoked. "Don't pretend you're concentrating and can't talk. You're embarrassed the fish is getting the best of you," they teased.

In a series of gasps, Jason choked out, "Fuck you, I'll be one ahead in overall catches starting tomorrow." And he started gasping the 'wahoo chant' and pumped the rod and reeled like a fanatic. It still took another half-hour before Cheesy skillfully slid the gaff under the fish's head and jerked it up and onto *Sassy*.

Jason collapsed in the chair. His arms felt like jelly and he could barely mutter, "Wahoo, wahoo." But the satisfied smile said it all. "I'll be ready tomorrow, suckers," he roared. "Uh-huh, one up on you mothers!"

Hanging on the scale, the fish moved the gauge to 46 kilos. Jason was back slapped and shook in celebration. "First fish over a hundred pounds. Just barely, but…"

Jason cut them off, "But I'm the new kid in town, and I got the most fish and biggest fish. Give me some water, please." Someone handed him a chilled bottle while Duncan found the deck-wash bucket and made a smooth move. He cleverly filled it more than halfway and then drenched the worn-out Jason.

"Oh!" Jason yelled. "I'd usually bitch up a storm soaking my good threads, but hey, toss another on me. I'm tuckered."

The crew were all smiles. Like moms and wives, when the anglers are happy, everyone's happy.

The sportfisher motored in. As they rounded the point to Sunset Bay, the men woke from their self-imposed stupor and muttered a uniform, "Wow!"

After bathing and choosing beds, the fishermen found enough energy to sit at the two picnic tables. The sun was sinking into pinks, corals, and purples. The air was cooler, especially since they were damp from the showers and sunburned.

With the change in plans, Cassy had stayed home and was busy grilling chunks of the wahoo. Everyone was enjoying pieces raw with wasabi and soy that Mia served as appetizers.

"Never get this anywhere but here," Tim said. "The freshest of fresh. Wahoo is a very fragile fish. Have to eat it within two days. Doesn't ship well."

"What's the deal," Duncan nudged Dag. "All of you on the wagon? Are we breaking a taboo sucking down suds?"

"Nah, just dad," Dag replied. "He made a promise, so we made one also, won't drink to tempt."

"We aren't causing problems?"

"Hell no, we want you to get tuned up quick and fall asleep early. Less hassle for us," Dag laughed. "No, when we're in town, we'll share some rum, or if you guys can stay awake long enough for Harry to crash."

"Not tonight anyway," Duncan admitted. "Our asses are kicked. Long red-eye flight, sun, fish, sun, beer, sun. Wow, and Mia's your sister?"

"No, we just rent her. She's the maid," Dag chuckled. "Yep, Mia's the youngest. Watch out," he smiled and winked, "We're a protective family. We'll protect you from her."

The usual topic arose. "So, Harry, what's the biggest you've caught here?" Jason asked.

"Well…" Harry started.

Tim was quick. "823 on the town's scales, 1985. Right, Dad?"

"Yeah, hated to kill that one, but it was a tournament and won the guy a new pickup truck. South of here, off Grenada. Good fish, fought like hell. But, hey, we got plenty of big fish other than marlin."

"Dad got three ninety-pound bull dorados and a 565-pound bluefin tuna," Mia added indifferently as she brought two more beers.

"Sometimes I think blue marlin are overrated," Dag said.

"Over-fished," was Harry's comment

"That too, but I still get a bigger thrill of landing a dorado on spinning gear rather than cranking in a billfish," Dag explained.

"Fishing," Carlos was buzzed, "it's like, like a war between two dimensions…"

"Here we go again, inter-dimensional warfare," Duncan chuckled. "Carlos, do you have to?"

"No, really think about it." Carlos slurred, "The fish are swimming around in the wet dimension."

"Well, yes, that's obvious," Cheesy agreed.

"And we lure them and drag them into the dry world. Sometimes they're lucky to be returned to their watery dimension. Other times, they get eaten. We are their ET's. Like UFO abductions."

"Have you been smoking that local stuff?" Harry guffawed. "He got any more of those, ah, interesting perspectives? This is gonna be quite a week."

"I was talking to your son. Says you fished all the way down from the States," Duncan asked. "Where do you think is the best?"

"Right there." Harry's arm shot out to the west beyond Rapid Point.

"That good, so special?" Jason was lying on the lawn, looking up at the evening sky.

"Oh, I fished the North Drop-off at St. Thomas, and the edge of the Saba Bank in the early seventies. Right now, where we took you today is better than those places were back then. Eat and sleep, fellows. I'm calling it quits after dinner. You said you want to see the sunrise over the blue Caribbean. To accommodate your request, we gotta get up and out at five. The girls are packing breakfast with bottles of coffee and lunch sandwiches. We'll be packing more beers from now on." Harry winked, slapped Carlos on his shoulder, and took the stairs to his bedroom.

^^^^^^^^^^

Fishing is all about attracting fish. That's from where the word 'lure' is derived; lure the fish to you. Standing on shore casting live bait or a fancy 'lure' into a pool or stream, it's all about presentation. On a motor cruiser, miles away from the shore, in the middle of the vast blue sea, it is about attracting or bringing the game fish from the depths. The sound of the props is the first wake up call. Usually, a captain will steer the boat in a wide, half-kilometer circle or an elongated figure eight, again and again, to ring the fish dinner bell.

To get a quick response, if fish are nearby, some fishermen drop a chum slick, fish guts mixed with vegetable oil. The oil stays on the surface and marks the spot. They work their boat in a circle around that chum slick. Harry didn't bother with the stinky stuff, too messy, and often would start a puking convention.

At daybreak, their boat was rolling two miles west of Union, surrounded by all the shades of blue that remained of the previous night. The sea was flat with just a slight refreshing breeze. Jovial spirits prevailed among clients and crew. Dag kept the engines plowing at eight knots, calling the fish for breakfast.

In the natural food chain order of things, bigger fish look for the sparkles and sounds of smaller fish. Years ago, fishermen started increasing their catch by using attraction devices, known as teasers. Artificial, big, hookless baits replicate schools of fingerlings (finger-size fish) fish. Harry stocked large wooden hookless lures with mirror pieces glued on. The big decoys flashed as they spun in the prop wash, usually set to follow two waves back. A foot-long fake bait would quickly have the mirrors smashed by either bill swipes or chomps.

Like everything, sportfishing teaser lures evolved into extra-large lures cast from multi-colored reflective plastics that made an enormous bubble wake from a concave nose. Duncan produced two ultra-modern teasers from the team's tackle box. One of the teaser's hollow chambers had ball bearings that made a dinner bell rattle noise. He packed a second, vented chamber with crushed ballyhoo.

"Out on the open sea, you must bring the fish to you," Duncan muttered.

"If you say so, you're the boss. But there's no guarantee this will stay out there for long. A good teaser is meant to get hit," Cheesy assured.

"Don't worry, Mr. Chessman, that's what we brought them for. If they do the trick, they're worth the money."

They would troll regular deep-sea gear out and back, hooking nice fish, nice wahoos and sizable yellowfin tunas. At a certain time or distance, Harry would give a nod and the heavy stuff would be reeled in.

The fishermen had their saltwater fly gear ready and stood poised at the transom. All eyes watched for a fish to appear in the wake behind a teaser. Harry had his hands on the port side mirrored bait and Cheesy minded the starboard. Once they raised a fish, they'd pull in the hookless lure and the fly fisherman would feed out his shiny streamer. Dag would cut the engines at the precise moment the fish was about to hit.

It's called fly fishing because of the reel and the long thin rod originally with hand tied 'fly' baits. It was more basic, purist, and damn difficult. The extreme light-tackle meant heavy-duty fights. The rod and reel were so expensive, they should have been gold plated. Harry never had an angler stand and flick a dry fly. Saltwater fish wanted smaller saltwater fish to eat and didn't suck bugs from the surface.

If they wanted to know the purist point of view, per Harry, use a damn handline. Forget about the rod and reel together. As basic as it gets. The line is wrapped around a spool, locals called a yo-yo. If you were onshore, you threw out the line like the cowboys worked a lasso, whipping it over your head. At sea, you just dropped it over the side, either anchored or drifting. But Harry had somehow discovered the patience and resolve. He kept his mouth shut, opinions to himself, and counted the angler's money.

"Looks like you've done this before?" Jason asked Harry.

"For your information, Sunset Bay holds the Caribbean record for a 44-pound dorado…" Harry started.

Tim finished not so much interrupting as much as reciting, "And a 38-pound kingfish on flies."

"No kidding!" Carlos was astounded

"What was it like, bringing in a dancing gold dorado on a fly rod?" Duncan asked Dag.

"Brought in many on spinning gear. Big thrills. This one was great to see, but I didn't catch it." Dag declared, "It was my sister Mia. She caught them both."

"Really?!" That shocked all three fishermen.

"Impressed the hell out of me," Harry said and continued in a mutter, "still dealing with that. Mia can fish."

They all took a turn climbing onto the tower with Tim to scout for fish. Jason spotted one in the stern wakes and elbowed Tim.

"Dag, got one about twenty meters back. Oh, oh, it's moving

fast. Dad, Cheese, get ready to pull in the teasers."

Seconds later the bill was whipping at the port teaser as Harry pulled in the line hand over hand.

Dag nodded to everyone and cut the throttles. Carlos fed out a long yellow feather streamer. The billfish made a pass, but didn't hit the streamer.

"Wait, wait, leave it there. Let out some more line," Harry advised. "Dag, goose the engines a bit."

The sportfisher lurched forward and then Dag pulled back the throttles again. The streamer was visible about thirty feet behind. No one said a word. They just watched and got to see the bill shoot straight up from the depths as it took the bait.

"Release the drag; let it take all the line it wants," Cheesy narrating while he continually filmed the action. "It's a sail!"

Carlos froze and watched the long fish stretch out and dance across the waves. With the engines idling, the only sound was the reel screaming out endless line. Dag eased into reverse to help close the distance. The game was to touch the six-foot leader attached to the mono line. That made it a catch. With a big fish, light tackle, and inexperienced fisherman, the fight wouldn't last long.

"It's a sail! Watch your drag!" Harry repeated the advice as the fish again leaped high, twisted its body while shaking its big-eyed head, and spit the hook.

"That's what we came for," Duncan said as he patted Carlos on his shoulders.

"Good fight, Carl," Jason called from the tower. "Better luck next time."

"Close, but no cigar," Carlos moaned.

"A bit of advice, fellows," Harry counseled, "no drag. Feed the line out and keep it taut between your fingers. On this tackle, you don't want the fish to feel anything. Feed him so he swallows the hook. This ain't like the big rod and reel stuff; you can't set the hook. The fish has got to swallow it."

"Aye, aye, Captain Harry, lesson learned the hard way," Carlos replied.

The routine began again; the teasers were set as Dag motored ahead.

The private fly fishing tournament continued through four hot, nearly windless days. The billfish seemed to boycott; but each angler was happy as they'd been busy. Optimism prevailed with sunny days and relatively calm seas. Each hooked at least ten dolphins and had landed two, all reasonable size. Carlos landed the biggest at eleven kilos. The weight didn't matter except as a side bet, unless the contest finished in a tie.

Jason sulked on the side bench, perturbed his latest sparkling golden bull dorado had somehow broken the leader only six meters from the transom. If he could have cranked in only a bit more, Cheesy, always at the ready, could have touched the leader or even gaffed the fish to give him the lead.

"Duncan Kelley steps up. Folks, it's his turn at the transom." Carlos announced in a sportscaster's tone. "Day five of the first Team Wahoo saltwater international fly fishing tournament extraordinaire, Kelley has boated two fish, but so have his valiant opponents. The contest remains a stalemate. Can he do it; land another?"

A school of flying fish broke off through a wave to the west. Tim had the area focused with his binoculars. "Dag, about ten degrees to port," he directed, and never taking the glasses off that spot. "Got a bill, port side, about twenty meters back!" Tim shouted. "Finally got what you've been waiting for."

The boat dropped to idle as Duncan kissed his silver Mylar streamer and said, "Do your job. Come on, fishie! Make my day!" He fed out his streamer watching for any sign of the big fish. Suddenly the reel was being stripped of line. Shocked, Duncan staggered, fumbling with the reel, trying to get control.

Cheesy grabbed the angler around the waist. "Try not to get ruffled. Control your breathing."

His lightweight, nine-foot rod was bent until the rod tip touched the sea. "Who the fuck are you, Cheesy the Zen Master?" Duncan gasped. "I thought you were making me famous with the GoPro?"

"No, but I know what works; control your anxiety before you control that fish. This one's got nice size. Don't worry, Jason's keeping track with the digital."

Duncan gulped some breaths, calmed, and let out more line. He found better footing as he wedged against the port stern corner.

From the tower, Tim yelled, "Looks like you hooked a white marlin. Plenty of room to work him. You know the routine, keep the line from touching the gunwales."

They felt the boat slip into gear and Dag began a slow wide turn to port, following the marlin. "Everyone, eyes wide open. Follow where the line enters the water. I can't see that well from this station."

"I'll steer from up here," Tim said.

"Yeah, I'm coming up there with you. Better for the dramatic wide action shots," Jason yelled. "Get that bill to dance!"

"Oh sure," Duncan replied in a stern voice. "I would if I could. But better for me to dance to the bank with your money. Ha!"

"I'm climbing up there, too," Carlos joined.

The long, slender fish shot out of the sea thirty meters off the stern and danced for a few seconds. It showed only a black dorsal fin and no stripes.

"Are you sure it's a marlin and not a sail?" Duncan asked.

"Absolutely," Dag replied, "because there's no sail, only a thin dorsal. Don't concern yourself with what it is; land the mother!"

They were all excited except Harry. He sat in the fighting chair and stayed out of the confusion. Dag and Cheesy were shoulder to shoulder with Duncan. The rod stayed bent, but as Tim backed down, Duncan regained some line.

"Play him; don't worry about a thing. Tim's better at maneuvering than I am," Dag whispered. "You got this one, just take it easy."

Duncan started cranking like a madman as the marlin turned and rushed toward the boat.

Twenty minutes later, after more than a hundred digital close-ups, Cheesy stretched and touched the marlin's bill and snipped the leader to free the fish. Amid back slaps and handshakes, Duncan rose from taking a bow and bear-hugged Cheesy.

"I don't know where that breath control shit came from, but it worked." He kissed the older Brit on the cheek. "That got me my first bill. I owe you, buddy."

"Think nothing of it," Cheesy mumbled and grinned, "Until, perhaps tipping time."

"That was something, yahoo, Team Wahoo! I don't fucking care if it cost me ten K, watching everyone work to boat that fish. Hell, it was fucking worth it!" Jason was exuberant. "Let's go into town to celebrate. Dinner's on us. That will give your lovely wife and daughter some time off."

"Don't know how to explain this, but every dinner is on you," Harry beamed. "Count me out. I'm sure Cassy would love a night off. She won't, no, she won't want to make the trip."

"Come on, Harry, I'd like to hear more of your stories," Duncan cajoled.

"Plenty of time for that over the next two days," Harry said. "Not me. Tonight will be for R and R, not as young as I used to be. But hey, take my kids. With you and them gone, that'll make it better for snoozing. More stories tomorrow."

"What do you say?" Duncan looked at the crew.

"I'd love to but need to spend some quality time with my wife," Cheesy backed out. "You understand. But you can use my skiff rather than take *Sassy* all the way around. Drop me off and come get me in the AM."

"I'm there. We've been so busy lately; I could enjoy a night out on the town. It'll be no problem talking Mia into it," Tim agreed.

"You can count on that and me too. Feel good to blow off a bit of steam," Dag smiled.

The Chessman's skiff was tight with six. It was good that evening was flat calm as they rounded Queensbury Point and saw Clifton's streetlamps.

The talk was of fishing until Mia said, "Enough with this macho shit. Cool it. I don't know about my brothers, but I'd rather hear about places where you're from or where you've traveled. Believe it or not, we fucking live, breathe, and eat fishing. Forget it for tonight, huh? Give me a fucking break!"

"Okay, okay, got you," Duncan placated. "Where do you recommend?"

"Well, we don't have many options. Mom's restaurant, Curly's, is the best. Plus, it's guaranteed they'll That's a really nice ut up with our shit talk," Dag said. "There's Fred's or Lulu's, but at Curly's, you just got to tip... tip well. This is all included on your charter tab. Mom will enjoy a rare evening alone at home, but believe me, Chef Honoré will put a smile on your face that starts at your belly. We called from offshore, he's waiting with barbecue, pulled pork, and definitely fish with the coldest beer. They've chilled two crates of greenies in the freezer, so there's plenty of brews to go around."

"Sounds good," Carlos and Jason echoed as the skiff found the dock. The walk along deserted Main Street took only minutes to find Granma's.

"It must have been great growing up here," Duncan assumed.

"Yeah, sure, but small towns, small minds," Tim reacted. "That's kind of what our problem is now. Seems the island decided we should vacate our home and Sunset Bay for a hotel. Progress."

"I kind of know where you're coming from. I was lucky to get away from Guatemala. Beautiful where I grew up, but mucho problemas," Carlos interjected. "I miss it. You never had a car?"

"Harry wouldn't pollute," Mia replied. "It's okay to smoke

petrol on the sea, but we bicycled everywhere. Didn't come to town so much. No reason."

"All the local boys chasing…" Duncan started.

"There was no chase, because there was no chance," Mia cut him off. "Local boy, then local father, maybe a husband. And that'd keep this girl on this rock where she didn't want to stay."

"So, where have you…" Again, Duncan was interrupted.

Mia coughed and cleared her throat. "I own a sailing yacht, a luxury catamaran, chartering in the Lesser Antilles."

"This is mom's place, Granma's. Guess? Yep, it was our Granma Gretchen's restaurant," Tim bowed as a maître d. "Please make yourself at home."

The street in front of Granma's had the flair of the American old west with a hitching post and water trough originally for the donkey and bison carts, but now refreshed only the street dogs. The red sunset reflected off the front wall of thick, aged, golden bamboo. The awning that spanned the street-side also served as the hinged shutter that folded down at closing time.

The interior walls were a collage of sporting posters of West Indies Cricket greats or Manchester United players. Single bulb fluorescents illuminated the interior; one flickered seemingly to the beat of the continuous reggae. The group split and sat easily at two of the broad, wood tables. The far wall was also open to vent a wide grill. A tall, dark man, dressed in a white apron, wearing a pillowy chef's hat, nodded his head and spread his arms wide.

Honoré beckoned them to sit. "Great to see you all tonight. Glad you called ahead, Mr. Dag," he sighed, "You can see not many other customers out and about."

Jason walked over and extended his hand, "What's on the menu for tonight?" He wrinkled his face, "We've been eating a lot of fish this week."

"Well, the wife's got some curry goat back on the stove, but I'll tell you right off, it's spicy. And I'm ready to put some nice chicken on the barbecue. Was waiting for you to start so it don't dry out. And, fo' sure, we got some fish to grill." Honoré grinned, "Fish you might have hooked. Also have boiled green bananas, rice and beans, slaw salad, and flan for dessert."

Carlos joined and said, "Bring it all; my mouth is watering. Where's the beer?"

"I'll serve the drinks," Tim offered. "You all want beer? Got some good kill devil local rum."

Duncan ordered, "I'll try a Cuba Libre."

"Me too," came from Mia and Dag.

"What's that?" Jason asked.

"Rum and coke."

"You know what, I'm feeling good. Think I'd like to try a tame one, just a smidgen of rum, if you please."

"Oh, the boy's gonna get wild tonight," Carlos joked. "Haven't seen you have a cocktail since the end of our efficiency course."

"I'm being efficient," Jason nodded, "Damn efficient. We have two days remaining. Looks like a three-way tie."

"Wait a minute, I'm leading," Duncan shouted.

"You're only leading the fly rod division. Pardon me, but I have the biggest and most fish," Jason bragged. "Thus, a reason to p-a-r-t-y!" He slapped his thigh and started singing, "Get down tonight, get down tonight!"

"And he hasn't had a sip yet," Carlos laughed.

"How's the family Honoré? I know we haven't come around much since we've been back?" Dag asked.

The tall dark-skinned man shook his head, "No problem, no problem. I got eyes and ears and know what's happening out at Sunset. You all got your hands full. Mammie, come out and say hi." A slender, graying West Indian woman wearing a white headscarf came from the kitchen and said hello. "The wife is helping with her sweet hand. Wait 'til you taste that curry. You all been gone a while, years and years. Daughter Minnie is a dentist in Toronto. Believe that! And Scampy, he was accepted by the US Coast Guard. We real proud of the both of them."

"Hey, bartender," Duncan catcalled Tim with a whistle, "You think we're lightweights; another round if you please."

Mia suggested, "Would you like to try rum with our local coconut water?"

Jason was already grinning, "Sounds good."

"Fix me one, too," Carlos said.

Mia attended to those drinks while Tim divvied out beers and then joined Mammie in the kitchen to load the platters with food.

"Mia dear, how you be girl? Good to see you back. Vacationing?"

"Not quite, Mam, helping my parents."

"Heard about all their legal problems. Regular nest of wasps."

"Harry, Dad, probably caused it."

"No, the ways I hear it, I think Ban Franklin is behind it."

"Huh?"

"Ben Franklin. Money, girl, US money."

"Isn't that the root of all evil?" Mia smiled.

"One of the seven deadly sins. An' we got the other six here, too!" Mammie giggled.

As the meal progressed, talk centered on the guests and Tim's living abroad. Mammie tended their table with bowls and platters of steaming food while Honoré worked the grill. Rum and beer flowed as reggae was interspersed with some Jimmy Buffett in the background. During the evening, two other tables filled with local men sipping beers, eating barbecue, and conversing loudly. All the other local customers sprouted dreadlocks and knew the St. Claires, yet they exchanged no pleasantries.

"Hey, sweet mama, how 'bout getting us some service. We need more beers." One local approached and tapped Mia on the shoulder.

"Yeah, some service," came from the second table. Mia looked and saw Mammie was shoulder deep scrubbing pots and pans.

"Okay, always the waitress, just can't get away from it. What would you like?" Mia smiled.

"Beers all 'round."

"Bring that sweet thing over here, too." The rude comment wasn't missed.

"Good food huh, you guys satisfied? Maybe time to get a round for the road," Dag said to his table. The evening was getting a slight edge, a rough edge.

"Whatever," Jason said, grinning from the alcohol. "Still early."

"Not much else going on. Town's quiet," Dag reminded.

"Turn off this punk, white boatie shit music and play some Jamaican dub," the oldest dread shouted.

"Watch your mouth. You boys know I don't condone that language," Honoré returned.

"So, youse make dem whites feel at home, but not us?" Another at the dread table shouted.

"Why talk so? Where do you see whites? Nothing 'bout feeling… what? You didn't hear Jimmy Cliff and Peter Tosh minutes ago?" Honoré moved away from the grill. "You guys are dreads, not Rastas. Rastafarians love all."

"This isn't about feeling anything. If you want to talk so, go home and while you're there learn some home-taught manners," Mia announced as the rum moved her mouth.

"Yo, sweet ting. You should be friendlier. Don't talk so if you can't back up them words," the graying dread they knew as Foxy stood and approached Mia.

"Yo!" Mia shot back, "You should smell better! And you know us, we St. Claires never say anything, we can't back up!" Mia was pissed.

"Smart mouth, huh? Plenty ways to cure that," Foxy laughed and grabbed her arm.

Mia twisted away as Tim rose, ready for a confrontation. All the patrons started drunken, anxious movements. Honoré ducked back into the kitchen. Dag rose and got between his brother and sister and the dread Foxy, now backed by a few more of his friends.

"Whoa! What's wrong here? We're all Union Islanders. These are our guests. Please don't give them the wrong idea about our home," Tim said.

"This attitude stuff happens all the time. Beer flows, people get excited. Nothing to get upset over," Dag said to his anglers while two more dreads rose to confront Tim.

"You're her bros, right?" One said, slightly staggering, pointing wavering fingers.

"Yeah, you're Tony. You know me, all of us. Come on, man," Tim said, continuing to be diplomatic.

"We all know everybody," Tony slurred. "You know us, and we know you. But you didn't even say a hello, mon."

"Hello!" Mia cupped his ear and shouted.

"Your man, Honoré, here was just speaking about manners. That's plain disrespect."

"Please. Okay, you're right, we're wrong. Hello, really missed seeing you around. Everything good at home?" Mia asked her baby girl's voice. "Still dating your sheep?"

"Wise-assed white bitch! You livin' on the utter side, robbin' the island, and now, and now ya rubbin' our faces!" the eldest dread, Foxy, shouted.

"Listen, please, can we make amends with a round of drinks?"

"Nice, that would be nice, real nice," Tony slurred.

"As long as everybody, and I mean everybody, is drinking them somewhere else," Honoré required, standing arms crossed holding a big cricket bat. "I don't want no trouble, and I don't need no arguing. This is a friendly establishment, not a dive rum shop. In the future, if you carrying an attitude, carry it some other place. Hear me?" None of the dreads wanted to argue with the bigger man.

"Your family's a bunch of sissy, pussy asses," Foxy muttered to Tim.

"Hey, it's cool. Enjoy the last round. We're leaving," Tim said, wringing his hands together.

Dag made an exaggerated movement to look at his watch and motioned for the anglers to get a move on.

"Time to go if we're still planning be at the drop at daybreak. Let's go out to the boat."

"So, what's with you, nigger?" Tony, the dread, said loudly to Jason. "These white boys and the Rican, they letting you keep company with them? Or you carrying their bags, nigger?"

"Friend, you have mistaken me for someone else," Jason said calmly.

"We ain't mistaking nuthin'. You de nigger fo' dis crew," Tony kept at it. "Get me a cup of ice, nigger!"

"Come on guys, we've known each other our entire lives. What's up with the attitude, now? These are our guests," Dag said again. "Come on, don't give them the wrong impression of our island."

"Your island?" Another dread shouted. Everyone was standing. "Huh, might as well be, cause your mama and papa keeping de best for you, for you, Dog-boy! Leaving the rest of us to scrape."

"Looks like scraping hasn't been too good lately," Mia piped.

"I warned you, you smart-mouthed bitch!" Foxy made a move to grab at her again, but she moved aside and Tim slid in face to face.

"Boy, don't..." Foxy threatened.

Tim pointed his finger in the dread's face, "No! You don't! This is over."

"You always was a pussy ass, Tiny Timmy."

"Hey, let it go! This is all minor stuff. I'm not taking any offense. Whatever you got going on, I'm sorry for it, but me, my brother, and sister, and our friends have nothing to do with anything you're thinking. So, let it go."

"Don't peepee from bein' scared, Timmy," Tony laughed. He thrust his arms forward to push Tim, but the muscular St. Claire grabbed the man's extended arms and sharply pulled the dread across the table, noisily clearing it of plates and bottles. Two other dreads stepped up both holding empty beers. Tim rabbit punched both, crumbling them to the floor. Foxy reached for something in his pocket, but Mia smashed him across the face with a serving tray.

The melee was on. All the dreads still standing were moving in wielding bottles and chairs. With a grin, Jason gave the Tarzan yell, slapped one with his open left hand, and then landed his right, flat palm against the ribs, doubling him over so the locks were shaking as the man gagged up his beers. Jason wrenched the puking head backward and said, "You were very, very rude to me." Then he pulled the head down, kneed him in the face, sprawling him ass over teacups, knocking over the table.

Tony spit blood on Carlos, "Screw you, you fucking spic."

"Man, you're already down," Carlos answered.

"I said, screw you!" Tony tried to pull himself up against a chair.

"Not too smart to be bad talking while you're crawling around the floor." Carlos lifted the dread, looked him in his bloodshot eyes and slammed him with a right. It was so hard Tony bounced off the bamboo wall, rattling the building.

The other dreads put up their hands, palms out, showing they wanted no more of what had been dealt to their buddies. No more words were exchanged. Quickly, amid mumbles and grumbles, they lifted and carried out those that had fallen in the brief fight.

"Sorry for the mess," Dag said. "Honoré, my sincere apologies."

"Not you, them was spoiling for trouble." Mammie grinning while chewing on a fingernail said, "They found some. We'll clean up this mess," she moved her finger to her lips. "And if Cassy hears about this, it wasn't from us."

Each of the anglers presented Honoré and Mammie with a wad of bills amid handshakes and hugs, continually complimenting the delicious food and ambiance. They were all smiles as they took the quick walk to the skiff.

Once each carefully found their seat, Tim tugged the pull start and then twisted a few wires; the single bulb lamp atop the outboard came on. "Want people to see us," he said. "We only have a foot of freeboard, the top of the gunwales to the water, for you landlubbers. Don't jostle much, and we'll stay dry."

"You know those guys?" Duncan said to Dag.

"Went to school with them, not that they finished. Most, I think, now call themselves fishermen. They hustle, smuggle, mostly toking weed, and dreaming of better days they aren't willing or capable of working towards."

"But don't you see them all the time? I mean, it seems like a small place," Carlos asked. "Same shit back in Guat. I see guys who were school chums and didn't progress from smoking dope. Angry at everyone, never realizing they're only angry at themselves."

"Yeah, but we don't live here. We're just back because our parents are having some problems," Mia huffed. "That attitude, those fucking bad manners, dirty, unwashed, Marley wannabes, don't have a clue about anything. That's what drove me out of here."

"I don't understand," Carlos said and slid an arm around Mia's back. "You have a dream business, fantastic location, spectacular boat. What problems? These guys must be in the minority. Can't be many that dumb?"

"No, well, kind of, yes. A hotel wants to buy our bay. The island thinks we're cheating everyone by not wanting to sell. And we are kind of over the proverbial barrel with the government." Tim explained, shouting over the sound of the outboard as he revved it to round the point, heading away from the last streetlight.

A louder roar blasted from the blackness. A speedboat, darted alongside the skiff, maybe two meters off their port side. The speeder swerved and kicked up a wake that violently rolled the packed, flat-bottom boat.

"Holy shit!" Jason bawled, "Didn't they see our light? Wow, maybe they did and veered off at the last moment. Wow, I think we were lucky you had the light."

"Who was that? Kalaloo?" Mia screamed.

"Can't say, couldn't see, moving too fast," Dag answered as calmly as possible. "Took me by surprise. Yeah, you're probably right, Jason. They must have seen us and pulled away. Lots of big boats out here at night. Could have been Kal, but probably someone moving towards another island, maybe Canouan or St. Vincent."

"Running at night with no lights? That's both illegal and dangerous. Didn't he see our light?" Duncan gasped.

"Drunk or not paying attention. Somebody's always speeding around. Maybe don't want to be seen," Tim excused. "Lots of stuff moving from island to island, not paying customs duties."

From behind their skiff, the speeding boat appeared again; this time thundering along the port side, creating another wake that soaked the six and had four inches of water sloshing around their feet.

"Holy shit!" Jason bellowed. "This isn't funny." He moved and spewed out his dinner and drinks. The series of loud gags didn't help the situation.

"Bastard's playing with us," Dag said, holding onto Jason by the shoulders.

"Anything we can do?" Carlos asked.

Tim handed a plastic gallon jug with the top sliced off. "Use this to bail."

The speeding boat flashed on its bow lights and was flying

towards a direct head-on impact, but at the last instant spun away. This wake threw up the skiff's bow and almost flipped it. The St. Claires each grabbed an angler and held them in the small craft.

With an arm chop, Dag broke off their running light from the top of the motor. "I'll buy Cheesy a new one tomorrow. Everyone hold on tight, and keep quiet."

This time the bigger boat approached from the stern, slightly slower with more lights on what had to be on a radar mount. Within meters, the vessel spun and throttled up as it careened along the skiff's starboard side. The bigger boat's wake made it seem it'd brushed the skiff. Mia swung a paddle and smashed two of its sidelights.

"When you buy Cheese a light, get him a paddle for me," Mia breathed.

"Got to say, you're a gutsy woman," Carlos hugged her. "Smart move, Dag, might make it a little harder to see."

"Pull on the life jackets, just in case," Dag ordered. "This wasn't funny in the beginning and now, it's really pissing me off. Someone's going to pay heavily for this!"

"Okay, okay, they'll pay later," Tim cautioned as he steered closer to the shoreline. "I might have to get him a new prop; they probably won't see our profile against the darker island."

"In case?" Duncan muttered. "If he hits us, we'll be chum from his props. I saw three big outboards on it as they pulled away."

"Shh, quiet," Dag whispered. "In case he has shitty aim. If he wanted to hit us, we'd be lucky to be swimming now. Nah, he just wants to scare us, maybe flip us over. Don't worry, he doesn't want to scratch his gelcoat. Without a marker light, we might hide, or we might just become an accident."

"Yeah," Mia agreed in a whisper. "My money's it's the same assholes who were in Curly's. They don't have the courage for any more face to face. This is their idea of scare tactics. They're sitting out there waiting for us to make some noise so they can place us."

The boat sped by again and the skiff was rocked by the wake, but it was off in the distance and only its lights were visible. Tim continued to motor slowly until they could see the tall single bulb over their dock. He glided to the pier. Mia and Dag wrapped the cleats and helped their passengers.

Duncan, on his knees, kissed the dock, "We came for safe thrills." Everyone heard him sigh, "I guess that's what this was."

"Hey, ah, let's keep this to our group. No sense bringing Harry and mom in on this," Dag said. "We'll handle this later, in our own way."

"Yes, we will," Tim nodded. "And payback's a bitch. Tomorrow, when we get fuel, we'll see if any boats have lights broken. Hey, how about a nightcap? We have some greenies still on Cassy."

Carlos was holding Mia's hand, "Sounds like a plan. You grew up here with this tension?"

"Before we left," Mia answered squeezing the hand, "things weren't like this. It was calm, tranquil, boring. Now everyone's geared up because of greed."

"Man, oh, man," Jason added as he lay prone on the dock and washed his face with saltwater. "Those guys were as bad as Mississippi rednecks. Never thought I'd encounter racism here."

"Oh, it's not racism. Just plain stupidity," Dag replied. "It's easier for guys like them to blame anybody else why they aren't successful. Some will do anything for money. Sell anything."

"Drugs?" Jason gurgled as he washed his mouth with seawater.

"Sure thing, fortunes are built from white dust here. Before that, it was pot," Tim replied. "Most of the richest men in these islands made their fortunes smuggling something, now the get rich scheme is running coke."

"They don't care what happens to their island?" Duncan asked. "That shit is the ticket to destruction."

"What's the word, rationalization? Someone will bring it in, so it might as well be a local making the bucks," Mia countered. "His family does well, a few businesses spring up, hey, and everyone knows who does what here. Times change, the neighbors don't speak up, mostly out of fear."

"I could never understand that. You'd think they'd want to keep everything beautiful," Carlos reasoned.

"Your beauty makes them hate," Mia continued. "Once VCR movies began being rented, one movie was one movie too much."

"What?" Duncan questioned as he drained his beer. "Almost lights out for this fisherman."

"Soon as they saw someplace else, they wanted to be there, and not here," she explained. "See a gangster movie, they all are sporting gold chains, and then what does everybody want? Gold chains!"

"I remember seeing Robinson Crusoe," Tim laughed. "And all I wanted was to be rescued."

"You ever hear the joke about a man who dies and goes to Hell," Dag related. "The devil tells him to pack his bags as he's going to our island. The man says, 'great, I was just there on vacation.' The devil says, 'now you have to live there!'"

"Christ! You make this place sound horrible. I would gladly have traded places with you."

"That's the point, we didn't know any better," Tim replied. "Sure, you think, oh man, living on a tropical island would be so cool. Dudes, it's only cool if you got seriously deep pockets. Unless you want to live like a local, and tonight you saw a great slice of the local culture or rather lack of; everything costs."

"Now, our family is being squeezed in that money vice," Mia sadly sighed. "Never thought they'd all turn against us. I know that's what Harry said, but he always exaggerates. Now we know, and I don't want to be here, but we must."

"Or we lose everything," Dag finished.

"There are worse places," Duncan slurred.

"Yeah, they are cold and wet," Tim countered.

"Look, if we're going to fish tomorrow, we'd better call it a night. I'll sleep on the boat with you, Tim. These assholes might try something. You never know."

"All right, fishermen, follow me." Mia took the lead as they staggered to the house.

Once inside Duncan and Jason were the walking zombies and found their beds. Carlos followed Mia into the kitchen. "So, how much has the hotel offered for your bay?"

With only the small stove light on, the stars were visible looking towards the dock. "Half a million. Taxes and other government duties will cut that. Mom and Harry paid almost that much from Granpop."

"This place is worth at least five million. Did they counter?"

"I don't think so. It's a sticky ball of wax with the government, our uncle, and who knows what else is going on behind the scenes."

Carlos found a water bottle and poured a glass of water. "How come you always call your mother, mom, but your father, Harry?"

"I thought you were a designer, not a shrink?" Mia asked.

"Just wondered, that's all. Harry seems like a friendly guy."

"Harry fishes. He only thinks fish. He only respects those who fish and catch big fish." Mia looked out the bay window at the late moonrise, "If he met you on your turf, he wouldn't have a thing in common with you. Harry is more a fisherman than my father."

"Okay, that's easy to understand. But you must admit, he put together an impressive place here."

"Humph! Easy for another fisher-man," Mia emphasized 'man'. "Try being the only girl in a fishing family. I never had dolls."

"But we were told you had several fishing records?" Carlos moved closer.

"Yep, and you see who's cleaning the house and making the beds, and not out with you on charter."

"Not by choice? Come out with us tomorrow and show us your style," Carlos pleaded.

"Style? I don't think so. Harry doesn't like me to fish, not ladylike enough. Or women shouldn't intrude. After all, it is fisher–men."

"Aw, come on. Give us some pointers. It'll be fun; besides, we're paying."

"We'll see, in the morning," Mia slipped into her little girl's voice.

"You're quite the woman, Mia. I like the way you handled yourself in the restaurant. You didn't back down." He moved to her side and leaned to kiss her. Mia stuck up her hands between them. Carlos expected to be pushed aside, but was instead she grabbed his collar and pulled him into a tight embrace.

Mia kissed hard, twisting her lips, "Let's see your style."

"Everyone should believe in something.
I believe I'll go fishing," Henry David Thoreau

CHAPTER ELEVEN

Another early start, but the anglers were sprawled on their beds until Dag did his rooster crow routine. Minding reputations, Carlos used the escape route from Mia's second-floor bedroom, down the lattice, and he made his way to *Sassy*. His two compatriots looked like the limping wounded as they stumbled to the dock in the darkness.

"Didn't we just go to bed?" Jason asked as he looked at his watch. "It was eleven when we made it back last night."

"Well, I can see my kids are breaking you in," Harry laughed. "Spend a few months here fishing and carousing, you'll be good with only a few hours of shut-eye. For years I would…" He realized no one wanted to hear his boozing tales. "Yes, get some water in you. Drink as much as possible."

Dag maneuvered against the side of Cheesy's yacht, and the older Brit made a graceful leap. With a guffaw after a survey of clients and crew, "I can see a good time was had by all. Be an exceptional day of fishing. Yes, sir, I feel positive in predicting chumming. Where's Tim?"

Mia appeared from the forward berth wearing a hooded jersey under a big, floppy straw hat. "Hey, Cheese, you're bright and chipperfor half-past five. Tim and me traded this morning. He's helping mom."

"Eww!" Was all Harry had to say and started baiting the deep-sea rods.

"And look at you, my dear, smiling while the poor fellows are barely holding it together. This is sleeping in for me. I usually am the first to the boat, except for the boys," Cheese hooted, "whom I've had to awaken every morning of late."

"You forget, I had plenty of practice drinking with guests on my catamaran and then rise and shine to bake fresh biscuits for breakfast."

"Yeah, well, keep it down, okay," Harry asked. "You're on today. Show 'em your stuff, sweetheart."

"Harry, that's so nice of you to let me come along." She said as she sat regally in the fighting chair while her father and Cheese placed the baited trolling rods in their holders. As the tip of the orange sun peaked out from the ocean, Mia got the first strike and quickly reeled in a nice kingfish. Between the thumping with the wooden bat, the roll as Dag slowed the boat, combined with a crosswind dousing some diesel exhaust, Jason and Duncan were chumming on separate sides of *Sassy*.

"Looks like you had a bit too much fun last night, my friend," Cheesy concluded as he handed a packet of saltines to Jason. "Here, chew some of these crackers. They usually settle one's tummy."

The youngest fisherman man stuffed a few in his mouth, chewed, and then regained his position at the rail. Heaving more into the sea, "This is no good. I'd better lie down."

"If you go below, it could make it worse. Lay down on the bench'" Harry advised as he fed out one of the teasers.

As the sun cleared the water, Mia pulled off her hoodie to reveal an old-fashioned, broad, black bikini. Even though, the suit probably belonged to her mother, the daughter perfectly filled it.

"Talk about another teaser," Dag hissed.

"Hey, that's your sister," Harry barked. "She's getting a day off."

"You sure you don't want to try the heavy gear today?" He said to Duncan. "Might have a better chance sitting chair than standing, wobbling on the deck. Feel that breeze? She's coming out of the north. That means with the east-west current we'll have a decent chop before noon."

"No, thanks for the advice; we've got a bet riding."

"And we're tied," Jason said without moving his arm that had been shielding his eyes.

"I'm holding you to some more stories, Harry," Duncan replied.

"Oh, no!" Cheesy, Dag, and Mia shouted.

"Hey, if the man wants stories, he's paying. Let's see, my grandfather…"

"Fished with Zane Grey," Cheesy finished that sentence.

"Really? The famous western writer?" Carlos asked.

"Few people know that Zane Grey started sportfishing." Harry was in his glory. "The man went to New Zealand and Tahiti. Yes, sir, he caught the first thousand-pound marlin off Tahiti. The story is that sharks took off a few chunks, and it still weighed over a grand. That's what they called big fish back then, granders. Those must have been fantastic days."

"Those were the days." Mia, Cheesy and Dag harmonized as Mia took the position as the spotter in the tower.

"Hey, I hope someday you tell stories about me," Harry sighed. "Yeah, my grandfather talked about losing entire, big billfish to sharks, in one gulp."

"What's the biggest shark you've encountered?" Duncan egged

Harry on.

"Have to be that orca we saw chewing on that floating dead whale," Cheesy offered.

"Was almost as long as this boat. Damn close. We skedaddled in a hurry," Harry smiled. "Wish we'd had a camera that day. No one ever believed us. Anyway, my grandfather fished the world while fishing was spectacular. Told about Mr. Grey catching one so big that it snapped the rod, so they tied the line on the next pole, but that made too much line for the reel. They had to pull that monster fish in by hand."

"It went four hundred pounds," Dag and Cheesy recited in unison.

"So, he got your father," Carlos paused, "hooked?"

"Ah, my Dad caught his first billfish when he was eight," Harry tilted his head and winked up at the billowing clouds. "It's in our blood." He slapped Dag on the shoulder, "Isn't it?"

"Like a nasty infection," Dag smirked.

"My Dad taught me, I taught Dag and Tim," he paused and looked up at the tower, "and Mia. I caught mine at eleven."

"Thanks for including me," she quipped. "Mine was thirteen, Tim's twelve, and Dag's nine."

"Sweetheart, you're a natural," Harry beamed.

"Yeah, sure," was her rapid comeback. "Hey, hey," Mia shouted, "Billfish coming towards the starboard teaser, maybe thirty meters behind it. Somebody better get ready."

"J, it's your turn," Duncan mumbled with little gusto.

"You take it," Jason replied with even less enthusiasm and didn't move.

"Somebody better step up," Harry chided, "come on, suck it up!"

"Okay, okay." Jason pumped some deep breaths and grabbed his rod from the overhead rack. It took him a half a minute to find a firm stance. He wiped his sweaty face with his left hand and flipped out a red streamer with his right. There was no tension to his line. The boat's wake pulled the wet fly directly towards the fish. Jason wasn't ready for the instant strike.

The small, ninety-pound sailfish blasted out of the waves. He lost his footing and stumbled as his rod bent while the line tore off the reel. Everyone, but for him, saw the sailfish twist and roll the leader around its bill. One sharp jump straight up, and snap... the rod tip bounced. The fish had snapped the line. Jason staggered and slumped into the fighting chair.

"Short and sweet," Carlos uttered.

"No, short and sour," Jason voiced as he crawled back to the side bench.

"Say, guys, can I get in on this bet? I mean just for the fish caught today?" Mia yelled from the tower. "Say five hundred bucks, unless that's too steep for you?"

Duncan and Carlos smiled and nodded their heads in agreement. Jason waved his right-hand thumbs up.

"Sure thing, pretty woman," Carlos winked.

The day progressed as Harry had predicted, with a wind chop opposite the current, but the fishing progressed fast. Shortly after seven, Jason had lost the first, a small sail. Within forty-five minutes, Carlos and Duncan simultaneously hooked good sized dolphin after the crew located a school by diving birds. The two fought to keep their fish separated on either side. Duncan stayed on the port side and Carlos struggled with his off the starboard stern.

Harry worked with Carlos, instructing him to keep the rod tip as high as possible and work his line in slowly, but steadily. The twenty-three-pound bull was solidly hooked. Harry did a superb job of gaffing it. Duncan's took another twenty minutes of thrashing and with Carlos' fish already boated, Dag maneuvered the boat to cut the distance. The second dolphin was two pounds lighter.

"Fellows, thanks, we'll be eating mahi mahi for a while," Cheesy smiled as he removed Duncan's fish from the hanging scale.

The fishermen didn't touch the prepared breakfast sandwiches. Harry and Dag had seconds. "Looks like it's your turn, Mia. I'll take the tower and scout," Harry offered with a groan at every rung as he climbed the ladder.

Mia brought her rod from below. She looked the part, deeply tanned in her conservative, black two-piece, big Jackie O sunglasses, with a few lures hooked to her straw hat. She opened a small tackle box and finally decided to use a red-headed white streamer rigged with two hooks. With a small file, she sharpened the barbs until they easily sank into her thumbnail. Her smirk said it all, "Lesson numero uno, sharp, long-shank, forged hooks. Right, Harry?"

"Un-huh," her father agreed. "That was my first lesson. Don't be a dull guy fishing with a dull hook."

"Well, would you look at that, a Redington rod and reel combo, first-class a few years back. This girl doesn't fool around," Duncan admired.

Mia tilted her head and looked up from under the floppy hat with a posed smile. "Harry, remember when you bought me this for my fourteen birthday? Really signified my coming of age." She carefully unrolled and attached a new wire leader to the line.

"What size is your line?" Carlos asked.

"Sixteen."

"Wow," both Duncan and Carlos uttered, and they an effort to bow. "You are the saltwater master," Carlos continued and Jason pulled himself up to look. "I'm using twelve. Damn, I am the novice."

"Me too," Duncan disclosed. "Hmm, the difference is clear. This lady knows the territory."

With a wrinkled face, Mia explained, "No sense in trying to keep the line invisible. This isn't a perfectly clear freshwater stream. There's plenty of bubbles churning in the prop wash." She grinned, "I'm going for the big boys, not puny fish. Cheese, please let out the teasers, say about another two waves farther back. Harry, nothing out there yet?"

"Not yet, darling. Don't worry, I'll let you know. Dag, try running a figure eight."

"Hey, I think family's getting special attention," Duncan complained.

"Not really," Dag countered. "We've been doing it for you off and on, alternating between tight and broad circles, always along the drop-off. Come here and watch the depth sounder. See," Dag explained, "this is the forty-fathom line. It drops off here to about a couple thousand, but our sounder only registers up to two thousand… on a good day, meaning flat calm, no surface bouncing and we're going slow, under four knots."

"And you've been doing the same for us?" Carlos asked.

"Absolutely," Cheesy answered. "This is all about you, the anglers, the fishermen, the clients," he paused and exclaimed, "the tip! If you don't catch your fill, then you're not pleased with our services. Every day you've had several hookups each. Not the boat's fault, if you, well, I won't go there," Cheese smiled, "if the fish are so damn strong, they break the lines!"

It was after eleven and they were running north of Union. "I won't lie to you. I know these waters," Mia said regally from the chair. "I'm sure you've been here several times this week, but you know nothing about the lineups. Dad, Cheese, and Dag do. They brought you here, but I have my place."

"Line ups?" Jason quipped. "This isn't about the last night's culprits?"

"What about last night?" Harry chirped.

"Nothing, nothing, dad," Mia quickly replied. "No. Watch. See the south end of that island? That's Canouan, line it up with that big rock, you can barely see it, Sail Rock farther out to the east. Now, look south and see the northeast tip of Mayreau just tickling that distant island; that's Palm. Well, when all those points coincide, it's my favorite fishing spot. What's the depth, bro?"

"Reading 100 fathoms, 600 feet deep for you fellows," Dag corrected. "Man, this is bringing back the fantastic old times when we had our own competitions."

"Now, I say the fishing prayer," Mia spread her arms evangelically, tilted her head upward, and shouted, "Jesus, Jehovah, Neptune, Poseidon, Allah, Mohammed, Confucius, Buddha, please give me a fish!"

The men were smiling with heads bouncing in merry agreement.

"Yes, gentlemen, that's my girl, one of the ultimate showmen, ah, show, ah, show persons," Harry proclaimed.

It was another twenty minutes until he shouted, adjusting the binoculars, "Birds, a bunch of black frigates, gulls, boobies, and white tropic birds. Could be tuna-time. It looks like the school's heading west. My advice, ah, you know, come up far ahead. Fellows, I think you all should get ready. Big, lots of fish, and the most birds we've seen this week."

Instantly, the deck became busy. Jason pulled himself together, poured a bottle of water over his head, and stood at attention, holding his long rod straight up.

"Carlos, you're the last in the rotation. How about helping with the teasers? My crew is about to give you a free lesson."

"Sure thing, Captain Harry, just say when."

Dag goosed the diesels and closed the distance in a matter of minutes. A swarm of big black, pterodactyl-looking birds circled above a narrow stretch of ocean that was churning with rapidly moving fish chomping smaller, slower fish. With excellent timing, one or two of the birds would dive straight down, level out less than a meter above the sea's surface, and snatch a fresh morsel off the waves. A game of tag usually would ensue between two frigates or they would swoop against the smaller, long-tailed, white tropic bird. The brown boobies were plunging into the water everywhere.

"What's the deal with the frigates?" Duncan asked. "I've never seen them resting on the ocean. Can't swim or what?"

"More like, or what," Cheesy replied. "The frigates can't touch the water. Another of God's jokes. Their feathers aren't waterproof. Read an article; they tracked one that flew continuously for over two months."

"How the hell can they do that?" Jason inquired.

"Seems they sleep a minute on and off as they are soaring," Dag contributed. "Had a bird watcher on board in CR. Said they can shut off half their brain and although they're flying, they're sleeping half the time."

"Hey, enough with the Audubon Society meeting!" Mia exclaimed. "Any fish, dad?"

"Oh, I was listening, interesting stuff about the frigates., Harry smiled. "Yeah, I've got my eyes peeled. If you throw out now, probably only hook a small tunny."

Dag throttled up and aimed directly ahead of the center of the two acres or more of fish. It was easy to spot the diving birds. The fish were in such a feeding frenzy that the sea's surface appeared to be boiling with activity. This was Neptune's navy, probably three schools of fish, six-inch fingerlings or sardines, maybe squid, with two-foot long bonito tunas gulping them, and fifteen kilos and bigger yellowfin tuna with some bigger bull dorados filling their bellies chomping anything they choose.

The air force was the graceful white long-tailed tropicbirds snatching bait from the wave tips, the cumbersome web-footed brown booby diving deep alongside a few gulls. The huge black frigates bullied all the birds with their sharp talons, snatching from others' beaks.

Duncan joined Harry spotting from the tower. Everyone else aboard scanned the surface for something big from the depths, cutting through the schools.

"Starboard teaser," Duncan shouted. "Watch it, watch it, there; see the bill. Oh, my god!" Duncan yelled, "It's got to be huge."

"Yep, wait, wait, there it goes; knew it had to roll trying to snatch your big-assed, space-age monstrosity," Harry lauded Duncan's teaser. "Carlos, pull it in nice and slowly. Try not to spook this guy. We're looking at some serious fun here." He grinned, "And Mia knows what to do. Baby doll, this is a biggie."

Mia tossed the streamer into the wake as Dag cut back on the throttle and slowed the boat by gradual increments. The combination perfectly placed the streamer ahead of the thrashing bill. Mia was locked on, focused, and cleverly kept the streamer just ahead of the fish. With a snap of the big tail, the marlin shot forward and gulped it, soaring in the air between the wave troughs. (Replayed later, Cheesy captured the moment perfectly with the digital. The blue's mouth gaped open and they could see the white streamer being swallowed.)

"One, two, three, four," Mia counted while hastily pulling line off her reel. "Ten, eleven, twelve…"

And the fish soared straight up; its tail cleared the water by two feet.

"Oh, my fucking god!" Carlos bellowed, "It's got to be fifteen feet long!"

The massive fish fell backward and smashed against the surface. Mia's rod bent and bounced as she dumped as much line as she could to keep the marlin from feeling any pressure. She was hoping for a second gulp that would hook the streamer into softer throat tissue than the hard mouth.

"He's too big!" Mia cried.

"Never thought I'd hear that from you!" Dag laughed as he called Harry to take control from the upper steering station.

"Help me; somebody twist the chair around." In perfect form, Mia stood against the back of the chair for support and used the entire rear deck to play the fish while Harry reversed in small, finessed arcs.

Slowly, Mia gained on the massive fish. Suddenly the pole curved into a severe arc and the reel screamed feeding line as the fish headed in a different direction. She kept her composure and continually moved to have the rod directly facing the fish.

"Keep it cool," Carlos urged. "Want some water?"

"Yeah, tilt the bottle." She gulped and coughed. The blue changed its mind and charged the boat. Mia slipped once as she frantically cranked the reel. Carlos secured her with a grab around her waist.

Mia shrugged with a wink, "Team spirit, huh?" She laughed, "You will still be down five big ones."

"Damn, girl, I'd easily pay that to see this anytime. You're one toughie. Jason is getting all this on our camera. You got biceps, quads, and other memorable body parts bulging. Add that to what Chessman captures, I think these will be my late night fantasy flicks."

She whispered with a giggle, "Another sick fuck, fish porn! I know what I want to see bulge, later."

"Pay attention. Stop gabbing," Harry admonished. "This fish could be some record. You never know."

In unison, fishermen and crew, "Aye-aye, skip."

Dag sided over to the couple, smiled and elbowed Carlos, "Told you we'd protect you."

Runs, rushes, dives, and jumps. The fish fought hard for another ninety minutes as Harry expertly maneuvered to cut the distance as much as possible.

"He's tiring," Cheesy professed. "How about you, Mia?"

"Who? Me? I'm thinking how I'm gonna spend all the money I'm winning."

Jason cut in, "Land this one so I can get another chance."

"Okay, hear that, Harry?" Mia called. "Let's show them how it's done." She jumped down from the chair, moved to the stern rail, and nimbly straddled it. Carlos and Dag stayed close in case the fish either pulled or charged her, and she lost her balance.

Harry plowed in reverse as Mia spun the reel incredibly fast, always guiding the incoming line so the reel didn't overly fill on one side and foul, stalling the mechanism. Mia wasn't so much showing off as demonstrating her skill. She wasn't a natural like Dag or Harry. She'd been away from fishing for years and had to think through every step.

Down and up and down and up, her rod bobbed. The marlin was cooperating. Cheesy took a break from filming to look at his watch. "Better land him, getting on to two. Give these blokes enough time for one more chance each." He focused the GoPro as Mia turned to him and shrugged a nod. Jason had rallied and found enough gusto to endure the rocking at the tower beside Duncan and Harry maneuvering from the upper steering station. Carlos was beside Mia, keeping a watchful eye as her safety belt. Dag was at port stern ready to grab the leader if it appeared. All eyes and cameras were focused on the frothy water off the stern as Harry slowly reversed.

"I see him, I see him!" Duncan shouted. "Look, that reflection, that fucking long reflection, that's him."

"Yes, yes," Jason yammered excited, "Look, there's the bill, right there, three waves back."

"Mia," Harry called, "steady and brace yourself. This is a fun, but Cheese is right, it's cutting into our clients' time. I'm gonna blast the diesels one good burst and shut her down. Dag, you ready?"

"Absolutely!"

Carlos joined as he held Mia by her tanned thigh. "Me too, bring it on! But don't rush things on our account. This is fair and square. We all had our time." He rolled his head, "It would be nice to wet another line."

Harry swallowed hard with his body twisted so he could aim his reverse tactic. "Okay, here goes."

The twin Caterpillars roared for five seconds while Mia reeled like the crazy woman she was. Dag leaned far out over the stern. The reverse push blew off his ball cap, and his long hair drifted as if he were on a motorcycle. Then the boat sagged as Harry cut the throttles and shouted, "Now, fight 'em kid!"

"There it is." At least two waves back, Mia and Dag saw the leader. The bill was only ten feet off the stern, with big, black, round eyes peering, trying to understand what was happening to it. The massive fish wasn't thrashing and appeared tired.

Dag touched the leader, holding it, he turned with a broad smile, "You beat him, sis! And look, he knows it."

"Hey, there's my streamer. Can you?"

Before she finished, Dag deftly stretched even further and snatched the hook with his side-cutter pliers. It took one strong flick of his wrist to free the fish and the blue marlin slid back into the blue Caribbean. Everyone was church quiet, in awe, watching the huge fish roll on its side and then raise its bill as if agreeing it had been a good fight. And maybe it was waving as a combined thanks for permitting it to swim away.

"God damn, god damn, god damn! That was fucking hot. We were just in Animal Fucking Planet!" Jason shouted with glee, "No one will ever top this! Mia, thank you, thank you."

"Yes, I totally agree. You are the ninja warrior, fisherwoman extraordinaire, to be praised every time fish tales are told!" Duncan bellowed. "Yes sir," he nudged Captain Harry, "Let's get back on track. I don't mind losing five Bens for that lesson, but would like to feel another tugging on my line."

"Who wouldn't?" Harry smiled and pointed as he upped the throttles, "Dag and Cheesy's already got the teasers out. Get your ass down there. Now, who's up next? Jason?"

"J, your turn," Carlos yelled. "I'll pay another five if you can top that battle, or you Dunc. Damn, man oh man, that was hot, whew," he exhaled. "That was something special. Mia, you are one of a kind." He went to the cooler and distributed Heinekens. "Sour stomach or not, here's to the lady of the day!"

All bottles were raised in appreciation.

"Fellows, I know compliments are due. I'm good," Mia explained, "Always have been, always will be. Patience, I got from my parents. Took a lot to put up with Harry." She raised her beer and toasted her father. "Thanks, dad; that was some par excellent boat work." Then she chugged the greenie and asked for another. "But I am no longer your 'little girl'. Come on, Harry, look at me." She did a pirouette and ended with a Swan Lake ballet move, kneeling with arms outstretched.

"Well, no, honey, as much as I hate to, I'll admit it. You're not a girl anymore, not so little, but still my... and mom's little girl. Has to be... always. Mia, that's how we think of you," melodramatics from the upper steering station. "Dag, take the helm." Harry turned and wiped his eyes before raising the binoculars. "I'll go back to scouting again."

After watching Mia provide everyone with a lesson in the fine art of saltwater, extreme light tackle, the anglers were eager to get another hookup. Jason had pulled himself together after gulping more aspirins and multi-vitamins. He shed his Team Wahoo shirt and leaned against the stern; muscular arms outstretched.

"What was that prayer you said, Mia? Jesus, Mohammed, Confucius?" He asked.

Mia obliged and got all the anglers to recite after her. Harry, Dag, and Cheesy already knew it by heart. It had been the St. Claire family prayer for at least three generations. Team Wahoo grabbed hands and chanted, "Jesus, Jehovah, Neptune, Poseidon, Allah, Mohammed, Confucius, Buddha, please give me a fish!"

"You know, you've lost your copyright to that prayer. Our team will chant it 'til the end of days," Carlos laughed. "But when asked for the origin, it will always be Union Island Mia." They locked eyes, and for a few seconds were oblivious of the others.

"Better change that," Mia replied. "As soon as this shit with the bay is behind us, I'm heading back to my catamaran in the BVI. I've got a captain chartering it for me now, as we speak, but I miss it. Not the charter guests, and all that day in day out bullshit, but I really don't like the day in day out bullshit here. Catch my drift, macho man?"

The mustached man nodded approval and spoke very low directly into her ear, "Let's make some time to chat more... later," Carlos slipped into his professional business voice, "over lunch, detail a timeline, crunch some numbers." He looked around and furtively grabbed her hand. "I'm really fed up with what I do and where I do it. This environment," he tugged her hand as he craned his head towards hers, "is stimulating. It's what I was born to. You know what I mean? I left a place just like this, tropical; traded it for grim weather at least six months a year. I'm ready for a change." He whispered, "and financially able. I want to feel free again."

She gave his hand a squeeze and dropped it. "Yes, I do, but Carlos, you're never free on a boat. There is always something to keep you busy."

"Hmm, like I said, let's talk about it."

Another conversation began when Duncan climbed the tower and was beside Harry. "We've been thinking. Maybe we could get together and financially help your situation. We're all bachelors with money in the bank and great credit. No question, the fishing is great."

The VHF squawked a government weather advisory. Harry turned a few knobs for better reception. "Better talk to Tim. He's our financial advisor. Quiet, please, all of you. If the government is broadcasting about the weather, best we listen."

The radio hissed static and garbled words. Harry pressed a button, and the transmission became audible to all.

"Tropical storm Monique is now at 9 degrees north latitude 54 degrees west longitude moving north-northwest at eight miles an hour. Monique is very developed and could have hurricane winds of at least 75 mph tomorrow."

"Well mates, it looks like you picked the perfect week. Seems the shit is coming," Cheesy nudged Jason. "Doesn't sound good. But it'll be at least a few days of meandering, probably bounce off Barbados. Where are you making connections?"

"We fly from here to Antigua tomorrow night. Layover there and then Miami."

"In that case, not a problem at all. This storm won't be a problem for us for at least another three days," Cheesy estimated.

"Just as soon as we get ahead. Now it's Mother Nature," Harry mumbled as he scanned the horizon for more birds.

"What do you in the case of a storm?" Duncan asked.

"We all drive to Florida!" Harry joked. "Batten the hatches, buddy, and wait it out." He drew a deep breath. "Been through many, a dozen and more. Sit tight, nail everything down. Put *Sassy* onto her mooring or…" He paused, "make a run for it. Get everyone on board and head to where the storm ain't. Used to be Venezuela, but now with all the turmoil there, pirates would pick us clean."

"Come on, pirates?" Duncan mocked. "There are no pirates anymore."

"What? You don't watch the news, read the papers, or what's, ah, that Google thing. Hell yes, there's pirates and southwest of here they're stealing and killing. Times are tough all along the Venzie coast."

"Come on, Captain Harry, chin up. Storm Monique might miss you. If I could squeeze a few more days of vacation, I'd be willing to stay and ride it out. It sounds like a safe adventure."

"Duncan, best you guys get out while you can. Those who never experienced a powerful storm can realize what it's all about. The blow only lasts, ah, maybe a day. But the aftermath without electricity, the cleanup, rebuild, business downtime, airport closed, schools; that's months. You're a businessman. Consider the logistics of getting the materials to patch and rebuild transported to little Podunk, Union Island. If we're lucky, they'll be shipped up from Trinidad. That is if that Monique doesn't also crank that island. Time, it's all about time," Harry breathed, "Fucking time. It's cutting into our fishing time and the clock is ticking. This means, at the least, a few charters will cancel."

The day finished nearly perfectly with each of the clients picking up another fish. Jason grinned with his twenty-eight-pound kingfish that overshadowed another twenty-two-pound dolphin Duncan hooked. Carlos didn't have any luck raising a fish for his light tackle, but on the run back to Sunset, a sixty-three-pound wahoo struck the heavy gear. That fight lasted so long they arrived at the dock with a backdrop of a beautiful orange and vermillion twilight.

Still feeling the previous evening's intoxication, beers weren't a priority. The three guests showered, 'coffeed up,' and packed for departure directly after the next day's fishing.

Duncan and Jason walked to the dock and queried Tim, who was wiping down the boat, about perhaps assisting financially. "That's a really nice offer, but I think we'll make it. Dad doesn't want to sell shares or have partners unless absolutely necessary." Tim answered. "This bay has been in the family for eighty years, mom's family. Harry'd like to keep it that way, privately owned. But you never know, we might call you."

"Oh, I can understand that. We could do some type of loan or whatever you decide. This has been a fantastic week. The best fishing ever. Hate to see your operation fall under the wheels of a big corporation like so many others have," Duncan returned.

"I agree," Jason added. "I know I'll be back. Can't beat the ambiance." He laughed, "Just stay out of town. Ah, even that will calm down, you'll see. The fishing, well, fucking fantastic. We're all shamed by your sister's lessons today." He shouted, "I'm leading in the biggest fish and most!" He slung his arm over Duncan's shoulder. "New guy luck, huh?"

"We'll see tomorrow. I'm heading back for chow," Duncan said.

"Think I'll hang with Tim for a while. My stomach is still churning. Might eat crackers for a few more days, ha-ha," Jason laughed.

The talk at the picnic table dinner was all about the weather. Attention was to the big, portable, short wave radio tracking Monique interspersed with tales of past hurricanes. Carlos sat across from Mia, who tended chicken and fish on the grill while Cassy finished the salad. Harry and Dag brought out the bowls of side dishes of boiled and fried cassava and rice and beans.

"You can all talk about storms, but Hurricane Stan on October '05 hit my hometown in Guatemala. We got twenty inches of rain and the Santa Ana volcano erupted next door in El Salvador at exactly the same time. That killed maybe five thousand," Carlos remembered, reverently dropping his voice. "That was a textbook case of just when you think it can't get any worse; POW, you get pounded with a combination punch!"

Cheesy sipped an iced tea. "Mother Nature's pissed at what we've done to her planet. Trying to get us to clean up or get us out. Me and the missus, we've been through some hard blows on the yacht. Learn to roll with it. Like being in a blender for a day or two. As long as the mast stays and hooks hold, you know it's going to be over, so you just ride it out." The ruddy, red-faced man hugged his thin wife. "Right, Verena, honey?"

The slight woman nodded her head in agreement as she sipped a hot tea. "Bloody right, we were off Barbados in 1980, August it was, when that prick Allen blew through. Category three it was. Thought we were in a washing machine. All we could do was brace ourselves and hang on. Couldn't even lie down. The motion would throw you off the bunk." She grabbed Cheesy's hand and squeezed. "But we made it and we'll do okay in this Monique bitch."

"What's the plan, dad?" Dag asked.

"The usual; button up the house, close the shutters. Tomorrow, after dropping these gents off at the airport, top off the tanks and fill the extra gerry jugs," Harry listed. "Then we'll pick up what we can from around the yard and store it in the house. Good thing we had the big clean up a few months ago. Not much lying around that can bash us as hurricane rocket projectiles."

"Mia and I will put some easy grub together that doesn't need refrigeration," Cassy offered. "Then I have to do the same at the restaurant," she sighed. "Lots of fish in the freezer. I'll give it away or we'll have a big barbecue for the town after Monique passes."

"If the looters don't steal it." Harry quipped and with wide eyes explained, "That's the routine these days, isn't it? Free everything after a natural disaster. Anarchy takes over from law and order?"

"Come on, Harry," Cheesy chided. "Everyone knows everyone on this salty rock. Can't picture roving gangs of armed looters."

"Hey, Mother Nature and Human Nature, which is the most destructive?" Harry returned. "Anyway, what difference does it make?" He looked directly at Cassy.

"I'll check with Tim about the insurance. Where is he?"

"Still hosing down on *Sassy*. Got Jason helping, probably talking business propositions," Duncan got in.

"After we are certain how the storm is tracking, we'll put her out on the big three-point mooring," Harry prescribed.

"I checked them all when we started the clean up. Got extra shackles, chain and swivels if we need them. I'll do a quick dive morning after tomorrow. Check the big one and second-biggest for your yacht, Cheese," Dag responded. "Good, inch thick, nylon, double painters on each, half-inch chain. Shouldn't be anything to worry about… as long as the pumps work."

"We've got two extra backup pumps, redundant systems on our girl," Cheesy described. "Can't have too many pumps, with screens, extra switches. It'll be okay. Got new batteries. To tell the truth," he sighed, "I hate storms, but also love them. Makes one take a better look at everything. There's the before and the after."

"Aftermath," Mia finally joined. "We tied my catamaran to three separate moorings, up in Virgin Gorda Sound. Should be okay as long as she doesn't kite."

"Kite?" Carlos asked.

"The wind gets under wide flatboats, the area between the pontoons, lifts them, kites them and pitches them over." Mia's hand wiped some sweat off her brow from the heated grill. "It's insured to the max."

"I'd love to see your charter boat," Carlos injected quietly.

Perfunctory, Mia replied, "Go online, Stray Cat dot com." She winked, "Give you a discount, as I already know you." She whispered with another wink and a nudge, "In the Biblical sense."

"Chow down boys and girls," Harry instructed. "Got a fishing contest to complete bright and early and then see you off." He raised his glass of iced tea, "I truly commend you as fishermen and all-around nice guys."

"Here, here, raise your glasses blokes and ladies. This was the very best charter is many years. Team Wahoo is okie dokie," Cheesy toasted, and all hands were up clinking drinks.

"Well," Carlos sized up the situation, "I'm exhausted after a long night and an exciting day. Soon as I eat, I'm heading for the sack." Discretely, he reached under the table and squeezed Mia's thigh.

She cupped her hands together as in prayer, looked him in the eyes and smiled seductively, "If you can keep your eyes open long enough, I can show you my brochures and website."

"Oh," Dag chuckled, "is that like 'your etchings?'" He dodged her elbow. "I better get Tim and Jason. Somehow they must have lost track of time."

^^^^^^^^^

The five o'clock plane was on schedule and the three statesiders made it with minutes to spare. At the end of the final day, they declared the Team Wahoo private tournament a tie. Jason scored the biggest fish, Duncan, with a flurry of five successful hookups in a school of dorado on the last day, captured the most fish. Carlos caught the biggest on light fly tackle. It was also fairly obvious to a very silent and discreet Jason and Duncan, that his unused bed meant he had captured Mia.

Harry circled while ashore goodbyes scattered among promises to return, along with endearments to keep in touch, echoed in the boarding area. Jason hugged Tim while Dag and Cheesy assisted with the luggage during a constant chat.

"Thanks, Cheese, I'll edit our digital videos and photos and send you a copy. Be great for your website. You can bet your sunburned ass that we'll be watching it when the snow flies. Like to stay and all that, but got to get back to the old salt mine," Carlos paused, "while you enjoy the salt air." He slapped the elder Brit on his back.

"Don't worry, sonny," Cheese waxed. "I have a feeling you'll return soon. As far as the salt air, maybe two days from now, it will be stinging at 90 miles an hour! Off you go and we got to get the boat fueled before the dock closes."

"Adios," Dag said and pulled Tim from a long handshake with his dark, muscular friend. They trotted to Cheesy's skiff. Harry was pacing, head bowed in deep thought.

"What are you thinking about, Harry, with such a dour look?" Cheesy asked.

"Not thinking, Cheese, praying. Giving our fish prayer a recite, and maybe it might help swing things our way. Haven't seen the inside of a church since that last bitter meeting with the choir and a long, long time before that. If we get this blow dead-on, well, a little help from the big guy up above couldn't hurt. All my work, er, all our work, everything hangs in the balance of the next few days. If Lady Luck,

Jesus, Jehovah, Neptune, Poseidon, Allah, Mohammed, Buddha and Confucius smile or frown tells the tale." Harry forced a grin, "We'll give it our best. That's all we can do. To the fuel dock."

"The fellows got off safely. Likable group, for American businessmen," Cheese said.

"Hopefully, they know enough business, they can help us out," Dag offered.

"Don't count on that. They're fishermen and all fishermen are bullshitters," Harry bellowed. "Believe me, I know. Everything is, see you again, we'll be in touch." He made a sour face. "This situation is all on us."

Tim was smiling, "You might be right, pops, but those guys quizzed me for numbers and I emailed them a prospectus. I was flat out that Sunset isn't taking in partners, but we would sell stock, limited. Like you always say, Harry, only time will tell."

As expected, there was a line of boats waiting to top off their tanks. Dag and Cheese volunteered to shop for what necessities might remain on the shelves. They returned with arms filled with bags of snacks and found they were only one pirogue behind in the queue. Amazingly, Harry had kept his cool.

"Ah, caught between the devil Monique and the deep blue sea," Harry scratched at his bald spot that he liked to call his 'tree line'. "Most are talking about making a run for it to the southern safe haven of Trinidad. What do you think about running down south?"

"I don't know. Your call, dad, but we'd definitely be out of communication with you and another three or four days to return."

"Yeah, and mom would be sweating bullets. See your uncle anywhere?" Harry asked.

"Nope. The office door was closed, and we didn't think we had enough time to get into a talk-talk."

The boat guzzled sixty gallons and that brought her tankage to two hundred and forty with another seven five-gallon jugs strapped to the stern. With that much, *Sassy*'s Cats could idle for a few days and then, if necessary, still easily make a run to safety in Trinidad.

By dusk, Cassy, Mia, and Tim had shuttered the house and removed everything that could fly away from the grounds. Harry and Dag dismantled and removed the twelve-foot outriggers, so there was little on the sportfisher to catch the heavy wind.

Cheesy returned in his skiff and tied to the dock. He'd helped Verena carefully store most of their sentimental knickknacks from the shelves. They knew what to expect. If it wasn't secured in a locker, wrapped in paper, and stored in a plastic bag, consider it broken. The St. Claire's were doing the same, removing all their fishing tackle.

Tim joined the crew on the boat.

"Let's keep the two old rods so we can fish as soon as the Caribbean settles. That's when the fish will be starving," Dag grinned.

"Always fishing on your brain, bro," Tim reacted. "If we make it through the blow, we'll feel like we'd been in a barrel and went over Niagara Falls."

"What's this 'if' shit, huh?" Dag snarled and flexed his arms. "Me and you, Tim, I can see it now, two brothers withstand the frothing seas of Monique," he laughed.

"If it is like any other Frenchie woman," Cheese smiled, "you, ah, we might all get well fucked! "Have you developed a storm plan?"

"Just in case, take the old Avon inflatable and lash it securely inside this deck area. I know we got the emergency inflatable raft, but you can never have too much," Harry changed the tone. "I know you two ain't stupid." He looked at his boys with a serious glare. "This won't be easy. Don't do nuthin' dumb out there. Keep your life preservers on at all times. Don't make a move around the boat without your lanyard snatched to something solid, like the tower. That lanyard is your umbilical cord. You fall in, well, you can pull yourself or be pulled out. Hear me? Take this shit seriously! Radio contact with the house every thirty minutes, on the hour and the half so we know when to expect to hear from you. Your mother will be worrying up a stink. Maybe I should go out with you?"

"Better you stay with mom. She will worry, but if you're right there it'll be better," Tim reasoned. "No sense everyone getting bounced around. Dad, you're not as resilient as you used to be. The good jolts might break something."

"And my missus will also be worrying about you boys. I expect you'll be watching our *Moonchild*, too," Cheese added. "Each should have a flashlight and a flare gun. Keep them tied to you with a lanyard. My woman is making sandwiches with the other girls. You got the snacks and fruit we bought at the dock, but my feeling is your guts are going to be queasy at best. They have four thermoses of coffee for you."

"Okay, okay, we'll try to catch a few winks, four on, four off, but I believe it will be a thirty-hour stay-awake clip," Dag said as he and Tim neatly coiled extra anchors and secured them to the port and starboard stern gunwales. "I think after we put her on the mooring, I'll lay out three more anchors with plenty of slack."

"That's great for wind coming from the east, but once the storm passes, the sea will surge from the west," Harry reminded. "Seen it before, at least ten, maybe fifteen footers rolling into here. Hope our old dock can take those licks."

"I'll never forget those big swells from when we were kids. She wouldn't let us body surf. Mom was so worried when you took *Sassy* out into the open sea," Tim sighed.

"Had to," Harry said, "that boat is what makes our money."

"The insurance is paid up?" Tim asked.

"Come on, with everything else we owe? Insurance is the last mouth to feed. Like betting you're going to have shitty luck," Harry frowned. "When nothing happens, the agent gets the good luck and your money. When the bad luck happens and the shit hits the fan, you gotta fight to get back fifty cents on the dollar. Seen it too many times, insurance companies belly up after a big storm. No money they say, to pay for damages, never expected a storm this big, they say."

"Nothing is insured? Mom said to ask Tim. You can't be serious?" Dag gasped.

"Dag, time's been tough. Peter, Paul, and a lot of other bills had to be paid."

"I wish you'd have told us. We could have paid the policy," Tim grumbled.

"Cheer up. Now, now," Cheesy was lively. "The storm hasn't hit yet. Could always miss. Let's do our best."

"This morning Monique was cranking directly towards the Grenadines at least 80 mph," Dag informed.

"Could be worse," Cheese bounced.

"Cheese, you are the persistent optimist," Harry shook his friend's hand.

"If we do our best, by God, we'll make it. Chin up, chest out, like the stalwart men we are," Cheesy offered. Then in a deep, very British voice, "We have nothing to fear"

And the others chimed with a broad laugh of relief, "But fear itself."

Mia, Verena, and Cassy joined the group, and each added more storm info. "The new storm coordinates are: lat 10.5, long 58. Still barreling at us. The house is boarded up. We took everything inside that might blow away. Got lunches made."

"Good. I figure we'll start feeling it tonight. It should be trouble after midnight," Harry observed. "Cheesy, you need us to help to button up your boat?"

"Not really, we have her all tidied up, but could use a hand pulling the skiff out."

"Let's go!" Dag and Tim simultaneously shouted.

Everyone gathered in the kitchen. The windows were shuttered, closing off the view, yet almost everything was bright white and seemed to uplift spirits with optimism. They enjoyed a good meal of hearty vegetable soup.

Cheesy looked around and counted, "Lucky seven we are, maybe Magnificent Seven. Wasn't that a movie?" And raised his coffee and all toasted. "Two nights from now, we're barbecuing, and again enjoying each other's company."

"Here, here!" Rang from Mia.

The ladies cleared the table as the men moved to the living room to listen to the radio. Cassy dropped a spoon, and it clattered to the floor, breaking her mood. "I hate storms."

"Me too," Mia agreed. "But it'll be all right. Come on," she rolled her head from side to side as if loosening a tight neck. "No one here is a newbie. We've all been through this shit before and we're older now."

"There was a bad one in eighty, oh boy, do I remember Allen. Half of the town blew away. I recall my father giving everybody help to rebuild. It took years to recover. Clifton was never the same."

"Don't worry, Mom," Mia hugged her.

"Easy to say, hard to do. Better fill up everything we can with drinking water before they shut the electricity off and we don't have the pump. But we have the well; can always bucket it."

"I checked. We have two cylinders of propane for cooking," Mia replied.

"Damn, I forgot about that. We'd better bring the tanks inside." Dag instructed.

"Wait for the boys. We don't have to hurry; the storm is hours away."

"A storm lasts only hours, but it takes forever for... I remember the electricity was off for months," Tim said. "The school and the church lost roofs. Looking at it afterward, it was like a bomb exploded."

"Things are built better now," Verena countered.

"Sure, this house is almost thirty years old. What would we do if we lost it or the boat?" Cassy groaned.

"Start thinking about taking the hotel's offer," Mia whispered as she hugged Cassy.

"I'm going to the restaurant and see how far Honoré and

Mammie have gotten. They also have their own place to get secured." Cassy sighed, "Everyone and everything has to be secured… and it won't be. We always forget something… and the boys." She crumpled into a chair and rested her head in her hands at the table and sobbed. "Why, why now? We were so close!"

Mia and Verena sat on either side and rubbed Cassy's back. "Mom, we'll all be okay. Look, this is just another little bump in the road."

"Yes, girl, come on, shape up," Verena took over. "Can't be sobbing. Too soon for sobbing. Save it for later, if there's a good cause. You keep it under control, the emotions. I know how you feel, because I'm feeling the same. But you and I and Mia, we aren't the frilly girlie types. We are tough, just like our men are tough." Verena went for her shoulder bag and retrieved a flask. "Here, drink a jolt of that kick-ass Carriacou rum, Jack Iron." She raised it, gulped, and handed the bottle to Mia who swallowed and gasped.

"Damn, Verena, I'd forgotten how rough Jack is! Come on, Mom, have a belt."

With red eyes, Cassy rose and grabbed the bottle, threw her head back and gulped, wiping her mouth with the back of her hand, "You're right, damn straight, I'm bringing everyone else down showing emotions." She turned and blew her nose into the sink and in an 'Arnold' tone headed for the door, "I'll be back."

"Want company?" Mia asked.

"No, well, yes and no, Honoré is there. I called. He has the place almost buttoned up. I'll check just to be sure, seal the freezers and fridges with tape. Honoré had the good sense to freeze jugs of water so they'll keep things cold longer. Once I duct tape everything shut, should stay cold for probably three or four days at the outside without power. Figure the government will pull the switch early in the morning. Oh, there I go rattling on when I should be peddling."

She kissed Mia and Verena on their cheeks and mounted the old Schwinn. Cassy reached the mound where the road started to Clifton and turned back to look at the St. Claire homestead. "I'll be coming back in the dark," she grabbed her phone and snapped a photo. "Next time I see this it's all going to be…" She gulped and didn't finish because she chose not to jinx things.

The town was busier than Cassy expected. Her brother's hardware remained open and Sam waved as Cassy pedaled by. The sky was a menacing, cloudless purple and the wind was enough to have whitecaps lapping the shore. She carefully navigated around the self-concerned hustling mob, carrying what each felt necessary to survive the gale. Men balanced sheets of plywood on their heads and staggered, tilted sideways by wind gusts. Many were at a special tank filling jugs with pitch oil, kerosene, for their wick lamps. She courteously smiled, nodded, and waved to everyone. Few responded.

At the dock, Kid Kalaloo jumped from his speedboat and carefully placed the inflatable fenders for protection as the swells rocked it. His team of the two other dreadlocks had problems with their sea legs after the rough ride. Tony filled the fuel tanks. Foxy struggled not to get his legs broken while keeping the boat from bouncing above the fenders and scratching the pearl white paint or worse.

Sam was busy writing what townspeople were taking. Sam waved, relinquished his order tablet to the salesgirl, and pointed for Kal to meet him inside. They slid the glass doors closed, but it didn't shut out the noise from the crowd of babbling people haggling for materials. Every few minutes a wind gust would rattle the doors and everyone's nerves.

"Lookin' grim, boss. Weather turning to shit, real shit! Frothing out there along the reef stretching out from the airport." Kal stood with his hands on his hips as if ready to jump at a moment's notice. "Heard they closed the airstrip until future notice. Only one dumb fuck sailor still on a hook inside the reef."

"I ain't going nowhere. That dumb fuck's boat will be on the beach if he doesn't beat it out to sea. Me, I'm counting my blessings, helping others, and clearing my inventory. Let bubble butt Annie fill some orders." Sam sat back in his wooden desk chair with his hands gripping the armrests and anxiously rocked. "Better to sell it now at a discount than to have to give it away later as a good Samaritan. Where are you going to take your boat? Had them take mine and put it on the hard in Chaguaramas. Let the Trinis worry about it."

"Why do I have a feeling that you'll be ordering that bubble butt to put something hard somewhere later, boss?" Kid laughed. "I'll make a run to the southern tip of Grenada. My cousin promises he can haul it out whenever I get there. Saving me space in the boatyard. I'll camp out down there for a few days 'til the storm blows out."

"Kid… come here." The blasts of wind drowned out most of the outside conversations, but make people shout their material orders. Sam wanted to be certain no one else heard what he had to say. "This would be a perfect time to solve our problem with my brother-in-law. He'll have his sportfisher out on the mooring. Get those two guys with you to swim in and cut his boat's anchors loose. This storm will cover it up."

"You crazy!?"

"Listen, you said you'd do whatever it takes." Sam sat rigid and glared at the younger man.

"That's plain stupid. They'll see my boat and expect trouble," Kid reasoned.

"Use your head. They're gonna trust the mooring. If I know my sister; she'll want all her boys and hubby with her at home," Sam explained. "Wait till it gets a little darker. Drop those guys in the water close to the point. You don't have to go inside the bay with your boat."

Sam grabbed two polystyrene paddleboards and dive masks from the shelves. "And let them swim in with these if they need 'em.' Can't be that difficult to slice three or four nylon lines. Here," He pulled two new machetes from a wall rack. "Use these, they're guaranteed sharp. They paddle back out some and you pick 'em up. Then you're on your way to Grenada. Your boat's so fast, it should only take you about an hour to get south, out of the storm's danger zone. You want the hotel's water sports concession, don't you?"

"But I want to live to enjoy it. I ain't no little errand boy."

"Offer those two a grand each and there's five more to you. That give you… courage?"

"If it's worth five, it's worth ten, and you'll still be making a hundred times that," He growled.

"You're getting too good at business, Kid. Okay, deal." Sam's hand was grabbed and shook. "Don't mention me to those two dread head fuck ups."

"Boss, where you think they getting their payday from, me? Come on, we'll play this as quiet as possible. I trust them as much as anyone. Ten Bens is mo-ti-va-tion! They living on the promise of the hotel and work," Kid paused, "same as me."

Sam sighed, "Me too, Kid, me too. So, make it happen." He moved around his desk and hugged Kalaloo. "You're my right arm, in on everything, like the brother I never had. My sister, well, she only thinks about herself and always was my father's favorite, getting that whole fucking bay."

"Ah, boss, come on, you didn't do so bad with this store, the docks, and you got the house."

"Shut up!" Sam snapped. "Doesn't matter, I'm the one and only son. I should get and then I'll be the one giving. The daughter's husband should provide. He should have had to pay the family big bucks to marry Cassy. Instead Curly gave him that bay at a bargain price for Harry to take my sister. Sunset Bay is a lot of reasons to stay happily married."

"Whatever, whatever. You got your spring wound, boss. This is the time for keeping a clear head. Gonna be some wind coming, pushing big water. Last info says it is now a Cat 2 and still building over open water."

Turning to watch the bay, Sam said, "We'll handle it. Union Island will pull through. Always does."

"Okay," Kalaloo answered. Just one more thing, Boss, drop that kid shit. I ain't no kid no mo'." The younger man gave a chipper salute, spun around, and slid the door open. The first gust sent papers flying off Sam's desk.

"I'll get this straightened after the storm," Sam rubbed his hands together as talked to himself. "Got a feeling Miss Monique is going to straighten out a lot of things for me. One big storm can blow away a lot of problems."

"The restaurant looks about as good as it can. Take what you need for home, Mammie," Cassy directed. "I know you still got plenty of stuff to get organized around your place. Get a move on. I'll lock up here."

Big Honoré took off his white chef's toque and neatly folded it. Then he politely reached and encased Cassy in a bear hug. "It's gonna be alright, Ms. Cassy. You'll see. Hell yes, we'll get some wind and rain. Both much needed, I don't have to say what gets blown away wasn't built correct. Your place and our place tied down just right. Ain't gonna be no problem. You'll see. Don't worry yourself. The boys of yours and Harry, you can depend on them."

Mammie cut in, "And Mia, too. She's like a tree that bends with the wind, but never breaks. Yeah, all of you, and us, are like that. We lean when we got to lean. Don't worry Ms. Cass. In a few days we'll be here cookin' as usual."

"I know, it's just, well, things have been piling up. Feels like our luck's gone sour."

"Don't be talkin' like that, Miss Cass. That ain't so. It's just God figurin' we all need some hard time to appreciate the good times better," Honoré explained. "More than this storm is gonna blow thru. You'll see; in a few weeks all your problems will get sorted out and it will be smooth sailing and I do mean smooth."

Cassy hugged each again and took a deep breath, "I know you're right, but been a lot lately. I guess I should count my blessings that my family is all back home together again."

"That's it, Cass, count your blessings in spite of this Monique storm coming knocking. We'll keep in touch unless the cell tower goes… but it won't, so we'll call, and you call. Okay?" Mammie reminded.

"Definitely, now get yourselves home." They left and Cassy snapped the last padlocks to secure the shutters. She looked around at what had been her mother's pride and joy. She swallowed hard and snapped some 'before' photos. "Wish this were happier times." The metal bar across the front door took some wiggling to get it onto the hasp. "Okay, see you in a few days."

She looked up at the angry purple sky. "Mama, I know you're watching. Keep your place and our places safe." As she rode out of town, the crowds had dwindled to only a few stragglers and more than a couple were swigging from rum bottles. The way home was quicker pedaling with the wind at her back.

"I only make movies to finance my fishing,"
Lee Marvin

CHAPTER TWELVE

"What time is it now?" Harry asked.

"Ten minutes later than when you asked before, three-thirty," Mia answered. "Don't worry, Mom called, and she's on her way.

The St. Claire family was sitting on the dock, feeling it sway with every wave. Cheese and Verena sat relaxed on the porch, each savoring a small thin cigar.

"But look at that sky, so dark it could be night, except for the bands of lightning out there on the horizon," Harry winced. "Should have gone with her."

"We're waiting around to say our goodbyes. Like to get out there and properly set the anchors." Tim said.

"Not to worry, we can do it in pitch black," Dag vowed. "We'll set the two stern anchors, leave out a bunch of extra rope. It'll only take minutes to grab the mooring lines and we're done. Then enjoy some coffee and sandwiches. Call it, heads or tails, for the first watch."

"Heads, but what difference will it make? You can't sleep in this slop." Tim replied.

"I can, damn straight. Look, there's Mom's bike light. See it, bouncing around. She's hitting every bump. She's made it. Come on, Tim, get in our hugs and let her tell us how worried she'll be and then we can get off the dock," Dag answered.

In a few minutes, Cassy rolled the bike onto the dock. "Boys, I'd rather you took her out and came back in. Paddle the old inflatable," Cassy said between long hugs.

"We'll be all right. Just need to keep the old girl running, so if the storm turns, we'll be able to head her out."

"That's madness. You could drown. Secure the boat and join us at the house," She insisted.

"Mother, we'll be all right," Tim reassured as the broadest lightning flashed, followed by a loud crack of thunder.

"Better listen to your mother." Harry smiled and jerked to another loud crack of thunder. "It's almost six. Last coordinates put it passing Barbados."

The first rain squall began pelting them.

"Don't worry," Tim hugged both parents and pulled on his yellow rain slicker. "We'll stay on the radio. If it gets terrible, we must head out to the open water."

"Then it might be too late. *Sassy* can ride it out alone. I don't…" Cassy pleaded.

"Okay, Mom, okay. Now you get to the house before you're all drenched," Dag said as he unwrapped the dock lines. Harry extended handshakes with winks and nods to both his sons, slid his arm around his wife, and hustled Cassy into the house.

"Sticking me here, huh?" Mia squealed. "That means I got to listen to all the moans and groans for days."

"Yeah, but they love you more, and would worry too much if their only daughter was out in this blow," Tim reasoned.

"Blow this! You both owe me. Be careful out there." She sent them kisses that got lost in the squall. "Seriously, keep on the radio otherwise our two 'rents will drive me even crazier. God be with you," she yelled. "Never take off your life jackets." Mia threw both hands up waving the middle fingers as she ran towards the house.

"Okay, bro, get up on the bow and keep a lookout for anything floating. The last thing we need is to wrap something in the props. It would really be the last thing," Dag warned as the fishing boat bounced up as she busted into the growing ocean swells. "Shouldn't be anything, but keep the boat hook with you. Only take a few minutes until we're at the mooring," he shouted over the weather and motor noise.

"I can see *Moonchild*. Cheese's boat is riding nice. She won't swing into us, will she?" Tim yelled back.

"Not to worry, me-son, unless she breaks loose. Talk later, when you're back in the cockpit," Dag said as he maneuvered the wheel and the spotlight. "Wait for my signal to grab the mooring lines. Keep pointing at the ball!" Dag shouted.

Slowly, pointing to the west, he brought the bow directly up to the mooring ball. Then Dag reversed to the south and threw out one plow anchor off the starboard stern. He ran back to the wheel after quickly wrapping that line on the midship cleat. The wind tried to swing the boat to the north, competing against the force of the sea. He watched and reversed to port, ran and threw the second stern hook.

Tim's wet face came around the windscreen, "What the fuck are you doing?"

"Set the stern two anchors. You grab the mooring lines and then we'll adjust our position. The force of Mother Nature has probably set them already," Dag was jabbering. "Grab the lines!"

It took Dag only minutes to have *Sassy* secured on a three-point anchor system. The hardest part was keeping their balance in the swells as the wind rolled the boat side to side while the swells rocked it bow to stern. She was bouncing constantly. It was like a very serious version of a carnival funhouse. Every step necessitated a handhold.

Tim crawled from the bow, hugging the side railing. "Storm's building up, huh?"

"Some," Dag was busy adjusting the length of the stern anchors. "These can be our saviors or our downfall. Anytime we engage the transmission, got to be certain there's no slack in these anchor lines. They'll be enough trash floating out here, can't wrap a prop with one of our own lines."

"I hear you. I heard you the first time," Tim wiped his face. "You could have waited and I would have helped."

Dag hugged Tim. "Bro, I do this and it's all matter of fact. Same as you and the computer, but different. You know what I mean. You had to be on the bow to keep the mooring ball in sight so I could line her up. Same as the props, one anchor can foul another and they're both useless."

"What now?" Tim asked.

"Got Dramamine? Rolly-turvy now, gonna get worse. Rack out if you can. I got the first watch. Six-thirty, dark as hell. Sundown should be in an hour. Go below and try to get some shut-eye. I'll wake you in a few hours."

"Okay, you're sure there's nothing else that needs attention? Doubt I'll get any sleep."

"We checked the engines," Dag shook his head. "Now it's up to us to keep her right side up." He patted Tim on the shoulder. "Everything's okay."

Agilely cutting through the wave troughs, Kalaloo's high-performance, low profile, deep-vee hull was almost invisible. It surfed a six-foot wave until Kal could found protection in the lee of Rapid Point.

The two dreadlocked men tightly gripped the stainless rail on the boat's small dive platform. They were hesitant as they scoped out at the threatening water.

"Now, you want those Bens, or not? Get in the water and all ya gotta do is a simple thing; chop all the ropes holding that fishing boat. Probably got four anchors out, one in every direction." He paused, "Don't be afraid to chop anyone who gets in your way. This hurricane will cover up a lot of shit. Hear me?"

"Yeah, yeah, we hear you. But, damn Kid, that's a long swim. Yous sure there ain't nobody on that boat. Don't seem like they let it just hang there."

"Nah, boy, them St. Claires all got no balls. They 'fraid and at home, curled up with mommy and daddy. Don't worry."

"If no one's on it, then let's get right up against it," Foxy rankled.

"It's about people watching from shore just like I'm watching with these binos." They can't see you in the water."

"And you can? We putting our lives on the line for small money, trusting you with our welfare," Tony argued.

"When's the last time either of you dread-heads held even one Ben Franklin?" Kal shot back. "I can't anchor my boat in these swells, or I'd do it and save myself the money."

"It ain't your dough, we can bet on that, and also that you making money off our backs. We doing the risking. You sitting here nice and comfy," Foxy was almost crying.

"Look, it's one long surf. Pull your ass up onto that boogie board and ride it in. I'll be watching every move. Once I see you wave, I'll come in, but you gotta swim this way some. Come on, you know my boat can't be seen close to what's supposed to look like an accident. Keep the boogie board tied to you. You don't have to do no diving or nuthin'. Chop them ropes at the waterline," Kalaloo made a face wrinkling his lips, "This is for bigger money down the line. Don't worry, I got your back."

"Counting on that, Kid," Foxy stuttered.

"Don't call me Kid!" He shoved both of the dreads backward into the froth. Both clawed to the surface, coughing.

"Just chop the anchor lines and think about how you're gonna to spend the grand." Kal turned his back on them and opened another Heineken as they kicked towards the powerboat. He glanced at his dive watch, half-past five.

Ashore, the St. Claires and Chessmans were making the best of a very stressful time, fawning relaxation with an endless trivial conversation. Mia was lying on her back, sprawled on the living room, floor surrounded by the big, antique, tube model Zenith shortwave radio, a modern Grundig multi-band radio, and her phone.

The Chessmans had sunk comfortably into the cushions of the wicker couch. Verena had her head on Cheesy's shoulder and they held hands as if on their first date. Cassy was in the wicker chair closest to the kitchen. They were playing what could have been the world's longest game of Scrabble.

"What is that word, 'flapjack'?" Verena asked. "I've never heard of it. Mia, I think you're trying to sneak one over on an older Brit couple."

"You've heard of pancake, well, the same thing," Mia rolled over and found that her phone still had Google. "See?"

"Okay," Verena pinched Cheesy's arm, "You ever hear of flapjacks?"

"Oh, I believe I read it once, perhaps in a Jack London story."

Harry occasionally walked out the side door and got drenched. He'd only glimpse *Sassy* every time a bolt of lightning snaked across the black sky. Inside, he paced across the bayside set of kitchen windows.

"What's the time now?" He asked.

"Harry, my dear friend, I'm sure you've got a watch somewhere in your collection of gifts, if you were too frugal to purchase one. And damn it, you have a cell phone; that always has the time and lights up," Cheese reminded. "Me and the girls are playing word games. Come on, join us. Your sons are A-OK. Not a thing to worry about."

"Five-fifty, Harry," Mia said, "Ten minutes from another weather tracking report. Hope to hell the meteorologists got off their butts and have some new info. Those guys up in Kingston worry more about covering their own asses that providing the most recent info to the people."

"Oh, Mia, can't blame anyone for putting themselves first, or their families, in times like this," Cassy almost scolded. "Got to have some empathy, share the feelings you have."

"Oh, no, Mia's right. Take a civil servant job, so be civil and serve," Harry warned. "We need to know where Monique is, lat, long, and wind speed."

Mia clicked her cell phone at precisely six. "Well, the tower's still standing. Happy and surprised we still have current," she said as she swiped the screen. "Oh, oh, oh…" Her voice trailed off.

"What? Mia, what's that damn phone saying?" Cassy clamored.

Mia sat up and cleared her throat, "Monique hit Barbados and tore a path across the south of the island. BBC's last report has a sustained wind speed more than 110 mph. Tore a path from Grantley Adams Airport to Bridgetown. Headed directly west." She exhaled a long breath.

"That means what?" Cassy asked.

"Only a Cat Two," Verena tried to say almost cheerfully.

Harry cut in, "No disrespect, Verena, but never, never say only in front of a Category two. If it is sustained that means the gusts go another fifty to sixty or more. And it's a bullet coming directly for Union."

"Come on Harry, more optimism," Cheese bayed. "Don't make it sound like we're doomed. Come on, man, for God's sake, lighten up! A category two will blow through, out to sea quick. Could even pass north."

Just then the lights went out. "I see your point, Cheese. So does Vinlec." Harry swallowed hard. As he paced, he shook his head and wrung his hands. "Got a lot riding 'tween now and Christmas. Yeah, that's about our deadline. Dead-line sounds about right. We're in line with fucking Monique and our business is dead!"

"Dad!" Mia stood and put her arms around him. "You got nothing to worry about. Don't stress yourself into a heart attack."

Mia began lighting the glass chimney wick lamps. The room suddenly felt warmer as the shadows danced on the walls with the breeze.

"Hey, everyone's saying: Harry, you got nothing to worry about! Well, my dearest daughter, I do have a shitload to worry about. First, all our lives, second, this house, our homestead. Then *Sassy* and the business we built for the last twenty-some years. Please, don't tell me I have nothing to worry about. I don't have the energy to start over. Might be all I have left just to rebuild." He exhaled hard and sank into a chair.

"Mia's right, Harry," Cassy spoke up. "You're getting yourself all riled up, and the storm hasn't hit us yet. I'm worried, but let's pull together. Tim and Dag, call them and see what's happening. They'll be the best judges of how fierce the storm is." She walked over and sat on the floor beside her husband and hugged his bare legs.

Mia handed her an old, red railroad-style lantern.

"Curly gave us this as a wedding present; remember, Harry?" Cassy laughed. "Said if you ever lost your temper with me, light this to help you look for it. Forgot about that until now. My father had a sense of humor." She lifted it and held it towards the center of the room. "Okay, whose turn is it? What's the last word?"

At that moment, the wind had more power than the sea. It howled and whistled through the tuna tower as the anchor lines groaned at the combined pressure. The waves constantly pounded the hull. Many parts of the sportfisher creaked, and the aluminum tower accompanied with more than a few rattles.

Tim rolled over, opened his heavy eyes to the bleak darkness and only saw Dag on the opposing bunk with a small penlight bouncing around as he played with the radio.

"Didn't want to wake you, bro; tried to be as quiet as possible," Dag said.

"Yeah, it's about as quiet as a library in here," Tim replied. "What are you up to? What the fuck is that light?"

"Headlamp, buddy, a hands-free headlamp. Here," Dag tossed Tim an elastic contraption. "Strap it on your noggin. Makes it easier to locate each other in the darkness."

"Feels like a jockstrap. Where the switch? Okay, I got it. We look like..." Tim laughed, "What do we look like? You got on an orange life jacket, over a yellow slicker, and white safety harnesses under everything. Not quite a fashion statement."

"I look like a survivor. We aren't dummies. Get yours on," Dag said seriously. "Checking radio frequencies. Barbados is getting creamed. Monique roared down the southern coast. Found two ham operators still on the air. Must have generators. All power's off there and sounds like almost every antenna has snapped."

"Holy shit!" Tim breathed.

"That's all to be expected. Looked out a while ago and no lights at our house. Vinlec must have pulled the plug."

"Wouldn't see much as it's all shuttered up. We don't seem to be bouncing as much as before." Tim buckled his safety harness before he pulled on his yellow raincoat.

"I think this is what they call the calm before the storm," Dag answered. He opened up a big, red plastic canister and dumped two flare guns and cartridges on the bed. "Hey, remember what Cheesy said; keep a flare gun on you at all times. Don't go anywhere without your safety line clipped onto something solid." Tim stepped back, took a pistol, and placed it in his coat's side pocket.

"Always enjoyed listening to accounts of the storms hitting other islands," Tim muttered. "This will be big news when I get back to jolly old London."

"Wait; it's six o'clock. Let's listen to the National Weather Center."

The radio had static, but was clear enough to recognize that shit had hit the fan in Barbados and the fan was spinning towards Union.

'This is the National Oceanic and Atmospheric Administration. At one o'clock GMT Hurricane Monique passed over the island of Barbados, registering sustained winds of one hundred and twenty mph.

Tracking stations in Florida predict that the storm's force is still increasing.' Blasts of static from lightening and the combined thunder broke the transmission. 'Emergency shelters are full. Only two radio stations remain operational. All others have lost their antennas. The present position of the eye is 13.21N, 59.55W. All vessels should take appropriate precautions. Next broadcast in 30 minutes.'

"Phew! Holy shit! Doesn't sound good." Dag sank back onto the bouncing V-berth bunk. "What do you think?"

Tim steadied himself and sat on the stairs at the hatch. He found a thermos tucked at the edge of the bunk and cautiously poured a cup of coffee amid the bumps and jerks. He carefully handed it to his brother and then poured one for himself. "What're our options? Take *Sassy* out to the open water now? We can't leave her. What if a wave broached her or her pumps failed? *Sassy*'s family."

"I know what you mean. We need her to fish another day, but we've got to be careful. This could become a dangerous business, little brother."

"Hey, what part of me looks little?" Tim remarked. "Become dangerous? Hey, I'm not little or stupid. I knew this would get hairy. But also, a night never to forget. Me and you, bro, me and you."

"Yeah, yeah, yeah, we'll be okay, because we've got each other's back. I wanted to chat with you about something, your weight training, I guess. Don't know how to put it?"

"What about it? I've been working out."

"Saw you and Jason. You switch over to the other team?" Dag asked.

"What? What other team?"

"You know, I'm not prejudiced," Dag grinned.

The boat lurched with a different twist, as if she dropped off a ledge. The hull made a hollow sound when it skimmed off a wave and landed solidly. Both felt it and bolted to get out of the cabin. As the hatch opened, the wind caught their rain hoods and blew them back. It took a few minutes to catch their balance topside. They had to fight the direct force of the wind in their faces combined with the wet, slippery, rolling deck.

"Snap your safety line around something solid!" Dag shouted as he clipped himself to the starboard post of the tuna tower. Tim maneuvered around the inflatable and snapped his lanyard at the handgrip on the port gunnel.

Their boat lit up, reflecting a series of lightning bolts.

"Something's wrong," Dag yelled. The sportfisher wasn't sitting the way he expected. "Check the stern-port anchor. Can't believe we're dragging."

Tim felt nothing but slack as he pulled in only a short section of the anchor rope. The end was frayed where it had been hacked. He held it up for Dag to see. "What the fuck!"

Slowly, with handholds, Dag carefully moved to the starboard stern. He peered over the side into the churning sea and his headlamp beamed on a wet head of dreadlocks sawing with a broad knife at the anchor line. "Hey! Hey! What the…" The head tilted back and the face was revealed in the lamp's beam. "Tony, you mother fucker!"

Tony locked his eyes on Dag and continued to saw at the line as fast as possible as he rose and fell with the constant swells.

In a fishing move, Dag grabbed the gaff mounted along the stern, swung as if he intended to grab a fish, but intentionally pointed the hook away. He smacked the dread solidly on the back of his head. On the next swing of the gaff, Tony reached out with one hand, grabbed the pole, and yanked Dag overboard into the wild, dark swirling water.

Realizing what was coming and that his safety line was hooked, Dag gulped a breath before he hit the black, surging sea. He had his hands outstretched to protect against any debris floating or a crazy man with a long knife.

This was a risky situation for Tony, and he knew it. A few minutes more and he would have cut the second anchor line. But when it was cut, there would be nothing else for him to hang on to. He knew he'd be floating at the mercy of the storm in the pitching waves, but he would get a payday for screwing the St. Claires. The first blow across the back of his head from the gaff really rang his bell. Maybe he should have drifted away, but Dag had seen his face.

Slashing wildly with the machete in the turbulent water, Tony struck something solid. It was total blackness except for the bright light that his opponent was wearing. That was his target, but it was all blurry with the saltwater burning in his eyes.

The life jacket bounced Dag to the surface. With a lucky grab, he secured his position by grasping the top end of the anchor line. He felt two sharp blows on his left arm and that located Tony's body. Dag coiled his legs and let go with a double leg kick and solidly hit the dread chest-high, causing him to drop the knife. Even above the howling wind, he heard a gasp and gagging. Dropping from the anchor rope, he caught Tony in a choke hold.

This was life and death. His right arm ached from the new wounds. His left squeezed Tony's neck and considered putting him away once and for all. With a slick move, Dag looped the slack of his safety line around Tony's neck and let the surging sea apply pressure. All he had to do was hold on.

Following the shock of the loss of the stern anchor, Tim crawled to the bow to check those lines. It was slow going, belling along the port side safety rail. He hadn't seen his brother flip into the darkness as he knelt at the bow to inspect the mooring lines. The loops were stretched out tight at the bow cleats. He peered over to see the mooring ball. His head beam lit up Foxy, straddling the big, floating ball with his arms and legs coiled around one line for support as he sawed at the other.

"Dag! Dag!" Tim screamed. "Foxy, you mother!"

Grinning or grimacing, Tony had his teeth bared, hanging on the mooring line. "Think yous can stop me, Tiny Tim?" The man snarled.

Tim reached into his coat pocket. He raised the red plastic pistol, cocking the hammer of the flare gun. For a split second, they watched each other. He drew a bead on the dread. "Yes! I think so!" The fireball hit Foxy square on the right side of his head, at his ear. The phosphorus flare was so hot it set the wet locks aflame. The older West Indian screamed, dropped from the line. Tim watched the small, intense white flame as the raging sea carried the villain away with arms flailing.

"Tim! Tim!" He barely heard his brother's voice over the wind and smacking waves. Carefully gathering his lanyard, Tim crawled on his belly. He worked hand over hand and inched slowly around the windscreen to the port side and then moved across the slick, pitching deck. He followed his brother's safety line.

Looking over the stern, Dag's left arm had Tony and was viciously punching him with his right. They were floating at the length of Dag's safety line. The West Indian had his nose and lips split, gushing blood.

"Pull this bastard up! Don't be careful! I've got his throat wrapped with my safety line! If it snaps his fucking neck, too fucking bad!" Dag roared as the two men rode the waves up and down.

Tony heard the words and didn't know what to do. The half-inch nylon was cutting into his throat. Breathing wasn't easy. He couldn't protect his face from Dag's blows and try to loosen the noose. It was tightening on his windpipe. The rough seas were slapping him against the fiberglass hull. He relaxed and let himself be lifted.

Tim knelt and got his arms under Tony's shoulders and slowly raised the man over the stern, wary not to tumble into the sea himself.

"Don't worry about hurtin' the asshole," Dag shouted as he struggled to pull himself over the stern. "Mother fucker!" Dag kicked the prone man. "Don't take your eyes off this prick. Where's the first aid kit?" Dag's right arm was dripping blood from two long gashes. "Fucker got in some swipes with his long knife."

"Oh-oh, bro, that looks bad."

"Not as bad as Tony's gonna be when I'm through with him." Thunder clapped in response as the winds' howling increased. Talking was possible; hearing was nearly impossible. Dag slapped the dread in the forehead with the flat palm of his good hand. "What the fuck is wrong with you? Who put you up to such nastiness?"

"Punk thought a knife would save him." Tim wrapped the culprit with the thick monofilament line they used for the teasers. "Tough guy. Hey, Dag, in the same locker as the first aid, see if there's a roll of duct tape." Tim rolled the villain onto his back, exposing his face to the weather and saltwater surging up through the scuppers.

Dag slid backward across the deck as a set of huge rollers pummeled *Sassy*. He had the kit and the gray tape. "We're gonna wrap you up and maybe throw you back. You're too small to keep. Hey, bro, I caught that piece of shit Foxy sawing the mooring lines at the bow." He turned to help Dag with the bandage.

"How bad is it?" Dag asked.

"I shot that fuckhead with a flare. He's drifting now. I think at least he lost an ear. One mooring line is good, the other's sliced about halfway through."

"I meant my arm."

Tim cautiously moved forward, helping his brother reach the slight shelter behind the windscreen. He grabbed Dag's arm and examined the cuts. The rain had washed it clean, but the blood kept coming. "Looks like he didn't scrape any muscle, only a couple slices through the skin. Probably could use stitches. Get over by the steering wheel, where there's some protection and I'll wrap it with gauze. Might as well use the duct tape, too."

"Son of a bitch! You will pay for this!" Dag staggered and kicked Tony again. It was difficult to tell if he even moved, *Sassy* was lurching so much.

"If our boat sinks, so do you!" Tim punched Tony and knocked him out.

"Let him lay there. He can't drown with his head up like that. And fuck him if he does," Dag yelled. "Let's get me bandaged."

The radio's constant crackling static parted to Harry's voice. Their father was shouting to be heard. "Hey, how bad is it out there? I thought you were coming ashore? You've got our mother in tears!"

"Sorry. Negative on that. Everything's... all right... so far. We'll keep in radio contact." Tim transmitted. "*Sassy*'s riding better than expected. It's all good."

Cassy's voice was next. "Are you sure? Boys, this is a powerful storm. Mia's radio says we have about six hours until the eye should be over Union."

"Mom, we know, we know. We're listening to the same advisories. Believe us, we have everything under control," Tim said as he glanced at Tony wrapped up, lying motionless at the stern, and Dag lying on the forward bench holding up his bloody wrapped arm. "Everything will be okay. We'll transmit again in another thirty minutes. Okay, mom, dad, Mia, Cheeses, we love you." He switched off.

"Getting kind of corny there, bro," Dag managed.

"Giving 'em what they want to hear," Tim said firmly.

A string of lightning lit up Sunset Bay. If anyone had been looking, they'd have seen Kalaloo's white boat bouncing on the black sea. He needed a flashlight to read his watch. Seven; an hour and a half and no signal from his two accomplices. He let his powerful craft be pushed by the pounding sea deeper into the bay to make a last search.

"Crack! Ba-boom! Ba-boom!" Lightening was rapid fire now. The high-velocity winds projected the thunder. The jagged flashes of light revealed the sportfishing boat riding the rollers at the same angle as the Brit's sailboat.

He ducked behind his small windshield and rubbed his stubbled jaw. "Mother fuck. Them clowns didn't do shit. Probably huddled onshore under a big rock. Dumb asses." He sighed heavily, "Boss ain't gonna like this, but fuck it. I'm heading out of here, pronto."

He gunned his engines and bucked up and down the series of tall waves to clear the point. The size of the sea diminished slightly after he escaped the confines of the bay. The last weather predicted the storm to hit the big time before midnight. The GPS bearing said it would take fifty-five minutes to round the southeast point of Grenada. More power, Kalaloo planned to be there in thirty.

The Sunset Bay house no-smoking rule was lifted during Monique. The Cheeses enjoyed aromatic, thin cigars and had given one to Mia. They smoked nervously. The side door suddenly opened and

Harry's entrance startled everyone. No one had noticed him going outside. Both the wind slamming the door closed and the heavy, wet gusts shook the group from their stupors. He lightly groaned as he shed his raincoat. His thinning, wet hair gave him the sick puppy look.

"How'd you sneak out?" Cassy asked.

"I didn't sneak anywhere. You were all involved in your word game. I walked out the front door. Getting breezy out there. If I had a bar of soap, be time for a bath," Harry wheezed. "Both our boats are still riding where they're supposed to be. I guess that's some consolation. Don't like it in here; nothing to see through the shuttered windows." He bumped Cheesy for a puff.

"Sit down. Try to relax. Harry, this isn't so bad. Remember, it will end. Every night is followed by a dawn. So will this one." Verena lamented with a yawn. She and Cheesy had committed their fate to providence and were on the edge of sleep.

Illuminated by the wick lantern, still lying on her back encircled by her radios, phone, ashtrays, and coffee cups, Mia looked like a steam engine puffing away on her cigar. Cassy propelled the rocking chair, back and forth, back and forth.

"How are they?" Cassy nervously asked.

"Everything looks okay. Anything new on the shortwave, Mia?" Harry said between long drags on the tobacco stick. Cheesy prepared another for himself.

"Not much except Barbados got creamed. Eastside of Grenada is reporting power lines down with a ten-foot surge. Nothing unusual for a storm like Monique. Upgraded to a Cat three, but they analyzed and say she's a compact storm, powerful, and moving quickly, fifteen miles an hour or better."

"Oh, Harry!" Cassy whined.

"Not to worry. That's all good news, moving fast, that is. Cat three, well, what's the difference after Cat 2? Another twenty miles an hour sustained winds. It's the gusts that get you. If one catches something just right," his voice trailed off. "The boys are strong and they know the sea as good as me. Dag checked the moorings. Everything'll be okay, you'll see. Just wait. Gotta be patient. Listen to me, huh, giving advice on patience."

"But you're at least smart enough to be here, inside," Cassy remarked.

"Mom, Dag and Tim will make it with *Sassy*. The downside is we'll all have to listen to their stories," Mia tried to joke.

"Yeah," Cheesy chimed. "We'll be hearing about this forever."

Ba-Boom! Crash! Something big slammed into the house and shook the ground floor.

"What the hell was that!?" Cassy screamed, but never stopped rocking.

"Sounds like Mother Nature is remodeling," Mia answered as chipper as possible.

"We'll see tomorrow. That's soon enough. Got to expect…" Harry joined.

His words were cut off as a tree crashed through the living room window, to the right of the main door. More sounds of breaking glass followed. Harry turned slowly, not fast enough to get out of the way of the tree that smashed through the living windows. It pinned him in the chair.

It sent the shutter flying like a Frisbee. It just missed Mia and the Cheeses. Everything that didn't weigh much in the room suddenly levitated and plastered against the far wall. Lamps tipped and slammed the floor, but there was no fire. Dishes slid off the table. The house creaked as it stretched with the powerful gusts.

The chilling wind instantly made the house uncomfortable and everyone simultaneously gasped, "Damn!"

"How about a bit of help here. Help!"

With the first gust of wet wind, Mia bounded from the floor. She snagged Cassy's hand. They hustled to where Harry had been sitting. They could hear him bitching.

"I'm in the tree! I can see you! God damn it! I can't lift it alone. Okay, come on. But watch where you step, some broken sharp shit got to be on the floor. My guess, it's our West Indian cherry tree."

"Okay, okay," Cassy timidly repeated until Cheesy joined and pushed her out of the way.

"Come on, Mia, feel for the biggest branch you can find. Get down and lift with your legs, not your back," Cheesy instructed. "Harry, can you move at all?"

"Sure, I can. I'm not paralyzed, but the trees got me pinned in the chair against the wall."

"Okay, on three, one, two," amid a few groans, Harry slid out of the chair to the floor and pushed his way through the smaller branches. The weather was swirling around. Everything in the house seemed to be moving.

Harry was breathing hard. He made one step and almost collapsed. His right leg was badly scraped and bruised; his knee swelling. "Mother of God! Sitting in my own living room, and I get creamed! That means it's time to head for our panic room, the bath. Anyone need to use the facilities before we make it home for the next few hours?" Harry was back in charge.

"I gotta go. Too much coffee," Mia waved her hand.

"Me too,' Verena admitted.

"Okay, me and Cheesy will do our business out here. Make a checkup. I think we can pee through the new window Monique made. Stay here."

'Come on, matey, you know what they say about peeing into the wind. Your leg good enough to get outside?" Cheesy pulled on his slicker, snugged the hood, and flicked on his flashlight. He became Harry's crutch. Bouncing off the table and chairs, they made their way through the kitchen to the side door. It wasn't easy. Harry was more dragging his leg than limping. With their flashlights, they surveyed what damage they could see from the inside. Most of the front porch roof was gone. The few timbers left were folded around the cherry tree.

"Not worth contemplating it now, my friend," Cheesy shouted over the wind.

Harry rolled his tongue around his mouth and nodded as he put his weight against the side door. The wind won and pushed him back a few steps. In rugby style, Cheesy pushed Harry through.

"Ah, I agree, Cheese." Harry unzipped and tried to discern where the wind wasn't coming from before he let loose. "Sort of got to expect some damage." He talked loud enough to be heard above the storm, but didn't want the women to hear.

"Ah," both sighed to bladder relief. "Out here, doesn't seem like one-ten or one-twenty," Cheese said. "Not pleasant, but not pelting. We're holding our footing. I am anyway."

"Don't know what you're holding, but I'm holding my pecker," Harry laughed. "You and Verena have had the right attitude all along, chin up, and hi-de-ho. 'Que será, será, and all that Spanish shit, too. Carpe fucking diem, huh? Ain't this the shits?"

"I think it's Italian," Cheesy shrugged as the wind's whirling force pushed them farther back towards the dock. "Your boys, they're excellent seamen. I trust they, and both our boats, will be okay. Everything and everyone will have some wear and tear after this whore Monique moves out," he shouted.

"Yeah," Harry scrunched up and wiped his face, grimacing with every step. "Just bad timing. That's the worst part." A wicked gust knocked them to their knees. "Hey partner, let's get inside. No room for stupid tonight."

The wind twisted them around and in a blast of lightning, they saw the dock, or what remained. The waves had smashed the two main cross braces off the pilings. Harry bounced as if trying to jog, and the wind slammed him down.

Cheesy made it upright and extended a hand. "Get up, Harry. Can't fix it now. Take only a day or two to nail it back together. Don't fret the small stuff, Harry. Remember, as long as you and your loved ones are still sucking air, it's all small stuff."

A deafening blast of thunder boomed instantaneously with the lightning flash. As they rose from the ground, they glimpsed both vessels hanging in line, rising and falling among the gigantic roller waves.

"That's where they're supposed to be," Cheesy uttered before another gust knocked him sideways.

With a cringing grimace, Harry spread his aching knees in a squat and levered his friend up. "Come on, we got to get our asses where the wind ain't blowing so strong. I want to radio the boys."

The two men locked arms and lurched their steps, trying to slant their weight against the wind. Unfortunately, the wind swirled and knocked them down and askew several times before they crawled back into the recently ventilated house.

"Radio here doesn't look so good, Harry," Cheesy said as he discovered a three-inch tree limb had cracked the white plastic case. "Ah, don't worry, Verena's got our portable handheld." He gave a look of assurance, "You'll be able to tune them in on it."

"Yeah, our handheld's around here somewhere, but, damn, I forgot to charge it. There's always something. I could use a belt of rum about now," Harry confessed.

"Couldn't we all? One would lead to two and two would lead to no leaders. We need to be stalwart for the ladies."

"I guess you're right. Cheese, you ever get tired of always being right?" Harry laughed and clapped his buddy on the shoulder.

"What do you think?" Dag muttered.

"I think the bitch is still building." They'd stripped down to their soaked shirts and were sitting in the V berth, shivering. Their headlamps didn't brighten their spirits. Dread Tony was lying with his face against the wall with his hands and feet wrapped with silver duct tape.

"I agree, but the eye will be here soon. It'll settle for a bit, then." Dag chuckled as he rubbed the bloody bandage on his forearm. "Doesn't feel like a washing machine. More like a whirling blender."

"Don't know about you, but with these lamps and the complete blackness, I feel like I'm in some kind of mine. Confined, claustrophobic."

"What do you want it to be, coal? Let's fantasize big; we're in a gold mine. Well, the lights keep your arms free to use," Dag said as he poked Tony. "I needed my hands free to see where this son of a bitch was. Looks like it's stopped bleeding."

"Hard to tell. You aren't leaking, so maybe it stopped. Want me to wrap it again? What time is it? I haven't heard from our shore patrol in a while. I tried radioing about an hour ago."

"Eleven-forty-five. Remember mom said that the eye should pass between midnight and one." Dag used his good arm to tune the radio. "Nothing. Maybe they only come on, on the hour."

They sat quietly until midnight. The radio crackled to life with the St. Vincent Emergency frequency. 'All stations, on land and at sea: be advised Hurricane Monique is now centered approximately five kilometers south-southeast of Kingston with sustained winds exceeding two hundred kilometers an hour moving west-northwest at approximately twenty-two kilometers an hour. This is an extremely dangerous storm. Take all precautions. Do not be out in the elements. This message will be repeated with updates every half hour. God is with us all.'

"Wowee zowee, bro, this doesn't sound good. Looks like the eye is somewhere east, close, still cranking to us," Tim said sadly. "What do you think we should do?"

"Maybe bend over and kiss our asses goodbye," Dag tried to chuckle, but instead coughed. "I don't know, but when the rear wall comes through after the eye, for a while it's going to be, I don't know, bad. Sorry, with this arm, don't know how much help I'll be. Don't know, don't know," he stammered, "don't know shit about now, except we are in the shit!"

"Hey, we got our life jackets, safety lines, still more flares. You know the program; hold on tight with your undamaged hand. I checked the bilge about an hour ago when you were crashed. Everything is okay. Engines are running smooth. Fuel needles haven't moved much. Pumps are working like charms." Tim chewed on his thumbnail and sighed, "Coffee?"

"Yep, better try to gulp it now." At the first swig, the boat lurched, and the coffee went flying. "Damn, perfect timing. Glad it wasn't steaming hot, and that I'm already soaked," Dag scoffed. "Remember, it can always be worse."

"Where did you learn how to see the bright side?" Tim asked.

"Lots and lots of bumpy fishing charters with caballeros retching. Even as captain, I always had to be the one to hose and scrub. About now, I'm feeling glad I missed dinner."

"We got sandwiches," Tim offered.

"Missed my point, bro, all this rolling, my stomach is in ejection mode," Dag belched.

"Can't believe seadog Dag would ever puke."

"Everyone has their limit. I'm close now," Dag rolled his eyes. "We're bouncing up, slamming down, twisting, rolling, man oh man. I think it's time to go. Put all our safety gear on again."

"I agree. You radio Dad and I'll drop the mooring," Tim stood bracing himself.

Dag found the radio's microphone as Tim headed back on deck. Again, he clipped his safety line between lurches.

"Sunset Bay come in." The radio squawked with static. "This is *Sassy.* Come in, Sunset Bay. Sunset Bay!"

"Sunset Bay, come back." The signal was weak and only audible because he was in the V berth. Dag was glad he'd connected with Mia. "How's it going out there? Over"

"Everything is peachy, just peachy. How's the house taking it? Over."

"Little of this and a little of that. Nothing that a few nails won't cure. Power's off. Can't watch TV. How's are you two? Who puked all ready? Over."

"I think it's calming down. Sis, it's so nice out here, I talked Timmy into going out fishing. Just in case you wake up and see us gone. Over."

"Be careful. Very careful. You're the only brothers I've got. Over."

"Roger that. Keep the radio on. We'll try to call on the hour. Be back for breakfast. After dawn will be the best fishing ever."

"I'll have coffee and pancakes. Be careful, promise. Over"

"Promise. See you in the daylight. *Sassy* out."

Dag slogged his way topside. The deck was awash with rollers breaking over the stern. He snapped his safety line close to Tim's. They put their hooded heads together. "Sounds like they're making it okay onshore."

"Same as us, saying what we want to hear. But I think we got to go. Seas coming big from the east, from the shore, and meeting the massive ones coming around the point into the bay; piling up. And they're meeting right where we are. I dumped the stern anchor. Can you handle the wheel?" Tim asked. "When I let loose from the mooring, it's got to be fast and we can't tangle one. What do you think, hard port or starboard?"

"You let her loose, I'll let the wind push us for a few seconds, and we should be out of the way of our lines. I can handle our boat with no hands. Fast is my middle name."

"That's what all the girls say." Tim switched on the big spotlight and lit up the bow. "Keep your eyes on me."

"Hey, what girls have you been talking to? Tim, be careful."

"Always." They clasped hands.

Tim worked around the windscreen to the foredeck, holding tight to the stainless rail, always mindful of his safety line. Movement was tough, bulked up with the life vest. Even with his headlight, the sleeting rain made vision almost impossible. It was like staring at a power washer. Squinting didn't help.

Bellying, he made it to the bow. Tim had to sit to get enough control to remove the mooring lines from the cleats. The wind and the sea had him beat. He couldn't loosen them. A wave broke over the starboard side, slammed, and flattened him, pushing his face into the fiberglass. Luckily, he remained conscious.

As he was feeling his surely broken nose, Dag engaged the transmission and edged forward, reducing the pressure on the mooring lines. Tim's eyes were watering. Using the Braille method, he could pry off both ropes. He swallowed hard. This was something new, not what he'd expected. *Sassy* was freed to face the storm on the open ocean.

He felt the throttle drop as he turned and crawled back to the steering station. Once Tim rounded the windscreen, Dag throttled up.

"Hold on! Let's get the hell out of here. I don't know where we're going. Here, the way we were bouncing, twisting, and rolling, isn't the best place to be," Dag shouted.

"What about *Moonchild*?"

"Cheesy's yacht will be all right. Got a much deeper keel. Think it draws six feet. We draw draws two."

"Got ya! I'll use the spot to watch what's coming." They both held on as the sportfisher bucked against the waves.

"Can you see anything? I can't. I'm using a compass heading. Hold on, I'll blast through the cut, and then we should get out of this slop."

"I'm holding, boss, I'm holding."

"Out there, it won't be a walk in the park, but the sea's not so confused. Most waves are traveling the same way. We just got to be conscious of when the storm's rear wall comes through. I plan on making a big, wide swing to the south. The last forecast said it was running west-northwest. Figure we'll end up somewhere south and west of Grenada."

"As long as *Sassy* is still right-side up tomorrow morning, I don't care where," Tim kept working the spotlight.

"You okay? Your nose isn't looking so good," Dag joked.

Tim checked his teeth with his free hand. "Nothing a cold beer and a warm woman wouldn't cure."

"Same here. Glad to hear that. Seeing anything?"

"Just black water," Tim was again serious.

A colossal wave broke and the boat shuddered. Water flowed everywhere on the deck. They were about to pass the point. Tim shined the spotlight on the rocks off starboard. "Oh, oh, I think we're climbing a mountain," Dag predicted. "Hold on!"

Bam! The brothers couldn't see it, but their boat went almost straight up, vertical, and luckily the wind pushed her nose forward. The sportfisher fell her length. When the hull was in the air, the engines suddenly accelerated as the props cavitated. Once *Sassy* fell, she tumbled into a huge wave trough and rolled on her port side, the twin props caught and shot her up on another wave crest. It was a miracle she righted again. Dag held the wheel.

"Holy shit!" Tim screamed.

"Hold the fuck on! This is gonna be one long fucking night."

"If people concentrated on the really important things in life, there'd be a shortage of fishing poles." Doug Larson

CHAPTER THIRTEEN

Through a few tiny slits in the continuous gray, a glimmer of a pink sun appeared. The wind had dropped off to a stiff breeze, but enough to keep the house creaking along with an occasional bang.

The panic room had done its job. With yawns and groans, the five untwisted from a tangled pile. Harry woke first. His posterior sat on the cold ceramic tile base of the shower stall with his upper body crooked, leaning against the wall of the shower stall. He snaked his good leg between Cassy and Mia. They wrapped the bruised right knee in a towel and it was stiff along the shower wall. He sniffed and sneezed, finally found the roll of toilet paper, and loudly blew his nose.

"Bad alarm, bad alarm." Mia shook her fist in the air, "Too early, too early. Even lying on this cold, damp concrete, I need a couple more hours."

Verena coughed, "Here, here, I second that." She snuggled closer to Cheesy, who was wedged between the toilet and the vanity.

"I'll make coffee, you all try to sleep." Cassy pulled herself up and on tiptoes peered out of the small bathroom window. "It's light already, sort of gray, not black anymore." She turned and gave her hand to Harry to help him stand.

Harry moaned as he moved his right leg. In a smooth move, he pulled Cassy into a tight embrace with a solid, lusty kiss. "No matter what you see outside, inside, it's all upside, there's no downside since we're all safe, uninjured, and alive."

"I know, I know," Cassy sighed loudly and allowed herself to be his crutch as they made their way to the kitchen. It was more than the usual disorder after a long night. Soggy, half-eaten sandwiches, stale crackers, and chips had been blown off the table and littered the floor. The big change was the top branches of the cherry tree sticking through the doorway from the living room. She staggered and caught herself. "Oh my, oh my." Cassy sat down and just stared at the treetop.

Harry limped his way around her. "I'll say it again; everything's going to be okay. Where'd you hide the coffee?" He dumped out the little that remained in the pot and refilled the percolator with bottled water. It took a few matches before he got a stove burner lit. "See, darling, we're cooking with gas again. The tanks didn't get blown or washed away." He rinsed the cups he could find with water from another gallon jug. He sighed, "We'll be up and running again in no time."

Cheese was behind him at the hallway door. "That's the spirit and Mr. Caffeine will further inspire us. That banging must be an upstairs shutter."

"Do we still have an upstairs?" Cassy asked.

"Certainly, my dear, I'll go look as soon as I find my rubber boots. Bound to be some sharpies lying in wait for my tender footsies," Cheesy mumbled.

"Wait for a cup," Harry sort of ordered as the percolator started making the pleasurable bubbling noise. "No need to rush out." He pointed Cheesy to another chair, but the Brit grabbed a broom and began sweeping. "Sit down," Harry said.

"Aye, aye, Captain, but I must respectfully decline. Might as well sweep as I search out my booties. The kitchen held up well. Ah, there's my white Wellingtons. Can't misplace those. Cost me almost twenty-five pounds. Wonder how they got under this cabinet?"

"Will ya quit babbling? You got your boots; here's your coffee. You want moo?" Harry snapped. "Hey, Cass, we got any of those elastic bandages?" He wrinkled his nose, "Might help a bit."

"Black will be fine. I see the storm didn't improve your morning demeanor at all, admiral. If you don't have any elastic, I know we have Ace bandages on our sailboat. One is especially for knees," Cheesy answered over his shoulder as he opened the side door and peered at his yacht. "*Moonchild,* our lady is still afloat. I can only imagine the mess below decks."

Cassy pushed Cheesy out of her way. "Where's *Sassy*? Where are Dag and Tim?" she cried.

Harry rolled his head and poked Cheesy in his gut. "Had to be in such a hurry, just had to open the door. Now you got her all worked up. Drink your fucking coffee and keep quiet."

"Shut up, Harry! Damn right, the only thing on my mind, since we are all together, is our boys. Cheesy, I apologize for him." Cassy leaned deflated against the wall. "Where are they?"

After several gulps of coffee, Harry used a broomstick for support. He limped a few careful barefoot steps farther down the sidewalk to where he could see the entire bay. "Well, sweetheart, our boat's not washed onshore. I know she didn't sink at the mooring if Cheese's boat is still there. The boys must have taken her for a ride."

"I'll bet it was quite a ride," Cheesy mumbled.

"Thought you were busy drinking your coffee?" Harry said.

Mia walked up loudly yawning and startled Cassy with a hug

from behind. "Mom, I guess I forgot to tell you. Last night, Tim called and said they had to take her off the mooring. Inside the bay was too wild."

"But if the Chessman's boat made it?"

Cheesy answered, "Depth, probably because your fishing boat is riding on the surface and our sailboat has about five tons of lead in her keel that goes down seven feet. That stabilizes her. Why we chose that yacht, with a big deep, full keel."

"So, where are they? Are they safe?" Cassy rattled off.

With a smug look, Harry tried to be convincing, "We laid out a plan before the storm. If it got to where they felt it was getting too bad inside the bay, no protection, they were to head southwest and swing back east, as soon as the sea fell."

"I'll try to raise them on the radio," Mia said as she filled a cup. The radio was dead. "Damn, I guess I passed out with it switched on. Oh, mom, those two, Dag and Tim, are good. Probably drinking cold greenies in Grenada or Polars in Venezuela."

"About now that sounds good, very good." Harry licked his lips.

A second-floor shutter that had been banging suddenly crashed to the ground and broke the mood. Cassy sobbed.

Wearing a long robe, with coffee and a small cigar in hand, Verena appeared calm, as if there had not been a tempest the previous night. She coughed and said, "Woman, now is not the time for tears, but smiles. We have been blessed with another day and fresh opportunities. Look at the beauty. The sun will beam here soon."

"Yeah, yeah, yeah, you and Cheesy here should get on the preaching circuit," Harry barked as he gathered Cassy in his arms while trying to support both with his broomstick cane. His good leg slipped, and they both hit the wet ground. "Crying is excellent therapy, sometimes. Right, babe? Cry your eyes out, if it'll make you feel better." He deposited her on the cast iron lawn bench that had been too heavy to move by hand or by the storm.

Harry knelt close, "But babe, you're crying without good reason. I know you want to let off some steam from all the stress, but you're making us all sad when we should be happy. We survived," He slid his hand along his leg, "With only a few scrapes and bruises. Come on, you and I know damn well the boys and the boat made it through. We're tough!"

Her body twisted with jolting sobs and Harry prodded. "Cass! Stop that! *Sassy* is strong and running better than new. Both those boys were born to the sea and can run that boat with their eyes closed."

Harry stood and hugged Mia, "Tell your mom, us St. Claires are tough. Tough like, ah, yeah, tough like coconuts. Yeah, we roll with the wind. Sure, a few scrapes and bruises, but we end up okay."

"Coconuts, yeah, Harry, you're a real coconut," Cheesy chuckled.

Mia sat and consoled Cassy, "We'll get the boys on Cheesy's portable. But you know the antennas are down everywhere and what isn't down is being jammed with calls. They're okay. Come on, mom, cheer up." Mia sighed, "Let's look at the dam… at how well we made out."

"Yeah, Cass, you never liked the old porch, anyway." Again, Harry tried to show the bright side. "And now everything will get a bright coat of paint." Wobbling, he braced himself with the heavy bench and pulled his wife up. Using her for support with his arm around her waist, they led the group walked around to the front of the house.

It was difficult to see the upside, knowing they had zero insurance. The cherry tree had smashed the front porch and only the last two outside pillars stood. The tree had broken everything and left it in a pile that blocked the front entry.

"You were lucky it didn't hit the main roof. I think they call porches, sacrificial. You know, gone with the wind," Cheesy attempted to be humorous. No one was laughing. "The house is still standing with the roof attached, that's the important thing. Only a few windows to repair, and the electric line, and…"

"Shut up. Please. Cheese, you're my buddy and we'll make a detailed work list this afternoon," Harry advised as the Brit couple walked off alone. "Materials will be scarce. When the boys get back probably make a run to Trinidad and load up with lumber, roofing, and paint."

"No, we won't," Cassy again lost her composure. "Oh my God! We'll never…"

"Yes, we will! The place needed fixing up, anyway. I never liked that old porch. This one will be better with a full wrap-around veranda. What them Hawaiians call, ah, a lanai. You'll see. Everything will be better."

"Look, the sun's breaking through, mom," Mia pointed to radiant beams of clear light shooting through the gray clouds, as if it had been scripted. "Like Verena was saying, a new day dawns. Mom, I'd ask you not to worry, but I know you have to. I'm worried too, but I just feel, no, nope, I know they're okay."

"I'm really worried about them," Cassy got out between gulps of air as she fought to stop crying. "Harry, what if… I just… I just think they should have stayed with us."

"Them two are okay, you can bet on it. Soon as it calms, we'll see *Sassy* purring around the point."

"I hope so," Cassy whimpered, "I hope so."

"Well, look at it. Still too rough to come back in yet. Probably be two or three days."

Mia offered. "Come on, mom, let's go into the kitchen and start a cleanup. Keep busy, make things look better. We'll cook a tasty meal. That'll cheer you up. Those two clowns are okay." Mia gave Cassy her hip so her mother could lean on her for support.

Harry hobbled towards the Chessmans where they were trying to roll their skiff over. "Sorry about all of that. But a bit too much for the girl to take. I know you meant well with all the philosophy. Let me help before you strain something."

"Harry, we know you," Verena said curtly, but with a smile. "Yes, we try to always be positive. Carter here, even more than me."

"Hmm, I haven't heard your first name in what, five, maybe ten years, Cheesy. The wind didn't move your skiff an inch and look at what it's done to our house."

The three stood and viewed the new, Monique revised, Sunset Bay. Green had disappeared. Brown and dull gray remained. All vegetation had been fiercely stripped of leaves and blown out to sea. Bare, wet rocks were revealed on the cliffs. Other than the smashed porch and three front windows demolished by the tree, two light poles carrying the main electrical lines were down.

The bay was a murky brown covered with leaves and trash. The waves were still rolling in, tipped with white caps. Lots of foam and debris marked the bay's edges. Only the grim, weathered pilings remained of the dock. It needed a complete rebuild.

As soon as they got their launch flipped over, all three buckled to the increased gravity of the situation and took seats along the skiff's side rail.

Cheesy lit more of the small, thin cigars for each. Harry put his arm around Verena and gave her a hug. "I know I'm a bear and I apologize for my words before. All I can hear now are your words echoing, it can always be worse."

"I feel honored," Verena said as she took a pull of smoke. "Aren't many people over the years who've gotten an apology from Harry St. Claire." The older woman giggled. "Few know you better than us."

"Here's to that," Cheesy interjected with a slap on his captain's shoulders.

"But you're correct. A few thousand and the place is all spiffy again. Getting electric out here will take a forever and a day," he sighed. "Can probably cut the dock boards by hand." Another sigh, "Sure hope the boys are okay."

"They are, they are. Don't fret. Let's get down to business and make your place shipshape again. We'll give you a couple hours and then you all can come out and relax and enjoy a sunset from *Moonchild*. We have less to organize," Cheesy playfully shook Harry.

He rubbed his jaw. Harry sat in thought for a moment and nodded his head. "Yes sir, I got a chainsaw and just remembered where it is. Hope I got oil-gas."

"Got a tank right here," Cheesy shook his skiff's gas tank. More where that came from on our boat. Get your saw and we'll make kindling out of that intruding cherry tree."

"Sounds like the plan."

^^^^^^^^^

Everything, wind, water, and *Sassy* were going in mixed directions. Monique had whipped the sea to chocolate milk and added tree leaves and palm fronds as sprinkles. One breeze blew stiff from the north followed by gusts from the east. Waves shook the hull on every side.

Dawn broke slowly. The sky gradually lightened to a bleak gray, warmed slightly with tiny specs of the pinkish sun. The wind was blowing better than twenty and still making long white caps on the wave edges. The weather was improving, but after last night, anything would be better. The boat wasn't lurching or bouncing miserably, but cutting through the waves as she was designed to do.

The chart navigator finally started working. Since they'd bolted from Sunset all the electronics had been on the blink. Falling off too many steep waves had knocked something loose. Suddenly, Tim's blurred concentration at the seas through his sleepy eyes focused as the GPS buzzer went off. Dag struggled to get up from the front bench. Both were grubby and soaking wet. They acted and looked hungover.

"What's that, Tim, room service?" Dag laughed with a long yawn. He stretched and groaned at the bloody gauze on his forearm. "Wow, can't believe I could rack out, bouncing around in this slop. Must have caught at least a couple hours."

"How's the arm?"

"About the same as your face. You know you got a good pair of shiners!"

"You went under about two and it's almost seven now. All I've been doing is sliding off crests and surfing through wave troughs. Monique's still got things churned up. Sea's dropped a little." Tim looked haggard at the wheel. "Think we still have one full thermos of coffee down below. "Nothing's been operational, 'til now. No autopilot, GPS, radar, depth sounder, radio. Couldn't leave the helm."

"Aye, Captain Ahab, we ain't looking for the white whale. We're looking for a green island or an island that was green until last night." Dag had regained his sense of humor. "Been going in circles, or what?"

"Trying to keep a course of 185, almost directly south. Never had to touch the throttles, kept the engines at three thousand RPM. I have no idea what our distance over ground has been. Add in current, wind, who knows? Both radio antennas snapped. I wasn't able to raise anything. Damn, the CD player is out, no tunes."

"But I'll never forget the night. Total E-ticket all the way," Dag smiled. "Glad the diesels never stalled. We'd be floating on slivers of fiberglass if she'd have wrapped something in her prop coming out of the bay. For that luck, we must light some candles in church when we get back."

"When did you find religion?" Tim asked.

"Since last night. Could have easily gone the other way, you know."

"I got you. We'd better get you back so your arm can get stitched up." Dag looked lost in thought and missed what Tim had said.

After a few moans and ouches, Dag returned from the V berth with the last full thermos. "Almost forgot about the critter we got wrapped up down there. Smells like he shit himself." Dag poured two cups of coffee. "It ain't steaming, but will help."

"Let that prick Tony roll in his own turds," Tim said as he gulped some coffee. "Wonder how Foxy made out after that twenty-five mm flare blasted the side of his head? Here, your turn, take the wheel. I got to sit down."

Dag checked the instruments, pushed a few buttons, and their boat made some whirring sounds. The wheel turned by itself. "Okay, autopilot's working. According to Mr. GPS, we're at approximately 12.44 north and 62.45 west," Dag scratched his head. "Wow, wind and currents, rough calculations, we're 90 miles to St. Georges, Grenada. Got to go southeast.

"What, not go back to Union? It's got to be about the same distance."

"I figure we can get fuel easier and hopefully get in touch with the folks. Bring whatever they need. How's your cell phone? Any charge? Mine's dead."

"Same here. Now, it's sort of reasonable out here, daylight anyway, I'll hook both of them to the twelve-volt system." Tim pulled himself to the chart plotter, read the screen, and pushed a few buttons. "St. Georges, huh? Says at our current speed of six knots, we'll be there late afternoon. Think we can goose her a bit, maybe do nine?"

"Nah, like to, but who knows what's floating out here? At six we bump, at nine we might poke a hole," Dag explained.

"Got ya," Tim agreed. "What are we going to do about our prisoner? Dump him out here? Sink or swim?"

"Hey, that's not a bad idea. Fuck him," Dag recommended. "Never figure these guys out. We mind our business and they mind our business."

"It's like you said the other night," Tim answered. "It is all about envy, and they always want an excuse for failing. Look, if we'd have been born to another family, it could have all been different."

"Nah, no way. We got what it takes. Hey, you got amnesia?" Dag crossed. "We didn't have it so easy growing up, but we made it. Got legitimate professions, you do, sort of anyway."

Tim went below. In minutes, he dragged a howling Tony up the steps by his hair and deposited him directly to the stern. Tim flicked open his knife. Tony's bloodshot eyes were wide as Tim held the blade to the dread's chin. Then he slowly snipped the fishing line that wrapped the prisoner. His hand and feet were still tight with duct tape.

"Gonna do you a favor," Tim whispered in the dread's ear, "Giving you a life jacket." He pushed the straps under Tony's arms and around his waist. "Don't want you to drown."

The man had lived a rough and tumble thirty years and his face showed it. He lay against the stern wall, sniveling and moaning, but held a bitter stare. He spat some blood and cracked, "Water."

"Oh, you want water. Thirsty?" Tim chuckled. "Cut the engines, bro."

Sassy slowed, rolling in the choppy seas. Tim attached one of the safety lines to Tony's life jacket.

"What? What? I just want a drink of water."

Tim lifted the prone man above his head. "Here's water." Tony made a big splash. The orange life jacket kept his head above the brown Caribbean. He was bobbing up and down, getting slapped hard by every wave, towed by the safety line only two meters back. "Help me! Help. I don't wanna die."

"They say dead men tell no stories," Dag grinned. "If you tell us everything you know, then maybe you won't be a dead man. Hey, dummy, no one knows you're here. Whoever you're working for thinks you're dead, drowned already. Talk or I'm cutting you loose and pulling away. Who knows, maybe you'll float to Aruba or Bonaire, but you won't be alive when you get there."

"Please, please," Tony gagged.

"Believe what my brother said, they say dead men tell no tales. Your friends must want you dead to send you out on a night like last night. Not too smart, huh? Swimming in a Cat three hurricane. You broke all the rules last night"

"What… rules?"

"Tell us what you know, or I put the boat in reverse," Dag's grin had stretched into a broad smile. He was enjoying this. "You'll be sucked under and the props will chew your ass up."

"Why did you want to cut our boat loose?" Tim asked. "Huh, you piece of shit, tell us who put you up to it or I swear, I'll…" The boat was in neutral and Tim accelerated until Tony was engulfed in black diesel smoke. "Grind you up like hamburger. Then the sharks eat your stupid ass, piece by piece."

"No! No!" Tony screamed.

"No, what?"

"No, me don't want to die."

"Start talking," Tim tugged the dread closer to the boat. "If I like what you tell me, you get to ride in the V berth again." He unfolded his penknife. "If you lie to me, oh, well."

Tony remained tight-lipped.

"Dumb fuck, see this line that's dragging you! It's much thinner than the one you cut that was holding this boat in the storm." Tim held up his knife. "And this is a lot sharper than the blade you had."

"Start talking!" Dag echoed.

It was after eleven when the sun finally burned off the haze and revealed a light blue sky. It was hot and super humid. It was a breeze now; the breeze dropped to less than fifteen. The storm was sucking all the wind to the north, leaving only humidity. Motoring east, the white decks were too hot for bare feet. Dag had put out two rods with chrome spoon baits flashing on top of the murky sea. The dread Tony was nowhere to be seen. The brothers were silent from nervous exhaustion.

Finally, Tim pulled himself up from the front bench and looked at his watch. "Hot, huh? Past noon. I'm about out of energy." He stood and was glad to see the profile of an island ahead. "Think we're about twenty miles west of Grenada. Your arm feel okay?"

"Not bad, you should have been a nurse."

"Keep it up and you'll really need a nurse. Think it's calm enough to make for a harbor?"

"Lots of shit in the water. Where you want to head, St. Georges, or go around Point Saline to St. Davids?"

"Well, you ought to see a doctor. St. Georges is a better chance to find a clinic open."

"Yeah, don't want to be out here another night." Dag found the binoculars. "I'll keep watch while you steer. Head a few points north, looks like we got some trees in the water. Wait, looks like something, like a hull, capsized. Holy shit, someone's waving."

"Where?"

"Over there," Dag pointed. "See it? I know, lots of brown water, but it's the shiny spot; the sun's reflecting off the hull."

Tim stared into the distance, spun the wheel to port, and headed north. "Who only has a white hull? No green or blue anti-fouling bottom paint?"

"Careful, might be more stuff in the water coming up to it," Dag advised as he kept scanning with the binoculars. "You won't believe this. Look!" He handed the glasses to Tim and took over the helm.

"God works in mysterious ways," Tim whispered. "I see what you mean about lighting some candles."

The engines slowed and Dag put the boat into neutral and drifted to the overturned boat. Even upside down, it was easy to tell it was long and sleek. A weak hand waved from a prone, face down body straddling the hull as they approached. When the man rolled over, it was Kid Kalaloo.

Slowly Dag came near and reversed, as a precaution to not hit the overturned boat and damage *Sassy*. Kal dragged himself to a sitting position with his legs riding the Vee hull.

"Kal, is that you?" Tim shouted. "What happened? You okay?"

"Now that I see you, things are better, much better. You guys are life savers." He struggled to stand, but couldn't. "Don't really know what happened. Must have shot off a big wave. Flipped."

"Oh yeah, there were some mega ones out here last night," Dag smiled. "Come on, we'll give you a lift."

"Thought I was gonna be shark food." Kal flopped into the water and doggy-paddled to the St. Claire's boat.

"Not yet, anyway," Tim muttered as he extended his hand to pull the man on board.

Kalaloo stood shakily, wobbled, and collapsed into the fighting chair. Tim handed him a bottle of water and he gulped it until he choked. Kal poured the rest of the water over his head. "Look, I know you're doing the best by coming by, but think you could tow my boat. It's all I got."

"Aw, yeah. We can understand that. I mean, look at what we went through to save ours. This boat is our bread and butter." He handed him a rope. "Tie this on the bow. We're headed for St. Georges." Dag maneuvered their stern close as possible to the capsized boat.

"I'll help you out," Tim said, "I can use a swim to cool off." Within a few minutes, they were slowly towing Kal's flipped speedboat.

In a half an hour, Kal regained enough strength and composure to walk. He looked over Dag's shoulder at the instrument readouts. "Wow man, that's a nasty cut, you got."

"Yeah, headed to the clinic," Dag smiled. "Lots of sharp shit bouncing around last night."

"Got more water?"

"Down in the cabin," Tim directed. "Got plenty of big, cold bottles. Open the fridge."

"Okay, if I have one? I'll bring up a couple."

"That would be nice. Sure, can use a cold drink about now," Tim smiled.

Kal opened the hatch and stepped down into the V berth. "What? Hey!" He yelled when he saw Tony lying on the port side bunk, trussed and gagged with duct tape. Something bumped his shoulder, and he turned to face the barrel of a flare gun held by Tim. "What the Hell?!"

"Hell's where you might end up. Isn't it funny how things work out? Your buddy, Tony, told us you would pay him to cut *Sassy* loose. What's with that?" Tim asked, still smiling.

"Think anybody would miss your rotten ass after a storm like this?" Dag intervened. "Maybe we ought to put you and your buddy back on your hull and tow you the other way, out to sea?"

"It ain't like that! Please!" Kal pleaded.

"He said please. Did you hear him say please?" Dag laughed.

"I heard him; it almost sounded like he was begging," Tim

chuckled. "Worthless air sucker."

"Come on, guys. Okay!" Kal scrunched down as if he fainted, then suddenly sprang and connected a fist with Dag's jaw. "I ain't going down easy! You two fuckers ain't getting me, I'm getting you."

One roundhouse swing from Tim's right flattened Kal. Lifting him up, he got three more jabs for Tim's personal enjoyment that had him coughing blood. The West Indian drew his legs into a ball when Dag connected with a shot to Kal's groin. There was no struggle as they bound him with tape the same as Tony.

"Damn, we should do a commercial for Duct Tape," Tim sniggered. "God gives and God takes away. Ever hear that?" He said to a quiet Kal as he wrapped a rope around his waist. "Well, it seems God gave you to us. Now we can take you away."

With a jerk, Dag used his good left and pulled Kal bouncing up the few steps and through the hatch. The two brothers laughed at him lying flat on the deck.

"Now, Kid, we know you don't have a problem directly with us. We'll give you the same chance your buddy, Tony, had. Tell us who put you up to this. Here and now, we own your ass. This," Dag hesitated, "is life and death. Your life or your death."

"Yeah," Tim slowly said for effect, "No guilt on us for dropping your ass in the deep, out here. We finish ahead. We found your boat and get salvage rights. That money will come in handy now. Figure, we get an easy ten grand for your go-fast." Tim sucked a deep breath, "And you end up D-E-A-fucking-D! Dead!"

"I ain't saying nuthin'," Kal growled.

"Got some balls, huh? But sore ones, and no brains. You are our toy, asshole. We can do with you whatever we want." Dag laughed, "Tony held out... for one swim."

"You wouldn't!?"

"How can I best explain this to you? Hmm? You're the fucking bait," Tim said as he did a repeat; lifted Kal and tossed him over the stern. The attached line paid out a few meters. They watched from the stern as Kal tried to keep his head above water. Every few seconds, he gagged loudly as he took a breath and also sucked in seawater.

"Oh, damn it, Dag, we forgot to put the life jacket on Kal." Tim pulled their wide-eyed, gasping victim to the stern.

"That's what Tony said at first, but after a few minutes, he blabbed." It was Dag's turn to interrogate, "Tell us about the hotel people. That's who it was, wasn't it?"

"Never!" Kal answered as they pulled him up and strapped him into a life jacket.

Tim pulled the tow rope tight and spun Kal around. "Just checking there's no mention of our boat or business on that life jacket." Then he pushed him back into the brown sea. Tim released the line towing Kal's boat and dropped it into the water.

"Oops! Damn clumsy of me. Dag, you better put the boat in reverse so I can pick up the rope."

They used the same maneuver that convinced Tony to spill his guts rather than get chewed by our props. Dag reversed the boat and swung wide, just missing the still coughing Kal floating prone in the sea.

"Bro, sorry, clumsy today. Missed the rope again. Pull forward and back down again. I'll get it this time."

Dag shifted gears, a shot forward, and then he spun the wheel, barely missing Kal.

"Okay! Okay!" Kal gurgled.

"See, that's exactly what Tony said. Could have saved yourself a lot of drama."

^^^^^^^^^

Monique had moved on to be an active problem in Puerto Rico and Hispaniola. In the northern Grenadines, the problem was Monique's residue. Nearly all government offices and businesses were indefinitely closed. Many roofs had become kites and crash landed on the east side of Mount Campbell. Schools were closed. The airport was scheduled to reopen after a week and then only for government services.

It would take weeks to access and estimate the damages. It would take much longer to locate the funds for repairs. Churches got the quickest attention. Not that worship and prayer needed a roof, but churches became the hub of activity, communications, and first aid.

The optimist's view was the high winds had provided Clifton with both a thorough and necessary cleaning with some redevelopment. Lots of labor jobs would be available. Most of the work, though, would be done for free or for meals. The upside, if there was one, had the island's hundred thousand people again working together. Electric was still off. Poles were down everywhere. The first order of business, get the power grid operational. Electric was crucial for the rebuild.

The storm seas had smashed the municipal pier in several places. It would be 'somewhat' serviceable as soon as a crane barge removed the accumulated debris. Petit Bay and Ashton Harbor were filled with wreckage. Poorly prepared vessels were now unattractive parts of the beach-scapes.

At Curly's, the monstrous rollers had lifted and twisted parts of the dock; the fuel pumps were tilted, and part of the roof was missing, as was the proprietor and his team for the first days. During that time, some looting of 'necessities' had occurred. Residents, already hurting economically, were reusing any serviceable building materials they could find. A dry place to sleep was the first order of business.

The souvenir and T-shirt signs had mostly blown out to sea. Tourism would be nil for months. The initial sightseers would be insurance agents. Dive operations changed their focus from vacationers to assisting the underwater clean up. Fishermen had the best livelihood if they had pulled their boats far enough on shore and survived the tidal surge.

St. Claires and the Chessmans had Sunset Bay livable again after two days. No outsider visited or called. The boys had not checked in, but that was understandable because of the loss of communications. On Union, not one cell phone tower had survived Monique's windy wrath. Cassy tried to keep her mind occupied by busying her body. She and Mia worked the day hours straightening the home's interior. Opening the shutters was the best improvement. Their daily chat was more about memories than current events.

It was uncomfortable. There was only a slight breeze with high humidity. The rains created puddles that bred loads of pesky mosquitoes. They cleared a spot on their beach and swims became the best aspect of the workday coffee break. They cooked sumptuous meals from their kitchen freezer, knowing that it soon had to be emptied. Without electricity everything would spoil.

Moonchild was reorganized in six hours and became the charging station for phones and tools. The Chessmans lent their hands to the Sunset Bay effort. Harry, with his bandaged knee, traded off the chainsaw work every hour with Cheesy. One cut while the other dragged off the pieces. It took only a day until they'd removed the tree trunk and were using hammers and pry bars to pull apart the broken porch. They stapled trash bags over the ruined windows. Nightfall, the second day after Monique, it was almost home sweet home again. But the boys were still absent.

During the first cup of coffee, Cassy prodded Harry and Mia, "Let's all go to Clifton. I haven't heard from Honoré or Mammie. I didn't really expect them to come over here. I've got to check on the restaurant, if it didn't blow away."

"Won't lie, babe, I'm exhausted."

"Me too, mom," Mia sighed and then relented, "but I'll ride over with you on Dag's bike."

"Come on, Harry, it'll be fun. We'll make a big cook. Check all the damage and see how the recovery is progressing."

"I can save my energy, sit here, and tell you about the recovery; it isn't happening," Harry paused, "yet. Too soon. I'm sure the capital, Kingston is getting the main attention. Once they get things running up there, they'll start sending crews to the other islands. Canouan, with those big hotels and Bequia will get the first attention. Maybe in a month, six weeks, some government white shirts will appear around Union."

Harry seemed to catch himself as he viewed the open bay. He was worried about Tim and Dag and couldn't let it show. "Okay, I'm with you. Let's see just how bad Monique squeezed this rock. It'll take me longer, but I'll meet you. Save me a bowl of soup."

The women bicycled around town for half an hour. It was depressing. Every street had piles of smelly garbage. Zero vehicles were moving. People who weren't occupied with fixing or cleaning their own properties, sat quietly in the shade, most swatting at mosquitoes. The buzzing bloodsuckers made nighttime sleep difficult.

The town was quiet except every block possessed a few noisy gas generators providing comfort and entertainment for only a privileged few. Cassy wondered why they'd never purchased a portable generator for times such as this. Then she remembered they hadn't even bought insurance. Harry never considered a 'downside,' particularly when he was enjoying 'the upside,' usually intoxicated. She stopped and told herself to forget yesterday and tomorrows, enjoy and only live in the present. Cassy was finally starting to understand Verena. They'd make it through all these problems, no matter what. Nothing was insurmountable; she only wanted to be certain Tim and Dag were safe.

The wait at the police station took another half an hour. Cassy felt it mandatory to put out a missing persons alert for her sons and their boat. They knew Officer Comstock, who promised to forward the bulletin to the St. Vincent and Grenada Coast Guards and Police as soon as they re-established communications.

Mother and daughter rode quietly, intimidated and frightened by the storm's destruction. Unexpectedly, they heard a plane and checked out the airfield. Surprisingly, it was cleared and a small six-seater bounced incoming along the wet asphalt runway. Mia biked over as the pilot led two officials to the office. She told the pilot about her brothers on *Sassy*.

The restaurant was essentially undamaged. The roof and shutters were intact. An energetic thief had pried open the back door and absconded with some of the beer and rum stock. The robber may have either been conscientious of others and left some behind, or had planned on coming back. More probable, the thief was somewhere close by, sleeping off the free drunk.

When the shutters were lifted, Cassy's dismal mood brightened with the light that flooded her restaurant. She sighed and happily snagged the floor-sweeping Mia into a tight embrace. They danced with the broom between them to an old calypso rhythm that Cassy hummed and mumbled the few lyrics she remembered. Their swaying, bouncing, and twirling was to Shadow's *Bassman*.

"Come on, Mia," Cassy belted out, "you must remember this song. If I don't want to dance, the Baseman has me in a trance. Pow, pow, pow, pow, he's driving me crazy! I don't want to; I don't want to! I gotta dance!" Cassy was laughing, shouting out the chorus.

"Miss Cass, what's happening? Good fo' you! You get into the rum stock?" It was Honoré peeking in the front window. "You singing Bassman? What?" The big man strutted into the room and started his rendition of the song. He knew every word, and he stayed in tune as he pranced about holding their hands and dancing along. This went on for a few minutes until the women fell giggling onto chairs.

"Glad to see you happy and smiling, Miss Cass and Mia. That storm was a mean one. Me and Mammie scrunched down in our bathtub and recited our prayers until we see the sky finally get gray again and the last of that lightning and thunder. Yes, mama, Monique was a baddie." He shook all over as if trying to shake off the storm's residue. "You make out okay?"

"Monique gave the house a slight remodel, but all-in-all we were blessed." Cassy's smile faded, "But Dag and Tim took our boat somewhere and we've lost contact."

Honoré went to the fridge and returned with three beers. "Either you been drinking hard before I reached, or someone helped themselves. Anyway, here's to you, and," he touched bottles with Mia, "and you and your boys. They'll be back. Hell's bells, everyone's out of touch right now. That's the real misery of these storms. First, people worry about the storm coming and then worry after about everyone who they can't phone. A week or so, everything be up and running again." He caught himself after a long drink, "But Dag and Tim, not to worry 'bout them; they're seadogs, through and through."

He drained the beer and looked around. "Things good here, 'cept for maybe a lil' packrat taking some alcohol. What's the plan?"

Mia stood, "Another cold beer sounds good; anyone else join me? They're gonna get warm." She returned with a next round. "Now, this is what I'm talking about; I'm craving a party."

"That's a brilliant idea," Cassy agreed. "Honoré, think you can borrow a small generator so we can have music? Might as well try to cheer up our friends, customers, and hell, everyone else. We were planning to make a big soup and give away our frozen stock before it goes bad. Let's put a festive flair to it, call it…"

"Mom, we don't have to call it anything. Word will spread quick of free, hot food. And you're so right, might be the best PR for the St. Claire family yet."

"Un-huh, be nicer if the boys were here with us. But I feel they're okay, tied up to a dock somewhere. Oh, oh, here comes trouble, your father."

"Ah, dad's sober; he's a sweetheart," Mia was wearing a beer grin and ran over and hugged a limping Harry.

Mia assisted her father to a chair beside the front window where he could watch Main Street. Cassy had several large chunks of slightly frozen fish in the sink.

"We're feeling like a party; how about you?" Cassy asked.

"Why not? But I can't dance," Harry laughed. "Knee don't have a damn thing to do with it. You know, I never had any rhythm. What's this? Looks like the party started without me?" Harry asked as he saw the green bottles on the table.

The big chef carried a gas generator to the rear of the restaurant and plugged in the CD player. Cassy chose only old calypsos from the stack. The vacant air filled with cheerful music. Honoré had found his chef's hat and began contentedly chopping vegetables while singing along.

"Honoré, how's things? Everything go okay with you and Mammie? Monique was a bitch, huh?"

"Well, you knows how it is, Mr. Harry, things are good, but always could be better and we all damn lucky, 'cause could have been worse, much worse. Me and the missus are blessed to have our roof and slight damage. How'd you make out?"

"I'm sure the girls already told you," Harry propped his sore leg on a chair and wiggled around until he was comfortable. He thumped his bandaged knee. "This is the worst of it. Tree blew into the house and pinned me. Like you said, it could have been a lot worse." Harry turned and stared out at the bay, "Waiting on our sons to rendezvous back here."

The big chef brought Harry a steaming cup of instant coffee. "You and I knows your boys doing 'bout the same thing as we are. They on a waterfront, probably down Grenada ways, and sipping some beers and rum, chatting up young ladies." He smiled, "We both lucky to have good, solid families." He knocked Harry's cup with his Heineken, "Here's to better days in every way."

Harry sipped the coffee and agreed. "Yes, we are lucky. Now look over there at Curly's. Seems our relative is just unlocking after the storm. You going to invite Sam for soup?" He directed at Cassy.

"Why not? He's family, a friend, and if anyone needs to see our good side, it's Sammy," she replied.

"Harrumph," Harry cleared his throat and spit out the window. "Guess you're right. Scarbeaux Hardware probably will have its busiest days ever. Look at people running to it! Bet he draws more people than your free soup!" Harry laughed. "But yours will smell better!"

"So, we're both helping people. Nothing wrong in that," Mia obliged. "Probably Uncle Sam's doing the same as us, giving stuff away free."

They watched as Sam nailed some prices on the store's front wall.

"Look, your uncle's in his glory. You'd think he'd be helping his friends. Instead, I think he's upped the prices. Yep, I'm pretty sure that roofing was ten dollars less a sheet a week ago."

"Does it matter?" Mia asked.

"Well, damn it, yes. It's profiteering. Making money because others are suffering."

"So, let him prosper. It's his karma," she said seriously. "He'll give us the best price or we'll get what we need somewhere else."

"With what, your good looks?" Harry sighed, "Our house is down, the boys and the boat somewhere, and we can even pay the government fines, let alone repair the damages."

Cheesy and Verena drew everyone's attention as they slowly navigated their skiff through the debris and tied to the dock.

"Everybody looks sparkling and chipper today," Verena hailed the lot. "Seems the storm cleaned up the town a bit."

"You make it around the point okay?" Cassy inquired. "Must be lots of stuff floating."

Cheesy performed his ritual nose wrinkle, "Not much, maybe a dozen boats grounded, but not yours." He was quick to say. "More floating garbage than usual. Funny, no one's out fishing. But gladly trade prosperity for this less noisy town. No noisy motorcycles. How's the leg?"

"Got a bit of an ache after making my way across to here, but that's expected. I ache after that distance with two good wheels under me."

"Looks like this side of the island took the brunt of the storm," Verena said. "Any word from the boys?"

"No, not a word yet." Cassy began wringing her hands in her apron. "We notified the police, who notified the coast guard, but their boats down."

"As usual," Harry commented.

"But I talked to the first and, so far, the only plane that landed. The pilot promised to keep an eye open for them, and to radio the other airlines to do the same," Mia contributed. "He seemed so nice, promised to make calls to our boat via the VHF frequency as he flies up and down the chain."

"Say it again and again," Cheesy observed, "I'm certain that your lads are all right."

"Yeah, sure. Probably sipping a cold beer right now. Bet they're in Grenada. That's where I'd go." Harry said.

Mia brought a tray of coffee.

"Tea, please. If you have it," the Chessmans asked.

"Was one of the few things that got wet," Mia replied and squeezed brown water from the box of tea bags.

"They'll do all right," Cheesy replied. He elbowed Harry to look at the fuel pumps almost laid over by the storm. "It'll be awhile before other boats can get into here."

"Yeah, probably put a big dent in Tim's plan to have a tournament," Harry said low and serious. "No phone, no electricity, no dock, no tournament, no payday," he paused and dropped his voice, "no business, no more."

"Timothy was planning for the end of November and it's just become October," Cheesy stated as he sipped his tea. "Adequate time to make the repairs."

"Adequate, my ass, Cheese, do you believe in Santa Claus and the Tooth Fairy?" Harry half-smiled, "Recognize where you are; nothing gets done quick around here."

"No, I believe in hard work, diligent effort. If the spirit is willing. We, you and I, can push the effort. Would help to enlist your brother-in-law."

"Here, here!" Verena raised her teacup in a toast. "What can I do to help?"

"Talking about getting the municipal docks up and running again. Not much, except a crane barge can help that," Harry explained.

"Well, I just might know someone who knows someone in the BVI," Mia offered. "Hmm, hey, I'm going back and try to catch that pilot again. Maybe he can get a message to this commercial dive company I know."

"Come on, Verena," Cassy handed her an apron. "We've drafted you as a replacement." Honoré stacked loaves of skillet bread as Cassy wrote, free hot lunch on the blackboard usually meant for that day's menu. "Grab a ladle."

"Free lunch for as long as it lasts!" Cassy shouted and clanged a small bell.

"Here we are paupers and she's giving food away."

"Harry, without electric for refrigeration, everything will spoil anyway," Cheesy answered.

"Last I knew, these people hated us, now we're feeding the enemy while Sammy over there makes a mint."

"Aw, Harry, don't forget, we're all friends here. This is a small island," Verena followed. "Every good you do comes back to you."

"If I had my way, I'd wait for the food to rot a day or two more," he mumbled.

"Hush your mouth! That's mean," Cassy reprimanded. "You'll see, when we need help, it will be there."

"Have you all been asleep for the last few months? Nobody'll help us do anything except pack to leave."

"Maybe we should reconsider the hotel's offer?" Cassy said calmly.

"We might have to," Harry sighed hard, to be heard, "just so we have something to pack besides our hats."

"Harry, who was the American ballplayer who said it isn't over until it's over?" Verena perked in her heaviest British accent, "Chin up my good man."

"Our boat's gone along with our two sons, out there somewhere," Harry moaned as he clutched the chair to stand. "Our house is in awful shape. I'm hobbling around. No boat, no boys, no money, and I'm a gimp! And probably no tournament. I've already stolen everything Peter had stashed to pay Paul. And you, 'chin up, pip, pip,' bah!"

CHAPTER FOURTEEN

St. George's, Grenada had miraculously escaped Monique's grip. The keyhole harbor only suffered from its waters muddied from runoff due to heavy rains. On the north side of the quay, along the concrete wharf, the inter-island ferry boats sat quietly waiting for notice that various docks were again open for business.

On the bay's south side, alongside a concrete pier at the new marina, they tied the sportfisher trailing Kalaloo's flipped speed boat. The St. Claire brothers enjoyed beers in the cabin's shade and each sprawled on the deck with a folded towel as a pillow. They'd spent the morning at the clinic. Dag's arm was neatly bandaged and in a sling. A strip of white adhesive tape now separated Tim's black eyes.

"That Doc did an okay job, huh? Says you shouldn't have any nerve damage." Tim passed his brother another beer, "And no charge. They figured it was a Monique bite."

"It was; so's yours. Come on, you're as lucky as me, nothing can dent your thick noggin," Dag laughed, finally cheerful after days of stress. He pulled himself up and looked at Kal's overturned hull. "You think we should have taken those guys to the police? Foxy and Tony could have killed us. And Kalaloo pushed them to do it."

"Nah, they were stupid and greedy. Now they know we're serious," Tim replied. "And we did a good deed saving Kal's boat. He owes us… if we decide not to claim the right of salvage. He's still sweating."

"Supposed to get a crane here in tomorrow to yank his go-fast out of the water. I wonder if he can save those outboards?" Dag thought out loud.

"All that boat only needs is a new owner. They'll dry it out, shine it up, but the saltwater fucked all the wiring and electronics," Tim added. "If my credit card works, we should buy what we need for *Sassy*, two new antennas, some polish, and wax."

"Brilliant idea, but it can wait. My eyes are as heavy as my ass. The bunk is calling," Dag said as he drained another greenie.

"It's the bullshit that disturbs me. A fucking conspiracy on our island, Union, against us, the St. Claires. Dad was correct for once and not paranoid. Well, maybe a little paranoid, but rightfully so." Tim continued slurring his words as he pulled himself up with a loud yawn, "Yeah, a few hours of shut-eye won't hurt. I'm exhausted. While you were getting wrapped, the receptionist listened to my hard luck Monique tale and let me use the office phone. Couldn't get through to Union. All the antennas and lines must be down. The folks are probably going nuts. Dad's wondering if *Sassy* made it. We're second."

"You're starting to sound like Mia," Dag accused with another noisy yawn. "Well, I just hope the storm didn't rough them up too much."

"Ah, they're all right," Tim assured. "Mom and Dad have been through a lot. And Mia, well, she's her own private hurricane. But I've noticed she's matured since her significant other offed himself."

"Everything's going to be all right," Dag sang off-key Bob Marley as he straightened out his bunk and drained his beer. "Duerme ahora, mi hermano. Sleep good."

The brothers bumped fists.

In a dream, he was fighting several men who were trying to set the boat on fire; Tim flailed his arms. In reality, he knocked an empty beer to the floor in the V berth. That was a suitable alarm for the St. Claire brothers.

"Holy shit! What time did we crash yesterday? Before noon, right? Hell's bells, it's almost seven now."

"So, we got eight hours; that's good," Dag calculated.

"No, bro, I said yesterday. It's 7 the next morning. We slept almost a day." Chilly moist air hit them as they staggered on deck.

"Don't know about you, but I could still sleep for another day, but we better head back. Looks like the sea has calmed. Mom's probably worried sick."

In a second wake up attempt, Tim grabbed the deck hose and splashed his head.

"Hey, don't get my bandage wet," Dag said as he ducked to the far side, near the steering station. "When you're through making yourself almost presentable, let's have breakfast here, at the marina, and then we can check the electronics store for what we need to keep *Sassy* in good shape. We know we're gonna get nada on Union, or pay through the nose. I'll check the engine fluids and clean the engine water intake strainer. We had to suck up a lot of garbage. Don't want the Caterpillars overheating. I'll do it now so we'll be ready. Then all we'll need is to top off the fuel."

"Sounds like a plan. We never touched all the jerry jugs. We'll be good for a few trips if we have to locate materials for repairs."

"Let's hope we don't need to do anything but fish," Dag flashed a goofy smile. "Hey, Cheesy's optimism has rubbed off. Better get some ice," he paused, "for all the fish we're gonna catch and all the beer. Those greenies sure bring out the optimism."

The installation of the new antennas took only an hour. With scenic Fort George on the starboard, just after ten, they left the harbor for the open sea, and then headed north past the cruise ship dock.

"That is the ruination of all we hold sacred in the Caribbean," Tim bawled over the sound of the diesels. "Fucking cruise ships, I hate them. Remember when we woke up and there was one in our backyard anchored off Mayreau? Little Saltwhistle Bay jammed with a cruise ship. Only three hundred people live on Mayreau and three thousand yahoo tourists show up to play on the beach for a day. Fucked with everyone's head; they believed the cruise ship visits would make them fantastically wealthy overnight."

"Yeah, but they call it progress, state-of-the-art tourism. All-inclusive, all you can stuff down your gullet to be happy at sea and only in port a few hours. No reason anymore to stay in a hotel," Dag replied. "They are like cockroaches, everywhere. Now they're carrying passengers near to both the North and South Poles, disturbing nature. Hey, take over while I put out some spoons."

"You want to waste time fishing?" Tim argued. "Thought we were headed home as fast as possible?"

"Brother, you never waste time fishing. I didn't say slow down, just that I'm dragging some spoon baits, flashing in the water. Something hits, well, yeah, we slow, because fresh fish will be a premium now. And," Dag preached, "after a storm, fishing is always good."

Once the two rods were locked in, Dag brought up two beers. "And as long as *Sassy's* running, we have a cold box and cold beers." They toasted. "What do you want to do about what Kalaloo told us?"

"Not a thing," Tim answered.

"Nothing?" Dag made a puking sound.

"Now we know for certain that Uncle Sam's working against us, we might surprise him."

"How are we going to surprise anybody? Kalaloo will tell him what happened."

"In a business sense, I think it might be better we speak with Uncle privately," Tim rationalized. "If Mom and Dad find out, life will be miserable on the island. No one will talk to anyone, a war."

"I guess you're right," Dag waved his bandaged arm. "I won't be much help if he gets tough."

Tim did a muscle flex. "I don't think I'll need any help except moral support."

"You been taking steroids?"

"Dag, you know me, I always go to extremes. Worked my ass off at Shearsome to succeed and exercise was the logical and healthiest way to fight the stress."

"What? No desire for feminine companionship?" Dag asked. "That's my best stress reliever, senoritas! I thought you'd be married by now."

"That's you, I'm different," Tim countered. "Always have been. Marry who? I don't meet women."

"Yeah, but, ah, did you get a little more different?" Dag inquired. "I saw you with Jason. Looked, ah, different."

"I don't need to explain myself!" Tim snapped. "I'm in with a diverse group in London. We apply to our physical and mental selves. Jason has the same attitude. He and I will stay in touch. Next subject."

Dag sat quietly for a few minutes watching the chrome spoons flashing in their wake and said, "Like they say, bro, whatever floats your boat." They both laughed and lightened the moment. "I'm getting a beer, want one? No breathalyzer out here."

"Okay, okay, give me a beer," Tim slowed to a smooth six knots. "I know, Dag's Rule, if a boat's moving, we ought to be fishing. And you're right, by the time we land, it'll have been four days without electric current and fresh fish will taste good."

Dag nodded his head in quiet agreement. Tim slid in a Beatles CD and started shaking his butt to 'Money.' He did a Tom Cruise shuffle across the deck mouthing the words: 'The best things in life are free, but you can give them to the birds and bees, I need money, that's what I want.' The brothers howled with laughter.

Everything was back, almost the way it should be. The bright ball of the sun enriched a cloudless sky. The overhead blue was several shades lighter than the calmed, dark blue Caribbean Sea. Monique had stripped the greenery and anything that could be blown away from Grenada's northwest coast. The leaves and trash left an ugly, thick ring on the shore at the high-water level.

Autopilot controlled the fishing boat as both brothers relaxed. There was no other marine traffic. They were still exhausted from the wild night with Monique. Only a few birds checked out the flashing baits. Tim sat in the captain's chair and considered possible business tactics to foil their not-so-loving Uncle Sammy. He scanned the VHF marine radio for any signals and found one ham still operative. His brother was slouched asleep in the fighting chair when a big kingfish swallowed one of the spoon baits.

Dag tried to set the hook, but his arm wasn't up to it. He took the helm while Tim landed the fish.

"That was fast, no fooling around, Tim. A couple more like that and we'll have a payday. That king was starving, he gulped the lure so far down it's hooked in his gills."

The fish were hungry as Dag had predicted. Taking the most direct route, Tim steered over the drop-off out in the deep water. They landed all five blackfin tunas they'd hooked on feathers. Two barracudas hit the spoons and they still made it to Union island in only four hours.

"Holy shit!" Dag shouted as they saw the island's hillsides picked clean of anything green. Many entire roofs that the wind had separated and even some smaller buildings lay crumpled, littering the side of Mt. Talbot.

Tim opened two more beers, "Here's hoping Sunset Bay looks better than this."

*Sas*sy slowed as they entered their bay. *Moonchild* was resting unscathed at anchor. The first glimpse of their homestead was the ruined dock.

"Be careful, could be a lot of shit floating, submerged just beneath the surface," Dag cautioned. "Might as well do a spin so they see us. Then we'll come back out and grab the mooring. I'm sure Cheesy will give us a lift."

"Jee-sus, the dock, trees, the porch, man-oh-man, we're gonna be b-u-s-y!"

In neutral, the sportfisher coasted slowly, and Tim blew the horn for five short blasts. "Hey, that's the danger signal," Dag said.

"Yep, that'll wake everyone up."

The side door swung open, and Mia bolted out. She didn't stop, dove into the bay, and swam toward their sportfisher. Harry followed her out of the house, limping to the shoreline. Cassy was last out and joined him, waving her arms.

"Where have you two assholes been hiding?" Mia shouted as she pulled herself up onto the dive platform. Dag handed her a beer. "Thanks. I can use it and a few more." She tilted her head and drained the bottle. "Left me cooped up with the Harry and Cassy sideshow. You two had them worried silly," Mia's mouth motored on. "Well? Holy cow! Look at your arm and your face. How'd that happen?"

"Hey, take it easy," Tim hugged her. Dag joined with a one arm effort and explained, "We rode it out, no problem. Got a few scrapes, finally made it to St. Georges, and got some sleep."

"Bet you guys got beat to shit! That was some storm. Well, you can see Monique did some remodeling around here. Mom's frantic and Harry's talking doom. No phone, so no business."

"Not to worry, sis. Got it all figured out," Tim explained. "I still have the satellite phone. We couldn't call you because there are no antennas here. I can do some business. It's kind of expensive when I'm not chatting with my office. On the way up, I used the boat's VHF radio and was lucky enough to hit on a ham radio operator in Grenada. He was one of the few whose antenna made it through the storm. We chatted a while. Most of Grenada still has telephones and the Internet. He agreed to call the States and forward all the information to the International Game Fishing Association. We'll keep in touch through *Sassy's* VHF. I think we can pull off the tournament. That should get our asses out of the fire."

After a long burp, Mia hugged Tim, "You must be adopted because nobody else in this family thinks the same as you do."

"Stay close and it might rub off on you," Tim said and lifted his sister off the deck and tossed her into the bay. "Won't have room for you in Cheesy's dinghy with all our fish. We'd better get ashore before Dad has a heart attack."

Cheesy and Verena motored to the sportfisher and carried the men ashore. A myriad of hugs and hellos accompanied the censored version of the brothers' escape from Monique. Cassy finally relaxed with her family again intact. Without electricity, sunset was truly lights out. Everyone crashed early and slept soundly.

Shortly after dawn, a perpetually smiling Cassy had coffee perking for a homespun, aromatic wake up. Mia scrambled eggs as her mother fried cornbread pancakes. The nourishment fueled the breakfast discussion of the many how, when, where and what questions everyone asked.

The condition of Dag's arm was the first consideration; his sister cleaned and wrapped it. "Don't worry; I'm not gonna just sit and watch. I can still lift, carry, and do some prying with my left. Won't be too good at nailing as a leftie. Dad, you and Cheesy really busted ass around here, sawing up the tree that hit the house. How's your leg feeling?"

"Not bad, but neither one of us will play basketball for a few weeks," Harry laughed as he sipped his third cup of coffee.

Tim and Mia began writing a work list with the dock being the easiest to repair. "We have enough bolts and nails remaining from our last repairs," Tim remembered. "I think we can use what good boards remain from the porch roof."

"Sounds like a plan," Harry agreed. "Cheesy and Verena will be in. Nothing else going on. Their small freezer on *Moonchild* is keeping some stuff cold for us. They were happy to get fresh fish last night."

"Let's go back out later. I feel like fishing," Mia said. "I'll walk around the Bay and see what I can scrounge. Lots of stuff floated in. What isn't good, I'll pile up and we can burn the trash later. I'll pitch in on the dock."

"Well, there's still water in our well, for me, it is laundry day," Cassy spoke. "I'll do it in tubs like we used to. The tropical sun will have it dried in no time. We can use some fresh clothes."

"Aye, aye, skipper," Harry chanted. "Let's go. Sooner we get the jobs finished, the sooner the fishing begins. We can repair the porch and windows down the road. Sunset Bay needs to be ready to fish. You really think we'll be able to communicate with the prospective anglers, Tim?"

"Monique slowed things, but she didn't stop anything. I've got my sat phone and also have an arrangement with Mr. Compton, who lives somewhere around the Point Saline Airport. We planned to talk on the VHF every afternoon at four." Tim gave a wink combined with a nod. "I figure the best reception will be offshore. We might as well be fishing. What's the status of Curly's fuel dock?"

"When we were at the restaurant the day after, the pumps looked like the Leaning Tower of Pisa," Harry offered, "but I'm certain that is a priority for everyone. Ol' Sammy will figure some way to sell fuel. It's got to be like gold now. Maybe me and Cheese will head that way when you go out dragging baits."

"What, you're not coming with us?" Mia was shocked.

"Young lady, contrary to popular belief, I don't want to be hobbling around forever. If I take a slide on the wet deck and crack this knee again, well, might have to fit me up for a wooden peg leg."

"My, oh, my, never thought the day would come when my husband would take common sense over going fishing," Cassy quipped as she stood behind him and rubbed his shoulders, "Who knows, you might mature one of these days."

"What's the point in maturing?" Harry smiled. "Just don't want to be an invalid. You three catch fish and I'll trade them off for diesel."

"Dad," Tim was serious. "No commotion with Sam, okay? We need fuel and materials for repairs. As soon as diesel's available, we'll motor there after fishing. I want to have a chat with Unc, alone."

"I've said before, Tim, you're the man with the plan," Harry grinned. "Now, let's get to work; it's almost seven. Be hot soon."

The morning went according to schedule. The coordinated effort had the dock serviceable. It wasn't pretty, but it was stable. They could tie alongside after they returned from the afternoon's fishing. Mia was beaming after landing seven dorados and drinking as many beers.

Cheesy and Harry had the charcoal ready as soon as they cleaned the first bull. Verena set the picnic tables with two kerosene lamps for light.

"These days seem to flash by," she said. "I'm not sewing much because of the usual distractions."

"Hey, I'm not even thinking about the restaurant anymore. I don't know if that's good or bad?" Cassy asked. "You're lucky, you have a generator on board. No sense planning anything in town until the current is flowing again."

Cheesy brought a platter of fish from off the grill, and Harry had a bowl of baked potatoes.

"Thank you for what we are about to receive," Verena solemnly said.

"Amen," resounded.

"And, here's a no thank you for everything else you've dumped on us," Harry said looking upward. Then he asked his kids, "So, the fish were hitting?"

"Oh yeah, it was thick with dorados," Mia spoke. "Seems like they're running. Like to find that school again."

"Hmm, late in the year, but I guess after the storm. Motor them over to Clifton tomorrow and sell or trade 'em," Harry continued.

"Better we give some fish to the town council to distribute," Cassy recommended.

"Ahoy, Madame Rockefeller, who's paying for fuel?" Harry asked.

"Harry, can't you think of it as doing the community a service for once?" Cassy returned.

"Be all right if it was just once, but if you give it to the council, we won't get no credit," Harry answered.

"You do what you want with these, dad. What we catch tomorrow, I'll give some away and make certain that people know who it comes from. We'll go out early tomorrow morning and then take the catch to town. We need to get some materials to finish the dock, redo the porch, and glass for the windows."

"Been thinking; changed my mind. Don't want you buying anything from Sam. Over my dead body, we're not paying his inflated prices."

"Sam is family," Tim nodded to his brother. "I'll bet he'll give us a break."

"Maybe I should talk to him," Cassy offered.

"Let's give businessman Tim the opportunity to cut a deal," Dag said.

"Son, take what I said to heart," Harry bayed. "I don't want one red cent to go to Sam. Besides that, we ain't got no red, blue, or yellow cents."

"Don't worry; let me handle Uncle Sam," Tim dropped into a Godfather accent. "I'll make him an offer he can't refuse."

^^^^^^^^^^

Every day had a similar program, more cleanup, more repairs, more fishing. The togetherness effort had revitalized everyone's energy and optimism. After setting fire to more of the previous day's piles of sea trash, Mia followed Dag's step by step directions and captured dozens of nice ballyhoo with the throw net.

Armed with fresh bait, that afternoon *Sassy* was packed with everyone, including Cheesy, Verena, Cassy, and Hop-a-Long Harry. And it turned out to be a stellar afternoon. About halfway to the drop-off, Dag saw a cloud of birds diving around a floating patch of Sargasso grass.

Tim twice steered a figure eight, sweeping only a boat length away from the weeds. Minutes before three, the first rod bent, followed by the others. Cheesy and Harry both screamed, "Fish on!"

They'd located a nice school of dorados. That provoked the usual Chinese fire drill, as the excitement of screaming reels had everyone scampering around the deck. They either grabbed a rod or ducked out of the way. Shouts of directions, anticipation, and frustration reverberated across the boat. Cassy brought her brilliant golden bull dorado in first. Harry played mate, as Dag was unable, and Cheesy fought with another fish. With a nice swoop, Harry gaffed it, and the other three.

"Okay," Mia roared as she took off her Penn ball cap. "Get your beer money out, most fish and biggest fish. Put it right here, ten EC from each. Come on, cough it up! No losers, because we're all going to be sucking down greenies later. Winners don't have to pay. How's that?"

"I'm in, already the three ladies each have a fish," Verena

boasted. "Let's get another wager, ladies versus the men. And we'll even spot you an extra... fisher-person."

"Hell, me with a bum knee and Dag with a bad arm, shit, together we only add up to one man, so it's even teams. Game on!" Harry hooted.

The day only got better. Tim steered, Dag spotted, while Harry and Cheesy snapped on fresh bait. Cassy and Mia rigged a few ballyhoos before the reels started screaming again. Harry grabbed one and settled into the fighting chair. Dag climbed from the tower and took the wheel so Tim could have his turn to fight one. Mia and Verena quickly reeled in small ten-pound blackfin tunas.

Harry kept his sore knee as straight as possible, and off of the chair's footrest, so it got no pressure. That raised the degree of difficulty a few points. With the rod in the center gimbaled holder, he could pump and crank, punctuated with considerable grunts and groans. Then the fish broke water; launched in a high arc. In a genuine Kodachrome moment, the massive bull dorado leaped so high it somehow eclipsed the afternoon sun.

"God damn," Harry yelled, "that's a fifty-kilo fish, if I ever saw one. Mine's off the stern now. Where's yours, Tim?"

"Mine's off the starboard," Tim reacted, his strong arms bulging from the force of fighting a similar-sized fish without a chair for support. "Haven't seen him yet, but he's got some weight." Tim steadily cranked his reel between pumps of the rod.

"Come on, you two, don't fuck around. Get them in so we can get our lines back out there again," Mia lauded.

"Nothing like a foul mouth cheerleader," Harry grunted as he gained some line on his fish. "Okay, Cheese, gaff this fish before it tangles with Tim's."

"Mine's here, too. Jeez Louise, this might be a hair bigger than yours," Tim shouted as he saw the length of his fish.

"Mia," Dag coached, "Grab the flying gaff. Yeah, the hooked pole with the rope."

"Big bro, I know what a flying gaff is. I'm no stranger to this," Mia scoffed. "Hope my little ass has enough weight to sink the broad hook. Whew," she shook her head as she viewed Tim's fish zigzagging through the water. "Don't think I can swing and lift a fish that size in one move."

Cassy stood between Tim and Mia. "Swing the gaff when I say. You know enough to sink that big hook behind the head, so we don't cut the line. Tim, bring that fish over here. Keep the rod tip straight up."

At that moment, Cheesy sunk the gaff and hoisted Harry's fish. The huge dorado bounced on the stern deck; but then all attention turned to the starboard action.

Tim dipped his rod twice and pumped like a madman coming up. "Now!"

Mia leaned over the gunwale, holding the big gaff straight in front of her. Her stare locked on the fish and she swung the hook downward. It sunk deep into the fish's broad back behind the head. The dorado lunged upward with a twist. As intended, the big gaff hook separated from the rod, and the fish swam, secured with the attached line. Cassy held several wraps and slowly she and Mia pulled the fish to the boat. Tim handed his rod to Dag and proudly strained to lift his prize into the boat.

The crew huddled together, looking at the two huge golden fish. The scene went quiet for a few moments. The squawks of the birds and the diesel engines went mute. Only deep breaths could be heard.

Harry broke the silence by slapping Tim on the back. "Son, I got to say, yours is bigger, not by much, but bigger. What's going on here? Are we fishermen or farmers? There's fish out there; let's bait up." Harry raised his hand and high-fived everyone, shouting, "Ballyhoo, ballyhoo! That's what I'm talking about. This is a St. Claire," he caught himself, "and Chessman moment."

In gentlemanly fashion, the ladies won with two extra fish. Tim got the biggest weight at 45 kilos, two heavier than his father's.

As they headed to Clifton, Harry and Cheesy watched the sunset from the stern. "Damn, thought they were both over a hundred pounds," Harry confessed. "Must be getting old. The eyes aren't registering like they used to."

Cheesy hugged him. "Shut up, Cappy, you were only off one measly pound on Tim's and five on yours. Our scale could be off that much. Both lost water weight after they croaked. You know that, partner. You're as good today as I've ever seen you cranking with one flat tire. You still on the wagon?" He whispered.

Harry let loose a long sigh, "Forever and ever, that's what it looks like Cheesy. Things are going too good to let Rita screw it up."

"Rita?" Cheesy questioned.

"Rita, you know Rita, R-I-T-A, Rum - Is - The - Answer. Think Cass's right, I've finally matured."

"Never, never happen," Cheesy squawked as they hugged. Then both cracked up with laughter.

It was almost dark when they tied alongside Clifton's main dock. The government crews must have been out in force as there was no trash visible. The public works crew had strained even the sea along the docks of floating garbage. The cleanliness gave it the air of a new beginning.

The lights shining down from the tuna tower illuminated *Sassy*. Verena relaxed in the fighting chair while Cheesy filled the diesel tanks. The pumps had been unbolted and lifted from the crumpled dock and moved to where they'd cast a fresh piece of concrete. A generator hummed from inside Curly's warehouse.

Mia and Dag set up a butcher shop on the dock and sliced up fish. Harry and Cassy waved for passers-by to approach. Word rapidly circulated and a small crowd gathered, each brandishing a plastic bag, hoping for fresh fish for dinner.

Tim boldly walked into Curly's Hardware, directly to his uncle's office carrying Sunset Bay Fishing Tournament posters. Sam was sitting behind his big roll-top desk, which was covered with stacks of papers. The older man had his reading glasses off in his left hand while he rubbed his forehead with the other. He smiled a welcome and waved Tim to sit.

Sam avoided eye contact for a bit, then resigned that he had to deal with the issue.

"Stress is getting to me, Tim. The weather, business, almost all of my helpers have disappeared." Sam paused and his words hung in the air, "You had some good luck running from the storm, huh? Heard that the house took some licks."

"Everything will work out. It was kind of exciting riding it out at sea. Never know what to expect during a storm like that. Bring out the best and…" Tim purposely paused for emphasis, "and worst in people. Me and Dag held up okay. No real wear and tear on our boat. That's how we make our living, fishing, but you know that. Mom's house is what I came to talk about. First, may I tape up these tournament posters; you know, somewhere visible from the fuel docks?"

"You're still thinking of putting on a fishing tournament?" Sam asked. "After Monique and who knows what weather is waiting in the Atlantic? This would be the time to reconsider the offer to buy the bay. I could be the intermediary and maybe could get the offer increased."

"Everything's still a go for the tournament. It's IGFA sanctioned, you know. As far as the hotel, well, I don't think they'd want to give us more money thinking the storm has us on the ropes. They'd try to low ball."

"But I could try. After all, Cass and me are the same blood, just different mothers." Sam looked closely at the fishing poster and frowned, "Thanksgiving tournament, huh? You guys are down and almost counted out. I'm trying to help cut your losses. Wise up and give up."

"Got to try," Tim beamed a broad, but pasted smile. "That's what I want to talk about." He turned and shut the office door. "Dad doesn't want us to do any business with you."

"Harry, hmm, well, he could be right this time. It might not be wise to fix up the place if you're going to sell. The deadline is getting close. The storm had to cut into your bailout money."

"Not that badly. Everything cuts into this and cuts into that." Tim presented a knowing nod as he picked up a machete similar to what he's seen Foxy with. "Hey, we need some extra labor, you know donkey work. You see those two dreads, Foxy and Tony, around?"

Sam rubbed his jaw and with closed eyes, he answered, "Didn't you hear me? I said, my help has disappeared."

"Oh, didn't realize they worked for you," Tim was coy. "What I want is for you to give us the materials we need."

"I can give you a discount, say fifteen, no, I'll make it twenty percent."

"No, I mean a total discount," Tim paused for effect. "Absolutely free."

"What? Why?" Sam half gasped, half stuttered. "Ah, you're family, but the best I can do is give them to you at cost plus ten percent."

"Uncle, exactly that," Tim leaned over the desk on his muscular arms, "Because we are family and Granpop's probably doing the twist in his coffin right now."

"I think your big business school has gone to your head," Sam smirked.

"Uncle, and I say that very loosely," Tim lost his smile and snarled, "you should be happy I don't take a two by four to the side of your head, you black-hearted, back-stabbing prick!"

"Tim!" Sam pushed his chair back from the desk, putting a little more distance between him and his nephew. "I'm busy, come back tomorrow when you cool down. Quit talking foolishness and throwing around empty threats."

In a wide sweep, Tim cleared the desk of its mounds of papers. "Now you're not so busy. You think my threats are empty? Uncle, have you seen Kalaloo lately; because he told us everything. Every fucking thing! There are two ways we can do this. You can comply with my demands and make a gift of everything we need. Then Mom and Dad, and everyone in the town may never know how you tried to kill us. Then, keep your fucking nose in your own business, and leave us," Tim paused, "and the bay, alone."

"Whew, whew, whew, whoa there, Tim. That's quite an accusation. How about fuck you, your demands, and your half-caste family!" Sam bellowed. "Huh, how's that sound, you, you, punk!"

"Accusation? Accusation is a big word from your small, greedy mind, you black-hearted prick."

Sam made a move to rise and grab a machete.

"Sit down! Sit the fuck down, now! Make another move and I will fuck you up. If you don't think I can, go for the long knife," Tim barked. "I always thought you were a nice guy and Dad had it all wrong, but he read you perfect."

"I don't have to listen." He tried to rise, and Tim's hand shot out and thumped Sam hard in the chest. He sank, cowering, into his padded chair, gagging on his breaths.

"Yes, you do! If you refuse and want to argue, I'll personally have your ass thrown in jail. I'll use everything to keep you there because you premeditatedly planned a murder. You tried to kill both Dag and me and scuttle *Sassy*. I have two witnesses that will testify. So, Uncle, what's your answer?"

"You think you can barge in here and blackmail me," Sam fumed. "You're just an educated punk, Timmy."

Tim snatched Sam by the wrists and twisted. Sam's body convulsed; he couldn't pull away. Finally, he cried out. "Enough! Enough!"

"It'll never be enough, Sam, for what you've tried to do to your own sister, our mother, who has never even said a cross word to you. We all showed you respect." Tim flung Sam back, and he crashed and slid down the wall with what sounded like a sob.

"Nobody calls me Timmy." Muscles flexed, Tim took deep breaths in an attempt to regain his control, but it was a lost cause. "Mother fucker, you can't call me anything, Uncle. If you even think for a moment that I won't have you arrested, you better think again. To work against your own flesh and blood, you're fucking trash. The town believed you about the hotel and the opportunities. But the opportunities were just for you. You greedy son of a bitch! Stand up! Quit bawling like a baby. If I had been intent on hurting you, you'd be bloody by now. I'm not like you. As you said, different mothers must have caused the difference." For a stinging rebuke, Tim added, "Take it any way you want to; you're more like your mother than our Granpop. And you see where that got her. Your mother had to start over and lived on the edge of town after she was caught cheating! You didn't even live with her. You chose the better life with Granpop."

Sam's didn't have any reply. Dazed by the intensity of Tim's words, he just sat and stared. Slowly, he pulled himself up. Tim watched for any movement to grab a pistol or a club.

"At least I'm giving you a choice," Tim returned to a calmer tone.

After a few coughs, Sam stood with his hands folded as if in reverence. "I never meant for anyone to get hurt. It all got out of hand."

"Crashing our boat wouldn't kill us all?! Forget about the hotel! Forget about everything," Tim decisively stated, "and we might do the same. Now, write an invoice, carte blanche, everything we want for nada, not a fucking cent. Write it!"

"Okay, I agree." He hand printed what Tim said and signed it. "Load up what you need." Sam extended his hand to shake. "Deal? No more mention of what went down?"

"Uncle, you're too much," Tim laughed. He grabbed Sam's right hand and squeezed until Sam cried out. "You're trash Sam, absolute trash. But I'll be honorable and keep quiet. Dag, too, no one knows but us and a few people in Grenada. If you so much as fart and I smell it, I swear, I'll be up your ass so fast. We'll be back tomorrow and start ferrying the materials. Don't forget what I said."

The Sunset Bay crew had distributed their catch with enough saved for another grilled dinner. Everyone was waiting for Tim. He'd grabbed two crates of Heineken on his way out of Sam's store.

"Now that's what I'm talking about," Mia praised. As she and Dag each grabbed a crate before Tim hopped on the boat. Everyone was all ears, patiently waiting for Tim's explanation of the meeting.

He tried to look sad but couldn't fight back the smile. "We're getting it all!"

"Doesn't anyone listen to me anymore," Harry lectured. "I said that we had no money for repairs and I specifically said that I didn't want to give Sam any business."

"Dad, I heard you, but Uncle is giving us anything we need… as a gift. Yeah, it was a gift to you and Mom.

"Your ass, a gift!" Harry roared. "Sam only knows about giving people one thing, especially the St. Claires, the shaft!"

"Harry, your lad cut a good deal, lighten up," Cheesy said. Then he and Verena started dancing an infectious jig. In seconds, everyone except Harry was bouncing around, high-fives flourished.

"Cheesy, the only good deal with Sam, is no deal," Harry snipped, annoyed.

"Really," Tim explained, "everything's absolutely free. Uncle realizes the family ties. He said he felt really bad about our problems and wanted to help. So, we're actually doing him a favor by taking the wood and roofing. It's easing his conscience."

"Well, I'll be damned," Harry sprouted a grin. "Ah, you still can't trust him though. Probably got something up his sleeve. He'll be calling the police, saying we stole all this. Next thing Sammy swears his 'help' bought him shares into our business. He probably thinks he's one of our 'partners'."

"Can't do any of that. I got the open work order receipted, dated, and signed. Here, read it." Tim unfolded the paper in his shirt pocket.

"I can't believe it. Maybe miracles do happen. But even so, don't trust him, you hear me, don't trust Sam at all. If he tells you it's a nice day, go look before you leave without an umbrella."

That brought a laugh from everyone as they pulled slowly from the dock. Harry had the wheel and Dag found Tim staring off the stern at the few lights that remained in Clifton.

"Pulled it off, huh?" Dag whispered.

"Worked like I said it would. The prick folded under pressure."

"No cojones. What's next?" the older brother quizzed.

"Fix the house, fix the tournament, fix the folks, be one happy family again."

"Since when? I must have missed that." Dag snapped. They both chuckled.

They made daily runs loaded with materials from Curly's Hardware. Sam never made himself visible. His bubble-butt secretary/assistant, Annie, made invoices for all the supplies. The brothers loaded the sportfisher carefully and didn't leave a mark on the shiny white fiberglass.

Two nights following Sam's pledge of assistance, the siblings held a business meeting after Harry and Cassy went to bed. The three sat at the outside picnic table illuminated by two kerosene lamps. A blank-faced Mia used the calculator on her phone and scribbled numbers in a ledger. Tim worked away on his laptop. Dag kept all supplied with chilled beers from *Sassy*.

"After reviewing all of our expenditures," she swatted at pesky mosquitoes, "we still need about forty thousand US."

"And we have only ten weeks to raise it," Dag tuned in.

"Okay, Monique hit us a little harder than expected," Tim granted. "She put a dent in our progress, but it's only a slight dent. We lost some income with three weeks of canceled charters, but so far we have sixteen boats confirmed for the tournament a month away."

"Any messages from Duncan or Carlos? They offered to help?" Mia asked. "I thought they might want to return for the tournament."

"Nothing yet," Tim joked. "I imagined Carlos would have been back in touch with you. After all, you got touchy-feely close?"

"My phone's not working; you know that."

"Yes, we'd better run to Grenada to make some calls to our few sponsors, and check the bank to be certain that the tourney entrance fees have all been deposited," Tim directed. "We need to put up some posters."

"Who's providing the prizes?" Dag inquired.

"Who else? FineBraid Fishing Line and the International Game Fishing Association are the two main sponsors. For that, we get hype in whatever fishing magazines that kiss up to FineBraid, and FineBraid will match our first prize and the organizational costs. Penn Reels was considering joining the sponsors," Tim ran on, "Then there's the usual, the beer company, rum distillery, department of tourism, with a couple of hotels, and the local airlines. But… the prize money comes directly from the entrance fees."

"Ah, what are we making from this?" Mia asked.

"Public relations," Tim was short.

"Can we take that to the bank?" Dag said wide-eyed. "I thought we'd get a sizeable chunk of change out of this tourney?"

"Hopefully, we won't have to," Tim addressed. "I'm hoping that the banks will be represented by fishing teams."

"Take me along to Grenada and I'll drum up some more contestants. How much is the first prize?" Mia asked.

"The entrance is seven hundred a boat and three hundred a fisherman," Tim rattled off. "For that, they can win twenty-five percent of the entrance for best boat and best fisherman. That leaves second and third to split another quarter, and we get the last quarter for organizing."

"I missed the prize. How much did you say?" Dag leaned forward.

"First for the best boat, you know, most billfish, is about ten grand. The biggest billfish is another ten. Rich enough to bring in the big boats," Tim reasoned.

"I agree. Anyone who's ever fished these waters will want to come. I'll send some emails to the marinas and people I know in Venezuela. That's close enough for devoted fishermen to cruise here."

"Yeah, but they have to have the entrance. It'll keep out some little guys, but next year we'll have two tourneys. One in the spring for dorados, no one does that, and our billfish are around when the US has Thanksgiving." Tim explained. "Once we get this project moving, it'll make Sunset Bay famous."

"Yeah, now we're only a legend in Harry's mind," Dag laughed.

"How much do we take home?" Mia probed.

"Figure on twenty boats, including us. Three fishermen per boat, that puts us at thirty thousand minus our fees. Figure our share being about five, to be safe, matched by FineBraid, so we make ten."

"All this work for ten, not forty? Where do you expect to get the other thirty?" Dag asked.

"Don't worry, I'll get it covered, if necessary, out of my pocket. But it would be nicer and excellent PR if our team won. Plus, if we catch a blue marlin over a thousand pounds the IGFA has a standing tournament prize of a hundred grand US and a new Mercedes."

"Wishful thinking," Mia replied. "Mercedes on Union?"

"Dreamer," came from Dag.

"We could take all the money if we landed Junish," Mia chimed.

"Another dreamer," Dag added.

"You think he's still alive?" Tim sat up. "I always wondered if he was that big or if we were just that small when we saw him?"

"That was a big fucking fish, even though we were little kids. Ever hear Harry and Cheesy talk about it? It's like they saw God that day." Mia went on, "What could kill it, unless it died of old age. If someone caught Junish we'd have heard, wouldn't we?"

"Somebody'd be bragging. Junish is the biggest that I've ever seen. My arm's down, and Dad's out of commission," Dag sulked. "So, it'll be you two."

"And Cheesy," Mia smiled.

"We'll be there for moral support. I guess I could captain and Dad could be the cheerleader."

"Please… Harry cheering or explaining our faults?" Mia scolded.

"Come on, Mia, lighten up on Harry," Dag excused. "He's trying and has come a long way during the last few months, and got back in Mom's good graces by staying off the bottle."

"Harry's trying. Harry's always trying." Mia whined.

"We're all trying. It's working out," Tim coaxed. "We're almost a family again."

"Almost, and that's like horseshoes, but more like hand grenades," she grinned.

∧∧∧∧∧∧∧∧∧

They had nearly completed the repairs to Sunset Bay Fish Camp. Almost, always almost, because, as Harry expounded, their bay was a work of art in continual progress. It would only get better and better. He relaxed on the new, half-built veranda that extended around the house. The dock was better than new.

Even Harry was stroking a paintbrush with everyone else. Cassy had chosen a fresh, light tan for the house and burnt orange for the trim. Curly's Hardware had it delivered, special order, from Grenada. He sat in the shade of the partially constructed porch and rolled his head to a tune he hummed, 'Here's a little song I wrote. You might want to sing it note for note. Don't worry, be happy. In every life we have some trouble, but when you worry you make it double. Don't worry, be happy. Don't worry, be happy now.'

"Aren't we happy and chipper! Didn't realize you knew the words to any song. Don't believe I've ever heard you singing before?" Cheesy said as he sat next to his best friend and grabbed an extra brush.

"Well, buddy, I was just getting out of high school. 1988, Bobby McFerrin had this big hit. Shit, I thought I was on top of the world, back then."

"And yes, everything's worked out magnificently." He continued, "Don't think I've ever seen you so happy. And painting the house? I thought you hated painting?"

"Used to dislike a lot of things, domestic things, I guess they're called. Always put fishing, and, I guess, fucking off as a priority. My kids have an attitude, and my attitude might be the reason Sam is hell-bent on screwing us over," Harry lamented. "Hoping this tourney might turn a lot of things around. Might help me pull my head out of my ass. Don't figure Tim or Mia will stick around, but who knows? Like to hand things over to Dag, if he'd take it. Union is probably too small for all of them now."

"Cool yourself, Skip. Remember 'que será, será.'"

"Why do you have to always hit me with some foreign language shit? Huh?"

"Whatever will be will be," Cheesy translated. "Don't get your boxers in a twist. You're the man who knows fishing. It might be time to collect all our notes and put them all together into a book. Harry's Memoirs, I can see it now, a best seller."

"Fuck you! Grab your fucking brush and start stroking it rather than me." They both laughed.

"The tournament is closing in and we have to have the house ready. Do you think there's enough quality guest house space on storm stomped Union?" Tim worried.

"Don't sweat it, most of the fishermen will pinch a penny and sleep on their charter boat," Dag answered. "What we're doing now is more important. This run to Grenada will help get publicity. They have crummy newspapers, but you and I can hit the radio and TV. You know, feed them human interest; Union Island rejuvenated after Mo-fucking-nique."

"You two do what you want, I guarantee I'll get more anglers and boats," Mia attested. "The news services are too broad. You need specialized coercion, and I am specialized!" she laughed. "Wait and see."

"Little sister, do your thing." The brothers broke into the Isley Brothers hit. "Do your thing, do what you wanna do, we can't tell you who to sock it to."

"Yeah, go ahead and make fun. You'll see," Mia defended. "Just wait and see. And, yeah, I remember that song. Granpop had that old vinyl and practically wore it out on birthdays. Remember? He'd wear that crazy orange shirt with black lizards printed on it and be shuffling his feet to it." Mia continued the lyrics, "I'm not trying to run your life, I know you wanna do what's right. Give your love now, to whoever you choose. How can you lose, with the stuff you use now?" She beamed a smile and nodded to her brothers, "That's exactly what I'm saying!"

The St. Claires were about a half-mile west of the fishing village of Guayave, in deep water, dragging two baits. It was just after eight in the morning. By nine, they'd be at the dock in St. Georges. Their plan was to spend the day chatting in town. Then, they'd spin around to the few marinas on the south coast of Grenada to drum up interest in Sunset Bay's fledgling tournament. The previous week the boys had made a three-day run fishing north. They stopped to hype their tourney among the anglers at Le Marin in southern Martinique, Rodney Bay in St Lucia, then Kingston, Bequia, and Canouan. They added twelve more definite paid-in-full boats with more anglers to come. Everyone said the same thing; they loved to fish those waters off Union; the tournament had reasonable entrance fees, and the prize was worthy.

"The more boats and anglers we get, the better, right? Or are there some limits?" Mia continued.

"No limits, just where in the hell are we going to have the daily ceremonies? That's something I haven't totally figured out," Tim pondered. "Originally, I thought we'd have ten to twenty boats, I mean, that's a lot for any tournament, and this is a new one. But the whole fucking Caribbean either knows Harry personally or has heard of the fantastic fishing off Union. Since it is out of the way, no resorts close, other than Canouan, few have ever fished our drop-off."

"Uncle Sammy will make out again like a bandit selling fuel and supplies. Mom's restaurant is operational again. She'll cater and probably most boats will eat there. That'll probably piss off some townies, but fuck 'em," Dag sneered. "This initial tournament will show them what the St. Claires can do. Personally, I'm impressed, and I've been in a few, pushing probably twenty. Most tournaments have about fifteen boats."

They ran through all the big venues and decided that the airport had the biggest sheltered area that hadn't been severely damaged in the hurricane.

"I'm certain I can get the government's help," Tim said. "Probably have to change the name next year to The Union Island Billfish Tournament."

Mia strutted across the deck. "And I'm certain I can drum up even more fishermen. Anyone want to make a wager?"

"What's this with you and gambling?" Dag inquired.

"Life's a gamble," Mia curtly replied. "I like monetary incentives. No different than you two. Dag, you get tips and I'm sure you get bonuses for outstanding work, Tim."

"Okay, what's reasonable? Dinner on us if you get five more boats?" Dag asked.

"Dinner was a given," Mia countered. "I haven't heard any place for me in the tournament organization. Shit, I had to invite myself along on this trip. You left me at home when you went to Martinique. Didn't even ask, just took off."

"Hey, I'm sorry, you're right, I'm wrong," Tim apologized. "I didn't know you were interested. What would you like to do?"

"Say, just say, I get ten more to boats come up from Grenada; that will be a third more. Increase our profit share considerably." Mia thought out loud. "I want to be master of ceremonies."

"Done," Tim immediately replied. "That's great. You take the microphone." He shook his hands in the air. "I never wanted to do it, anyway."

Mia beamed a smile and moved between her two brothers and draped an arm over each. "Thanks, I'll be happy to be part of Team St. Claire. I'll make you proud."

"You always have," Dag hugged her.

They found a lucky berth at St. Georges Marina. The docks were packed with sailboats, motor yachts, and mega yachts.

"I guess everyone believes the storm season is over," Tim assessed. "Look at some of these yachts, they dwarf our boat. Big money people run out of places to spend it."

"Big toys for big boys. Speaking of which, looks like Kalaloo's' boat is over there," Dag pointed. Two West Indians were replacing the powerheads on the outboards. The white hull was along the path to the marina's exit. One mechanic saw them and beat it to the exit first.

"I think that was Kal," Dag said with a laugh. "I don't think he likes us anymore. And after we saved him and his boat from destruction."

Tim chuckled, "Always remember, no good deed goes unpunished."

The two men walked until they found an instant printer and reproduced a hundred photocopies of the tournament information.

Mia did a ten-minute, total makeover in the V berth before she started on her mission of drumming up more anglers. Dressed in a black miniskirt, black halter top, topped with a black Fedora, Mia turned every man's and a few women's heads. She took a taxi to the top of Young Street and walked into the Commonwealth Bank, directly to the managing vice president's office, removed her hat and big sunglasses, and pulled a tournament poster from her stylish messenger bag.

"Mr. Hodge, remember me?" She asked a dapper man in his late forties wearing a light gray linen suit sitting behind an impressive mahogany desk. The walls of his office were tastefully adorned with mounted fish, photographs of fish, and fishing rods. A photo of his wife and children sat on his desk.

The man slowly eyed every inch of Mia, his brow wrinkled, before negatively shaking his head.

"Sure you do, Sunset Bay Fish Camp, ah, come on, you know my father Harry."

"Ah hah," Hodge's head bobbed as he connected a few memories. "You are a St. Claire, young lady? Ah, I haven't fished with Harry and Cheesy yet this year. I'd heard rumors they'd sold Sunset Bay to developers. Wait a minute, you're little Mia? You've been away for what, five years?"

"You're correct." She primped, "Not so little anymore. Yes, been away too long. But you're wrong about our fishing resort. It's open for business. Harry took a little sabbatical and then there was Monique. We're back in action again." She crossed and uncrossed her long, tanned legs.

"What can I do with, ah, for you, Ms. St. Claire?"

"Please, Mia, Mr. Hodge, I'd like to take you fishing?"

The man stood and waved his right arm, "Well, fishing is… one of my passions. I do have other passions. I thoroughly enjoy fishing with your father and Cheesy. Like this bank, they're a regular Caribbean institution."

He walked and described some of his catches. Mia was attentive and leaned forward to give him a better view.

"Everybody knows how great the fishing is around Union. Well, it's time to return. Sunset Bay is providing a Blue Marlin tournament in a few weeks, and we'd like to have all the local anglers represented. Perhaps you could mention it to your friends. We'd love to have you participate."

"I'd love to… participate."

"Can I count on it?"

"What's the prize?"

"At least a quarter of the entrance fees. More anglers, more boats, more prize money. My brothers and I, well, the entire family, have organized this to be one of the best tournaments in the Caribbean. FineBraid Line is working with us and the IGFA. As it stands now, the prize should be at least ten thousand US, but probably more. Perhaps Commonwealth Bank could be a partial sponsor?"

"What would a sponsorship involve?"

Mia stood and leaned over the desk. "Put up some flyers in the bank, maybe contribute a paltry amount, say, five thousand?"

"EC?"

"US, everything must be in US," she was making it up as fast as she moved along. "Because we have anglers coming from many countries. American is the common currency."

Hodge scrutinized the tournament poster and studied Mia for a minute. "Hmm, what's the worthy cause? The bank can't just contribute money. That would be giving it away. Has to be for a good cause."

She didn't hesitate, "For the preservation and conservation of billfish in the Grenadines, catch and release. You know Harry, my father, has always been a true conservationist. He put this tourney together to teach other boat captains to save the billfish, especially marlins."

"Ah, a fishing tournament to help save the fish. Now that is a grand idea," Hodge grinned. "A Thanksgiving Tournament, the third weekend in November. Hmm, yes, you can count on it."

"Thank you, you won't regret it." Mia beamed, and as she rose from the chair, "When can we expect a check?"

A big ledger of bank checks opened on his desk. "Who do I make this payable to?"

"Sunset Bay Billfish Tournament. In fact, why don't I open an operating account here?"

Hodge nodded. "I'll have my assistant help you." He pushed a button and a waving young lady ushered smiling Mia to the counter. The vice president clicked his cell phone, "Simon, you ready to try out that new reel?"

Mia hit every bank, restaurant, and store along Young Street delivering posters and shaking hands practically in rhythm with her posterior. She continued the same sponsorship spiel until four that afternoon, their prearranged rendezvous. Pushing a shopping cart filled with beer, she drew more stares.

"What the…?" Tim was stunned by his sister. "I, ah, we left you in a long white T-shirt and wowee!"

She handed the beers and carefully stepped onto the boat. "You know as well as anyone, Tim, you must dress for success." Mia wore a fake frown as she threw off her hat, "How many new anglers did you guys get?"

Dag bragged, "Four more boats. Right here, walking these docks. Sorry, sis, we can talk the talk and walk the walk."

"Walk on this!" Mia unfolded her middle finger, then broke into a smile, "Sorry about what?" She opened her bag and pulled out neat manila envelopes, each with a signed sponsorship agreement and the deposits. "Talk about walking," she made a clown face. "I walked in a different direction, additional sponsorships. All of Grenada wants to help Sunset Bay and Union Island rebuild. And they all want to fish the billfish to save the billfish."

"What!?" Both men broke up with laughter.

"Just what I said; this tournament has to have a cause. The first one that came to mind was saving the billfish. Shit, we gotta save something, might as well be the big blues. For that, we get big green!" Mia flashed a wallet full of deposit slips. "It was easy - easy. Fishermen are a unique breed of addicts."

"I can't believe that you got eleven more boats registered with another five possibles." Tim stammered as he reviewed her papers, "For a new tournament, this might be one of the best attended."

"Remember what that bank robber said, I forget his name. If you want money, go to the banks. There are six different banks along Young Street, then there's KFC, McDonalds, and two grocery chains. My good luck was that all the big dogs were at work today."

"Bosses come in on Mondays to check the weekend's receipts," Tim said as if it was a business rule. "That was lucky timing."

"But, Mia, you must have really sold it," Dag toasted her with a beer. "I'll say it was a miracle."

"Miracle, not quite." She squirmed on the bench seat until her miniskirt rode further up her legs. She leaned forward and made a toot, blowing across her beer bottle. "The luck is male chauvinism. It's always fisher-m-e-n. All the business heads were men. Combine the two and you have an egomaniac who likes nature, the sea, fishing, the thrill of conquest against big fish, and they all consider themselves womanizers. If you're a top dog on an island, you must have a boat. Then to get bragging rights at the marina, you must bring in either beautiful women, big fish, or both," Mia snickered. "I let them think I was available to go fishing." She punched Dag's shoulder, "Technique. It's always, bait, presentation, and technique."

"Ever thought about a career in sales?" Tim laughed. "Maybe a motivational speaker?"

"Believe me, I can motivate, motivate, motivate."

"Yeah, sis, motivate and get me another beer."

Diverman Hank on author's boat with 38 kg Sailfish off Canouan, SVG.

CHAPTER FIFTEEN

The surprise was Mia, the cohesive factor of the St. Claire family. Sour words and nasty talk had ceased; everyone exhibited only a positive attitude. This was a unified effort. Even though they knew they could pay the fines, Sunset Bay Fish Club was reaching for posterity by presenting a quality tournament. It was the initial trial run contest, but they had registered more boats with more anglers than any other tournament south of Puerto Rico.

All Tim had to do was to tie all the many strings together in fine fashion, with attention to detail. He knew he had valid excuses for any slackness, Monique and the general, 'no hurry, not my job, mon,' Eastern Caribbean attitude. The fishermen weren't expecting to find thrills on Union. They'd paid for a fun weekend catching fish. That included partying, drinking rum, and telling tales together, the camaraderie of fishermen.

The government had graciously approved the locations and venues. The Coast Guard would transport the Prime Minister and Minister of Fisheries for a brief talk about aquatic conservation that included cocktails from several donated cases of locally distilled rum.

From the marinas he'd worked on his way west along the South American north coast, Dag enticed a Latin contingent to take part. It included a five boat Venzie flotilla, one from Panama, and one from Guyana. The numbers were increasing. The tournament was getting close to the fifty boat mark.

Ms. St. Claire coddled the Grenada sponsors and anglers with two more visits. Both times she greeted her clients with a piece of fresh fish caught on the quick run south from Union to St. Georges. The dorado, tuna, and 'cuda pieces let all know this was about fishing. Her attire modified into subtle-sexy, wearing the Sunset Bay khaki uniform always accented with an orange silk scarf. She pulled off being the model fisherwoman identity nearly as perfect as her mother.

Each time she visited a different brother was her escort. That way, every participant knew every organizer, every second-generation St. Claire fisher-person. Next year, no crystal ball knew where anyone would be. Tim, maybe England, Dag, maybe Costa Rica, and Mia was the biggest question. To stay prepared, they kept quadruple copies of the tournament's comprehensive records with contact numbers, email addresses, boat names, clubs, associations, down to favorite baits.

The next step was to have a successful tournament. That needed smooth weather and plenty of hookups.

∧∧∧∧∧∧∧∧∧

Thursday, November seventeenth, three weeks ahead of the deadline to pay the fines and get a new license, was the inauguration Sunset Bay Billfish Tournament. The most boats in many years were anchored off Clifton. Twenty-three had found berths along the repaired municipal pier and docks. Mia's sponsors and the herd of IGFA judges anchored outside in Sunset Bay. Had to have the judges; this wasn't small prize money. The top boat and angler would win at least fifteen thousand US dollars each plus prizes donated by the sponsors.

Union Island and Clifton were also back on track. The airport added two extra flights each day for that weekend. Two fishing families flew in on private charters. The limited guesthouses, which Tim had told people to prepare, were filled. A few entrepreneurs were making money in their restaurants, and everyone on the small island wore a festive smile, at least for a few days. Beer and rum started flowing on Thursday evening at the opening ceremonies.

The airport portico was designed to provide shelter for passengers of the four small airlines that plied the Southern Grenadines. On its best day ever, the airport had held only a quarter of the two hundred and fifty anglers and crew, plus all the vendors and helpers. They had recruited every table and chair in Clifton for the patchwork seating arrangements. More than a dozen grills and extra-large igloo coolers lined the perimeter. Many were on a lend-lease from hotels in Bequia and Canouan, along with suitable cook and waiter attire. The institutions of the St. Vincent Grenadines worked together to make this event a success.

Cassy and Verena distributed handy drawstring Sunset Bay Tournament bags, all embossed by FineBraid Fishing Line, to every angler and captain. The fishermen had been instructed to bring their own libations to this initial function. That way no one could complain they drank more than they'd wanted and missed fish because their fishing skills were diminished. That was Harry's idea, BYOB, and the anglers showed up flaunting delicious fifteen and twenty-year-old rums. One of the event's sponsors supplied ice and soda. Locals from the church ushered, tended the dinghies, and served the 'also donated' appetizers of 'saltfish bakes' and curried chicken rotis.

A steel pan trio made excellent music and provided drum rolls for each introduction.

At the head table, facing a mass of one hundred fifty-eight registered fishermen, with another hundred plus captains and crew, sat the St. Claires and Chessmans. Nearly everyone wore the free tournament T-shirt. Even Harry and Cheesy had changed from their standard khaki for that evening.

"So, that's about it, everyone knows the rules, it's tag and release. If you get a thousand-plus, unfortunately, that's got to be weighed. Looks like we'll have excellent weather. Good luck and great fishing." Mia received standing applause.

Harry shocked everyone by rising and taking the podium. Tidied, with his gray ponytail neatly trimmed, he saluted his audience. The knee was better, but still was painful; not one hundred percent. "Most of us have fished together at one time or another. I want to thank everybody, for coming to make this the first annual a success," he coughed and looked around, "for the Union Island and Sunset Bay Tournament. Enjoy yourself, that's what this is all about, good fun and entertaining competition."

"The fishing starts at eight AM with the traditional captain's swim." Everyone laughed, knowing they had to come ashore to sign in and then swim back to their boat. "Yes sir, all your asses are gonna be bright-eyed from doing the Australian crawl. I won't be getting wet." He pointed to Dag who still had his right arm wrapped, "My son, the one-arm bandit, will skipper Sassy this season. I hope. Monique screwed up my right knee." He raised his bandaged knee, did a one-leg stagger, and almost lost his balance.

The crowd roared and began a chant, "Harry! Harry! Harry!" Fewer voices continued, "Cheesy, Cheesy, Cheesy! The Englishman stood, performed a distinguished bow at the waist, and as he straightened, pulled up his wife for an introduction.

Harry caught himself, "What's wrong with me, I didn't introduce my better half and all my much better parts." He grabbed Cassy and pulled her up, "This is my lovely wife, Cassandra, the person behind the St. Claire Sunset Bay Fish Camp. This is Timothy with as much brains as muscle, and you can see he's got a load of both. Don't know whose side that comes from? He's returned from Jolly old London to get a tan and help his family. This tournament is his idea."

"Next, this is our eldest Dag, also an extreme fisherman, same as me, fish lust. And this is Mia, our youngest also luckily takes after her mother with brains, brawn, beauty, and…" Harry paused, looked at her and a big smile took over his face. He shook his head, chuckling, "Yeah, Mia also has fish-lust. Watch out for her, fellow anglers, Mia is a fishing force to be reckoned with. Those of you who have already met her, now realize it is all about her technique. It's always bait, presentation, and technique."

Mia stood, posed, flexing her biceps, while the crowd politely snickered.

"We got forty-two Caribbean boats from as far away as Puerto Rico, Venezuela, and Panama. As of this moment, we have more than 150 anglers vying for a top prize of," Harry paused and gracefully blew his nose, "ten thousand to the best angler, ten thousand for the best boat, ten thousand for the biggest blue marlin. Nothing to sneeze at. Good luck. Drink your own tonight, get a good rest. See you back here again at the sign-in, 7 AM. Oh, by the way, the BYOB tonight is my idea. Don't want to hear any bitching about headaches. Tomorrow night booze is free from sunset until eleven. After all," he paused for effect, "this is the First Annual Sunset Bay," he paused again, "and Union Island Fishing Tournament."

Honoré and Mammie with several local women barbecued pork, chicken, and fish. The St. Claire siblings circulated separately through the crowd. Cassy accompanied by Verena and a church group served the hungry anglers. Sam slipped up behind Cassy and startled her,

"Looks like your tournament is a success, Sis," Sam smiled. "I wish you the best." Cassy silently nodded in shock of seeing him at the event since he'd shunned her family since the storm.

With a few followers, Sam walked over and equally stunned Harry. The latter stood and not only extended his hand to his brother-in-law but drew him into a long, very public hug. Harry broke away and rattled his spoon against his water glass to get the participants' attention.

"Fellow fishermen, this is my brother-in-law, Sam Scarbeaux. We like to call him Uncle Sam because he gets your money at the fuel dock and fishing supply, AKA Curly's Hardware." There was a slight patter of applause as the contestants were enjoying the delicious food.

"Holding court, Harry?"

"Hmm, Samuel, you fishing in this?"

"Yes, sir, too much money not to. I'd like you to meet the owner of *Temptress*, the boat I'm on, Mr. Van Gell."

The slim, well attired, bearded man extended his hand. Harry hesitated, but shook. "Pleased, I'm sure. Beautiful place you have here."

Tim appeared at his father's side and answered, "We like it."

"Ever thought of selling?" Van Gell leered at both men and then turned to the crowd. "With a big franchise hotel on Union, you could have this many people every week."

"Once in a great while, a crowd is okay. Every day would ruin the, ah, um, ambiance," Harry said as he strained to see the flashy woman in Van Gell and Sam's group. "If we sold out, where would we go? This is the best fishing."

"With enough money, you could find someplace, I'm sure," the hotel man taunted.

Dag appeared, chewing on a sauce-dripping chicken leg. "That's why you're looking here? I mean, did you just sell someplace as sweet as this and want a replacement?" Mouthing the chicken bone, he grabbed Sam's and Van Gell's hands with his greasy shake. "I'm Dag, Tim's the deal-maker; right Unc? I fish."

"Oh, I buy and sell many places," Van Gell searched for something to wipe off the sauce. He reached into the FineBraid bag and used the tournament shirt.

"Ah, a real live wheeler-dealer," Tim said as he draped his heavy arm over the hotelier. "Right here in River City, ah, Sunset Bay. Come on, come with me, Van-de-bilt, um, Van Guy, Van Dam, what is your name?" Tim maneuvered him away from the stage.

"Beatrice, is that you? Beatrice Thorpe? I didn't know you fished," Harry said when he recognized the woman with Sam and Van Gell. Deeply tanned, she wore a tight white bikini top with a short white sarong. It announced she spent her time in the gym and away from the dessert tray. It looks as though she wanted to catch something special. Nine women had signed to compete, but Beatrice was already trolling. She'd been the woman photographed nude on *Sassy*.

She politely kissed Harry on both cheeks. "So nice to see you again and sober," she coquettishly smiled.

"No, no, no, no kissing here!" Harry spun around searching the crowd and found Cassy chatting with her back to him. "I'm kind of foggy about the last time we met." He sat and tried to hide.

"You should be." She gave a penetrating, all-knowing stare.

Mia and Dag got on either side of the bleached blond. Mia asked, "Did you get a bag, a tournament kit, to hold all of your tricks?"

Dag, pretending to be intoxicated, draped a greasy paw over her shoulder. It left a visible handprint on her bikini bra as he pulled her into a discrete conversation, "You know, I always had a thing for older women."

Van Gell broke away from Tim and rushed over to separate Dag. "Lovely lady. Her husband handles my insurance. Gentlemen, please consider contacting my company if you contemplate selling." He handed out his cards, which each St. Claire visibly dropped.

"Well, it's been a rough year." Harry looked up with a dull face, "Sam can tell you all about that. But we'll let you know." Harry continued with more volume, "Beatrice might be lovely," he searched for the correct words. "But a lady," he shook his head, "never!"

^^^^^^^^^^

Daybreak had been an hour earlier. The westerly breeze was enough to be noticed and comfortably air-conditioned this morning. Townspeople, traditional early risers, milled around the waterfront watching the tournament activities. Few had any idea what to expect, except that it was a delightful break from the usual. The BBC came through very distinctly over the loudspeakers, "Beep, beep, beep. The time is 11 Greenwich Mean Time." Harry's voice followed, "Captains, to your boats."

Amid cheers and hoots, forty-two men splashed off the municipal dock, into Petit Bay, and swam to their idling boats. Attentive, not to cruise over a slow swimmer, the sportfishers idled from the harbor before accelerating west to the drop-off.

Cheesy climbed aboard and Tim tossed him a towel. "Shame Harry's leg's bad," Cheese muttered, "and your arm's hacked."

"He never was much for swimming; you know that Cheese," Dag contributed a steaming cup of tea. "Must be busting his balls to be aboard the St. Vincent committee boat with the Minister of Marine Affairs and all the press."

"Don't kid yourself, Harry enjoys drinking from the same bowl as the top dogs," Cheesy gave a sly smile. "In his mind, he'll always be the new guy, the outsider, no matter how many years he's been here. Our loveable Harry, may bark, growl, and even bite." Cheesy laughed, "Sometimes even his own tail, but he desires recognition; all avid sportsmen do. You three have given him something he craved."

"Okay, somehow, Tim, you designed the perfect therapy. I'll admit, Harry is much nicer when he isn't guzzling rum! This tournament is everything and more," Mia said and turned to address Sunset Bay's newest personnel. "Now it's in the hands of the IGFA officials. Right, what's your name, again?"

"Anthony Cavalardi, Tony," the International Game Fishing Tournament Observer (IGFTO) introduced himself for the second time. A trained and certified group had flown in from the States to watch the action on every boat. It was all about rules, keeping the anglers equal, and keeping the fish alive with catch and release. A short, thin man, with a graying goatee, Tony was an architect in Stateside life, but being a fishing judge got him around big fish action.

"Ready?" Dag asked before he pushed the throttles up. Clifton was disappearing around Mary's point. "Some will probably tail us, hoping that we know a secret spot. My strategy today is to go first go deep, we'll troll dead west for two hours, swing north, and then about noon we should have Mia's place on the GPS."

Mia nodded, "Sounds good. But with radar, depth-sounders, fish-finders, and every fresh, off-the-market electronic fishing toy, each has an equal chance," she posed. "But it's always sharp hooks, fresh bait, and proper presentation that catches fish."

Heading west, the deck had little shade. The wind picked up slightly as the sun rose in the sky, keeping the day relatively comfortable. It was a definite sunglass day; the sun was doubly bright in the clear sky and reflecting off the sea.

With the drop so close, boats were in the deep in less than half an hour. One, from Puerto Rico, hooked a small, two-hundred-pound marlin in shallow water, less than fifty meters. By ten o'clock, a few marlins had sore jaws. It would be a record catch day simply because this was the first day and the top score was being set. Potentially, it could be surpassed each of the next two days.

Sassy's crew dragged baits at seven knots for two hours, running a course of two hundred and ninety degrees, north of west. Mia and Tim were the designated fishers and would trade off after every hookup or on the hour.

In extremely deep water, too deep for the sonar to register the bottom, Dag brought the throttles down to what felt like creeping, five knots. Union was a speck capped by clouds and only a half dozen other boats were visible when Tim hooked their first marlin. It swallowed a silver and black bubble-head streamer. The action was just shy of twenty minutes before Cheesy touched the leader. As prescribed, they snapped many photos, and that satisfied IGFA Tony. The fish went three-fifty.

Rules were every hookup was radioed to the scorekeepers. "Sounds like a busy day. Six boats tagged two bills each," Dag relayed after placing his call.

"Anything big?" Mia asked what everyone aboard wanted to know.

"Biggest about five hundred, on *Temptress*." Dag said.

"Van Gell probably bought it and had it delivered," Tim laughed,

"I read they bring frozen fish to bass tournaments."

A small blue, rattled and shook Mia's rod, but only smacked the lure with its bill. She quickly loosened the drag and free spooled, but the fish never reappeared. She muttered a string of four-letter, not-ready-for-public-school words as she relinquished the fighting chair to Tim and joined Cheesy on the tower.

As planned, they circled the area they'd labeled as Mia's G Spot. In an hour and a half, brother and sister had each boated another medium-sized, two-fifty blue.

Mia lost another. The fish struck her lure and rocketed straight up only meters off the starboard side. With an intense convulsion, it arched its body with a mighty twisting thrust and threw the hook so hard it hit and rattled against *Sassy's* tower. Mia's scowl was her mood.

Observer Tony gave the okay to use a new jointed swivel lure Tim had brought. The lure was called a BB (Big Blue) Twenty-One. Each of the two sections was long and slender like two big, plastic minnows joined. Tim kept the big lure close to the boat, and all eyes watched it wiggle sensuously back and forth between the two prop wakes. When he locked it into the center rod holder on the chair, he released the drag and sent it back farther than the other baits.

"You better hope that swivel joint is made for monsters," Dag said as he returned to the wheel. "If something big hits, I prefer a single, long shank, forged hook on strong Monel wire. I'm just saying, that's me. I saw what the state-of-the-art newbies are using and they're catching…"

Tim interrupted, "We got three flat lines out rigged with bubbleheads with streamers and fat ballyhoos on forged hooks. Same on the planer line, running deep. Did you see how the second section wiggles like a fishtail on my lure? It's reflecting the sun in a different direction every time it moves. It can be another teaser bait. Hey, you're right; I agree, track-proven is the best, but I brought this to try. Tony, over there, says he'll sanction it."

"Yeah, bro, give it a go!" Dag was also enthusiastic. "I'm all for trying new stuff."

Ten minutes later, Mia yelled, pointing, "Big blue bill, slicing up a trough, heading for your new lure, Timmy."

He was already sitting in the chair, waiting. His left hand gripped the rod, his right was ready at the reel. He rashly released the drag and free spooled, using his thumb for friction. This way he could feel if the fish batted the lure. The line slowly paid out. He felt the first slight hit, probably the bill smacking the artificial. His thumb pressed tight on the reel's spool of mono when the lure took a solid hit. The line screamed off, blistering his skin on his thumb.

"Ouch, ouch, ouch, damn it," Tim barked as he locked the drag halfway, medium resistance. The fish kept taking line as Dag slowed the sportfisher. No one spoke or moved, just absorbed the moment.

In a split second, the line sagged. That meant either the fish got off or was charging the boat. Never losing sight of where his line entered the water, Tim maniacally cranked the reel's handle as if everything depended on holding this fish. His intense grip on the rod tightened all of his physique.

For several seconds, his concentration muted his immediate surroundings. Baboom! Sound returned when the enormous fish flexed its long head-to-tail muscles and shot out of the water. Tim thudded against the back of the chair as all tension disappeared from the rod. Not buckled to the chair, his body convulsed; he bounced against the chair back, and then he doubled over and collapsed, facing the stern. The rod, in the holder at the center of the fighting chair, prevented Tim from slamming against the deck.

The over-sized game fish continued to blast from the water. Cheesy and Mia hissed a combined loud gasp. It was like the second coming; everyone's mouth hung open. Dag managed a 'What the...' before he realized this was 'the' big marlin.

"Oh, my god!" Observer Tony choked; the moment overwhelmed him.

"Junish!" Shouted Dag as if calling at a pet dog to stop.

In auto-accident slow motion, the enormous billfish continued to rise as it tail-walked from port to starboard across the stern as though its big, round eyes were inspecting the vessel, captain, and crew. With a full twist, the sinewy silver and dark blue frame shook. It was so huge and so close the minute stripes and fine silver-green dots in the dark blue upper half were visible. This fish was a masterpiece.

The enormous fish shuddered, crooked its immense tail, and splashed all aboard. Its bill jerked backward and thrust again upward. Then pointing towards *Sassy*'s stern, the gigantic head whipped left, right, and forward. The fish spit the lure out. As if it had practiced the move, aimed at Tim in the chair; the artificial bait rattled across the deck.

The acrobatics finished when the monster fish performed a graceful backward arc and re-entered the blue sea. Adding insult, it waved its wide, silver tail twice before it disappeared.

"Wow! Wow! Wow! Wow!" Tony exclaimed. "That's the

mother of all blue marlin."

"And I lost him. Damn it!" Tim agonized.

"Tim, you couldn't possibly be ready for that… that huge mother fucker," Mia consoled. "No one could. I should have hauled in my small one."

"Haven't ever seen one that big in the southern Caribbean." Tony muttered, "You've seen him before?"

"Every couple of years," Cheesy wheezed. "Well, not every couple, I'm exaggerating, every five or so. This is late. I must look through our logs, but I think Junish makes his appearance is June or July."

"Duh, you think so?" Mia mouthed. "Gee, I wonder why we call it Junish? You forget, we were all together the first time we saw that Moby Dick monster marlin? That had to be almost twenty years ago."

"Almost exactly twenty. It looks like it's still growing. Wow!" Dag let out a big exhale, "I've seen a few four hundred kilo fish, and truthfully, not fish talk, Junish looks to be about double that. It's probably feeding," Dag chipped in.

"And you guys are professionals? Damn straight it's feeding; it damn well smacked our bait!" Mia argued. "Take a lot to fill Junish up."

"Sister, a huge fish like that looks for schools of tuna to chomp. We, ah, maybe Tim's super wiggler lure, pissed it off," Dag explained as he patted Tim on his shoulder, then gave him a playful slap on the back of his head. "If you're gonna piss off the big fucking fish best we make some improvements on your lure. Look!"

Dag pointed to Cheesy holding the jointed artificial. The fish had pulled the hooks straight. "Don't want to say I told you so, and it probably would have held a normal-sized marlin. Junish is a super fish and needs super-sized hooks."

"Yeah," Tim pulled his ball cap's brim down to shade his eyes. He splashed some cold water and rubbed his face. "You're right, fucking Boy Scout Dag, always fucking right," Tim huffed. "That fish was our payday, money, Mercedes, fame, and fortune. And I fucking lost it. Damn it!"

"This is just the first day," Cheesy calmed the tone. "We've got two more. Plenty of time to adapt and adjust."

Cheesy moved and put his arm over smaller Tony's shoulder. "Sir, you did not observe this, ah, monster fish today. Got me? What you saw did not happen."

"What? Why?" Tony stuttered.

"Because we don't want all the other boats up this way. If you blab, then the entire regatta will be out in force."

"Cheese's right," Dag continued as he and Mia circled the observer. "We'll give you all our digital footage after the tournament closes. You can show your buddies; that'll be great for Sunset Bay's business, but we need your promise to be discrete tonight and tomorrow. Can we count on that?"

"I'll only report it as a hookup. There's no reason to mention size. Yes, I can work with you on this. Don't think any rules are being broken," Tony agreed.

"Good. This evening, drink with us," Dag instructed. "Free-flowing rum usually means a lot of free-flowing shit talk."

"I don't drink," Tony answered. "I've been born again."

"Good," Tim said with a smile. He lifted the man and danced around. "Like you say, horseshoes and hand grenades, it was close. I can't wait to see what the GoPros captured. We'll get 'em tomorrow."

"Hey," Dag yelled. "Mia, in the chair, lines out; the day isn't over yet."

Tim studied his jointed lure for the remainder of the day and solicited ideas from all aboard. Two eyes screwed in, one in each section, held the weak hooks that were straightened. It was agreed to wire a swivel to those same eyes and attach long-shanked, super-strong forged hooks. They tested the movement and kept modifying it until satisfied it had regained the same productive wiggle.

^^^^^^^^^^

The second day of the tournament had considerably less action. Excellent sea and weather conditions had only produced an average of one marlin per boat.

Mia boated a nice three-hundred-pound marlin shortly after nine that morning. Everyone expected it to be a gangbuster day, but the higher the sun rose, the lower their expectations fell. Tim lost another after lunch. He dragged the lure all day, but it only drew attention from birds.

Mia's late afternoon hookup was unsuccessful. The fish never broke the surface, only went deep. It could have been a marlin or a huge wahoo.

The anglers paused as they passed the scoreboard on their way to the dinner buffet. The party continued with a calypso band crowding the small stage, playing a medley of classics by the Mighty Sparrow.

Mouthing the words to 'Drunk and Disorderly' while standing on a rickety, wooden step ladder, Honoré slowly printed the running scores.

SEA GHOST – FIVE
TEMPTRESS - FIVE
SASSY CASSY – FOUR
MAD HATTER – THREE
COURTESAN – THREE
BIGGEST FISH – TEMPTRESS – 480 LBS.

"What's up?" Harry sauntered over from the head table and joined the Sunset Bay gang. "Not too bad! The guys I rode with today couldn't catch a cold in an airport. I'm not along to give advice only to represent our business interest. I think the St. Vincent white shirts have changed their opinion about the necessity for a hotel."

"You've been politicking? That could be dangerous," Cheesy sparked a wide grin.

Harry wrinkled his face, "Oh, I know, leave it all to Timothy. Hey, I've learned, I swear, I only speak when spoken to, sit with my legs not crossed, and never eat with my fingers!" He laughed, "Come on, you guys, give the old man a break. We're doing okay, huh? Only one off the lead."

"Imagine if we'd hauled in Junish? Nobody could top us," Mia offered. "See you later, I got to go help Mom and Verena."

"How's she doing out there?" Harry inquired as Mia disappeared into the makeshift kitchen tent.

"Like a pro," Dag shot back, "Serious, maybe too serious. Today, no music, afraid it might scare away the fish. She wants to win. Mia wants the team to win, but in particular, she wants to win. I don't know who she needs to prove anything to. Wouldn't let us have a cold one until we came off the drop, into shallow water late this afternoon."

"I'm sort of with her," Tim agreed. "But a beer about two this afternoon would have tasted damn good. Hot out there. Don't think it would have cut into my abilities. But I lost one again today, and so did she."

"If we have a fine day tomorrow, we can still win," Dag reasoned. "Right Harry? Any secret touches you recommend?"

He shook his ponytail a few times thinking, "Has she been saying the fish prayer?"

"Well, now that you mention it, she hasn't," Tim said. "I wonder why?"

"I'd start with that," Harry recommended. "And pour the first beer overboard to give Neptune and Poseidon a buzz."

"You mean we need a monumental day, don't you? We've lost three fish. Those would have put us in the lead," Tim lamented. "If these boats don't pick up any more, yeah, maybe we stand a chance."

"Hey, that's our pond out there, Bro. We know it. Right?" Dag bragged, "We know every square meter. Maybe we'll get lucky and, ah, who knows, but it'll be a fantastic day tomorrow."

Cassy approached carrying a tray of small sandwiches.

"Well boys, not too bad. One fish away from a tie. You and Mia each caught one today. I bet you'll do the same or better tomorrow."

"No, mom; today only Mia brought one to the boat. I lost every one of my hookups."

"Our budget's so low the sandwiches gotta be tiny? And only one slice of bread?" Harry sheepishly asked as he grabbed two. "I'm hungry. These won't fill a cavity in a tooth."

"Harry, my dear husband, these are canapés, open face cocktail sandwiches. The buffet will begin in about half an hour. Don't stuff yourself; you have to speak, give the scoring," Cassy replied. "Go freshen up, at least splash some water to wash the salt off."

"Aye, aye," Harry saluted and half-skipped, half-danced through the crowd, shaking hands and always nodding in agreement.

"Your father's in his glory. We can never thank you enough, Tim, for having the vision and ability to create this," she spread her arms and almost spilled the tray of sandwiches. "You too, Dag. You helped us pull our butts out of the fire. And with Mia, we're a family again."

"Yes, mother, that's what it's all about." Dag pointed around, "Look what you gave us: we're all blessed."

Tim coughed and rolled his eyes as Cassy hugged her eldest. She turned and held Tim's face and kissed his cheek. She laughed, "Mia might be right; you might be adopted."

"Hey," Tim feigned offense. "I learned a lot from Granpop; give people what they want at a price they can afford. Do right by everyone and your days will be happy."

"That's so sweet of you to say that about Curly. My father was an exceptional man. He helped shape this island for the better. Many others came and tried to take advantage of our people." Cassy's voice quivered, "You boys and Mia are doing the best thing possible, working with everyone. Even Harry has given up goading people, and alcohol. I don't know how you did it, but miracles do happen."

"Yes, mom, we need one more miracle mañana," Tim said. "Two fish away from any money. The way it is now, with fuel, entrance fees, we need a few marlin and for the other boats to get only one."

"You'll get them. Think presentation and technique," Cassy reminded.

"Yeah, Mom, we'll get those damn fish," Dag mumbled as he grabbed the last three sandwiches from her tray.

"I can't believe this." Like a cymbal rattling, the empty tray clattered to the ground. Cassy walked to one of the center tables where Uncle Sam sat with a group. The brothers looked at each other. Tim thought she must have learned of his attempt on their boat. But that was impossible.

Instead, Cassy walked up to the well-dressed woman at the table. Congenially Cassy said, "Beatrice, I can't believe it. Beatrice Thorpe, it has been so long. I hope you've been well."

"Hello, Cassandra," the woman replied aloof.

"Are you in our tournament? I didn't see your name on the list of anglers, but then I wasn't looking. Are you here with your husband?"

"What? Ah, no, Theo had to work, the storm and all that."

Cassy leaned over and said directly so only those at the table would hear, "Try to keep your knickers on and your hands off of my husband. I still have that photo of you. You, you!"

"Cassandra," Beatrice tried to stand, but Sam grabbed her arm and pulled her back. She continued undaunted, "It was only a fun time. Harry probably doesn't even remember."

"Slut!" Cassy gave the woman a backhand slap. "Why should he remember you!?"

"Most men can't forget me," she said with a seductive tone as she rubbed her reddening cheek.

"You're with her?" Cassy directed to Van Gell. "Tell me what's so remarkable about silicone and dye!"

That spark caused a loud explosion. "Bitch! If you weren't so much of a cunt, Harry wouldn't have to look for a good time!"

The band was playing Sparrow's 'Jean and Dinah,' but Cassy became the center of entertainment. Beatrice tried to rise from her seat, but Sam and Van Gell held her arms. Cassy gave her a roundhouse punch that collapsed the woman onto the bench.

Cassy lifted the woman by her hair and slapped her again, "Better watch who you're calling a bitch, bitch!"

"Ladies, ladies please," Van Gell's face was all smile enjoying the ladies' argument. "Mrs. St. Claire, Mrs. Thorpe works for me as a personal secretary. Please control your temperament."

"Control her! Keep her away from me," Cassy was shaking, "and my family!"

"Mom," Mia hugged her. "Holy cow, that was some right-left combination."

Harry, on a limp-along trot, parted the crowd of anglers, and grabbed his wife's arms from behind, squeezing her in a hug. He lifted her up, feet dangling, and moved her out of the table area.

"Harry," Cassy was huffing, "did you know she was coming?!"

"Darling," he meekly cocked his head. "How would I? She's not listed as an angler."

"Just be sure!" Cassy fumed. After he released her, they walked outside. "You are finally getting out of the doghouse!"

"Arf, arf, arf!" Harry tried successfully to lighten the moment. "Good thing you never hit me like that. Probably would have given me a concussion."

Mia turned and watched as Cassy grabbed Harry's arm and walked in the dock's direction. She heard her mother, "Just don't give me any reason! Oh, that woman!"

Raised in Japan Pete and the author's father with
a 'chicken' dolphin St. Thomas, USVI

CHAPTER SIXTEEN

On the tournament's final day, Cassy's improvised restaurant at the airport consumed all the remaining eggs and bread on the island, and it wasn't enough. Honoré and Mammie saved the morning by concocting their tasty saltfish croquettes and saltfish buljol with skillet roti. They served the fishermen breakfast at six.

Seven captains still vied at a chance of winning the best boat. A few more successful hookups would tell the story. Nine boats were skunked with no fish and needed major miracles. It would be a heated workday, a solid eight hours of trolling, from eight until four. The awards ceremony was scheduled for five-thirty. Overnight, the wind had abated, and the temperature climbed from thirty degrees just after sunrise.

To keep things hopping and different, Tim had planned for the fleet to do a land rush start on the last day. All the boats were circling the drop-off when Harry shot the flare that signaled lines in the water. Many anglers who were yawning and gulping aspirins cringed when the fleet blasted their air horns in the affirmative.

"One thing we need for next year," Tim began as he stretched his torso to loosen up.

"What's that, chap?" Cheesy piped, putting out the port side rods. "Dancing girls, perhaps?"

"A drone for video, to capture all this action from above," Tim finished. "Dancing girls could also be added."

"I'm surprised I haven't read about anyone fishing with a drone, like they do kites," Dag wondered out loud. "Be easy, just put the same release clip as on an outrigger."

Mia set the two starboard lines, "Someone's already done it, I'm sure."

"Hey, Sis, what's the deal? How come no prayer during the last two days?" Dag asked.

She batted her eyes, "Saving it for if, and when we needed it. Okay, now we need some divine help. Come on, join hands. Dag, let Otto drive. Cheesy, Tim, get over here. Hey, fish-watcher, Tony, come on, let's not waste valuable time. Concentrate. Bow your heads in respect. Jesus, Jehovah, Neptune, Poseidon, Allah, Mohammed, Buddha, Confucius, please give us a fish."

Mia went to the ice chest, opened a beer for everyone, followed

Harry's program, and each diluted the Caribbean. "Neptune and Poseidon, that's for you. How about giving us a stellar day," Dag announced as he grabbed the wheel and switched off the autopilot.

Tim was first in the chair, and Mia was with Tony up in the tower. They yelled when they saw a marlin's dorsal fin cut across their wake. It batted at the two port side baits as if taste testing; then its bill smashed one of the mirrored teasers. Cheesy was dancing on the deck as Mia shouted from the tower which rod she expected it would hit. The marlin chomped the closest starboard lure. The reel screamed; Cheese twisted the butt out of the gunnel holder and handed it to Tim. Since the Junish, big fish incident, Tim routinely buckled himself to the chair.

Dag slowed and watched to be certain Tim had solidly set the hook before he put her in reverse. Bent over the rod, Tim cranked. The line came easily. Within ten minutes, Tony tagged it and Cheesy released it. Mia swung down from the tower and high fives went all around.

"My turn, my turn," she squealed as she set out two lines at the precise distance where she wanted them. Cheesy accepted a nod that his two rods were equal. Mia made the rounds, checking the drags before she yanked up the bait that was running deep, attached to the diving planer. Skillfully, enjoying being the center of attention, she changed the bubblehead lure with plastic streamers for a slim lead-headed, white horsehair, old-fashioned lure that streamed over a foot and carried two long hooks.

Everything readied again, Dag eased up to four knots and radioed in their success. "*Sassy Cassy* takes number five."

The boat stayed silent with everyone absorbed watching the trailing lines. It wasn't easy. Even with the best sunglasses, the glare was punishing.

The radio squawked. "*Courtesan* tags its fourth."

"Damn, we need a break!" Dag called out to whatever invisible forces might be listening.

Cheesy leaned against the forward cabin wall in the tiny shade and fiddled with the radio, pushing the scan button three times. Finally, it stopped on a weak frequency. The Englishman shook his head. "That's a bit of luck, good for us, bad for our competitor *Sea Ghost*. They threw a fan belt. They'll be stalled for at least half an hour, unless they try to run on one engine. Not good, too risky. Too bad. *Temptress* is still holding the largest."

"Unless someone lands a monster like we had the first day," rare words spouted from the usually silent Tony. "480 going to be hard to beat."

"Yeah, but there's plenty of biggies out here," Dag maintained. "They only get bigger by not getting caught."

"Hey! Birds! Birds! Off the starboard, a long way," Tim said and never took his eyes from the binoculars. "Aye, yai, yai, birds everywhere!" He spun in a three-sixty. "And no other boats in sight. About forty-five degrees off the starboard bow."

Dag spun the wheel and brought the boat up to seven knots.

"That looks good, yeah, do you see them now? Oh my god, this might be a school of tunas. You're gonna have to work some magic so we don't get hooked up with fish that don't add points."

"Got you, loud and clear," Dag replied. "Cheese, put out two more teasers. Tim, you want to run out your mechanical, wiggling marvel? Might as well pull out everything."

"And the kitchen sink," Cheesy hawed. "You ready, Missy?"

"Abso-fucking-lutely! Big fish, big fish, big fish!" She began an infectious chant. "Dagger, are you going to make a wide swing or cut through?"

"Swing north. Looks to me like the school is moving south. We want to pick up what's trailing them. I'll go behind and then do some circles. See how that works, then maybe a figure eight, cutting through the school. That's if we can keep up. Worse case, we get yellowfins. Anything else, young lady?"

"I'll 'young lady' you!"

Tony grinned at the brother-sister action. He graciously moved out of the way to the starboard side of the tower. Tim stood rigid on the port side deck glued to the binoculars. Cheesy was ready at the starboard stern. Mia balanced, standing on the chair, for a slightly better view, always ready to drop to the seat.

Birds, maybe a thousand, splashing, diving for the fry. Hundreds of webfoot brown boobies made up the greatest numbers, followed by gulls, some far-offshore pelicans, and graceful, slim white long-tailed tropic birds. The frigates circled high; then swooped to attack from above. The squawks and cries made a great soundtrack.

The center rod, attached to the deep-running planer, bounced, and then bent in a dangerous arc, pulled by tremendous strength, massive fish power. The gold Penn International reel peeled line with a harsh shriek. Mia's drop into the seat coincided with the fish's hard strike that wobbled the fighting chair.

Tim ran and cranked on the far starboard rod that had his wiggler. Suddenly, it was yanked tremendously hard, and he nearly lost his grip. Tim braced himself as the reel screamed. Cheesy, Mia, and Tim shouted, "Fish on!"

"Esta es una gran oportunidad de hacer mucho dinero. Muchachos, esto es un negocio serio. Caramba!" *{This is a great opportunity to make lots of money. Buddies, this is serious business. Get on it.}* Dag shouted with a decent Spanish accent, "Amigos, hagamos una fiesta ahora. Bailen, bailen! Señores, esto es serio! Metan el maldito pez end el bote! *{Friends, let's have a party now, dance, dance! Gentlemen, this is serious, get that damn fish into the boat!}* Get these fucking fish to the boat."

"Do your part Dagger," Mia yelled as she cranked and cranked. "Do your best to keep our lines separated."

"Sí, señorita, pero haz lo que tienes que hacer rápido! {Yes, but get your ass moving fast!}"

"Speak fucking English!" Mia ordered. "This is fishing, not a Berlitz Spanish course!"

"Si, um, yes, okay, sorry, I just got excited," Dag apologized. "We might have to cut one loose rather than lose both of them."

Cheesy felt for the knife on his belt.

"Whose is bigger?" Mia squeaked.

"Wrong question to ask men!" Cheesy laughed.

Tim didn't say anything. Cheesy had moved behind him and strapped him into a stand-up harness. Dag slowed, but inertia kept the sportfisher moving forward and able to maneuver.

"Hey, I'm actually getting somewhere," Mia reported. "It's coming. Cheese, where are you? Tony, get your tag pole ready!"

The small man dropped from the fish tower like he was a fireman ready to get on the ladder truck. Over his IGFA ball cap, he was wearing a small movie camera attached to an elastic head strap. "Yes, ma'am, you bring it in, and I'll do my part." He posed in the starboard stern corner, holding his tag stick like a spear.

"You gonna be okay, son?" Cheesy whispered to Tim.

"Yeah, yeah, I got this," Tim grunted, "I think. Go help Mia."

His sister pumped and reeled; sweat soaked her khaki shirt. Her neck muscles looked like they would explode with each crank. "Uh, uh, uh, it's coming, it's coming!" She groaned.

"Good thing, for a moment, I thought you were…" Dag let his words hang. He slipped into reverse. "Tim, try to keep your fish clear of the stern!"

Putting all of her strength into the next set of rod pumps, Mia moaned and groaned and finally, the bill appeared. Cheesy stretched out and almost went into the drink, but touched the leader. "Done! That's number six!" Cheesy announced.

Intently watching for the precise moment, Tony hit the blue marlin with the tag dart in the thick flesh just ahead of the dorsal fin. "Done, also done! I'll record it weighed three-fifty. Nice fish, Miss Mia. Nicely done. I must say, this is primo action. I'm impressed at the team effort."

Attention turned towards Tim, who was silent and not able to gain much on the fish. He was the stoic image of the mute, patient, fisherman. He stood upright, energizing every muscle just to stay even with his fish.

"Everybody ready? Backing down to port. You okay, Timmy?" Dag asked.

Between loud snorts for breaths, the words grumbled out. "I told you, no one calls me Timmy. No, I'm not all right. Cheese, help me move over to the chair."

The Englishman had relaxed a bit, rested on the stern for a minute after Mia's episode. He sighed and stood up. Mia unbuckled from the chair's shoulder harness. Tim cranked for thirty seconds before a much greater force pulled down on the rod. It was wrenched from his hands and out of the belt's rod holder. Instantly, Tim dove for the rod and barely snagged the butt with his left hand. Squirming on his belly, his right surrounded the crank, and his sore thumb pushed the drag lever forward. The fish kept taking line as the reel free spooled.

"Don't touch the rod! Help me to the chair, but don't fucking touch the rod. That'll be a disqualification. We need this fish!" Tim demanded. "Dag, Dag? Feels like a big one. I can't move him at all. Hope it's not a fucking tuna!"

"I'm backing down slow, tell me what you want?"

"Rum and coke, no, a gin and tonic," Tim's humor returned. "Okay, we can win big with this mother. Back, Dag, back, slow, easy, easy." Tim's hands were white-knuckled from his tight grip. Cheesy got the shoulder straps around Tim and then clipped a line on the reel as an added precaution.

"Fish isn't moving. That's good, huh, Dag? What do you think?"

"Hold on to that for dear life."

Tim sawed back and forth using the chair's gimbaled holder as the fulcrum.

"Move the boat! Forward. Fish's rising fast," Tim bellowed.

For the second time, Junish appeared like an ICBM launched from a sub, straight up. The body of this fish was at least six meters, and that didn't include the two-meter bill. Its recoil strength pushed it out of the water. There was plenty of air between the wide silver tail and their wake.

"Oh my God! It's got to be the same fish! Gigantic! Careful what you pray for," Tony mumbled.

Fully extended, flying, with the big lure visible, hanging from its mouth, Junish arched in a leap that bounded completely across their stern. Tim cranked, Dag maneuvered, while Cheesy, Mia, and the IGFA man stared wide-eyed and speechless.

The record-breaking fish bucked up through the waves and then rolled to the right. Somehow it twisted, changed direction, and swam directly away from the boat. They watched its huge dorsal move like a wrong way torpedo.

Mia moved beside the chair. She coached, "Hang on, Tim! What a fish!" Nervous, she began massaging her brother's broad shoulders.

"Reverse again!" Dag announced. "Careful with the drag, play it!"

"Oh shit, he's charging again. He's playing me!" Tim couldn't wind in line fast enough. The rod tip was back up, straight, with the slack line.

Continually watching the action, Dag slipped into neutral.

BOOM! Their boat rocked. The monster fish bounced against the stern and smashed into the small dive platform.

"I think he's pissed," Mia shrieked.

Junish sideswiped the port side and rocked *Sassy* again.

"Oh my God!" Tony squeaked. "Oh, my God! This can't be happening!"

The gigantic head suddenly appeared just meters off the stern. The long dark bill parried in a swirl and thrust, then dropped. The big black eyes seemed focused on the boat that was trying to capture it.

Dag released the wheel and turned to watch. The sportfisher was barely moving.

Fervidly, he reeled in line, but Tim's best efforts couldn't take up the slack. "I'm losing him, I'm losing him!" He cried, "What the…? It's, it's…"

The fish's entire enormous body appeared about five meters directly behind the boat, prone, not moving in the water. Its tail was a weather vane; the wind was coming with it. The fish may have been gauging the distance, deciding a new tactic, or summoning strength. Junish was not going to be taken.

It did what monster fish do, attack. The huge blue marlin zeroed in on the sportfisher. The massive tail made two sweeps, back and forth.

Imitating a juggernaut, the marlin charged so hard the water sprayed around the body. It was a surreal moment, only seconds to view the elegant, extreme heavyweight fight for its freedom.

Everyone paused, rigid, amazed, in respect, also in weird admiration. In a split second, two meters off their stern the marlin launched itself.

CRASH!

Later, all agreed they'd never heard a sound of such force before. Tony best described the force as the combination of a jarring auto collision and with the cracking sound of lightning striking a tree.

The strike was a triple, toppling, Cheese, Mia, and Tony. Dag's big bare feet somehow held his footing. Junish seemed to have aimed at Tim, strapped to the fighting chair. The long bill speared through the fiberglass transom and to within a foot of the chair.

Always thinking, Cheesy slid along the deck. His right hand shot out and grabbed the chair's armrest. With that for control, he shoved out with his left arm rigid and touched the leader.

"Done! That makes six!" Cheesy gasped. "Holy shit! Whew." He rolled away as the big marlin shook and shuddered the sportfisher with a series of twists.

Tony edged to the port corner, craned his camera-wearing-head, and examined the fish this crew had named Junish. "Could be a record? A world record blue marlin? You going to keep it?"

"How big?" Mia mouthed, taking photos with her camera.

"Biggest I've ever seen boated in thirty years," Tony muttered. "At least a thousand."

"Hate to kill him. We win, don't we?" Breathless, Tim continued to reel in the line, "I mean, ah, for the biggest fish?"

"Unless someone brings a whale painted blue with a long spear attached between its eyes," Tony replied. "But this could mean a hundred thousand and a Mercedes."

"Where would we drive?" Tim shook his head.

"But the money?" Tony asked.

"The money…" Mia and Cheesy choked out.

"We got pictures. They may be worth a thousand words and a thousand charters if people know Junish is still out here," Tim reasoned. "Plus, Sunset Bay is all about eco fishing."

"Oh, my," Tony was choking back tears, "A monster like this will draw the big playboys. Your act of conservation will get plenty of press, a lot of great press."

The marlin might have been unconscious for minutes from its

self-dealt blow. It ushered its strength, and the tail whipped side to side. More of *Sassy's* transom splintered, widening the hole until it slipped backward. Dag stepped to the stern, wire cutters in hand. He gave everyone a quick look and received nods all around.

Foolhardy or courageous, Dag leaned over the stern rail. Mia and Tony rushed and grabbed his legs. Eye to eye with Junish, "You are one big mother. Probably don't remember us from twenty years ago; take a good look. Now, I'm your salvation, but we'll be back fishing for you. You can bet on that!"

Dag snatched the hook with his pliers. Photos were snapped. Six-foot Dag was used to gauge the size. The fish may have been listening, but probably exhausted, or rational, and willing to have a human yank the hook from its jaw. No different from sitting in a dentist's chair.

The marlin's gills flexed like bellows. About a third of the gills were still in the water. The fish breaths made a gurgling sound. Its right eye stayed fixed, probably focused on the human prying in its mouth. Junish seemed to relax and accept the help.

"Damn it," Dag cursed. "No wonder it fought so hard; the hook is really lodged. Cheesy, get me the big set of wire cutters with the longer handles."

"Aye, aye," Staying a safe distance, the watchful Englishman passed the long-handled tool.

"Hey, sis, get a closeup of me and Junish," Dag twisted, looking up. His face was inches away from Junish's black eye. The fish remained motionless while Dag hammed it up. "Come on, for posterity," he winked.

"Okay, okay, I got several of you, pretty boy. You're immortalized beside this monster, granddaddy marlin. And a short video," Mia complied. "Now, cut that fish loose before..."

"Hold me!" Dag instructed as he bent and stretched further. Cheesy moved along Dag's side and gripped him with both arms around the waist.

"Got to get him loose before he attracts sharks. That would be horrible, Old Man and the Sea shit." Tim babbled, flustered, "I'm having serious problems getting out of the chair. What's with this harness?" He unsnapped a pair of straps only to discover they belonged to the stand-up belt.

The long nose of the pliers snatched the hook's shank. "Got me? Don't let me fall," Dag pleaded as he held the pliers with both hands and twisted. Dag exhaled a long, loud sigh; he kept working the hook sideways. The fish remained compliant.

Finally, after a loud grunt, Dag lifted his right hand, holding the big lure. They understood his wave and hauled him back to safety inside the boat. Dag sank back with an impish grin, spread-eagled on the deck. His hands held up, wiggling the mechanical bait in front of the massive bill that had speared *Sassy*. With hard breaths, he shook his head and rattled a nervous laugh.

Tim was still struggling to get out of the chair. Cheesy and Mia made their way around them and grabbed Junish's wedged bill.

"Never a dull moment," Cheesy wisecracked as they pushed. Probably, it was their hands touching it, but something shocked the fish to resume its struggle. The bill slanted more upward as the massive dark body, especially the tail, sank beneath the waves.

Grunts and groans, another push. The gigantic marlin assisted, moving its bill left to right, enlarging the hole in the transom. Tim finally burst free of the chair's nylon harness and squeezed between Cheese and Mia. With his legs wedged against the chair's footrest, he grabbed the bill with both hands and pushed.

Finally, the fish was free. It lay, motionless, on the surface for half a minute.

"We killed it?" Mia worried out loud. "Oh gosh, no, please."

"It's just stunned. Gave itself one hell of a blow. Me, I'd be dizzy," Cheesy joked.

"Come on, come on, Junish, don't die," Tim pleaded.

"Jesus, Jehovah," Dag sang as he gathered himself up from the deck. The others continued with him. "Neptune, Poseidon, Allah, Mohammed, Buddha, Confucius, please let this fish live!"

All five leaned over the stern. The fish's bill poked through the surface. The marlin curled left, and with a flex of its tail, disappeared.

"Hallelujah!" Tony shouted. "This, this… I captured it all on my GoPro. Ah, holy, ah, holy mackerel, no, no, holy marlin!"

"I don't know about holy, but that is one hell of a fish!" Mia yelled. "I want to be there when Harry hears."

"Harry can watch it. All the other fishermen, captains, crew, everyone on the island," Tony spewed contagious enthusiasm. "Tonight, tonight, I'll hook this up to a big screen. You get the digitals off your cameras. We'll show the greatest fishing moment of all time." He spread his arms like an evangelist, "Yes, I will."

"Maybe not the 'greatest,' but one of the greatest fishing moments," Dag qualified as he rubbed his face and poured a water bottle over his head. "The best is always yet to come. Right? That's what keeps you fishing!"

Suddenly, Mia cried, big sobs, with a big smile. Tim lifted and spun her around, making some nifty dance moves. Dag started the high fives with hugs that worked around the group. Cheesy did a little of his fancy jig footwork, amazing everyone by kicking up his heels on a wet deck. He tipped his ball cap with a bow as he opened the cooler and handed out beers.

They touched bottles. "Way to go, little brother," Dag started, but finished, "ah, way to go, younger brother."

"Could never have done it without such expert boatmanship," Tim beamed his toothy grin. "Made our boat a good dartboard. Learn that in Costa Rica?"

"Hey, what time is it?" Dag asked.

"Two-twenty," Tony replied.

"What are we, farmers or fishermen? Still time for more marlin," Dag laughed, "You ready, Mia?"

"Ready or not," Mia nodded. "What about the hole in our transom?"

"Far above the waterline. Going head-on into the waves. Shouldn't be a problem. We got good pumps and better luck, huh?"

"Letting out the lines, captain," Cheesy said working on the starboard while Mia did the port side.

"Not this one," Tim said, holding up his wiggler. "This is going on display."

"Agreed," echoed from the crew.

^^^^^^^^^

The school of fish and the flocks of birds had been forgotten during the heavyweight title action aboard *Sassy*. They'd vanished from sight. The fresh baits remained untouched. Dag steered a course that brought them to Clifton's dock shortly before four, triumphantly flying six marlin flags from the outriggers.

Tony made the ride home in the V berth, downloading his GoPro onto his laptop. Tim didn't permit anyone to touch their boat's cameras. Even after four beers, he was too nervous from the afternoon, and decided to download and edit only after he'd rested.

But Mia added her shots to the presentation. "We'll make believers," she swore, "out of the world of fishermen, that the world record billfish is still swimming somewhere off Union Island."

"Here, here!" The crew agreed.

The hole smashed through the transom quickly attracted a crowd and a myriad of questions. She and her crew got a freshwater washdown as Tony's improvised laptop showcased an irrefutable display.

The tournament's committee boat tied alongside and Harry made an awkward transfer to his boat. Oddly quiet, he gazed first at the six flags, then limped to the fighting chair, and stood holding onto its back. His head rotated back and forth, staring at the ventilated transom. "What the hell happened?"

"Had to be there, Skip," Cheese declared. "Seeing's believing! Wait 'til you watch the videos!"

"But the..." Harry was confused and stammered, "but the size of that hole looks like Dag backed into a telephone pole."

Dag placed his arm around his father. "Like Cheesy's saying, wait. The telephone pole came flying at us!"

Wearing his recharged camera, Tony captured the St. Claire family moment.

He shook his head, trying to comprehend the gash. Talking, so the crowd at the dock could hear, "Man, oh, man, what's a father to do? I give my kids, all grown up and mature, my pride and joy to run for a couple of days; now look at this! Whew," he turned with a big smile, and pulled all into a circle, his arms strained to surround his children and Cheesy. "And you return victorious! Not only the best fucking boat, but the biggest fucking fish! Come on, don't hold back. Tell your old man every detail! It was Junish, wasn't it?"

Cassy and Verena pushed through the onlookers and jumped aboard. With more hugs and kisses, Verena pointed to the damage and exclaimed to her husband, "I hope you got their license number!"

With a quick comeback, Tony grinned, "No, actually, we gave that fish a number." He fanned open his small notebook. "SC23742!" He set his laptop on the seat of the fighting chair and draped a towel for shade so they could see. "This will save a lot of explanation."

Lots of wows were heard with more, "Oh my," scattered among, "I never thought a fish could get that big," and "Whew, look at that!" The shots even mesmerized the crew who had lived the moment. Luckily, Tony had captured all the action, a total of thirty-seven minutes.

"Seemed like forever," Tim said with his arms around Cassy and Harry making another Kodak moment. "Yes, we're a fishing family. Come on, all of us, Cheese and Verena, get in this picture. Tony, you, too. Mia, give your camera to Mammie. This is our day!"

"We did it! You did it, I mean," Harry hugged Tim, then Mia, and grabbed the taller Dag and shook his hand. "So, what's the verdict? Fishing here better than Costa Rica?"

Dag let out a loud sigh, wrinkled his nose, and he nodded the affirmative. He whispered, "Might have to import some women. I'm missing my rice and beans and fried tostones."

Harry piped it up, "Honoré, Honoré, where are you? Hear that? You gotta spice up the rice for *Sassy's* next captain!"

^^^^^^^^^^

The tournament's final buffet was sumptuous. All anglers and crews attended alongside most of Union island and many of the government ministers from St. Vincent. They enjoyed three porkers spit-roasted, three sizable yellowfins wrapped in banana leaves and baked in the ground, and every chicken that could be bought was barbecued.

Local Haroun and imported Heineken beers, and Sunset Rum loosened all the tongues. The fishing chatter rose to a polite roar. Harry stood and tapped his water glass with his knife. "Okay, okay! Everyone get their belly filled? Everyone got a good buzz on?" he asked and got a howl of affirmatives.

"It's that time, folks, for the awards." Harry announced as he limped to the podium and grabbed the microphone.

On the wall, where the airport usually listed its few flights, were the tournament standings:

SASSY CASSY – ST. VINCENT - SIX
TEMPTRESS – PUERTO RICO – FIVE
COURTESAN - GRENADA – FIVE
MAD HATTER – ST. LUCIA – FOUR
SEA GHOST – US VIRGINS – FOUR
BIGGEST FISH–SASSY CASSY–ST. VINCENT–1000 PLUS LBS

"Gentlemen, ladies, old friends, new friends, this was a great tournament with sixty-six marlin tagged in three days. Every boat got action and thirty boats tagged at least one. That sounds like it ought to be a record, but the IGFA officials say it is the fifth-best tournament ever in the Caribbean. I've always said, a fifth is best."

"This is kind of embarrassing, but pleasant embarrassing. And believe me, I know the unpleasant variety of embarrassing!" That brought another laugh, and Harry continued, "The best boat is our own *Sassy Cassy*. The biggest fish, well you all saw what that beast did to the boat, also goes to the *Sassy*!" Harry pointed to Tony.

"I swear it was a monster, bigger than a thousand pounds, probably over fifteen-hundred. I didn't weigh it since its size made the weight apparent. And with the fish stuck through the boat's transom, it was impossible to attach a hanging scale. A possible world record, but the St. Claires decided to forego the usual photos of a majestic dead fish hanging with the anglers standing around." Tony nodded to the crew and reverently said, "They opted to be environmentally correct and release it. Absolutely the biggest I've ever seen. Some of you have seen my digitals. They'll be on display after this ceremony." With glee in his voice, Tony added, "And on my website forever!"

"That's why I'm embarrassed," Harry cut in, pointing to his family and the Chessmans. "My kids decided I didn't want the car or need the money, so they released it!" Harry's voice choked up. He took a playful, flat hand swipe at Tim's head.

"This is my number two son, responsible for this tournament and by tagging and releasing the biggest marlin, designated the best angler, Timothy St. Claire," Harry announced and turned away to wipe his face. "Come on Tim, stand and give a few words."

"I know many of you feel the home team always has the advantage, but truthfully we were lucky. My sister, Mia," Tim pulled her up, "has this prayer that we will now share with you. Mia, please?"

She raised her beer and saluted the anglers. "Not really my prayer, something we heard my father recite," she hesitated and smiled at her parents. "Please excuse me, got some beers in me, celebrating. So, Harry probably got it from his father, and it's probably been adapted over the generations. Don't have to bow your heads, unless you want to. Here goes: 'Jesus, Jehovah, Neptune, Poseidon, Allah, Mohammed, Buddha, Confucius, please give us a fish!' Oh, I should tell you," she started laughing, "we have a copyright on that. Every time you say it, send a dollar to Sunset Bay. Back to you, Tim."

"Yes, we said that prayer this morning and had one early hookup. You know our team had four through yesterday. We needed a miracle. It was our luck of finding the birds this afternoon. I mean," Tim was rushing his words, "two days ago, I think I hooked the same fish. My family first saw a monster marlin, it could have been the one we released today, when we were just out of diapers. I couldn't bear to kill it. Now we can fish for it again. I hope whoever hooks it next, is kind enough to just take photos and do the same release." He raised his beer and turned towards his father, "Here's to Harry St. Claire who's been preaching catch and release before anyone ever heard of environmentally friendly!"

The applause continued for minutes until Walter Van Gell began waving his arms. He began with gentle hand clapping. "Here, here. Like everyone, I truly enjoy a wonderful fish story. I for one want to say that I smell something fishy." He tilted his bearded face upwards and loudly sniffed, "I request the return of my entrance fees and I suggest that the rest of you do the same. You rigged this tournament from the beginning."

The room was silent. No one moved. Harry stood opposing Van Gell. Brother-in-law Sam, two other men, not crew, and Beatrice Thorpe surrounded the bearded hotelier.

"What? What are you saying? That we somehow had fish planted out there and they just snatched the bait? Come on! You aren't making any sense. Don't try to ruin a great event."

"Oh no, Mr. St. Claire. It is common knowledge that your finances are, hmm, tight, so to say. I request that the IGFA representative on your boat be investigated. I believe that you conspired and fixed this tournament. I also believe that you did not catch any fish today and certainly not a huge thousand pounder that was so magnanimously released. No other boat saw you catch it. You pounded the hole in your stern with a sledgehammer. Unfortunately, my stern hole isn't big enough to make me believe this farce. Now, I want my money returned or disqualify your boat!"

Harry stood, rubbing his jaw, staring at Van Gell. "Where's this coming from? You want to check my bank account before this tournament? Well, Mr. Van Gell, I got two words for you and they ain't Happy Birthday or Merry Christmas!"

For support, Cassy and the family stood with Harry. "What you're saying is… is unbelievable. You think we rigged it to win? I assure you…"

"Either disqualify your boat or return our money!" Van Gell shouted.

"You are ridiculous!" Tony joined the argument. "I saw the fish." He held up his laptop. "I have photos. You can measure it against the stern." He pointed to Dag, "Its body, just the body without the bill, is almost three times as long as our captain. Look at the digitals. I take offense of you challenging my word. I am honest."

"Photos," Van Gell paused, "today, photos and movies can be easily retouched. Your digital rendition was faked long before this tournament. Now, the St. Claires can pay off their debts with our money! No, I won't stand for it!"

The other anglers reacted with a sour rumble against the bearded

Van Gell.

"Go on, be suckers if you want, but I can tell a sham when I see one," he continued.

"If you can smell something fishy, I can smell sour grapes." Harry cocked his head to one side. "Bite me!"

"Here, here! Bite this!" shouted the anglers.

Van Gell stood on his chair and tried to quiet the room. "I want my entrance fees returned, immediately. Everyone's money should be reimbursed. Get out your checkbook, St. Claire! I demand it!"

Limping across the room, through the maze of tipsy anglers, Harry deliberately faced his opponent. "Demand my ass! Who are you but a spoiled, rich braggart! You are claiming that I and my sons, and the IGFA rigged this tournament? Do you realize how stupid that is?!" Tt incensed Harry. "I've been fishing here, in these waters, and this is my home and you swagger around and insult my family... why you!"

"Mr. St. Claire, your actions insult each participant's intelligence." Van Gell puffed up his chest and crowed, "You and your family are virtually destitute. This was a last gasp attempt to save your property. When other boats scored legitimate catches, your boat disappeared and then reappeared with another fairy tale of the big one that got away! I don't believe any of it."

"Mr. Van Gell," Tony said as he moved closer to Harry. "Whatever your name is? If that is your position, you will hear from my attorney. You have scandalously and maliciously smeared my good character. There's a timestamp on my digital recording. I guarantee it is one hundred percent authentic!"

"Everything can be faked. As far as I'm concerned, you're part and parcel with the St. Claire's plot. This is fraud. Fraud, I say! I'm calling in the authorities unless all fees are refunded."

"You're a wealthy man, a wheeler, and dealer." Harry moved so he was confronting Van Gell, who was still standing on his chair, "You're the money man behind the hotel planned for Sunset Bay, aren't you?"

"Why not give him his money, Harry?" Sam stood and suggested, "Defuse the situation. Deal with it later."

"Sammy, you're in his pocket, right? He practically owns you. What say you give him his money back? Didn't go so good for you, did it? Didn't drive us out as planned?" Harry scoffed as he returned to confront Van Gell. "Now I understand. You're the man, the man who caused us so many problems. One question, did Beatrice's husband sell you health insurance?"

"What?"

"Because you'll need it!" Harry leaned forward. He seemed to slip on his walking stick. He fell and tumbled toward Van Gell and toppled his opponent off of the chair. In a smooth move, Harry grabbed the white shirt to steady him. With perfect balance, he slammed Van Gell with a right to his jaw, followed by a left to his stomach. The bearded man stumbled backward, but Harry grabbed his beard and punched him again. Sprawled on the floor, the white shirt showed splotches of blood.

"Call me a liar, call my family cheats, you, you…"

"I'll get you!" Van Gell cried as he curled into a ball.

"No, you won't." Harry kicked at him. "Ouch, damn it, that's my bad knee!"

The two men, Spanish, sitting on either side of Van Gell, reacted too late. Perhaps they appreciated the humor or felt their arrogant boss deserved a few slaps. As Harry bent to favor his sore knee, the tallest reached an arm to shove the elder St. Claire off balance.

Many of the anglers were on their feet cheering for Harry and taunts at Van Gell. Sam rose and moved away from the ringside action.

Pushing his way through the crowded room, somehow Tim's approach hadn't been noticed by the bodyguards. He grabbed the arm of the man about to shove his father.

"Whoa there, buddy, that's my pop!" Tim jerked the arm hard, upward. Most of the crowd heard the snap; he'd dislocated the man's shoulder. For a few seconds, the bodyguard lay crumpled, but he sprang and head-butted Tim, who landed on a table.

The two were about to pummel Tim, who was momentarily blinded by the blood gushing again from his nose. The first man grabbed a bottle with his good arm to smash Tim. Mia threw herself into the fray with a good body block. As he recoiled to face his new adversary, she dropped him with a kick to his family jewels that would make any rugby player proud.

The second man was distracted by the pretty woman. He turned when Dag tapped his shoulder and met a flurry of punches. He ducked, snorted, and plowed his shoulder into the tallest St. Claire, skidding chairs and tables across the concrete floor.

Dag saw the second charge coming and pulled the man, throwing him down. The enraged bodyguard did an acrobatic leap and landed on his feet, ready for mayhem. He took a karate stance and threatened with his flat palms. He grunted, "Punks, now prepare to be taught manners!"

Tim ripped off his tournament T-shirt and wiped the blood from his face and did a Taxi Driver imitation, "You talking to me? You talking to me?"

The bodyguard, intimidated by Tim's physique, raised his hands to surrender.

"Nope, too late for that!" Tim roared. Van Gell's guard attempted to spin around with a kick. Tim sidestepped, feinted with his right, and connected with a left uppercut. That straightened his stunned rival for a targeted roundhouse right.

Harry had Van Gell by the shirt collar and dragged him across the floor. "You want our home so bad that you'd do anything. Get out of here and take your whore," he looked at Beatrice and grinned, "with you."

The woman had cautiously moved away from the fracas. Watching that she wasn't included, she retrieved her purse from a crumpled table. She turned and confronted the St. Claires. "I'm not... Harry and Cassy, I'm sorry." Beatrice pointed to Van Gell groveling at Harry's feet. "He had me mix something in your drink. That's why you don't remember me naked. I set up the camera and left the photo where I knew Cassy would find it. I'm so sorry. Van Gell threatened to cancel all business with my husband's company."

"You're a pathetic, greedy bitch," Cassy hissed.

"I'm sorry," the woman cowered.

"Sorry? Sorry doesn't cut it. If you know what's good for you, Sammy, drag your friends out of here," she continued. Cassy shook her finger at her brother, "On top of everything else, all your dirty tricks and conniving, when we win, you call us cheats! You should be ashamed of yourself. Did you forget that we're family? Get out!"

"I'm done with this," Sam said wiping his hands in the air. "Done, I apologize for poor judgment." He stuck his hand out and Cassy slapped it away.

"You, you think..." Cassy stammered, "Sam, how could you? For what? You wanted to ruin us? I'm your sister. For what gain?"

Sam shrugged and lifted Van Gell. Beatrice got under the bearded man's other arm to help him. The bodyguards slowly backed their way out, watching everyone as they hobbled to *Temptress*.

"Like I said, poor judgment. You and Harry never..."

"Never what?!" Cassy shot back. "Never what? Huh? Don't talk now, not another word!" Cassy turned towards the crowd of anglers, townspeople, and officials. "We're the St. Claires. We apologize for this disturbance. Family issues..."

Interrupting, with his arm around his wife, "Her family, not mine. I sincerely apologize for this, I guess all fishermen hate to be called liars, but when someone blames my family… well, you can see what happens."

Tim stepped up, blood still dripping from his cracked nose. He tenderly touched it, "Uh-huh, for the second time in a few months, I get a broken nose. Monique was the first." He laughed, looked around, and grabbed a standing bottle that still had some beer. He raised it high. "Whatever, this is the first Union Island Sunset Bay Marlin Tournament, the first of many." He smiled and pointed to Dag and Mia. "God knows, nobody will ever forget this one. Let's hope we still catch big billfish, but no more fistfights," he paused, "unless we set up a boxing ring!"

The room cheered.

Harry found his cane and tapped a tabletop. "I'm lucky to have a great wife and children. Sometimes fishing has gotten in the way of them, but… but no more. Sunset Bay is our home. Hopefully, we're going to expand… a little, and give some work to our neighbors, but no big hotels."

In a very serious tone, "You all see how money treats you, with no respect. We got a nice place here; and when I say we, I mean everybody who can enjoy the natural beauty."

Tim and Mia waved high fives.

Dag brought a round of beers. "Okay, everyone, drinks are on me, for the next five minutes so drink quick. Starting now! Oh, yeah," He had their attention. "Back to the prizes. Does anyone else want to argue about the *Sassy Cassy's* catches? I didn't think so."

Not the end –
Harry just hit restart

"There are always greater fish than you have caught, always the lure of greater task and achievement, always the inspiration to seek, to endure, to find."   -- Zane Grey

IGFA SALTWATER GAME FISH RECORDS
MARLIN
Atlantic Blue Marlin – 1,402 lbs. caught by Paulo Amorim - Brazil - 1992 – IGFA All Tackle Record

Pacific Blue Marlin - 1,376 lbs. caught by Jay de Beaubien – Hawaii - 1982 - IGFA All Tackle Record

Pacific Blue Marlin not recognized by IGFA – 1,805 caught by a charter group 1970 - Hawaii. This massive fish was not caught by one person alone, but a group including the boat captain and his daughter.

Pacific Black Marlin–1 ,560 lbs. Alfred Glassell Jr.-Peru - 1953

Pacific White Marlin – 181 lbs. - Evandro Coser - 1979 - Brazil

Extremely light tackle record fish - Leo Cloostermans - 573 lbs. Atlantic blue marlin caught on 4-lb.test line.

Atlantic blue marlin 248.5 lbs. caught on 6-lb.,

Atlantic blue marlin 381 lbs. caught on 8-lb.,

Atlantic blue marlin 604 lbs. caught on 12-lb.

SAILFISH
Atlantic Sailfish - 128 pounds, Bernadette Nicolson - Angola - 1994

TUNA
Bluefin Tuna - 1,496 lbs. Ken Fraser Nova Scotia – 1979

Yellowfin Tuna – 427 lbs. Guy Yocom – Mexico – 2012

Blackfin tuna -49.4 lbs. – Matt Pullen – Florida – 2006

Light tackle Tuna – yellowfin- 107 lbs. Trevor Hansen -South Africa largest ever caught on fly.

Biggest yellowfin but not IGFA recognized 445 lbs. – John Petruescu - California – a deck hand touched the rod while fighting the fish.

Wahoo -184 lbs. Sara Hayward – Mexico – 2005

Swordfish -1,182 lbs. – Louis Marron – Chile – 1953

Dorado (mahi-mahi) – 88 lbs. - Emily Seconi – Bahamas – 1998

Great White Shark – 2,664 lbs. - Alfred Dean – Australia – 1959 Biggest fish approved for an IGFA record.

Great White Shark - 3,450 lbs. - Donnie Braddick- Montauk, N.Y – 1986 not recognized by IGFA

About Ralph Trout

I was born lucky to be the only son of a Pennsylvania family. More good fortune was being raised on beautiful farm twenty miles northeast of Pittsburgh along the Allegheny River. I never forgot how cold the winters were and how long they remained. Warmer climes beckoned.

A degree from Pitt during the unsettling decade of the steel mills imploding meant little, except that construction paid better, somewhere other than Pittsburgh. As soon as I could, I moved to the warm tropics. I tried Hawaii, then made a move to St. Thomas, USVI and took over construction for a realtor. I made the Caribbean my home for thirty years. In the domino effect, I got hooked on sailing, scuba diving, fishing, rum, and all other types of fun under the tropical sun. Tank diving evolved from lobsters to sunken wrecks and treasure. Fishing grew from a weekend to two years dragging baits at nearly every island along the Caribbean chain on my trawler.

Jimmy Buffett sang it, *'the cannons don't thunder, nothing to plunder, I'm an over forty victim of fate.'* Living and working throughout the Caribbean in the '80s and'90s was fantastic surrounded by gorgeous women, countless boozers, smugglers, white-collar criminals, and know-it-all cruisers. Late summer and autumn, the storms blew through. Weathering one at sea in '99 was enough. In retrospect, the islands were the losers to unrestrained development. Tourism is a fickle monster.

The salty-life isn't for everyone; you must be a hearty sort. Plenty of couples split; islands are incredibly hard on women. But the small, saltwater rocks suited me. My tropical tales are convoluted memories enhanced as each year passes. My friend Rocky Mountain Earl professes, never let facts stall a good story.

The Caribbean Compass first took my stories. My fictional Caribbean tales include *The Wreck, Soucouyant – The Caribbean Vampire, Something Fishy, Soon Come – Divorce Caribbean Style.* When I learned the intricacies necessary to plant a tropical veggie garden, I shared the info in *The Caribbean Home Garden Guide.* My greatest adventure is *Road Trip: Huautla – The Mushroom Cult.* All of my books are available on Amazon.

www.ingramcontent.com/pod-product-compliance
Lightning Source LLC
Chambersburg PA
CBHW071307200626
46813CB00015B/484